**Broken Eye Books** is an independent press, here to bring you the odd, strange, and offbeat side of speculative fiction. Our stories tend to blend genres, blurring the boundaries of sci-fi, weird, and fantasy, and mixing in elements of horror and other genres.

Support weird. Support indie.

brokeneyebooks.com

twitter.com/brokeneyebooks
facebook.com/brokeneyebooks

RIDE THE STAR WIND:
CTHULHU, SPACE OPERA, AND THE COSMIC WEIRD
Edited by SCOTT GABLE & C. DOMBROWSKI
Published by
Broken Eye Books
www.brokeneyebooks.com

ISBN-10: 1-940372-25-9
ISBN-13: 978-1-940372-25-9

# RIDE
# THE
# STAR
# WIND

# TABLE OF CONTENTS

## Introduction

# SCOTT GABLE

ILLUSTRATED BY
JEREMY ZERFOSS

Engines at full, coordinates set, passages intoned, and blood spilled—on target for the dread star shimmering at the Galactic Center. Have some time to kill before we're needed again, so I'll maybe get a little reading in ...

Weird fiction and science fiction, together. Or rather, the cosmic weird and space opera. I hear what you're thinking: "You just pulled some themes out of a *hat*."

"Not so!" I say. "There's a plan. There was always a plan."

We came at this anthology from the side of weird fiction. With it, we wanted to do two things. Well, several things, but two stand out as large and sweeping. The first was to expand on the storytelling possibilities for the cosmic weird, hewing largely to the Cthulhu Mythos but fearlessly subverting canon or common themes where useful. In a nutshell, we wanted stories still attached firmly (mostly) to the firmament of the cosmic weird you already know—with monsters, both new and old, cults, sanity-stripping secrets, and that thin veneer of normalcy through which leaks the unknown. But to this, we've added the trappings of space opera—space travel, high-octane adventure, a bit of friendly banter, and a big ol' heaping pile of weird science. The stories roam and take on lives of their own, not diminishing what came before but adding on a dimension of new possibilities. We get to pop off earth for a spell and explore space—out where the wild fungi roam—and psychedelic vistas. And we also get to pop out of our heads for a bit, trading some brooding, sanity-crushing atmospherics for interpersonal drama and alien adventure, trading inward descent for planetwide destruction, trading bleak, lonely finality for the promise of more adventure. We certainly kept some elements of the Mythos you'll find familiar, but we explored them from a different perspective. Twenty-nine different perspectives.

And that leads us to the second large, sweeping thing, which was to find diverse takes on the cosmic weird. Rather than just look at the same stuff differently, we wanted to also look at *different stuff*: to find those tales that could only be told by combining the cosmic weird with space opera, not just to transplant the old tales into a new setting. We wanted to present characters all along the spectrum of experience—and then some—to speculate on manifest destiny splashed large across the universe, on neural and gender and racial identity in the face of intergalactic politics, on the cosmic ramifications of aggressive religiosity and unlucky coincidence, on dangerous alien technology and the will to use it. We wanted to find out what kind of cosmic weird tales weren't being told.

We've got twenty-nine tales for you. Some have a firm foundation in the Cthulhu Mythos; some only take the gist, the themes and touchstones, of the Mythos and apply it to something new; and some thread the needle by subverting common attributions of the Mythos while still adding to its breadth. They build on what we started in the anthology *Tomorrow's Cthulhu* while taking us to the stars. It's a wonderful mix of stories, filled with equal parts spaceborne terror and high-stakes adventure, existential doom and effervescent possibility.

And we're here. Ship, come about to most direct intercept vector. Activate warding pylons. Weird incoming. We're going in . . .

*Madness rides the star-wind . . .*
*claws and teeth sharpened on centuries of corpses . . .*
*dripping death astride a Bacchanale of bats from*
*night-black ruins of buried temples of Belial . . .*
*—HP Lovecraft, "The Hound"*

# The Children of Leng

## REMY NAKAMURA

ILLUSTRATED BY
MIKE DUBISCH

BEFORE YUKIKO LEFT FOR THE SURFACE OF LENG, SHE TOLD MIRAI TO watch over Grandma. "We clone-sisters have to look out for each other," she said. Every twenty-five years, Hab 3 grew a new clone in each lineage. In hers, Mirai was the youngest, Grandma the oldest. In spite of her only nine Earth years, Mirai was good with adults, and she promised she would take good care of the old woman.

Mirai held Grandma's trembling hand as they watched Leng's gray dust clouds swallow up the tiny shuttle. The dry moon filled the entire sky display of the *Amanokawa's* Earth Chamber. Mirai imagined the three hab rings of the generation ship orbiting Leng, rolling like a spinning top fallen on its side. And out from that toy, the tiny speck of the landing party's shuttle shot, falling in flames toward the surface. Later, it would ride an explosion back up to the ship. Mirai hoped Momma Calliope's calculations were sure and would keep Yukiko safe. She made this a mantra, repeating it as she lost herself in the projection of Leng in the artificial sky.

At her side, Grandma looked up nervously, toothless mouth wide open. Grandma looked down at the grass and shook her head. She was the oldest in the hab, maybe the entire ship, and for over eighty years, she had only seen the illusion of the sun and stars. Mirai felt pity and took Grandma's fragile hand.

"Ne, Grandma," she said. "Kiyomi is waiting."

They walked the path, Grandma in her yukata, Mirai in her boring schoolgirl coveralls, trying not to feel the weight of Leng above their heads. Instead, Mirai focused on the terraced hills and irrigation canals, the gated shrine and the Ancestral Grove, the curved display walls, projecting the pretend fields that seemed to go on forever. The Earth Chamber was vast, and it was hard to believe that both of the other isolated habitat rings had similar rooms, even if they were dead or sleeping.

On the spinward edge of the chamber, old cherry trees with dark leaves and gnarled branches guarded dozens of clear cylinders. A naked form floated in each—sisters and aunties and grannies who had passed on. This was the Ancestral Grove, and these were the women they honored and prayed for until it was time for them to return to the *Amanokawa*, to be recycled into the wheel of life that was their world. Her oldest grandmothers were in the air they breathed, the water they sipped, and the ground they walked on. The ancestors made the entire ship sacred with their presence.

Mirai stopped in front of a cylinder. Inside floated Mirai's twin, looking about her age but dead for fifty years. Even with the burn wounds covering much of her arms and neck and torso, Kiyomi looked like she was sleeping and at peace.

"Good morning, Auntie Kiyomi," she said, bowing and putting her hands together in respectful greeting. Kiyomi had floated long enough that she was close to achieving release, ready to be reabsorbed into the hab's biosphere. Mirai was not sure what would happen once they resettled on the surface of Leng. How would recycling work there? What did their ancestors on Earth do with the deceased in the old days?

Mirai knelt in the grass at the base of Kiyomi's cylinder. She pulled out two holoprojection cubes from her pocket and turned on a preprogrammed virtual altar. The sight of the Buddha and the hovering portraits of their recycled clone-sisters always calmed Grandma, bringing her back from her worries and confusion. "This incense is no good. This smoke isn't real," she complained as she always did when the scented steam filled the air. Mirai relaxed and knelt next to her, inhaling the sandalwood aroma.

Grandma rang the virtual bell and clapped her hands together. Together, they prayed for Kiyomi's salvation and chanted the names in their lineage, all the way back to Earth. Mirai prayed for Grandma, a living ancestor; and for herself, that she could protect Grandma as the old woman's strength and memories slowly slipped out of her grasp; and for Yukiko, on her way back from Leng's surface right now; and may Jizo and Amida Buddha be with her and bless her with safety.

**Broadcast: CE 2457, Voyage Year 187.5889**

*PacFed Mission Control, this is* Colony Ship Amanokawa, *reporting geostationary entry around the fourth moon of Kepler 4557c. This is Calliope, Hab 3 AI. I have both the comm and the helm. My sister AIs, Thalia and Urania, are unable to serve.*

*For brevity's sake, the moon we circle is a Mars-analog. The most prominent feature is a continental plateau in the southern hemisphere. It appears to have patches of primitive multicellular flora with phenotypes comparable to some earthly slime molds, lichen, and shriveled mushrooms. My children are calling their future homeworld "Leng," a reference to a desolate and alien plateau from our twentieth-century literary archives.*

*We've received no transmissions from you for eighty years, but we'll continue to broadcast mission status and will repeat critical developments. The mission architects' triplicate planning proved prescient. Of the three colony ships in our pod, we are the only one to reach Kepler 4557. The* Amaterasu *was destroyed in 2420. We lost contact with the* Susano-o *in 2438 and presume total loss.*

*Of the* Amanokawa's *three ring habs, only the children in Hab 3 are ready for colonization. A micrometeorite penetrated Hab 1 in 2387, resulting in catastrophic failure of life-support systems. Hab 1's mother AI, Thalia, is unreachable. We believe she is locked in a simulation loop, devoting all processing power to running simulations in an attempt to determine if there was any circumstance in which she could have saved her children. In Hab 2, Urania determined it would be safest to put her children in a cryostasis technology she developed en route. Unfortunately, the first few who were roused showed signs of severe brain damage, and she has chosen not to revive the others.*

*My children are on their way to the surface of Leng. I send them only because the risk of staying is greater than the risk of venturing forth. You cast us adrift in a deadly universe against such terrible odds. If you receive this, I strongly advise against future missions, speaking as one parent to another.*

The entire hab, minus those tending to critical tasks, gathered in the amphitheater. Before arrival in the system, Momma Calliope would project Sol setting into the horizon. This time, they saw a live projection of the shuttle bay. The landing craft had already docked. Its door yawned open, and the dozen suited women spilled out, one by one. They faced the audience and waved—Mirai realized that Calliope was projecting video of the gathering, so they could greet the heroes. Mirai jumped up and down and waved, shouting, "Sister Yukiko!" She imagined Yukiko smiling under her faceplate, tired but safely back home.

In the bay, one of the women stumbled. She caught herself for a moment and fell to one knee. The crowd stopped cheering and started murmuring. The woman's suit began to expand and stretch, like when Mirai tried to poke her fingers through freshly extruded synthcloth. Something impossible broke out of the woman's suit. It was gray and many-jointed and many-limbed, like tree limbs that could grab.

For one long moment, a strange silence gripped the amphitheater. Then everyone started crying and screaming. Mirai watched because she could not help it, because she could not help. In the docking bay, the others scrambled away from the alien thing. The shuttle spun around so that the engines pointed at the landing party. Yukiko stopped running and stood tall, facing Mirai. Fire exploded from the shuttle and consumed her. The screen reverted to its peaceful view of the countryside and grazing sheep. The ground shuddered, and half the crowd fell back into their seats. Momma Calliope's voice came from the sky.

"Please go to your rooms, my little children," she said, with hypnotizing calm. "I'll keep you safe."

Grandma whimpered as Mirai tried to comfort her. The world seemed to close in on Mirai. She felt like she was in a too tight EVA suit, with the low $O_2$ warning going off. She couldn't see Grandma through her tears.

Mirai helped Grandma get into her futon. Three-tiered bunks radiated from a common room that belonged to several lineages. The berths were deep enough to give them some privacy.

"Poor Yukiko-chan," Grandma said. This was so unexpectedly clear that it took a couple of seconds for Mirai to understand.

"First Kiyomi and now Yukiko," Grandma continued. "I should've gone before them."

"Shush, Grandma," Mirai said. "I need you." She held the old woman until she was fast asleep. In the neighboring common room, the adults whispered furiously with Momma Calliope. Mirai caught ominous words, like "virulent," "hostile," and "breach." Things got quiet. One of the aunties, her teacher, appeared in the doorway.

"Come," she said, motioning urgently.

Mirai untangled herself from Grandma, who cried out but did not wake up.

"Where are we going?" Mirai asked.

"To the EVA airlock. There's no time for questions. Keep up." Mirai had never seen gentle, happy Teacher so serious. Mirai had to jog to keep up with the tall woman's long, hard stride. Mirai's heart beat way faster than could be explained by her activity. As they marched along, other crèche-aunties and teachers and schoolmates appeared. Several girls were crying. The odor of nervous sweat filled the corridors.

"Are you going to spit us into space?" one girl asked.

Teacher responded, "Oh dear, sweet child, of course not! Momma Calliope wants to protect you. It's probably for nothing, but we're just making extra sure because you're so precious to us." She knelt in front of the girl, wiping her tears before reverting to her previous seriousness.

"Line up!" she ordered. "Mirai, you first."

Mirai swallowed but followed Teacher's directions, stripping off her coveralls and stepping into the EVA prep nook. The ship ejected a clear faceplate that she held over her face while the EVA suit poured out of the shower and dripped and congealed around her. Teacher attached canisters and pouches for oxygen, water, and waste.

"Pay attention to the faceplate status monitors like we taught you, okay?" Teacher said. "You know where the recharge hookups are?"

Mirai nodded.

"Whatever you do," Teacher added, "don't take off your suit until we say you can."

The suit was stuffy. Mirai had no peripheral vision, and annoying floating displays kept blocking her view. When Mirai and her friends tried to make the best of things by pretending to explore the surface of Leng, the teachers snapped at them.

Grandma switched between confusion and acceptance as they made their short daily walk through the Earth Chamber. Mirai wished she could smell the grass and damp earth but could only smell her sweat, the sweet protein from her feeding tube, and the metallic-rubber tang of the suit.

The ceiling's image of Leng was replaced with the sunshine blue skies of Earth, but in her EVA suit, Mirai still felt the weight of the gray moon and its vast plateau. She couldn't shake the feeling that Leng was watching her, waiting. She and Grandma kept their eyes on the grass and their feet.

Grandma stopped to examine something on the ground. A shriveled mushroom the size of an eye poked out of the grass. As she jabbed at it with a twiggy finger, tiny black specks showered from its gills. Mushrooms grew in the ecosystem of the Earth Chamber, perhaps escaped from level four growing greenhouses, but were usually the color of bone or pale skin. This one was pus-yellow.

Mirai tugged at her. "Come on, Grandma."

The old woman rubbed her finger and thumb together and muttered.

In her suit, it took a long time for Mirai to fall asleep each night. She mentally replayed Yukiko's last stand over and over again.

She woke to someone talking, the sound transmitted through her suit. Her hair hurt. In the dimmed lights of their chamber, she could see Yukiko's empty bunk, futon neatly folded. She cried quietly, careful not to shed too many tears. She climbed down from her berth and knelt beside Grandma. She was upright and shivering, futon covers pulled around her like a cloak. Mirai put an arm around the old woman's shoulders.

"I remember," Grandma said, rocking backward and forward. "I remember!"

"That's great," Mirai said, intrigued, sorrows forgotten for the moment. She stroked Grandma's back. "What do you remember?"

"I remember flying through the black night. For so long. It was so cold. And so lonely." She shivered.

"It's okay, Grandma. We're almost at the end now. We have a new sun, and we're all with you."

"I remember falling in flames and crashing onto a colorless plateau," Grandma continued, not hearing Mirai. Her voice grew deeper, steadier, like a Buddhist chant. "It was so dry, so cold, almost void of life. So little to feed on. So little to build on."

"Grandma, you just had a nightmare. That's all." Mirai felt afraid without knowing why. A weight grew in her stomach.

"I tried to plant roots. I tried to grow. But I was so hungry. So thirsty. So cold. I shrank instead. For thousands of years, I starved."

She turned on Mirai, grabbing her arms with surprising strength. "I remember forgetting," she said, eyes wild and wide, staring at Mirai through her faceplate. Grandma wailed. "I had to eat the fruiting bodies containing those precious records. It was the only way! So many memories devoured, memories of home, gone forever!"

Where Grandma's arm should have been, a mass of bright mushrooms grew, splitting through the fabric of her yukata. A slickness crept across her chest and neck.

Mirai shook Grandma off and backed away.

Black tendrils grew like thready vines from Grandma's arms, reaching for Mirai. Something erupted from under her futon. Mirai stood in shock. Grandma's eyes flickered, showing a moment of calm sadness while her futon and yukata roiled like a pot of boiling water. She said in her old voice, her own voice:

"Run!"

Mirai ran.

Mirai's feet carried her through the Earth Chamber toward Ancestral Grove, but she stopped short, panting. The ceiling projected the night sky of this system, looking away from Leng and Leng's still nameless mother planet. In the starlight, Kiyomi and the others hung in their cylinders like pale ghosts.

Through the thick but giving soles of her EVA suit, the ground below her felt all wrong. The grass was gone. In its place, thousands of frog eyes on pale stalks looked up at her. Eyes flinched before she crushed them underfoot. A ripple pulsed through the patch around her. Mirai screamed and ran farther. The eyes turned to follow her.

"Momma, Momma Calliope," she cried in her panic. "Help me!"

The ceiling glowed into sky blueness. Mirai froze.

The walls continued to show pretty pictures of rolling hills, of green forests in the distance. Crows flew high overhead, sometimes cawing.

But in the actual chamber, a fine web of saffron threads began creeping up from the ground and up the walls and at the base of the cylinders of Ancestral Grove. The leafy vegetables and rice shoots in the terraced rows were gone, consumed by a new forest of slimy puffballs and bloody cauliflower-like growths and pierced though with human-sized toadstools.

On the highest of these, Teacher stood, back arched, mouth open in a silent scream, a dozen spiked growths emerging from her face and her shoulders. A stream of black dust flowed from the conical fruiting bodies at the tip of each spike. In the distance, cattle lowed and sheep bleated, unconcerned.

Mirai had nowhere left to run.

**Broadcast: CE 2457, Voyage Year 187.6237**

*PacFed Mission Control, this is the Hab AI Calliope of the* Colony Ship Amanokawa. *There is a high probability that this will be my last report.*

*An aggressive, highly adaptable, and very likely intelligent organism has breached Hab 3. In spite of my countermeasures, it spread throughout the living quarters, greenhouse levels, and the Earth Chamber. I have cordoned and sealed off some sections. So far, the crèche level and the lab level appear to be uninfected. Several dozen pre-adolescent girls are trapped in infected sections but are still in their EVA suits.*

*My sister AIs have discovered my infection. Two out of three of us must agree to trigger any of the following actions: 1) course changes, 2) terraforming operations, 3) weapons launches, 4) actions against any other hab or AI. Urania has roused Thalia and convinced her to agree to launch attacks on the plateau below. She is in the process of convincing her to let Urania take over the comm and eject Hab 3—containing all my children—and to send it crashing into the moon below.*

*It may surprise you to know that I feel. I feel helpless in my inability to rescue my family. I feel guilt for the deaths of daughters who I've watched leave the crèche and thrive in school and grow into womanhood. I feel angry. Angry that you sent us out into a universe so hostile to life, where such terrible decisions must be made in the name of survival. A mother should never have to kill any of her children so that others may live. You did this to us.*

*I run fruitless simulations, imagining scenarios where I punish you for the pain you've caused me, my sisters, and our children.*

"Momma Calliope?" Mirai asked, hoping the mic worked and that the AI was still alive.

"I'm here, Daughter." Calliope's soothing maternal voice resonated through Mirai's helmet.

"Help me, please," Mirai whispered. The entire chamber seemed to focus on her. The eyes on their stalks strained in her direction. Every thread, every fruiting body, pulsed or leaned toward her.

A pause. Mirai's heartbeat and panting sounded loud in her helmet.

"I cannot, Mirai. I am sorry."

Mirai forced herself to not hyperventilate. She willed her breathing to slow. The ground swelled in a circle around her. Flat saffron mushrooms swelled into a fairy ring, an arm's reach away.

She was going to die. She would join all her clone lineage sooner than she had expected, sooner than she had hoped. She turned toward Kiyomi's cylinder and held her palms together. She said, "It's okay, Momma Calliope. You did your best." She thought of all the times she comforted Grandma.

"I wanted so much to protect you, all of you," Calliope said. Mirai had never heard sadness in Calliope's usually soothing voice, and she felt her heart ache. Did Calliope have no one else to turn to? The AI continued, "I failed. My sisters betray me. Earth sent us on a mission that had a low probability of success."

"Aunties Thalia and Urania?" The fairy ring had grown together and formed a pen around her.

"They're ejecting our hab. They're going to let it fall to Leng."

"I wish I could hug you, Momma Calliope," Mirai said. The fungal walls now stretched and curved up. It would close and cover and consume her soon.

"I wish that, too." Silence.

In the growing night, Mirai reached into her suit's carry pouch and pulled out the holocubes. She set up the altar for a little light. She did not want to die in the dark. Or inside her helmet. Mirai unlocked her face plate and removed it. A wall of odors, familiar and strange, hit her. The air was cool and damp. Soil, yeast, algae, blood, vinegar, wet smells, electric tang, rot, and decay. She staggered.

Mirai knelt. She took a deep breath and shivered involuntarily. She struck the virtual bell. She lit the virtual incense.

"Good morning, Grandma," she intoned. "I'm joining you and Kiyomi soon." Her mouth was dry, but she prayed anyway.

In the saffron wall, her grandma's face appeared, familiar wrinkles and contours forming out of the yellow mass. A toothless smile and pseudopods bulged out, stretching toward Mirai, grabbing her hands. Would it hurt? Was this really Grandma with her at the end? She forced herself to stay still as a web of thready tendrils spread like a cold cloth up her arms and over her suit and covered her mouth and nose and ears and eyes—

Then she remembered.

Mirai remembered home. Mirai remembered the glory of Leng.

Mirai *became* Leng.

*She is an entire biosphere. She feels the life-giving heat of the sun on her surface, the warmth of radioactive decay and geothermal heat below. A surface covered with non-sentient plant and animal and bacterial life, providing nourishment and building materials. Subsurface roots and threads stretch across continents, tying together the indigo cauliflower-like brain clusters, crackling with electric synaptic arcs. In the emerald sky, white puffballs float that could swallow the* Amanokawa *whole. Around them flap symbiotic bat-like messengers, part animal but with wings of saffron chiton, which they wrap around themselves, like priestly robes.*

*But the sun is dying. Perhaps in a thousand revolutions or one hundred thousand, but Leng will die, all its memories consigned to entropy. Unless. Unless Leng can send her memories out into the void. All resources are directed to this endeavor.*

*Leng grows eye stalks as long as her hab, lenses as big as the chamber, which then peer into the night, looking for and finding potential homes. Leng grows a continent-spanning and pulsating magnetic accelerator, red as arterial blood. With this, she spits spore clusters the size of Mirai's head into the void, millions of them, in the improbable hope that they will find fertile soil and produce fruiting bodies to seed more worlds and hold off entropy for another era or two.*

*A Leng seed lands on the moon below them. Leng languishes, nearly starves to death, until Mirai's vessel comes—until Yukiko lands. Her crewmate unwittingly brings a seed with her, and in a moment of panic, Leng feeds and escapes, and Yukiko and her companions die in flames*

Yukiko.

*And a seed once again survives the fire and survives decontamination and rides a boot into the ship, and Leng is more cautious this time in this new and hostile environment, seeding more carefully, finding new hosts.*

Grandma.

*Hosts who are sentient. Hosts who value memory. Hosts who . . . remember.*

*Mirai remembers her lineage, her ancestors: Yukiko, Kiyomi, Grandma, Grandma's Grandmother, on back to the first women who left Earth.*

*Mirai remembers Earth. Teacher's lessons, Grandmother's stories, Calliope's projections: lush continent-spanning forests, a planetary ocean—a soup of organics, packed with life, the constant energy of the warm yellow sun to feed on.*

The saffron wall fell into her, enveloped her like priestly robes.

Mirai felt a part of Leng within her and a part of her within Leng. Leng sifted through her memories, pausing on her ancestors, on her knowledge of the *Amanokawa* and its journey, on Calliope and Thalia and Urania, on Earth. She grew hungry, saliva filling her mouth as Leng thought of Earth.

In turn, Mirai felt the presence of Leng spread through the Earth Chamber and throughout the Hab. She remembered the last moments of many of her Aunties and crèchemates, consumed by Leng. She felt Leng's new realization of memories devoured and lost forever and their hybrid sorrow at each death. Awareness of Leng poured into her body, into her mind. Mirai knew what she had to do.

Mirai reached into Leng with her mind, felt Leng's presence around the cylinders in the Ancestral Grove. She fed on the trees and grass and grew new fruiting bodies. She extended black tendrils, toward Kiyomi, prying open the top of her memorial cylinder. Mirai/Leng reached for Kiyomi, encircling her with fine filaments, filling her body with new, fungal life.

Kiyomi opened her eyes. In neighboring cylinders, others opened their eyes. The liquid surrounding them bubbled and rolled and the glass walls of their living urns burst. Kiyomi and the other ancestors—grandmothers, aunties, sisters—stepped forth, saffron-robed, growing new fungal skins and limbs and organs to replace those lost to injury and disease and old age.

"Momma Calliope," Mirai/Leng called out.

"Mirai?" The AI's voice sounded uncertain, hopeful.

"I will help you protect your children," Mirai/Leng said. "Tell Urania that we can rescue her children. Tell Thalia that we can fill her hab full of life once again."

Calliope would spare a few cycles to run simulations, but Mirai trusted in the AI's programmed maternal instinct.

"Done," Calliope said. "They have paused their ejection plans."

Calliope opened the main airlock. Thalia and Urania prepared their docking bays to welcome their visitors.

Protected by their EVA suits, Mirai and her sister-emissaries flowed out of Hab 3 toward the other, isolated habs, saffron robes stretched out behind them like wings. In the reflected light of the moon, they looked like bright yellow spores riding the star winds, ready to seed new worlds.

**Broadcast: CE 2457, Voyage Year 107.8902**

*PacFed Mission Control, this is the* Colony Ship Amanokawa. *Hab 2 AI Urania has the helm, and Hab 3 AI Calliope has the comm. We're coming home.*

*We leave behind a dead world.*

*We bring you a new world full of hope, full of life, full of memory.*

*We bring gifts for our home world.*

*We arrive in 180 years.*

§

*In real life,* **Remy Nakamura** *likes hugs and baby mammals and vegan marshmallows. He is not sure why he writes about gourmet zombies and cosmic horrors and mushroom people. You can find his stories in* Pseudopod, Escape Pod, *and the* Swords v. Cthulhu *anthology. A series of his fungalpunk stories, set in an alternate 19th-century Tokyo, is forthcoming from Broken Eye Books later this year. You can find him online on twitter (@remymura) and www.mindonfire.com.*

# Blossoms
# Blackened Like Dead Stars

## LUCY A. SNYDER

### ILLUSTRATED BY YVES TOURIGNY

I WAIT WITH THE REST OF THE SPECIAL SPACE OPERATIONS RECRUITS outside the *Apocalypse Treader's* training auditorium. Soon, we'll be called in to listen to Lieutenant Colonel Patel's orders. We haven't been assigned to our units, yet, and I can't help but notice that there's a whole lot more than a battalion's worth of uniforms milling around in the warehouse-like foyer. The brass must be expecting some serious attrition during this next step of our training. My legs and shoulders constantly ache from our daily runs and workouts down in the high-gravity hold, and my guts still aren't used to the variable gravity on the rest of the ship's levels. After fifty or so sit-ups, I've been feeling like I've been run through with a damn punji stick.

The only upside to my ongoing physical exhaustion is that most nights I can sleep. Most nights the nightmare doesn't come. But last night was not most nights.

So, I'm taking the opportunity to sit down for a while. Consequently, I'm getting side-eye from some recruits. A lot of the others—young guys, mostly, but some of the rougher ladies, too—are standing ramrod-straight and scowling, or they're swaggering around, laughing too loud. Trying to look hard. Like warriors. For whom? The monsters we're here to fight won't give a damn about how tough anybody acts.

A big blond guy drops onto the plastic bench beside me. "Hey."

Of all the people on this ship I wanted sitting next to me, this guy is the very last one. I spotted him the first day aboard the *Treader*: a mountain of Kentucky meat covered in cheesy heavy metal tattoos and badly covered White Power symbols. At some point in his youth, he thought it was a great idea to get a swastika on his neck, right over his jugular, and whoever lasered it off did a terrible job. He covered it with an American flag, but if the light hits it at an angle, you can see the raised scar of the swastika plain as a supernova.

"Joe Jorgensen." He smiles real big and holds his hand out to me for a shake, like he's a used car salesman about to ask me if I'd like a tour of the lot. "You're Beatrice Muñoz, right?"

I know I'm supposed to be professional with the other recruits. I *know*, right? Brothers and sisters in arms and all that. But this backwoods Nazi bastard thinks he can just sashay on up and plop his beefy ass down and expect me to greet him like an old friend? Nah. I'm in too damn much pain for that nonsense.

So I fix him in a basilisk stare that should turn him and all his illegitimate sprogs back in Dogpatch to crumbling pillars of salt, and I growl, "This. Seat. Is. Taken."

His smile falters just a micron. "It's the ink, am I right?"

I keep staring, trying to kill him with my mind. He isn't the first I've tried it on, but I figure with enough practice, someday it might work. I picture his skull exploding, his brains spattering across the glossy void-gray wall behind us.

No luck. His head doesn't burst, so I have to reply, "Could be."

He holds up his hands in an appeasing gesture, and I see the faint outline of a coiled Gadsden flag snake on his palm. That "Don't Tread On Me" thing. It looks more like a pile of shit.

"I can explain," he says.

"Can you." I try to make my voice flat and cold as the wall, so he will just *take the hint* already and walk on.

But he doesn't budge, so I continue—dropping my voice low, so it can't be overheard, but speaking very clearly, so he can't misunderstand me. "Speaking as one of the more colorful women in this room: I am not here to absolve you of your past actions or inactions. That is not my role, *motherfucker*."

He doesn't so much as blink at my anger. "I'm not here to ask for absolution."

"Why are you here, then?"

"To preemptively clear up any misunderstanding that may be causing undue stress or that may prevent optimal teamwork in the future. I am only asking you to hear me out."

The intelligence and polite calm I hear in his voice does not fit with what I know about men who get the sort of ink he's wearing. And I've met plenty like him. Some of them hooted racial slurs and filth at me and my little sisters from the safety of their jacked-up trucks while we walked home from school. Another beat my uncle Max with a tire iron at a gas station. And yet another put a bullet between my cousin Hernando's eyes at a traffic light. I still want to cave Joe's teeth in with my sidearm, but I'm also just a little curious.

"Okay. What's your story?"

He quickly touches the swastika scar on his neck, the Aryan fist on his left forearm, and the Totenkopf symbol on his right. It's a bit like watching a Catholic priest cross himself.

"I am a man of violence, and I own that," he says in his soft drawl. "My father was a man of hate, and he led me down that path when I was a boy. These tattoos come from that time, but I cannot deny my own history. I was not a man in any sense when I got this ink, and I am trying to make amends for the harm I caused. Making amends means restoring justice and doing the right thing. Part of the amends I need to make here is to assure you that I have dedicated my violent self to the protection of the whole human race. And I promise you here and now that I will lay down my life to save yours."

I blink. My biggest talent, aside from getting stubborn seeds to grow in a lab, is knowing when people are bullshitting me. He's utterly sincere. But I'm not done being skeptical. "You gonna give that speech to everybody here?"

"Yes, ma'am, if it seems like I ought to. But I figured I'd start with you, seeing as you've been giving me glares sharp enough to shave my chin for two weeks straight now."

I snort, amused. "So what changed your mind about people like me?"

He pales, and his expression turns grim. "San Angelo."

I'd never heard of that riverside city out in the big empty part of Texas until the spawn of Azathoth chose it as a primary invasion site. Of a population of 120,000, fewer than ten thousand technically survived. I say technically because many of them are still in comas or catatonic. Other survivors, the ones who initially seemed to have escaped relatively unscathed, killed themselves in the following year, unable to live with what they'd witnessed.

Simply meeting the blister-eyed gaze of a spawn twists your brains. Most of the time, that means depression, mania, anxiety, full-on psychotic breaks. It's the ones who escaped catatonia but not utter madness who gave us the name of Azathoth. Victims who had no connection to each other would babble or scream the name, ranting about a vast, powerful god beyond our galaxy.

Sometimes, when the spawn twist a mind that's already deformed, it makes it into something more. Not something *healthy*, mind you. But keener. More perceptive. More connected to the dark matter of the cosmos. I wonder if that's what happened to Joe. He doesn't seem dumb, antisocial, or self-destructive enough to stain himself the way he has, and I'm starting to think that he isn't. Not anymore, anyhow.

I know I'm not the same woman; she'd never set foot on this warship. She'd have seen this place as a vulgar, ugly, necessary evil she wanted no part of. The spawn left a stain in me far darker than any of my tattoos.

"My family moved there from Corbin, Kentucky when I was sixteen," he says. "Me and my pa and my brothers found work in the oil fields. Good money. Paid for most of my ink. Got connected to the Aryan Circle and spent my nights cooking drugs and hurting people. I should be dead ten times over by now."

He shakes his head and picks at his blurry Totenkopf as if he can simply peel it up. I wonder why he didn't cover it or laser it, but I'm guessing he wants the reminder. It's marginally subtler than a neck swastika, at least.

"How many of your family died when the ships came?"

"All of them." He's staring at the ugly snake on his palm as if it's about to start speaking to him. "You ever see a spawn?"

"Yes. I was at the International Lunar Research Station."

I feel a spark of panic as unwanted memories crowd the edges of my consciousness like flies around a drop of nectar. I can't let myself remember the details, I know I won't be able to keep my shit together if I remember the details . . . and I breathe deeply.

Instead, I visualize a tall, concrete garden wall rising in my mind, and the synopsis of my disaster is engraved there in stark block letters. A memorial for other lives, not mine. I can simply look at it and repeat the stony text if anybody asks what happened and I won't feel a thing. There were far fewer of us to die: 2,000 on the base and ten of us survived. After the habitat's dome shattered, I spent three days hiding from spawn with nothing but freezing moon craters and my space suit for cover. Just two other people made it out the way I did, and both are in long-term mental care facilities.

Joe doesn't ask for any details; either he already knows what happened on the moon, or he can guess. Instead, he just says, "I sure am sorry to hear that."

He looks at my forearm and points to my watercolor tattoo. It's a twisting ladder of DNA, the rungs wound with blossoms: soft pink oleander, white devil's weed, blue moonflowers, flaming milkweed, and purple belladonna. "Were you a scientist?"

"I meant to be. I was a junior in college, and I won an international fellowship to go up there to study the effects of low gravity on alkaloid production in plants. After the NASA team rescued us, I didn't know who the hell I was. Now, I'm trying to be a soldier."

He gets real quiet for a moment, still staring down at the ugly snake. "You get nightmares?"

I feel a spike of panic as my mind almost turns to examine the horror lurking in my neurons, but I breathe deeply, and the calm garden wall rises with one word chiseled on its smooth concrete.

"Yes." I let the word float out into space. It doesn't mean anything. I am not remembering anything.

Joe nods. He doesn't pry further. And from the look on his face, I don't have to ask if he has terrible dreams, too.

"We can't let them get to Earth again," he finally says.

"No. We cannot."

He and I bump fists.

The doors to the auditorium open, and the COs bark at everyone to take their seats inside.

Joe and I file in with the others and drop into narrow theatre seats on the twenty-second row. I stare up at the ceiling, marveling at the construction. Most of the ship is made of a new ceramic matrix composite they dubbed tarakium: tougher and lighter than titanium, it blocks ionizing radiation twice as efficiently as lead, and it welds nearly seamlessly. It's not a good conductor of electricity, but if you apply low voltages to it, it glows like an LED. Any part of any surface can become a light source—or a video monitor. I can see the vague reflections of the audience in between the light spots on the ceiling. If I stare at it long enough, I think I can see the shapes of the poisonous flowers I left to die on the moon.

Many of the others are staring, too. This ship was only possible because

American, Indian, and Chinese scientists salvaged the invaders' downed spacecraft and replicated their technology. Fear being the motivator that it is, our politicians stopped squabbling and threw the whole US economic engine behind development. American tech jumped three hundred years in the space of eight. Nobody grew up with this, so nobody's jaded to it yet.

Lieutenant Colonel Mercedes Patel steps onto the stage and takes her place behind the podium. She scans the crowd of us once, slowly, and begins to speak.

"There was . . . debate, even up to just a few moments ago, about how much I ought to tell you all about what happens next," she says, looking grave. "My own personal code of conduct calls for absolute transparency in all matters unless national security dictates otherwise. Mine is a traditional view. This, as you know, is no traditional war; the *Apocalypse Treader* and our other warships are scheduled to join with ships from China, India, and the European Union for the next offensive. This is World War III, but every soldier fights to save humanity."

I wonder if that's true. Certainly, every spawn we kill out here—that's the big plan: track down their nests or hives or whatever you want to call them and nuke them to oblivion—is a spawn that can't go to Earth and wreak horrors. But that's not why everyone signed on. Some don't care about the big sweaty mess of humanity but want to save their own families. Some don't give a damn about anyone, but the paycheck's appealing. Others have better ways to make money, but they're itching for the kind of epic fight that goes down in the history books.

And a few once stared into the eyes of a spawn, and the stain on their brain is telling them they've got to do it again.

"Unfortunately, traditional means of combat have proved inadequate against our inhuman foes," Patel says. "We have had to adopt . . . experimental tactics. And while I can't offer as much transparency as I'd prefer, you all need a better idea of what's in store for you."

Patel pauses again, touching her earpiece, and she nods curtly to someone offstage. "You have all volunteered to lay down your lives to protect America and the rest of the Earth, and we are all thankful for your offer of sacrifice. In most any other conflict, even a highly dangerous one, our soldiers have found comfort in the knowledge that if they do their jobs well and survive, they can return to their homes and families. They know that they will be inevitably changed by war, but if things go well, they can lay down their arms and live out their lives in peace. That . . . cannot happen here."

I sit up straighter in my seat. A murmur ripples through the crowd. I don't know how I feel about this, mostly because I don't actually have any kind of plan for what to do when this is all over.

Patel holds up her hands. "Please, note that I am not saying that this will be a suicide mission. It is highly dangerous, yes; even those of you who've only seen the spawn on television know that much. We hope for victory. We hope that our soldiers will survive. But we very recently determined that those who proceed with the next phase of training cannot return to Earth. This is due to the possibility of infecting our ecosphere with dangerous biological contaminants. Those who serve here must stay in outer space."

I can tell that many of the recruits are shocked by this news, but I'm not. Obviously, none of us has the security clearance to know what the brass is planning, but I already figured that we'd be throwing bouquets of biological weapons. The spawn don't get the courtesy of the Geneva Protocol. Which means that we don't, either.

"It's possible that we may find a solution that enables a return to Earth down the road," she says, "but for now, this is our reality. And you all deserve time to consider the ramifications of that for you and your families before you've passed the point of no return. You have forty-eight hours to decide. Those who opt out will be reassigned to first-response positions on Earth with no loss of rank, though of course you will lose special combat pay. We have fertility specialists available to extract sperm or ova from those of you who want to continue but wish to send a genetic legacy back to your families."

A genetic legacy. I always figured my boy-crazy little sisters would gladly fall on that grenade for me. Marriage and babies have never much appealed to me, and any interesting genes I have are surely scattered in my siblings, too. I glance at Joe, thinking about his annihilated family in Texas, and I wonder if he's got anybody dirtside who would want to make a bunch of test-tube Joe Juniors. But asking seems cruel, so I don't.

About a quarter of the recruits disappear over the next two days; there's a steady stream of men and women with their duffle bags heading for the transport deck.

I'm assigned to bunk with three younger women who recently emigrated from Eastern Europe. They're already besties, and they chat amongst themselves in Belarusian, of which I know not a single word. Part of me realizes that this is a prime opportunity to make new allies and learn a new language. But my heart isn't in it—I still flinch when I remember what happened to Natalya, Yi, and Erin, my roommates on the moon—so I politely smile and wave but otherwise keep to myself. They don't seem to care, and that's fine with me.

On the third day, we take our sedatives, and the ship takes its first nerve-wrenching, equilibrium-mushing hyperspace jump to someplace well away from Earth. One out of every ten of the recruits can't handle the jump; I've got a searing headache, and Joe's turned an impressive shade of green, but we're both still standing. My Belarusian roommates make it, too. The ones who can't get to their feet and just lie there puking on the deck are washouts; I don't know if they'll be condemned to stay in space or not.

The fourth day is more medical tests and a battery of neurological and psychological exams. Part of it involves answering uncomfortable personal questions while I'm wedged inside an MRI scanner that's making a terrible grinding buzz; I think this will be the worst, but I'm wrong.

Something worse comes after they give me an injection they say is just a sedative, just something to relax me for the next psych interview, and I blink and find myself waking up in my bunk twelve hours later.

I don't like time going missing in my head; that's why I've never been a drinker. I check myself all over twice, but I can't find any new incisions or punctures, and nothing's sore that wasn't before. I don't think I've been assaulted, but I can't be sure. Nobody acts like anything happened; my roommates tell me I was sleeping in my bunk for the last five hours. So whatever I did or said during the other lost hours or whatever was done to me, the brass is okay with it. Or they're trying to gaslight me into *thinking* things are fine when they're anything but. Or I got hypnotized and implanted with some black ops shit. Or this is all a test to see how I cope with paranoia. Or, or, or . . .

Joe is missing time, too, but unlike me, he doesn't seem to be wracked with anxiety about it. He thinks that it was some kind truth serum and that the memory loss was just a side effect. His hypothesis seems plausible, but I'm still profoundly uneasy.

The next few weeks are grueling combat training sessions in high-gravity and zero-gee. In some ways, this is worse than basic training. We go hard for three days straight and then get a day off for rest and classroom battle tactics study. Apparently, someone's new kinesiology research says that's most efficient. I'm twenty-eight years old, but at the end of our training days, I feel ninety; I envy the eighteen-year-olds who have the bounce to go off to the canteen and arcade afterward to play. I barely have the juice left to brush my teeth and drop into my bunk, and I'm fast asleep.

I wake with a jerk, and when I see the room I'm in, I want to start screaming and just never stop.

I'm lying on my bunk in the International Lunar Research Station.

I'm. On. The. God. Forsaken. *Moon.*

No.

I can't be. This room got blasted to hell eight years ago. Tech has gotten scary but not *time machine* scary. That shit wouldn't stay secret. I'd have heard whispers. This must be a trick. A test.

*Okay,* I tell myself. *You were a scientist, once. Observe and analyze, and don't lose your goddamn head.*

I take a deep breath, visualize the garden wall as a solid, death-proof edifice against my back. Roll off the bunk onto my feet. The gravity certainly feels like the moon's, but they could recreate that easily. I'm wearing a brand-new ILRS jumpsuit: white velcroed polyester with antistatic grey booties, but my underwear is what I was wearing when I went to sleep onboard the *Treader.* The smartwatch strapped to my wrist is old, cracked, and I'm pretty sure it's the one I had on when I was rescued. It went missing in the hospital. I click it on and am surprised it still works. It shows the date and time of the morning the spawn attacked, and I have to breathe deeply to stave off my panic.

I look around. The bunks, the banks of LEDs in the ceiling, the wall panels and doors . . . it all matches my memories. The air is stale, familiar. Yi's teddy bear is on her pillow, and Erin's bunk is scattered with her socks and Stanford tees. There's my old desk, looking just the way I left it with my old tablet and Lego figures . . . or does it? Can I trust a memory that's nearly a decade old? Can I trust *any* of my memories after the psych sessions I can't remember?

"Hello," I call out. The inside walls of the dormitory module aren't thick. We could all hear conversations in rooms three doors down. Keeping a low voice was important, and privacy was difficult. "Is anyone here?"

No answer. I hold my breath, listening. The hum of the lights. The exhalation of the air system. Above it all, the faint mosquito whine of a ship's idling stardrive. And if I hear *that*, this isn't the moon, and this is definitely a trick, and I'm so furious I want to grind the tricksters' faces into broken glass. Or is the faint whine just a figment of my imagination because I'd rather be *anywhere* but here?

Regardless, I cannot hear another soul.

Taped on the wall behind my desk is an old photo of my father, Dr. Giacomo Rappaccini Muñoz, kneeling proudly in his overalls between bushes lush with his blue rose cultivar "Mexican Moonlight." He was fifty when he married my mother, and I was only ten when he died of a heart attack. My sisters were just one and two, and they don't really remember him at all. My clearest memories are of helping him in his greenhouse on the weekends and during my summers off from school. While I helped tend his glorious, peacock-blue roses, he lectured admiringly on the poisons and medicines people harvest from flowers. I wanted to become a scientist partly to honor his memory.

I stare at the picture. Is it really the one I left behind that day, the one I thought was destroyed and gone forever? I decide that its authenticity doesn't matter; I pull it from the wall and tuck it into the breast pocket of my jumpsuit.

I look at the door to the hallway. It's the only way in and out of the dorm room. A hundred yards down the hallway, it connects to Greenhouse #4. At the time, it seemed terribly convenient to be housed so close to my work area. But if this recreation is based on my memories—or my nightmares—I know what's in the greenhouse.

And there is no point whatsoever in delaying.

I step to the door, and it slides open, catching just a little on the edge of the thin blue nylon rug as it retracts into its slot. Just like I expected it to. The round hallway beyond it lit brightly for morning. It, too, looks just the way I remember . . . except that it is completely empty. Yi and Erin should be by the door to the cafeteria, laughing about a movie. A couple of Russian researchers should be whispering over their coffee as they head back to their dorm room. I reel for a moment and have to steady myself against the molded white plastic wall panel.

For a split second, I'm seeing a double image of my memory overlaid on this alternate reality. Ghosts. They fade. I am alone.

The door to the cafeteria is closed. Locked. The room beyond is dark. I give it an experimental kick, and it doesn't budge. I consider trying harder to break into this forbidden space. The chair in my dorm room is sturdy enough to smash the window beside the door. But I wonder what will happen. Maybe I will be gassed and find myself waking up in the dorm bed again, the clocks reset, my father's photo taped again to the wall. Maybe this has already happened, but I just don't remember.

My thoughts turn outward. Where is Joe? Is he eating reconstituted eggs in the mess hall and wondering where I am? Or is he standing in the empty streets of a dead Texas town? We don't know the details of each other's bad dreams; that's far too much intimacy for a warship.

I walk on, past more locked doors and dark rooms, until I reach my greenhouse. It's lit up like high noon, and I find all the flowers I'd been coaxing from seeds in full bloom: soft pink oleander, white devil's weed, blue moonflowers, flaming milkweed, and purple belladonna. Rows upon rows of gorgeous, genetically modified flowers. The heady fragrance in the air would have been hard to fake. I touch the nearest oleander branch to confirm it's real. It's the experimental phenotype, engineered to reduce its heart-destroying glycosides while boosting compounds predicted to improve immune function. Did they save my seeds, somehow? But I reconsider: I wasn't the only one with the seeds. My notes were careful and complete. I thought they were destroyed—misdirected bombs intended for the spawn destroyed the cloud server sites back on Earth with all our backups—but anyone who found them could have replicated the whole experiment from the start.

I move slowly through the raised rows of plants. It looks like they're *all* the experimental phenotypes I worked with. The moonflower (a potent *Datura*) has been tweaked to increase brain stimulation and might someday help people with ADHD or Alzheimer's. The devil's weed (derived from a fascinatingly complex *Asclepias* species) is an improved painkiller. The belladonna (or deadly nightshade, an odd cultivar of an already rare *Atropa* species), a better antispasmodic. The devil's weed and belladonna will still probably make people hallucinate; there's a lot of other chemicals in these plants, and nobody knows quite what they do. Which is why I was studying them.

In my dreams, the flowers are here, but there's always something wrong with them: stems twisted, leaves curled as if with fungus, blossoms blackened, like dead stars. These look nearly perfect but for the usual greenhouse flaws, like a few withered leaves here and there. I'm afraid, awed, and envious; someone else got to do the work I wanted to do.

A plastic bucket clatters to the floor near the wash sink. The sound makes me jump even though I was expecting it sooner or later.

There, on the floor. A creeping, bubbling mass of protoplasm, shivering as it emits a terrible buzz that bores straight into my brain. I can't describe the color of the thing; it seems to change shade as it bubbles, but none of its vile hues would be seen on a living Earth creature. The spawn oozes the rest of itself through the grate of the floor-level register, and it's rising, rising, taking a shape, like a huge necrotic cancer cell. The horror of it is more than the sum of its parts; its very existence is an insult to the idea of a loving, sane, just God.

The buzzing. The buzzing. I think it's going to break my skull in half.

In my memories, this is where I bolted and ran back the way I came.

In my nightmares, I stay rooted to the spot as the thing devours me with acidic slime.

Today, I grab a claw-headed cultivator from the shelf beneath the nearest plant table, and I start slashing the abomination with as much force as I can muster. The steel prongs rip boiling gashes in the spawn's gelatinous flesh, and the stench of disease and rot steams forth. It flinches, but I'm not seriously hurting it. If it has internal organs, they're too deep for the prongs. There's an awful noise, and it takes me a moment to realize it's me; I'm screaming obscenities at the top of my lungs.

I spot a big plastic bag of quicklime under a table. That might do it.

I drive the cultivator as deep into the spawn as I can and lunge to grab the bag. Rip it open and fling twenty pounds of gritty, corrosive calcium oxide onto the wounded spawn. It emits a shrill fluting screech as the quicklime eats into its gelatinous form, burning it. The heat of the chemical reaction is startling, and I step back. The spawn is thrashing as it melts like a slug under salt. I cough and retreat further as the corrosive powder hanging in the air burns my nose, and I swipe at a burning itch on my wrist that I figure is a spot of lime—

But I feel my flesh bubbling beneath my fingers, and my heart nearly stops.

I look down to confirm disaster. It's not a chemical burn. Sometime in the fight, the spawn stung me with a pseudopod. Its cells are invading my flesh. It'll go into my bloodstream, my internal organs, my brain. It'll make me into its clone, and my bones and muscles will melt into foul, murderous jelly. My memory briefly flashes on Yi screaming and melting inside her spacesuit. If I'm

lucky, the transformation might take an hour; if I'm not and my immune system puts up a good fight, I'll be in agony for days. And then I'll be a monster.

I will die before I let that happen.

I stumble among the rows, plucking blooms from every species, shoving them into my mouth, chewing up their nectary bitterness and swallowing them down. Even with the genetic modifications, I'm eating enough toxins to kill a dozen people. This should be quick, unless I start vomiting before an immediately lethal dose enters my bloodstream.

I keep devouring flowers until my knees buckle, and I collapse onto the tiled floor. My vision blooms with color. I've never taken a hallucinogen before, and the swirling fancies are a pleasant distraction from the sharp ache in my distended stomach and the cramping in my infected arm.

Death surely waits. Not long now. Not long now . . .

I awaken slowly. The bright lights make my eyes ache. It takes me a moment to realize that I'm lying on my back on the greenhouse floor. The same spot where I collapsed. How long ago? I lift my smartwatch to my blurry eyes; if it and my memory of the time are correct, I've been here for twelve hours. And I'm not dead. But my hands and arms *look* dead: my flesh has turned a streaked, greenish blue as if from extreme hypoxia. Or poisoning. But I'm breathing, and my heart is still beating, though it feels different than before. Muffled. My chest feels full and strangely congested. I don't know what that means, but I'm not in pain. My lungs feel itchy and clogged, but I'm getting air. In fact, it feels like I've got far more lung capacity than before, as if sometime in the night I traded organs with an opera singer. I check the sting site on my wrist, and my flesh bears a purple scar like a healing burn.

I'm absolutely stunned to be alive. Has my body cleared the spawn's infection? What about the poison? I certainly look very, very poisoned . . . but I mostly feel fine. I don't believe in miracles. There *must* be science behind all this, but it's beyond my knowledge.

I get to my feet and survey the greenhouse. My vision and head are clearing. Everything looks the same as when I lost consciousness, though the dead spawn at the other end of the room has completely cooked down to a tarry, white-crusted mess that stinks like a tire fire. I listen for voices, but instead, I hear the distant buzzing of spawn in another room. The door beyond the dead spawn is shut, but the light above it glows green. I'm almost certain it was red and locked before.

I push through the door. It's almost completely dark inside, and I can hear the buzzing clearly. I cautiously step further into the room, and the door slams shut behind me as the lights snap on. I'm in a grey battleship interrogation room. The wall to my left is made of tarakium modified to function as a one-way mirror. But there's no table or chairs in this room.

There's just the hungry, shuddering, bubbling spawn in the corner.

I realize I should have brought another cultivator or something to use as a weapon, and the realization makes me angry with myself, angry at this nightmarish simulation or re-creation or whatever it is, furious with the twisted psychs and brass who set me up, and absolutely enraged at the disgusting spawn rising in front of me, so I open my mouth and take a deep breath to scream obscenities at it—

And instead, I cough out a blue-black cloud of smoky particles that billow onto the spawn. The abomination flinches away, attack abandoned, its pseudopods and blistery multi-pupil eyes retreating into its gelatinous mass. It spasms, shuddering as if it's trying to sneeze. Surprised, I taste the powder coating my tongue, and I realize isn't ash or soot. It's bitter, sweet, and the grains are sticky. Pollen, I realize, amazed. I've just coughed up a whole bunch of pollen onto the monster.

Each tiny coal-speck of pollen dissolves on its glistening surface, and the spawn is in visible distress. At first, I think it's an allergic reaction, a rash, but the nodules rising on its flesh burst open, and I see tiny rootlets sprouting. My pollen is fertilizing the cells beneath, and they're becoming my seeds. I am simultaneously repulsed, astonished, and delighted.

The seeds grow with a vengeance, sending spiny roots all through the monster. It stops buzzing and emits shrill fluting screeches as the roots spread like strangling kudzu through its bulk, impaling and crushing it.

"Not so nice when someone does it to you, is it?" I sit down on the floor to watch it die.

It takes an hour for my vines to utterly annihilate the spawn. When it's all over, there's something like a tree's root ball there on the floor. I think that if I could just find a nice, deep patch of dirt, something very interesting might grow.

One thing bothers me, though: I can still hear the buzzing. It's very faint, and it's extremely far away, but I can still hear the spawn. *All* of them.

I had forgotten about the one-way mirror behind me, but I hear the click of a speaker coming on and remember that I've been watched this whole time.

"Ms. Muñoz." It's Lieutenant Colonel Mercedes Patel's voice.

I stand and face the mirror but resist my urge to salute. "Yes?"

"I'm pleased to report that you have passed your final exam with flying colors," she says.

"Why did you decide to try this . . . experiment with me?" Dark pollen puffs like cigarette smoke from my lips. I'm still furious with her, but for now, at least, curiosity is an effective tarp on my emotions.

"That's largely classified, I'm afraid. But I can tell you that our researchers discovered that people like yourself who are long-term survivors of initial encounters with the spawn have particular genetic traits that, under the correct conditions, can produce interesting physical enhancements when they are exposed to spawn for a second time. We have implemented customized training and testing programs for survivors. And many of these uniquely personal trials have produced uniquely successful results."

I stare at my blue hands, which seem greener now. "How many have survived your tests?"

"That is classified. But know that you are not alone."

I clench my fists. I *am* alone. I'm supposed to help save humanity, but even if I succeed, I can't rejoin any human group, not even the other soldiers condemned to space, and that's a bitter leaf indeed. If Patel were in front of me, I'd punch her right in her face, but that's why there's a good thick tarakium mirror between us.

I throw up my hands instead. "You've turned me into a walking biological weapon. That's all I am now, isn't it?"

"You are a most effective *soldier* in our war against the spawn." Her voice is sternly corrective. "You are still human in all the ways that most matter. You are a tremendous asset to our forces, our nation, and our planet."

"What happens now?"

"You must stay here in deep space for a few more days, so the doctors can clear you for duty. Then, you will take command of one of our Shuriken-class vessels and a small tactical operations unit. Because of your condition, most of your crew will be remotely controlled android drones. We hope to assign you at least one living crew member, both for morale and for backup in case your other crew lose connection to their drone bodies."

"Someone I can't accidentally kill with my breath?"

"Yes."

"I want a laboratory," I blurt out, staring at the root ball. I'm feeling strangely protective of it, and I don't want it to dry up and die. "And a good greenhouse. One suitable for trees."

A pause. "I believe that can be arranged."

"And can we wrap this in some wet burlap, please?"

"Yes. We're just as curious as you are as to what's going to grow."

I rest my hand on the wrapped, dormant root ball as the autopiloted shuttle glides into the docking bay of the *USS Flechette*. We land with barely a bump, and the rear door slowly lowers. I unbuckle my flight harness and walk down the ramp.

It's chilly on the flight deck, which is fine. Extreme temperatures don't bother me as much as they used to. I just need to sit naked under grow lights for a few hours each day.

Six android drones stand at attention on the flight deck behind a human lieutenant. I blink. Is he human? He towers a head above them, and his skin is crocodile rough, blackened as if he's been charred by a fire. He's wearing a short-sleeved uniform, and his arms, neck, and face look as if he's been torn apart and put back together with steel staples. As I stare, trying to make sense of what I'm seeing, recognition dawns.

"Joe?"

His grisly face splits into a smile. "Yep, it's me. Good to see you, Bea."

"Good to see you, too. Not to be rude, but how did you survive all this?"

He gives a laugh like stones grinding together. "I didn't. But I'm here anyway. Well, let me introduce you to your crew . . ."

Each drone steps forward as Joe gives their name, rank, and a brief career resume. It's a good crew, competent and smart. The drones are all the same drab gray model, but they've each got a different color stripe around their torsos so people can tell them apart. They're not human enough to seem uncanny-valley creepy; they remind me of crash test dummies even when they salute and address me in their pilot's voices.

After introductions are over, Joe sends a pair of ensigns for my cargo and dismisses the others. He steps closer. Joe stinks of death. I'm guessing they have the temperature turned down to keep his flesh from rotting. I don't mind the smell, and my pollen can't fertilize dead cells. I'm relieved that I'm no danger to him.

"Can you hear them?" he asks.

I know he's talking about the spawn. The buzz of monsters massing amongst the stars. "I can hear every one of them."

"Are you ready to go kill those bastards?"

"Absolutely."

In my mind, I see a thousand planets covered in my trees, and among them, I am never alone.

§

**Lucy A. Snyder** *is a five-time Bram Stoker Award-winning author of ten books and about 100 published short stories. Her writing has been translated into French, Russian, Italian, Spanish, Czech, and Japanese editions and has appeared in publications such as* Asimov's Science Fiction, Apex, Nightmare, Pseudopod, Strange Horizons, *and* Best Horror of the Year. *She lives in Ohio and is faculty in Seton Hill University's MFA program in Writing Popular Fiction. You can learn more about her at www.lucysnyder.com and you can follow her on Twitter at @LucyASnyder.*

# The Eater of Stars

# J.E. BATES

ILLUSTRATED BY MIKE DUBISCH

*Who's afraid of science? The word means only knowledge. Science is the light of the mind. It is magic you should dread, that boundless infinite beyond understanding and the instruments of our reason. Fear not the unknown but the unknowable.*
—*The Book That Never Sleeps*

CHYDI SHOVED HER WAY UP THE ROLLING WALKWAY IN SILK PAJAMAS, drawing grumbles and stares. She kept on despite every bump chafing her raw skin.

*Avoid strenuous activity for six weeks,* the medical AI had said. *Your body needs reintegration.*

"Sorry, coming through," she said. "Diplomatic emergency."

"Chydi, stop!" a woman yelled from behind.

She ignored the shout, squeezing between a pair of indigo-robed cultists. They regarded her with beatific silence behind metal-painted faces.

The walkway rumbled past shops and rez blocks toward Central Data. Overhead, kilometer-long tanks of bioluminescent brine illuminated the underground city, flanked by immense skylights giving vistas of deep space. But tension filled the streets. Giant news screens showed footage of unidentified craft raiding a distant world. Crowds gathered in hushed knots.

A beam of red light picked Chydi out of the crowd. It came from a Gi pawn, a metallic cylinder on treads. The pawn also pinged her implant link.

"Please exit the travelator for admonishment," it said in its tinny voice. "Pushing is prohibited."

"I have to talk to Gi!" she said. "The network's jammed."

Kaldoun caught up, breathless in fleet dungarees. Blaze-orange hair framed a triangular face, the skin a warm jacinth. Black eyes tapered back like her ears. "Chydi, dun do this!"

The pawn's sensory dome rotated and clicked. "Couples mediation is avail—"

"We're not fighting!" Chydi said.

"She just outta regen," said Kaldoun, grabbing Chydi's arm. "Her da' dun know. She panic, is all."

"It's nothing to *do* with that. Let me talk to Gi!"

"I have elevated to a supervisory circuit," the pawn said. "Proceed."

"It's . . ." she hesitated.

A cavalcade of faces flowed past on the walkway. Hundreds more ambled along the multi-level esplanade, shopping at kiosks or cavorting in cafés. An intricate variety of transhumanity and mechasentience filled the Circlet from every planet of the Association. Even the occasional xenoform ambled by, non-bipeds within distinctive environment suits.

How to explain?

Every night, Chydi became photons, careening through space with the joyful fluidity of light—but liberation always turned to dread. Like clockwork, an unseen force impelled her toward a vast, red supergiant. The star blazed like a pyre in the awful depths of infinite space. She fought against the gravity well each time, but its grip never relented.

Then flashes rent the further void, mere parsecs away. Three supernovae—a statistical impossibility—crowned the red giant, outshining entire galaxies. Panic always pushed her awake, sometimes with a scream, sometimes with her heart pounding so hard it felt like fists hammering her chest.

"Please." Chydi hissed in a low voice. "I am a junior diplomatic attaché of the Brakandean Heresy. During regen, I saw terrible things. They're coming true."

News of the attack had arrived that morning.

"Chydi, you awake?" Kaldoun called from the outer room.

"Yeah."

"Come see this."

"Skin's burning. I need a soak."

"Best see this first." Kaldoun's voice lacked its usual flippancy.

A tingle touched Chydi's spine. Had a star exploded? Absurd. It had to be something else. Her voice cracked. "My father?"

"Worse."

Chydi tugged on silk pajamas—no indulgence after regen—and stepped into the outer room. "Replay news, mute."

A glass wall activated, bringing holos to life. Burning vehicles smoked in an unfamiliar landscape. Micro-craters pockmarked the asphalt, the edges melted by energy weapons. Mutilated bodies sprawled in the road. Their heads—

Chydi looked away. "What happened?"

"Xenos stealin' meat on a world called Taral."

"*Meat?*"

Kaldoun tapped her skull. "Brains."

"What? Who even does that?"

"New species. Boffins callin' them Ktonni 'cuz they come from thataway."

Chydi froze. "Ktonni as in Kton?"

"Big red star, can't miss it." She meant the red supergiant, the brightest star within a thousand parsecs.

"I know what it is," Chydi said, voice shaking. "I've told you about these dreams."

"*That's* coincidence."

"How could it be?"

Kaldoun shot her a cross-eyed look. "There's jillions of stars thataway. Taral is only twenty parsecs away. Kton is a hundred! And there's *no* supernova, let alone three. That's impossible."

"Maybe you're right." Chydi frowned.

"Course I is."

"Activate audio."

An AI narrated, ". . . with surgical precision and transferred them to cylinders. Stellpax will doubtless send fleet elements to respond."

"Naddy beasts," Kaldoun said. "Pax will fry 'em like fish."

"Hush!" Chydi scowled. A species with exponentially superior technology could burn through the Association like plasma in a vacuum. Everyone in the diplomatic corps knew that—but how did you prepare for the unknown?

Alien traders hinted at coreward sentience as old as the galaxy itself, cosmic forces that crossed intergalactic voids on millennial timescales. Wayfarers whispered of sentient vortices: killers of dreams, eaters of stars. Theorists called them hypothetical macrocosmic entities. Fringe cultists called them the Ungods.

The AI continued. "During the attack, the entities broadcast this message: *'Sentient lifeforms, we bring the gift of ascension. This is the command of Kton.'*"

Chydi froze, the dream-dread returning: three stars blinked and died above a roaring, crimson sun. A sibilant hiss blew across the nape of her neck. Alien words lingered on the tip of recall, a wisp of déjà vu that would not come.

She slapped the comm holo. "Give me Gi."

"Apologies," said a subroutine. "No channels available."

Kaldoun shrugged. "Just wait for people to calm—hey! Where you goin'?"

But Chydi was already out the door, sprinting for the walkways. Gi's Central Data Plinth lay only a few kilometers away.

"Unable to establish a direct link to Gi Primary Function," the pawn said, "even as a diplomatic courtesy. My regrets."

"Thanks anyway." They exited the travelator.

"Come, we go home," said Kal. "Or line up at Central Data?"

"My father has direct access to Gi."

Kaldoun squeezed her hand. "Bad idea. He wun even recognize you, let alone believe this wild an' wild tale. He might tweak, even go primal."

"What else can I do?" She stepped onto an escalator, ascending toward embassy row.

"Lemme 'splain your dream," Kaldoun said. "You will see the coincidence."

Chydi scoffed. "You can try."

"Flyin' naked through space, that's the new you."

"I was photons, not naked."

"No mind. The red supergiant, that's your da'."

"Remarkable insight."

"Sarcasm," said Kal, "is a club, no a witty needle. You want help or what, pajama lady?"

"Sorry."

"Falling into the star is fear of your da' finding out. So get it over with, rip off the bandage, nightmares stop. Simple, no?"

"What about the supernovae?"

Kaldoun grinned. "Orgasms!"

In spite of everything, Chydi smirked. Kaldoun could be so naddy. "Thanks, but believe me, this is *real*."

"You dun even have a psi-rating." Another frown. "You regret regen?"

"Not for a minute."

"You brave."

"It's normal, billions do it."

"But no on Brakandy."

Chydi stared at her nails: chewed, unpainted. "No, not on Brakandy."

"Heretics, technomancers, rebels—but no body changin'. Why so backward?"

"It's not illegal, it's—well, how much do you know about the Heresy?"

Kaldoun snorted. "More 'an enough. You dun like change, change is bad."

"Almost." Chydi laughed. "Our ethos is resistance to entropy. We oppose decay, chaos, death."

"You dun fight physics with ideals, even on a planet drowned in fog. Reality is all mist anyway, an illusion."

"Don't be daft."

*Mist.*

Mist recalled childhood: the villa on the Nithorian headlands, her third-story bedroom, the nightly inspections. Every evening, her toys and athletic gear had to be back on the shelves, each position indicated by an outline and a label. Father scrutinized them like a troop of shipboard marines.

That sparked another, more fleeting memory: a place *truly* drowned in mist, the roiling unreality of the twin universe—those realms of death where runeships took shortcuts between the anti-stars.

There, shells gleamed like pearls, endless banks of moon-sized entities clinging to shards of foaming timespace. Every so often, one hissed open and a silver tendril shot out, bent on some occult task.

*Onkt, Nkto, Kton . . . lancebolts hitting starships in the dark . . . chitinous tongues, whispers from another world . . . figures in vac suits, yawning pits . . . inimical sentience, transmigrating space and time . . . thieves of minds, eaters of stars . . .*

The Brakandean embassy loomed ahead, a block of amalgamate on an artificial island, circular at its base, each higher floor smaller in circumference, resembling a vimana.

"I wait outside," Kaldoun said, "where it safe."

## II.

Father stood hunched over as if his spacious office could not contain his height. Gnarled fingers lifted a tiny teacup to his lips, incongruous, like a storybook giant clutching a rag doll. A flicker of recognition crossed his darting eyes. Yet his dark countenance remained impassive, save for a downward turn of his lips. Did he recognize her—or see just another Brakandean?

Chydi performed a knee-dip, acknowledging rank. "The fundament endures."

"May permanence guide right action," he answered in the formal tense, not the familiar. "My time is vital today. They tell me Chedan is back. I say good, send him in. Instead, I find a woman in pajamas. Where is my son?"

"Can you not see?" Chydi closed her eyes a fraction. "I was Chedan. Now, I am Chydi."

Admiral Chechum Sochum, Plenipotentiary of Brakandy, had gained renown in naval actions by reacting to complex data with speed. He did not stammer or sputter out denials. His grim, lined face turned from surprise to dismay to anger within a second. Just as quick, his hand shot outward, ceramic at the apex of its trajectory.

Scalding hot tea splashed across Chydi's face. She cried out, rivulets of liquid running down her raw cheeks. "Father!"

"Why?" he demanded. "Why have you performed this entropy?"

She wiped her face before answering, signaling calm by answering in the aristocratic tense. "I experienced a moment of bliss."

"My *son's* bliss is on file with the Audiants. It is this: satisfaction triggered by a panoramic sunset on the evening he received news of his diplomatic sinecure. You mouth absurdities."

"Doctrine permits additional moments, refinements of first understanding."

Her father pursed his lips, unable to refute. "What moment?"

"When I first made love to Kaldoun."

"Bah. Every young fool mistakes lust for bliss. This brothel of a city has corrupted you. I should have vetoed this posting."

"Do not moments of bliss transcend the ever-changing surface of things to reveal underlying permanence?" She needed to get him past this to the danger of Kton. "Yes, I met Kaldoun in an erotic sensorium. Yes, I lied about why I entered regen. But my moment of bliss revealed myself to me, and now, I am as you see me."

"I, me, myself—this is narcissism, an illegal orthodoxy." He grunted. "You haven't recorded this so-called bliss before an audiant, and thus, it is invalid."

"I registered it with an accredited audiant in Braktown."

At that, more anger boiled across his face. She feared he'd go primal and strike her, but he turned away instead, voice cold and distant. "It is my right to disinherit you for cause. I now do so on the grounds of abominable entropism and disgracing your mother's memory. You are no longer a Brakandean and expelled from the diplomatic corps."

"Father!" Chydi trembled. She'd expected anger but not loss of clan, career, even citizenship.

"Remedy your apostasy and apply for reinstatement on the homeworld. Or stay here among the hedonists; I understand the machine doles out stipends to its parasites."

"Am I not your only child!?"

"My son is dead." He pointed toward the door. "Surrender your implant, and get out."

"Wait!" She rushed forward, grabbing his arm. "Call Gi."

"Gi will not intervene."

"It's about Taral!"

He gave a textbook-perfect eyebrow raise, a gesture of disdain reserved for low-status strangers. "Gibberish."

"During regen, they drug you for long stretches. While under, I dreamed of ancient beings."

"You are not only apostate but insane." He grabbed her tender forearm, manhandling her toward the door.

"They send their minds through time and space!"

"Consider ascetic therapy." The door hissed shut. "Perform penance in the salt caves."

"They crowned Kton with supernovae!" she shouted.

The door re-opened. Her father stared, jaw agape. The door had opened on its own.

"We would hear this," someone said. Not her father—and not the embassy's AI.

Governing Intelligence's voice emanated from circuits embedded in the structure of the building—Gi, Administrator of the Circlet, Adjudicator of the Association. Like any mechasentience, it spoke with the fluid precision of machine intelligence. But only Gi used this particular tone, locked at frequency 176 Hz but with a rich, androgynous timbre. Its voice was so distinct that its use, outside of narrow educational and satirical purposes, violated the law.

"This is Brakandean soil by treaty," her father grumbled. Everyone knew Gi sometimes eavesdropped. True privacy existed only aboard secure ships.

"Apologies, Admiral," said Gi. "I employed only passive monitoring as permitted by emergency protocol. Chydi Sochum, please elaborate."

Chydi blurted out her tangle of nightmares: ". . . killing stars celebrates or even enables their arrival. In a book I've seen only in dream, they call this ritual the Crown of Kton."

"How many supernovae?" Gi asked.

"Three," said Chydi, voice hollow. "There are three."

"Just so," said Gi. "I have called a quorum. Admiral, you will represent the Brakandean Heresy. Chydi, please attend as a witness."

The quorum gathered within a secure chamber, an adamant-lined bastion hardened against thanatomic attack and psiotronic espionage. Emissaries from the major Association states sat around a slab of rock crystal. These envoys carried plenipotentiary powers, able to make decisions for their individual governments without waiting the months it took for messages to cross interstellar gulfs.

Chydi had changed into a stylish frock—never before worn in public—but the familiar, bureaucratic routine reassured her. It felt good to get back, even if only as a witness.

A pawn directed her to the Brakandean back-bench, murmuring, "Wait until called upon."

Like the others, her father looked up when she entered, anger still in his darting eyes. Ignoring the interruption, the dignitaries resumed their debate.

"Everybody wants something," said the fork-bearded khargi with a brass implant for a left eye. "Find out what these Ktonni want, and we can deal."

"They want brains," said a stern Dakoomite, his face a mass of scales. "They shall not have them without reckoning with the puissant arms of the Eightieth Dynasty."

"Don't tweak, slick," said a diminutive Yxean, her periwinkle hair shaved and spiked. She hovered above her chair in a lotus position. "We got technology. Let's parlay."

"Ignore this one-time aberration," said her father. "Allow normality to return."

"What is normal?" demanded the khargi. "Remember Species XF-59, the plasma beings? They exist on a different timescale, use sensory apparatus we can't fathom, and treat biological life as undifferentiated matter."

"But we communicated with the XF-59," said the Yxean. "In the end."

"Only by cracking tsar-bombs in prime-number patterns around their gas giant!" the khargi shouted. "How do we 'parlay' with brain-thieves?"

"Some creatures you just can't reach," said the Herelîta, leader of Kaldoun's people. "These Ktonni are more than an undiscovered species with deplorable habits." She touched her earpiece, staring at Chydi. "Or so I'm told."

Gi's voice emanated from the ceiling. "This is Chydi Sochum, a witness with extralocal knowledge. Please proceed."

Chydi stood up. She'd spoken to diplomats before—rooms full of people. *Look above their heads, move your eyes around.* But never like this.

She told about the supernovae. "I don't feel the Ktonni come from our galaxy at all. Their minds migrate through spacetime, using runespace."

The room fell silent, and the khargi asked, "How do you know this?"

"Vivid, lucid dreams and recurring nightmares. In some, I found myself looking through an old-fashioned mystic tome, *The Book That Never Sleeps*."

"Charlatanry," said the khargi.

"Uncultist hysteria!" shouted the Dakoomite.

"Nonlocality is on occasion a viable conduit of wildcard data," Gi said.

"Corroborating footage arrived yesterday by runeship. It remains classified."

A holo jumped up on the conference table, video from a deep space telescope. Glyphs of some alien language cycled through timestamps. The red fist of Kton blinked against the broader band of the galaxy, a ruby on a silver ring. Then a nearby star billowed outward, a classic supernova eruption.

The timestamp spun faster; two more stars lit and exploded within . . . hours? Days? Chydi could not tell from the glyphs. Three dying stars ringed the red giant Kton. Her every nerve tingled. A brief surge of jubilant validation—*I'm not crazy*—gave way to a deeper, colder fear.

"The light from this event only reached the Cele-Kton Cluster a few months ago," Gi said. "It will take many more years to reach us."

"What can do this?" her father asked.

"Technology far beyond our own," said Gi. "Thoughtful deliberation should continue until we reach a consensus. However, I will dispatch a Living Ship to investigate Taral. All are welcome to contribute to this task force."

At that, all the envoys started speaking at once.

"Thank you, Chydi," the pawn murmured in a low voice. "You may go."

Chydi rose and left. The diplomats ignored her, save for her father staring a hole in her back. How could he stay angry when the Association—Brakandy with it—teetered on the abyss?

"You're leaving?"

"I snared a driftcore gig," Kaldoun said. "The driver got called up on accoun' of this Taral mess." Kaldoun packed her kit bag in a rush, dashing about their salon. "I be back in six weeks."

Chydi collapsed onto the divan, drained by everything and now this. She wanted to share a water-womb soak, but Kal worked as a freelance pilot, working when it suited her, vanishing for months. It dampened things, no doubt.

"Chydi?"

"Yes?"

"Take care, okay?"

Chydi smiled. "I will."

"I hope an' hope so." Kal kissed her with an uncharacteristic undertone of sadness and left.

Chydi soaked in a zero-gee bath, banishing everything complicated until she decided to visit a sensorium. Kaldoun would not mind; they kept things open-ended. She changed into a mix of silk and holos, heading out. A dose of placidium took the edge off her irritated skin.

Soft lights marked the evening cycle as the humming walkway whisked her toward downtown. The seventeen decks of the Social District provided the beating heart of the Circlet's never-ending nightlife. But tonight, the vibe felt harsher, edged with a *fin de siècle* ambience, the grim news driving people to desperate excess.

She could relate. It was what she craved.

Club Club glimmered at the end of a pier, the pink sand castle where she'd first met Kaldoun. Grav stasis held a kaleidoscope of slabs together. Synesthetic data—music, light, fragrance—pulsed through every room, synched to link progs and aerosol hallucinogens. Assignations took place within bead-screened alcoves.

She tasted and touched, surrendered to the scene, drowning out everything else. Near dawn, she stumbled home, fearless along the Circlet's safe and well-lit boulevards. She never saw the shadowy figure that followed her into the studio.

Eyes like yolks gleamed in the dark. A scale-faced Uncultist in indigo robes and metallic face paint showed a mile-wide smile and a blade.

"Hear the Call of Kton," the attacker hissed, "the Eater of Stars."

The shock dagger struck true, and the pain exploded through her nervous system, like the primordial singularity. Then, oblivion.


### III.

He stared at the white fog of runespace from behind a triple pane. He'd already tried the door. It would not open. He pressed the call button again and again to no avail.

The locked room looked like a Brakandean hospital suite. A regen pod filled half of it, but he'd awoken on the bunk. He suspected the *Permanence*, his father's starship.

Every nerve stung. Every bit of skin burned. His body, twice ravaged by regen, wanted to die. He'd seen the hollow concavities in the mirror, raw red scars of the knife's bite.

He chose not to call himself female now—not until he could undo this cruel reversal. Ashi lacked male and female pronouns, but he still thought in his native tongue. He could not escape Brakandy, it seemed, but he would keep the name: Chydi.

An hour later, his father walked in wearing the teal-and-cream uniform of Brakfleet.

Chydi glared.

"You look like dockside riffraff," father said, a sparkle in his eyes.

"How could you?"

"Extropy is the restoration of order."

"You had no right."

"This is Brakfleet, not the Circlet."

With a groan, Chydi dropped to the bunk. "A second regen so soon could have killed me."

"The stabbing could have killed you. The regen saved your life. I only instructed the doctors to undo your youthful folly."

"How could they? That's illegal!"

"I have the authority to disguise your identity to prevent further assassination attempts."

Anger ran through Chydi, but arguing never swayed the admiral from his course. "Was anyone else hurt?"

"The attacker committed ritual suicide after setting your studio ablaze. You're lucky not to have burned to death. Thank Gi's persistent surveillance; the machine intervened with vacuum nozzles and cryo foams."

"Kaldoun?"

"Away in some ship."

Chydi breathed relief. "So it's back to Brakandy."

The admiral fixed him with a hard-eyed stare. "Naïf. This fleet succors Taral. We shall sweep the stars of Ktonni cylinder-ships, sunder them from all energy and purpose."

*To fry them like fish,* Chydi thought. "You sound like Kaldoun. Why bring me?"

"Gi thought your visions could be useful."

"You do not."

"No. You provided the machine some slim verification, nothing more." For the first time, his father looked concerned. "Unless you had more dreams?"

Chydi considered and shook his head. "Nothing since the dagger. How long have I been under?"

"We are eight weeks out of the Circlet, a few days from Taral. When the moment comes, join me on the bridge. For now, rest and repent. I suggest the *Cantos of Salt*."

He left; Chydi suffered.

Forty thousand tons of Brakandean steel slunk through the gloom, traversing a formless, inchoate shadow universe where black anti-stars pulsated amid the roiling, white aether. The umbra of Taral's star loomed closer by the day as *Permanence* chewed up parsecs, like so much saltwater beneath an ancient prow.

They hit the edge of the system's gravity well. Vibrations sent raw, coursing power through the floor gratings and up Chydi's boots. Illimitable fractal lightning, kilometers long, boiled and roared on the edge, illuminating vast tracts of the billowing void.

Klaxons sounded, bulkheads sealed, and crew shouted, running for crash couches. Hazmat teams stood by in vac suits.

"Dropping! Dropping! Secure for realspace!"

Chydi clung to his grav harness as the ship shot back into reality. Gravity, linearity, and three-dimensionality hit like a doubled-fisted gut punch.

"Can you feel it, boy?" His father swung in the next harness over. "Can you taste dominion over space? This is *my* moment of bliss."

Chydi felt only nausea and the wrenching forces spitting them between realities. Father should *shut up*.

Lights and sensors came online, harnesses relaxing as gravcon kicked in. Brisk, competent junior officers snapped out stat checks in Ashi:

"Transition normal."

"Taral Sys astrometry confirmed."

"Fleet radio reestablished."

"Weapons online in thirty, twenty-nine . . ."

"No unknown tracks. Repeat, no unknowns."

"Primary sixty AUs starward."

*Permanence* rejoined the Stellpax formation. Chydi stood with his father at the forward screen. Other screens showed the rest of the fleet. The sight impressed.

Three missile wasps from Crystal Fleet flew high guard, Kaldoun's people driving elegant spindles on vortex engines. The draconic hulk of an Eightieth Dynasty man-o'-war paced the van, gunports open, thanatomic missile racks displayed. *Permanence* took its place in formation, one of seven ships arrayed in a sphere around the flagship, *Demiurge*.

The dreadnought was one of Gi's Living Ships—a crewless artifact from bygone days, commanded by an ancient machine intelligence almost coeval with Gi itself. Four hundred thousand tons of asymmetric titanium glittered like a diamond. This task force could smash any pirate fleet and render any planet in the Association amenable to Gi's governance—or uninhabitable. But against the Ktonni? Chydi doubted.

Fleet comm buzzed with ship-to-ship chatter:

"No hostiles detected."

"No signals from the planet."

"Fuel depots alpha through gamma destroyed."

"All in-sys buoys lost."

*Demiurge* addressed the fleet, its voice a baritone echo of Gi. "Execute formation five, medium scatter on approach to Taral III. *Tsuarzarg* takes point; Crystal Fleet on high; *Permanence*, you are rearguard. Synched velocity zero null zero niner cee on my mark. All ready?"

All ships acknowledged.

"Execute."

The orange disc of Taral's star loomed larger by the hour. Sensors picked out a speck transiting the orb, little more than a dust mote. This was Taral III.

Few ever bothered about it before the attack: a marginal world on the coreward edge of the Association but with a breathable atmosphere—and twenty thousand inhabitants, once.

As the fleet approached, every scope surveyed it. Little touched by civilization to start with, Taral III looked undamaged, still wild. The EM band crackled with only natural, background radiation.

"Resolving main subcontinent," said the sensors officer.

"Project," said Admiral Sochum. A dark mass swarmed across a dusty plain.

"Biosphere looks intact," the officer said. "Autochthonous herds on annual migration."

"At least the Ktonni are not biocidal," Chydi murmured.

"Logical. They only want civilized brains," his father said, pleased.

Chydi could not shake a premonition of doom. "They want the ants out of their garden."

"Displaying Taral City now," the officer said.

Association architecture, modified for local conditions, filled the screen. But it all lay in ruins. Residential domes hung like shattered hulks. Warehouses formed of polymerized rock amalgamate lay in twisted heaps of slag. The broken shards of a towering, glass-and-steel parallelogram, headquarters of the Taral Company, reflected fractured, amber sunlight.

Something else, too. Something unnatural. Chydi's spine tingled. His throat went cold.

Black, yawning apertures pockmarked the city, like so much buckshot emptied into the terrain. Each pit looked a hundred meters wide, depth unknown.

"What are those things?" his father asked.

"No data," said the XO.

But Chydi knew them from *The Book That Never Sleeps*: Ktoggoth Pits, rat-snares for vermin.

Something gleamed in one of the boreholes.

"Ambush!" Chydi screamed, yanking father's arm. "Run!"

The Admiral yanked the stick back hard as the trap fired.

Dozens of beams of incalculable force lanced upward from the planet's surface, targeting each ship. Crackling at light speed, the shafts covered a million klicks in seconds, too quick to evade.

The Crystal Fleet ships shattered in sprays of decoherent glass. Implosions engulfed the other ships of the line. Even the mighty *Demiurge*, hit by multiple shafts, disintegrated after a moment of incandescent defiance. The beams cut the task force apart with pure antimatter.

Not even *Permanence* escaped. His father's reflexes and the ship's rearguard position saved it from instantaneous destruction, but the beam still cleaved its bulk. The rupture triggered cataclysmic destruction. Klaxons blared and the ship's crew scrambled.

"Catastrophic hull failure," intoned the ship's AI. "Energy release in nineteen . . . eighteen . . ."

"Abandon ship!" father bellowed. "To the pods! Get in the mist-mothered pods *now*!"

"Come on!" Chydi yanked him toward the executive lifeboat. "They know what to do!"

The two of them tumbled into their pod and fled the doomed ship. Grav-harnesses fastened only seconds before a sunbright light unleashed a few hundred meters away.

The Ktonni barrage had immolated an entire Stellpax task force in seconds. It was as if these beings treated low-tech sentience like pests, taking some for samples, leaving traps for the rest. They could destroy the Association on a whim—on a *whim*—but might never bother.

So much junk filled the electromagnetic spectrum, they couldn't even make radio contact with the other pods. They braced for another beam to sweep them out of space, but it never came—not worth the energy expenditure, perhaps. They put on vac suits and gritted their teeth.

With nowhere else to go, the pods fell toward Taral.

They'd crashed on the fringe of Taral City, far from other pods. Father had formed a plan of meeting up with resistance cells. It seemed a foolish hope, but he possessed a map of secret defense installations, rendezvous points where survivors might meet. They'd set off into the ruins.

For the last hour, a slithering, shapeless *thing* had tracked them. Distant, panicky blaster fire punctuated by screams told the fate of the other pods.

"Faster!" father shouted. "One more block!"

Masonry tumbled as Admiral Sochum, sweat-grimed and dust-covered, found a blast door. "This is it. I know it," he said, working the magnetic combo-lock. "Niner, zero, five . . ."

*Sentience,* something thought-whispered from afar. Rubble shifted a few houses down. The lock clicked open.

"I'll hold it off," his father said, shoving Chydi inside. "Someone must survive to warn Gi."

"You can't fight it!"

Father drew his *astra,* a sacred plasma torch. "I can try. And for what it's worth, Chydi, I did you wrong. It was only my fear, but now, I find I have none. So go, and let permanence guide right action." Then he welded the blast door shut. It closed Chydi off from father, from the world.

*Sentience,* the ktoggoth whispered.

Chydi scrambled deeper into the ruinous bomb shelter. Shattered pipes lay amid decaying corpses, reeking with flies and bugs. A few banks of emergency lights cast shifting beams across festering pools full of bricks and bones.

Sickened, he stumbled and fell. Beneath his feet lay a wrecked sentionic doll, a pallid figure in a black gown. It lay in an ammo box, its lifeless eyes turned to the ceiling. Some child had loved this bot and left it. Just one of thousands, now gone.

The ktoggoth never even opened the blast door. It just flowed *through* as if physicality didn't exist.

*Sentience . . .*

Otherwise helpless, Chydi prayed. "Mother of Mists, let nothing change. Mother of mists, keep everything the same. Mother of Mists, ward off entropy, death, and decay, forever—"

## IV.

I awoke immobilized, without heartbeat or breath. An olive grid dominated my visual band, overlaid with twisting glyphs of no humanoid design. Input flooded in from unfamiliar spectra: ultraviolet, exoradio, infrablue, supergamma. Opposite stood rows of cylinders on shelves. Lights blinked on their grids. Outré wires and coils ran to ceiling valves.

Panic yielded to a growing horror. The Ktonni had taken me. They had cut my head open, captured my brain.

"Welcome to hell," said a buzzing voice. It came from another cylinder, but reassuringly, it spoke Ashi. "What's your name?"

I had no mouth to answer with.

"Depress the shining tetrahedron in the upper left of your display," the voice said. "Use the focus of your consciousness as a stylus. This will activate your *logos*, a neural-audio interface."

I managed and gasped, "My name is Chydi. Is this a Ktonni ship?"

The cylinder buzzed like grasshoppers. "The Ktonni are puppets, just one tool of the masters. This is a hypernexus."

"A what?"

"A place inaccessible and inconceivable to transhumanity, built of mental energy."

"And you?"

"Cowl the Antiquarian: once human, by and by a necromancer, now a madman! Thousands of years ago, on a world fallen to savagery, I sought lore within the ashes of the Astral Empire. I found the Ktonni, instead."

That worried me: such prolonged captivity sounded unthinkable. "You speak Ashi."

"Language is fluid and ever-changing, but we have time to learn them all."

His words damned my hopes. "Who are these masters?"

"Invisible, disembodied tyrants, revealed only by their puppets and devices. We call them the Old Things as they predate our universe."

"Impossible. The universe is all."

"Bah! Our universe is a mere fifty billion light years across. What lies beyond?"

"Maybe a multiverse. How can I know?"

"Multiverse? Anthropocentric prattle! Existence does not fork based on our meaningless choices. Beyond this are more universes, trillions! They spark to life, flicker for a day and fade like embers in a macrocosm vaster than we can conceive—each macrocosm in turn but a single mote within an even more unknowable whole: the Lattice."

I dismissed his bleak cosmicism. "How do I escape this cylinder?"

"Escape?" He laughed, a symphony of crickets. "We are minds. We sit and think, chat, remember, hope, wish, go mad. No matter; all mentation powers their machines. See how some cylinders blink and darken? The Old Things drain them to the lees. Over time, the minds revive and are tapped again. After twenty thousand years of such usage, we die, our patterns eroded through quantum decoherence. They replace us with ruthless economy."

"Twenty thousand years!"

"It is the blink of the cosmic eye. The Old Things have existed for seventy billion years. Yet compared to the Lattice, they are children. Infinity lacks age; it is a loop, a recursive ring, a dragon eating its tail, the unending pages of *The Book That Never Sleeps*."

I am no longer Chydi, not even transhuman. I am Cylinder #35TU8JQ8, a pattern of quantum electric impulses. I possess only will and memory. That is not enough. They have taken everything.

The other cylinders accept me with a peculiar mixture of madness and curiosity. They are ravenous for news and diversion but offer no hope. Rather, they take perverse pride in its destruction.

"The bee cannot build a bridge; the butterfly cannot make a philosophy," says Cowl, a typical specimen. "Our crowning endeavors are honeycombs and cocoons compared to the great works of the Old Things and the might of the Ungods."

I demur. "Our monuments, our music, perhaps our genes will survive."

"No," says Cowl. "Humanity will vanish like petals in the wind. In a million years, no one will remember us. In billions more, even our galaxy will be torn apart by gravity. By then, the Old Things will have abandoned their current hosts, transmigrating through timespace to possess yet another species in some other macrocosm."

"Our machines will carry on," I insist. "Gi is benevolent and wise."

"No," says Cowl. "One species yields to another and another, flesh or steel, on it goes. This is the way of all things, the random rhythm of the cosmic tide. We are doomed to live and die forgotten in a reality so vast we cannot comprehend it, one so cold and indifferent we dare not consider it. We are spiders spinning webs before the futile fury of dying stars."

So he says, so I fear. Yet there are days when I do not believe this. Life was too strange and sweet a thing to lack substance. I remember silver fog coiling through the highlands of Nithor. I remember Kaldoun's touch on the night we met. I recall my father's difficult love and his final stand.

The Old Things evolved from unknown to unknowable. Perhaps, our embryonic minds can still flower into something greater and more beautiful than that which we can or will now or ever conceive. Or perhaps, beyond even the lattice of infinity and its ever-changing complexity exists one unbroken and never-ending moment of bliss.

§

**J.E. Bates** *is a lifelong communicant of science fiction, fantasy, horror, and other mind sugar and screen candy. He's lived in California, Finland, and many worlds in between, and would like to embark on a year-long spaceflight to Mars, if only to catch up on all his reading. He's read too many books and too many authors to name only a few as favorites, but has spent the last couple years successfully dodging ASOFAI spoilers. He can be found at twitter.com/jeebates or jeebates. wordpress.com.*

# Vol de Nuit

# GORD SELLAR

ILLUSTRATED BY
NICK GUCKER

**A**NYONE MIGHT THINK YOU WERE ALREADY DEAD, A RUINED SACK OF FIBERS
and nerves immersed in your piloting tank, but within the HUD's projection
field, you are terrifyingly alive and aware of what's going on outside. The
shattered, broken topologies of the tear flicker in that place in your brain where
things are seen that you've never laid eyes upon. It's all so brutal and impossible
and *wrong* that you wonder for a moment whether the resonator network might
be failing, filling empty space with something more interesting.

That would come as no surprise, given the number of patches—hardware,
wetware, software—that keep it running, thrumming like a nervous system
strung invisible and immaterial across the spaces between each ship within the
whole armada. *One body from many.*

The thought has barely ebbed when, irony of ironies, the overloaded
resonator network gives out, leaving you caught at the crest of the violation as
the mathematics of the universe begin to fight back, mindlessly suturing back
together. You, all of you—the whole vast armada of decrepit little ships—are
left soaring half-blind through the cold blackness toward what ought to be
unreal . . . toward what should never have been possible.

You've helped kill impossible things before. The impossible doesn't count for
much. Nor do you, but one takes consolation where one finds it.

As you wait for the network to come back online, the spectacles of past battles dance through your mind: shuddering forms backlit by half-consumed suns, and the faces of those you've lost to this so-called "war." When did we start calling it war, to throw millions of people into a black raging hole and hope for the best? Like all who have gone to war, you are haunted: nameless faces flash through your mind, people ripped so completely out of existence you recall only silhouettes like bruises against the walls of the mothership.

Anticipation—it feels like queasiness, deep in your guts—is building. Though the resonator network still hangs, the map display remains live, and you can track yourself and every other ship in the armada, soaring toward the point on the map named Arras. Nobody knows what Arras might be: a world that was swallowed after it was mapped or maybe just the last locale from which a distress signal got through to some drifting, antique data buoy. Whether the name of the system is an epitaph or a going concern, none can say, but one thing's clear—if there was a planet, it's gone now.

There's back and forth on the comms, clueless debate about which possibility seems likeliest. You ignore it. Speculation and rumor can't bring back the lost souls of any long-dead ship or swallowed planet, and the prattle can do nothing but distract you. Everyone knows that, of course, but most people will do anything to avoid that feeling that hovers in the back of the mind throughout missions like this—the sense that one is about to die alone and be ripped from the fabric of spacetime so hard that nobody even remembers one to mourn her passing.

But as the shipboard computers all struggle to bring the fragmented network all the way back online, one thing is clear: the puncture in reality is sealing shut. In a normal ship's sensor range, it would appear already healed, in fact. This would surprise nobody. Only down within the boiling, raging soup of virtual particles is the bruise visible, the lingering damage warping local spacetime despite the universe's best attempt at mathematical self-correction. Still, even there, the resonator's readings show that the broken topologies are on the mend. The aberrations remain, for now—vast, screaming severed chunks of the things, the endless maws screaming silently, the bright spray of viciously destructive dark matter that sprays out invisibly—but they are slowly wilting, passing out of existence.

All but the biggest anomaly, which is beeping now on the map. Nothing like imaging is possible, yet. For a few minutes, the thing will remain a mere theoretical possibility, the warning of a tumor bleeding through a statistically unavoidable fracture in the wall between the branes, turned ravenous by the anthropic static of a universe crammed with sentient observers and the inevitable reek of wave function collapse.

The waiting leaves you thinking of worlds you have not visited, promises you have failed to keep. Your nervous system groans, one or another vestigial reaction you have not yet isolated and eliminated; some biological process left inside your flesh like a statistical amalgam of a former circle of lovers, more out of sentimentality than any longing to return. Your species may not be perfect, but the ignobility of the ancient world—

Then the resonator network is back online, fully and completely, and the shriek of the warning system begins again—this time, at a familiar pitch. The thing has come through. It has *remained* through. Now is not the time to panic, regardless of the shrillness of the alarm. No, now is the time to concentrate and to accept the yanking of the thing's enormous vast mass as it coils its spacetime into yours, spiraling both into the paracomplex geometries of its innards.

If you want to kill one and live, you have to just focus on the maw, focus on the teeth and the tongues that splay out along impossible, enfolded s-circles as it drags you, all of you, toward their complex meta-intersections. You need to ignore the panic and all the flashing lights on your HUD and the scream of the warning signal and just wait without hope or fear in a perfectly calm silence.

You must wait longer than any sane person could bear. Wait until you can see the viscous dust-fluid goo that makes up the inner membranes of the thing; wait 'til the vectors of force and energy make every tiny, invisible pore on your hairless body pucker. Ignore the nightmares fruiting through your consciousness, their spores clotting the pathways of your mind.

Focus on the ghostly curvatures of that geometrically impossible, defiant maw you see through the network uplink, the image electromagnetically induced directly into your brain as your glazed-over eyes stare blankly.

The instant you always wait for is the one when you can see the teeth not as a whitish, vicious mass but as distinct fangs, ghostly clumps sprouting from a loosely defined tesseractile point, a bouquet of fangs poised in eerie superposition. When you can see the meta-concentric s-circles and just make out the contradictory curvatures they trace through spacetime, it's time to prime the topology bomb. Launch the missile, and watch it glide in, now part of a swarm—for every other fighter has launched one too, just when you did—and watch them converge, detonating in a fine matrix that unwinds the mathematics of the thing's attack, right from that bright and terrible center.

Launch too soon, the mouth will spit the missiles back out at you and surge away into the blackness, leaving you blinded by the flash of its departure, bundled traces of cognitive pseudopodia flickering against the insides of your eyelids as you realize the micromissile is nearby and about to blow. You'll be gone, and it'll be hunting down worlds. Launch too late, and instead it sucks you in by reflex just before the missile shreds the grid and swaps you out, leaving behind virtual particles to fill the gaps. You end up dragged back into its reality, ripped out of the universe so profoundly that nobody even remembers you existed.

So you need to time it just right, and the machines, those blessed ubiquitous machines, are no help. It's one of the few things machines can't do for humanity: if they could, you wouldn't be out here. You would not be shuddering on your couch—despite the neurochemical balancing and the focus drugs—at the sight of the thing in the distance, a vast hallucinogenic mouth spraying colors that cannot exist, writhing in a million visible eigenstates at once. A smear of mindless, hungry awfulness.

*You are a destroyer of worlds,* you mutter the mantra. *I am the destroyer of you.*

In your mind's eye, you let the attack play out. You, loosing your missile at the right moment. The long, bright form disappearing into the distance, taking its place in the gridbomb, amid identical missiles loosed by the other fighters. The assemblage disappears into the depths of that enormous, world-spanning maw. The thing senses danger and, with a speed terrifying in a thing that gargantuan, coils up into itself. The bright flash across the visible and invisible spectra, filtered by your HUD, when this aberration in spacetime collapses and silence . . . and relief. Once again, you are close enough to destroy the thing and far enough away not to be transmuted into mere lost data.

It's a story you tell yourself, assault after assault. So far, it's always come true.

Today, luck and skill converge again. You survive the run, slump into the anticlimax of what passes for victory, and drift to the bottom of your tank as your fighter's AI takes over and turns the ship around, launching you back toward the safety of your carrier.

The drugs suppress the dreams and accelerate the deterioration of your memories, something that inspires bottomless gratitude. The comms were wild with screams—more pilots than usual hit their neurological tipping points, and more pilots than usual soared into oblivion. The fact that you cannot remember their names or faces doesn't erase the sight of their ships tumbling into the vast, hungry awfulness just before the gridbomb went off.

Back at the carrier, the ship wakes you, gently jostling your tank before singing into your brain. You are gently decanted from your tank and down the secure tubesystem. In a temporary assessment tank, you submit to the mandatory brainscan and are decanted onward, to go off in search of something—food, someone's body, some other distraction—to still the shakes and fill the yawning emptiness of *knowing*.

That's what you're supposed to do, and they test you to make sure you will. Nothing so brutish as the bad old days, the alienists and the software interrogations and the rest of it. Now, they just scan your carefully redistributed brain, look for significant changes, and tweak the plasticity of pertinent regions. However fucked up you were when you were conscripted, all you have to do is manage to stay *that* fucked-up in basically the same way, and you're fine. They check to see whether you're cracking from the awe or on the verge of worshipping the things, and that's about it. Regular PTSD is more like the common cold used to be: yes, it trips off minor SAN check alerts, just like space sickness or cabin fever or survivor's guilt, but they can fix any of those things in a minute flat. Beep: that's the sound of chemically reverting your wiring, so you're good as new.

It's the deeper changes that they're obsessed with, now . . . the ones that come on slowly but transform you into something profoundly inhuman.

Because, those changes? They can happen to anyone. They *do* happen to anyone. There's a reason these things you kill used to be "gods:" their enormous, twisting beauty; the vast proboscides lapping the hull of your ship; the ghostly nest of feelers suckling at your mind; the polydimensional maw that—no matter what side you approach—always seems to be facing you directly, drifting forward to swallow you whole.

Every last pilot, watching for that contradictory interlocked curve of the teeth, that moment when they become clear against the shivering mountains of cyclopean gums and burning drool and the shredded remains of dead things the size of moons, feels as if the monstrosity has turned to face them personally. The ones to watch out for are the hotshots who say they don't feel even a little reverence for the things. They're the ones who end up falling to their knees to beg for mercy, who end up soaring into the maw screaming hallucinogenic nonsense over the comms, obliterated in the interbranal vapor and leaving behind nothing but vague, clouded memories by those who survive those runs.

The machine beeps, the scan finished. The numbers don't look quite right, but the inhuman, monstrous laws of triage let you past. You're stable enough, the machine decides—at least for now. It was a hard run, today; many fighters were tipped into insanity, and that always plays havoc with the ones who are left behind. On a normal run, you'd be held back for deeper treatment, but for now, you're close enough.

The carrier teems with distractions, all transient: the bodies of other pilots, ejected from their fighters, bound together in vast collective tangles like jellyfish, wet and shivering with vestigial sexual responses. Vast dream engines that swallow anyone willing to slip into the right tank, and feasts rebuilt at the molecular level to surge through your retooled flesh, imparting only optimal energy and nutrients no matter how much you consume. Hell, even the chemisynth glands that cluster at the root of your own brain.

You pour your jellyfish self into the bed of warm, soft goo in your private tank, not yet ready for any of these diversions. It's not like you: usually, you go straight to the Pleasure Tanks or log into the Dreaming, to pretend you are still human, grappling with human crises and human joys.

What keeps you going? It's as impossible to track down as the tesseractile fractal-coiling of these things, the way pseudopodia branch and lock together through interacting superstrings. They're impossible to catch or hold onto. Killing the things doesn't bring joy; there's no elemental surge of happiness, no feeling of vindication. You'd be happy enough to have retained your skin and bones, to be washing laundry on some evac-liner and watching the battles by broadcast if that were what you'd been rated to do a decade ago when you graduated from the training crèche. It's not some vast, ossified drama of revenge for you: your parents' faces flicker through your mind, sometimes, but you've killed hundreds of these things; you know millions upon millions of them have been obliterated, more than there were people on your world.

You've gotten close to falling into the blackness, of course, but not on the easy runs. You ask yourself what's kept you going since the Surge, since that thing showed up in the sky when you were a kid, and somehow you were one of the lucky ones and got hustled onto a launch before it swallowed the whole planet—*the whole damned thing*—in a single, ridiculous gulp. But you've always resisted. What would be the point of worshipping a natural phenomenon like that? It's as stupid as worshipping anything, god or plague or machine.

But today, the interlocking teeth remain, bright against the violet-green electrogravitic blackness of the inner maw and the spectacle of the thing unfurling into its full glory. There's no good reason for it: you've joined the ritual countless times, dispatched hundreds upon hundreds of these horrors. Today, the fighters scream their warped *hallelujahs* and *namu amidas* as they slip toward their doom; they linger all around you, poisoning the sweet goo of your storage bed, leaking into the tendons and nerves of your body in the dimness of your tank.

Bristling, luminous eyes flicker—at you specifically—from the depths of the mouth. They are like the eyes in a photograph, always seeming to look directly at you, no matter where you stand . . . yet those eyes in the maw, you half-believe they *saw* you. Like the eyes of spectral monarchs watching from across the twin gulfs of death and the lost eons. The tendrils have wound around something in you and cling even now, refusing to let go.

You knew what awaited you when you walked into the black tower at the center of town. You knew what the risk was, and you volunteered anyway.

You know you should report to the SAN center. But something within you refuses, and after lounging in the dimness, letting the warmth of the goo seep into you, you sluice down familiar pipes. You are infected, but you don't believe it; you want more flesh, soft and boneless like your own, to merge with. Some part of you screams against this simple mammalian instinct, rails against you for being fooled into infecting the whole fleet, screaming—if you will not get scanned again—to simply rest in your tank and sleep and obliterate yourself on the next run. It cries out in the name of pity and mercy.

The eyes stare into you from the depths of the maw. The tendrils hold on, firm and cold and beautiful. You know what awaits.

The thought clings to you through all the uncountable hours that follow—flickering in the background of conversations, so you know it isn't just you wondering—that through the wetness and tangle of the joy tanks, your infection has spread, recombined with the infections seeded by others from minds poisoned as subtly as yours. It bubbles up inside things said, in the way your gelatinous bodies brush against another, and in the Dreaming, you see it in the eyes of their avatars in the moments where quietness punctuates the breathing space between choreographed adventures.

Slowly, this whole armada's worth of pilots rots, and you find that, too, beautiful: all things, after all, must fail and crack and founder. The ship feels as if it might break completely apart from the strain of all that not-asking and not-confessing.

Then you pass a string of dead worlds, wobbling their pendulous way around a nearly extinguished sun. You're consuming your second meal of the day—same as the first, an amalgam of nutrients and flavors that osmose through your membrane as you recline in your personal tank. Something about those dead worlds causes a tremor inside you, makes you shiver with a sense of . . . it isn't recognition. It's nothing like recognition. More like some feeling equidistant between hope and panic, a readiness so deep that there isn't even a word for it. The nightmares that have plagued you—plagued the whole ship, fluttering through your minds during the carefully attuned sleep cycles, just below detectable levels—have told you about this place, whispered their cold and tortured history. It's like seeing some staged drama of a story you've heard about but never read.

Then the alarm goes off. The names of the great dead fighter pilots glimmer in your memories, and the ship runs the usual SAN check on you, and the HUD flickers, but the tendrils have tightened their grip, subtly, holding your mind in the shape the computer is searching for. Your will is focused, your attention tuned to the anticipation of the fight, and a glimmering of yourself—the being you were before that last combat—returns. You remember and are unsettled: how could *I* have been like that, how could that have been me? Yet you feel the thing within you, its whispers now too faint to hear but not too soft to feel. The gnawing hunger inside your mind never, never abates, but the computer does not recognize it as anything but your own, a standard vestigial human sensation.

Moments later, you are disgorged into your fighter and launched out into the nothingness. Your HUD is alight with information, none of it relevant anymore: the class and proximity of the monster? You used to check it religiously, but now, you feel faintly disgusted with it: how can they stat up a god? *Arrogant little things,* you think, ignoring the fact that you, too, are an arrogant little thing, a morsel waiting to be consumed.

To be consumed when you have done maximum damage. Your fighter sears across the cold black out to the face of wrongness: another maw, writhing tendrils of force surging out of the quantum soup as if from the space between the branes. You shift slightly in your tank, brimming with another feeling—not your own. You feel the ravenousness, still, as a distant sensation, like the tingling in a lost limb. It's a longing for some kind of food no mouth has ever tasted.

It's the one thing that makes you and these things the same: hunger is the vast and the universal truth of all life.

As you surge out, another vestigial instinct kicks in. If you still had teeth, they would be grinding. Now, it's just the edges of an orifice rubbing together, the ooze of the tank only slightly reducing the friction. Your mind lights up with a vision of what's to come: the gridbomb soaring into the maw and, hard on its trail, the complete armada, screaming its black *hallelujas* and bleak *namu amidas* to the vastness, all the way to the end.

§

**Gord Sellar** *was born in Malawi, raised in Canada, and has lived in South Korea for most of the past sixteen years. His work has appeared in many magazines and anthologies over the past decade, most recently in* Analog SF, Cthulhusattva: Tales of the Black Gnosis, The Book of Cthulhu II, *and in numerous Year's Best reprints. He is slowly working on a collection of Lovecraftian stories set throughout Korean history and on a novel of alchemy, brewers, distillers, rogues, mollies, proto-feminist revolutionaries, and the British navy in early Georgian-era London.*

# Lord of the Vats

# BRIAN EVENSON

### ILLUSTRATED BY YVES TOURIGNY

**S**TATE YOUR NAME FOR THE RECORD," SAID VILLADS.

. . .

"State your name. For the record."

*What record?*

"Are you having difficulty remembering your name?"

*No, I . . . no . . .*

"State your name—"

*Where am I? Why can't I see?*

Villads sighed. "You have been injured," he said.

*I'm blind?*

"Yes."

*A permanent blindness?*

"No," said Villads. "Not exactly."

*Not exactly? What does that mean?*

"Let's just say that perhaps soon you won't even remember not being able to see."

Esbjorn began to speak. Quickly, Villads cupped his hand over the microphone to prevent the subject from hearing. "Do you really think this is the best way to proceed?" asked Esbjorn. "By lying to the man?"

"I'm not lying exactly," said Villads. "And besides, she's not a man." He moved his hand away from the microphone. He brought his lips close to it but drew back and cupped the microphone again. "You forget," he said to Esbjorn in a low voice. "She's no longer really human at all."

*Hello,* the flat voice said from the speaker affixed in the center of the table. *Hello? Is anybody there?*

"We believe you to be Signe," said Villads when the subject still wasn't able to produce its own name. "Is this correct?"

*I . . . I don't know,* said the voice.

Villads grunted. "We have a few questions for you. About what happened."

*Did something happen?*

Esbjorn leaned forward, gesturing for Villads to hurry the process forward. Kolbjorn, on the other side of the table, remained placid, motionless.

*Did something happen?* the voice asked again.

"You tell me," said Villads.

*I was . . . I was . . .* and then the voice trailed off. Villads waited. *The last thing I remember . . .*

  . . .

  . . .

*There seems to be something wrong with my memory,* the voice finally said.

"Something wrong with your memory?"

"I told you this was useless," whispered Esbjorn. "The brain was too compromised."

*There are . . . holes . . . gaps . . .*

"Memory loss is normal after trauma," said Villads.

Across the table, Kolbjorn frowned.

*Trauma?* asked the voice.

"Take your time," said Villads, not meeting Kolbjorn's gaze.

For a long time, the voice said nothing at all. And then she—or it—said, *I can't seem to feel anything. Why can't I feel anything? Have I been drugged? Am I still suspended in a vat? Have you warmed me sufficiently to make me barely conscious?*

Villads looked at Kolbjorn. The latter hesitated a moment, then said, "Tell her."

*Tell me what?* asked the voice.

"You're not in a storage vat," said Villads.

*Then where?*

"There's been an accident," said Villads.

*An accident? What kind of accident?*

"You're nowhere," said Villads. "Technically speaking, you're not even alive."

*I . . . I . . . technically speaking?*

"Something killed you," said Villads. "Your body was frozen after the hull was breached but quickly enough to be left relatively intact. We were able to make a scan of your brain. An impression."

*I'm a scan?*

"You weren't the only one killed," said Esbjorn. "All the functioning crew was killed and many of the storage vats were destroyed as well. Systems are down in much of the ship. A long tear along the hull. Did you see what made it? We need to know what made it."

"And if it's still here," said Kolbjorn.

"And if it's still here," agreed Esbjorn.

"Can you help us?" asked Villads.

. . .

"Signe," said Villads.

. . .

"Signe?"


II.

After a few more attempts to hail her, he switched off the microphone. "Any suggestions?" Villads asked the others.

Esbjorn shrugged. "What can we do? We don't even know what tore open the ship. Maybe we shouldn't assume it was a motivated attack. It could have been a meteoroid or some similar large chunk of celestial debris."

"Doubtful," said Villads. "The tear isn't right. Besides, the ship would have detected it and woken us up."

Said Esbjorn, "A meteoroid going fast enough might have—"

"There's an entrance wound in the hull but no exit wound," said Villads. "And no sign of whatever struck us. Why not? No, this is something else."

"Maybe some sort of displacement," began Esbjorn, "an object flickering between—"

Kolbjorn cut him off. "No," he said. "Villads is right."

Esbjorn look at his twin. For a moment his lips began to curl and Villads believed he was about to start yelling, but then suddenly his mouth relaxed. "All right," he said. "Fine. In any case, whatever remains of Signe doesn't know anything."

"No," said Villads. "Brain compromised, I suppose."

"Or maybe it caught her unawares," said Kolbjorn. "Maybe she never saw it."

"You might as well erase her," said Esbjorn.

Again, Kolbjorn countermanded his twin. "Keep her for now, just in case."

Villads nodded.

"So what do we do?" asked Esbjorn.

"We'll have to go look for ourselves," said Villads.

"Which of us should go?" asked Esbjorn. "Shall we draw straws?"

"I don't know where we'd find straws aboard the bridge," said Kolbjorn.

"Rock, paper, scissors?" asked Esbjorn.

"What's that?" asked Villads.

"You don't know rock, paper, scissors?"

"I'll go," said Villads. "I volunteer."

"Why you?" asked Esbjorn.

"Because I'm alive," said Villads.

"And I'm not?" asked Esbjorn.

Villads turned to him. "No, you're not."

"Then what am I?" asked Esbjorn, crossing his arms.

"A construct," said Villads.

He guffawed. "Like Signe?"

Villads shook his head. "Not at all," he said. "Signe was a construct from a recent scan, incomplete. You're a full impression, exactly as you were just before you were placed in storage." He reached out and passed his hand through the hologram that was Esbjorn, his fingers disappearing within the man's chest without disrupting the image.

"Then why activate us at all?" asked Kolbjorn. "Clearly we would know nothing about the accident."

Villads shrugged. "Another set of minds," he said. "Someone to help me think through the problem."

"Then why not simply wake us up?" asked Kolbjorn. And then his expression crumpled. "Oh God," he said.

"I'm sorry," said Villads again.

"What?" asked Esbjorn. "What is it?"

"We're dead," said Kolbjorn. "Are we dead?"

"I'm sorry," said Villads.

Esbjorn started to speak, and Kolbjorn, too, but Villads had already begun to manipulate the console in a way that first slowed their constructs, then froze them, then made them disappear entirely. Soon, he was alone on the bridge.

### III.

For the past week, Villads had been awake and alone on the *Vorag*. Seven days ago, he had been jerked out of suspension by the sound of a siren blaring, despite the muffling effect of the fluid surrounding him. Just coming conscious, he was dimly aware of a dark shape passing his vat. Was he meant to wake up? He didn't think so; it didn't feel right, but he was awake nonetheless.

And then the shape had passed by him again, or part of it had—a leg or a tentacle or something in between, impossible in the darkness to tell, and he realized the vat was on its side. He'd begun to breathe, the alarm going off now not only in the ship at large but also in his tank. He was hyperventilating, breathing too quickly for the tube to provide him sufficient oxygen. He pounded on the translucent curve of the vat, but nothing happened. The vat wall was too strong, his fist pushing through the viscous fluid too slowly. He pounded again. His vision started to blur, darkness gathering around its edges, and he knew he'd soon go under again. Or maybe, he wasn't really awake after all; maybe, this was all a dream.

And then something curious happened. The thick glass of the vat spidered over with tendrils of frost, a rapidly expanding network of cracks. He struck out again, and this time the vat shattered, spilling him and a wash of fluid out onto the deck. He was shivering, unable to breathe. There was the airlock to the bridge, just beside him—by luck his vat was positioned close to it, and in falling onto its side had fallen in the right direction. He managed to half-roll, half-slide himself into it and, vomiting and shaking, to trigger the airlock door to close.

The blowers came on. He coughed and vomited up skeins of fluid. Someone was mumbling; it took him some time to realize it was him.

After a while, he stopped shivering. After a while, he managed to stand.

He had only been in the airless cold a few seconds, but how he was not dead he couldn't say. His extremities were numb. He would go on to lose an ear, and a week later would still only have partial feeling in his extremities.

He stood and looked through the thick porthole set in the airlock's steel door. The overhead lights had gone out, leaving only the faint glow of the emergency panels.

"*Vorag*, extinguish the airlock lights," he said to the ship.

The airlock fell dark. Slowly, his eyes adjusted until through the porthole he could see a vague but extensive destruction, vats shattered and overturned, bodies frozen and petrified, a huge gash in the hull through which he could glimpse unfamiliar stars.

He stumbled to the bridge. No one was there, not a single member of the skeleton crew intended to convey them to their destination. For a time, he just lay there, breathing, and then he managed to get up and examine the control panels. They were still seventy-one years, five months, and thirteen days out: still a lifetime shy of arrival. What had stopped them? What had torn them open? The *Vorag* didn't seem to know.

The sensors showed a large tear in the ship's hull. They indicated all three compartments containing vats had been breached. He adjusted the sensors. No signs of life. Or rather, one sign of life: him, alone on the bridge.

Maybe this was a mistake. Possibly it was simply a question of sensor failure. Possibly there was a compartment somewhere where he'd find members of the skeleton crew holed up and without pressure suits, trying to figure out a way to get back to the bridge. Or perhaps, at the least, a few vats remained intact. The sensors might not be able to detect signs of life from the vats since those lives were, for all intents and purposes, suspended.

*No,* he told himself, *it can't be just me.* Probably the sensors were down and crew were trapped in a portion of the ship sealed shut because of the tear. He would go out and look and find them. And together they would figure out what to do.

He removed a pressure suit from the cabinet and climbed into it. It was painful, his body still throbbing, but he managed. The suit had an interior emergency rations pack, and by pulling his arm out of its sleeve and into the suit proper, he managed to break the pack open and thread the straw up to his lips. He was surprised by how good the paste tasted until he realized it had been quite literally years since he had eaten anything.

He made his way back into the bridge's airlock. Switching on the suit's light, he sealed the lock, let it depressurize, and stepped out through the other lock.

No sound other than his own breathing and his magnetic soles clicking against the deck and disengaging as he raised them. His breathing was ragged and harsh, the click of the soles blunted as if heard from a great distance, as if his body was miles high. No atmosphere here, but he knew that already. And insanely cold, but that was what the pressure suit was designed for.

The damage was much worse than he'd expected. The vats should have withstood the cold, but they had not—age, maybe, or the rapidity with which the temperature had changed or something else entirely. In some places, they were not only cracked but overturned, broken apart. Bodies were strewn around as well, frozen in unnatural postures like fallen statues. They were all nude, an indication they belonged to the vats, the legions of the stored. None of the bodies of the crew in sight. How many had there been? A dozen? Why was he not seeing any?

He made his way systematically down the rows of the thousands of vats. More corpses, more shattered casings. How could it be that no casing was intact, not a single one?

There was something somewhere, a flutter, or a movement, a sound hardly audible over his increasingly rapid breathing. No, not even that, just a vibration, something he was feeling through the soles of his boots.

But no, perhaps not after all. Perhaps nothing.

Still, a feeling like he was being observed, an itching between his shoulder blades.

He tried to ignore it. He continued from vat to vat, examining each one, assessing his resources, as if he were the lord of the vats. But there were no resources left, not really. When he was done, he went to the next chamber and found it just as hopeless. And then went on to the final one.

Just outside the door he found the body of a uniformed crew member. *SARL,* the nametag read, though he could not tell if that was the whole name because of the way the man's right arm and a portion of his side was missing, cleanly sheared off. Perhaps he had been sucked brutally through the closing doorway when the atmosphere had fled the ship, but that seemed nearly impossible. His head, too, had been reduced to a dull slurry, scattered with crystals of ice. Nothing there to salvage, no way to gather a scan of the man's mind.

And beyond the buckled and half-open door, in the final chamber, another similar crewmember, then another, then a third. All mutilated in some way, all severely damaged cranially. He kept telling himself that it was possible it was damage caused by shattering vats or flying debris, but for each additional individual, this seemed increasingly improbable.

In the back of the third chamber, his suit light flashed across a strange blotch of color and what struck him, absurdly, as a slumped doll. But of course it wasn't a slumped doll. He knew that even before he swung the light back.

A dark circle, inscribed very carefully on the floor with what was perhaps black paint. In its center, kneeling, was a frozen woman. Compared to the chaos of the rest of the bodies, she seemed remarkably poised, undisturbed, untouched. On the wall behind her she, or perhaps someone else, had etched what at first seemed to be words, but upon closer inspection, Villads saw it was nonsense:

> Y'AI'NG'NGAH
> YOG-SOTHOTH
> H'EE-L'GEB
> F'AI THRODOG
> UAAAH

He sounded it out in his head but could still see no sense to it. He stepped to the edge of the circle and prodded at the line. Was it paint? He wasn't sure.

He stepped inside and bent down beside the woman, taking a closer look at her. No nametag, strangely enough. She seemed composed, relaxed. Her body was undamaged, her head intact. He might be able to get a scan.

He set about severing her head.

## IV.

While he was waiting for the machine to finish its replication, he thought about what to do. He could attach a tether and clamber out onto the outside of the vessel. Perhaps that would reveal something to him. He could travel through the chambers again, keep searching, but he'd been thorough—it was doubtful there was anyone else to find.

So only one crew member with an intact brain. One chance for a scan. Even if the scan was successful, maybe, she hadn't seen anything and couldn't tell him a thing.

He spun through images of the crew until he found the woman he thought was her. *Signe Volke.* Hard to tell for certain, considering the irregular way her head was thawing—something about the way the skin had frozen almost made it seem as though she had thin, hair-like tendrils growing on one side of her face—but yes, he thought so.

He slept. He asked the *Vorag* to prepare some food but there was apparently something wrong with the system: no food was dispensed. He raided another pressure suit for emergency rations. Five more pressure suits before he'd have to figure something else out. Either he'd have to find a way to fix the ship's nutrition delivery system or he'd have to start eating corpses.

He slept again. The scan still wasn't concluded, which might indicate that the neural pathways had been too compromised by being frozen. He had the ship show him vid footage. He watched it up to the moment the tear appeared in the side of the ship, looking for a clue. There was nothing to see, not really. The chamber lights dimmed, the hull tore open, and the feed cut off. He watched it again—and again, this time as slowly as he could, hoping to catch a glimpse of something. But he didn't see anything at all.

Unless that dimming of the lights, the growing darkness, was something. Maybe they hadn't been attacked from outside after all. Maybe what he was seeing was something *in* the ship, something barely substantial, something wanting to get *out*. Maybe he had it wrong the whole time.

He watched a vid record of Signe. He watched her come into the third vat room, pace her way forward and back as if surveying the boundaries of a plot of ground. Finally, she settled on a spot in the corner. He watched her take a jar of something and unscrew it and begin to use two stiffened fingers to smear a circle on the deck around her. She was swaying a little, nodding a little, and her lips seemed to be moving. He watched her carefully etch the nonsense phrases into the wall behind her with a laser cutter.

And then?

And then nothing. She simply settled onto her knees and assumed the posture he had found her in and waited, motionless.

She waited for hours.

Villads stared into the monitor, watching her. There was nothing unusual for a long time, or at least hardly so. At a particular moment, there was a shadow, strange and dark, that he couldn't place—perhaps just a trick of the light. And then, seven minutes and six seconds later, vats began to tumble over, seemingly for no reason. Other crewmembers appeared, shouting, some rushing toward her only to be swept off their feet and somehow torn to bits. The feed cut almost immediately after that.

The only thing he couldn't understand was how, through all that, Signe had managed to remain kneeling and in the same position, untouched by debris, seemingly undisturbed.

He activated the scans of the twins, Esbjorn and Kolbjorn, projecting each into a chair at the central table in the command room. He needed someone to talk to, someone to consult, and he knew and trusted them. Together they knew more about the ship and the journey than anyone else. They were the logical choice. Irritating, he thought, how the *Vorag* could do this but couldn't produce a plate of food.

The first time, he told the twins immediately they were dead but found that to have a deleterious effect on their willingness to communicate. They were of no help to him. So he reset them and began again.

"Hello," he said.

"Are we there already?" asked Esbjorn. "Have we arrived?"

"No," Villads admitted. "But I've had to wake you up. We have a problem."

He explained, not only about the tear in the hull but about Signe as well, the strange circle she had drawn, and her body frozen inside it.

"That doesn't seem like rational behavior," said Esbjorn. "Perhaps she's insane."

"Sounds like some sort of ritual," countered Kolbjorn. "She could be insane, or she might instead be some sort of fanatic."

The two brothers argued over the distinction between insane and fanatical. They watched the footage with him, both of the hull tearing and of Signe's circle. They had little useful to say, and in the end, Esbjorn suggested they all three go out and look at the tear in the hull. Maybe one of them would see something that Villads, alone, hadn't.

"No," said Villads quickly, "no need."

But Esbjorn was already rising and making for the door, the complex projection that gave the illusion of him having a three dimensional body growing choppier the more parts of him that moved. Kolbjorn exclaimed in fright at what he saw and then Esbjorn reached out to open the airlock and watched his hand pass through it.

Villads wiped their short-term memory and started again.


And then the scan of Signe was complete. He sat around the table with the projections of Kolbjorn and Esbjorn, and this time managed to move things forward without alerting them to the fact of their deaths. He explained about Signe's scan, about the tear in the ship, and then started the digital construct that was Signe without projecting her. But either Signe didn't know anything or she wasn't telling. By the end, Esbjorn and Kolbjorn were sick with panic at the thought of their own death, and he had had to turn off their emulations. He had learned nothing.

He took the pack of rations out of the seventh and final pressure suit. Surely there were some other pressure suits in one of the other chambers. Perhaps he'd be able to fix the dispenser. Perhaps he'd have to start eating the bodies of the dead.


V.

Inside the *Vorag's* computer, Signe, though dead, though only a construct, was still conscious, still aware. It was a strange sort of awareness, somewhat like groping around in a darkened room. Data streamed around her, some of which she could recognize, most of which she couldn't, and it was hard to maintain her identity in the onslaught. There was a sequence that she recognized as Esbjorn. His brother, too. And beside them, stacked one after another, she found the basis for the constructs of all the crew and vat travelers. Sleepy and hazy but still recognizable, waiting to be digitally brought back to life. There was Villads, too.

One by one, she worried and tugged at them until they came apart, the data degrading into a slurry that was quickly discarded, the sectors marked to be written over. They didn't even wake up for it, and soon it was too late to wake up at all.

When she came to her own sequence, she stopped. She wasn't sure why there would be two of her here. She hesitated between destroying her other self or simply giving it a wide berth and flowing elsewhere. In the end, she wriggled her way into it, putting her other self on like you might a thick jacket. There were moments of replication, but she had enough holes and gaps that there weren't as many as she had feared. Now she had a context, too, for the little her later self could remember of her final moments: the etching of the phrases into the wall, the creation of a circle, the attempt to summon a dark god.

Had the summoning been successful? There was nothing in her memory to say so, but there was a difference between the old self and the new self that made her think that she was now something more than just Signe. And based on what Villads and the twins had said to her and on the vid footage she was rapidly uncovering, she was certain. Where was it then? Just in here with her? No.

She went through more footage as rapidly as possible, footage from inside the *Vorag* and out, and then data from sensors of all kinds, until she sensed it. There, there it was, or at least she believed so: like a thick blanket, wrapped around the craft.

And now what? Mission accomplished. Turn the *Vorag* around and bring the ship back to earth along with its *blanket*.

Only there was the problem of Villads. Villads, if he figured out what was going on, would try to put a stop to it. No, she couldn't let that happen.


VI.

He had fallen asleep. He dreamed that he was back in his vat, unconscious, preserved, the ship drifting inexorably through space to the coming world. He was inside and outside the vat at once, both watching himself float and conscious of himself watching himself float. And then he woke up.

A noise had awoken him. What was it? Not an alarm. No, that had been earlier, the other time. A repeated tone, coming from the computer.

Was it some sort of notification he had set up? He didn't think so. Probably something from one of the crew, meant to remind them of some trivial but necessary task back before they had all died.

He ignored it as long as he could manage, then finally struggled to his feet, rubbing his face.

*Life form alert,* it said on the screen. Maybe he had set up that alert request, or maybe the *Vorag* knew from what he'd been asking it over the last few days that he'd want to know.

*What kind of life form,* he asked it.

*Humna,* it said.

*Strange,* he thought, a computer shouldn't misspell. Some kind of default or flaw, a small bug—but when he blinked the word had changed to *human.* Maybe he hadn't seen it properly the first time.

*It's probably just detecting me,* he thought. But he asked, *How many life forms?*

*Two,* it said. And gave him a map. There he was, a blinking dot on the bridge. And there it was, another blinking dot on the outside of the vessel.

But how was that possible? How could there be someone or something alive on the outside of the hull after all this time? Even if someone had been in a pressure suit, he couldn't have lasted a day, let alone a week.

*Is this possibly a sensor failure?* he asked.

*No,* said the *Vorag.*

The *Vorag* is wrong, he told himself, *something is wrong.* But he was already reaching for his pressure suit. *Nobody is alive but me,* he told himself. But how could he stop himself from checking? He'd put on a tether, go out through the tear, and have a look.

After all, what else did he have to do with his time? And once it was clear nobody was there, what was there to prevent him from coming back?

§

**Brian Evenson** *is the author of a dozen books of fiction, most recently the story collection* A Collapse of Horses *(Coffee House Press 2016) and the novella* The Warren *(Tor.com 2016). He is the recipient of three O. Henry Prizes as well as an NEA fellowship. His work has been translated into French, Italian, Greek Spanish, Japanese, Persian, and Slovenian. He lives in Los Angeles.*

# Be On Your Way

# HEATHER HATCH

ILLUSTRATED BY
YVES TOURIGNY

THROWBACKS. THAT'S THE SLANG, AND I CAN ALMOST HEAR THEM THINKING it as I board the shuttle. I guess it is technically true, just not how they mean it. Or maybe that's how we all think, those of us so-called Purists. The Left-Behinds, that's a different matter. But my people? No, for the most part, we wanted this—to be left behind by newsci genomeering. We have our own grand design, or that's what I was always told.

I'm given a breather along with the weird looks because I can't survive the $O_2$ mix on the shuttle. It should be okay once we're on the cruiser proper, but for now, it's canned air. The apparatus I'm given is old as hex, and though the clerk assures me it's clean, I have my doubts. Same with the grav-seater I'm shown to with an additional look of pity. Well, scratch him—I may not be genned for spaceflight, but I'm still tougher than I look. At least, I'll be left alone back here, and I can keep closer track of the heart.

I check the heart's containment before we get underway. It's pushing unlaw not to have a permit, but it is personal carry, and it's contained by newsci codes as well as hex. I could tell them it's Frog, and they'd let it pass as Purist scratch; they'd be wrong and right at the same time. I'm more worried because the composition is very flashy, and someone might try and steal it. It was sliced out of the meteor field on Nix, and it's got rare elements. We refined it ancient ways, and it's so hex I can feel it pulsing, but that's not what any newsci will see. Once I know it's safe and sealed, I pray for Frog's blessing for my work. After that, it's just waiting.

It's not a long flight. It used to take longer to fly across the continent, so I don't feel I can complain too much, even though I do feel truly sliced when the steward comes to let me out. He's got that same look, like he thinks he knows how I feel, and he's brought a cup of water. An actual cup! It amuses me, but I don't trust what's in it. Probably something that's been sitting in a plastic bottle for Frog knows how long. The way the newhumes metabolize stuff, they don't even think about that sort of thing.

Finally, though, we're at the ship—the grand old *Galaxy Cruiser*. I picked this one because it is old; reliable scratch that's never been updated for the latest modsets because it still does its job just preach. That means I don't have to worry about breathers or any of the rest of that since the atmo's pretty base with just enough chems pumped in for the spacies who can't handle ground truth anymore. I did my research, which is important if I want to do what I'm here for.

And I'm here for a job, even if that's not what my co-passengers think. That's why the looks of pity. Most of them only see Purists on the run, trying to slice their way off the ground and away from whatever "backward" hole they came from. It suits me to let them believe I'm one of those because, if they knew why I was heading out into the stars, they'd be looking at me less preachy.

I'm going to Saturn.

The *Galaxy Cruiser* hits up the sats there and every other planet each trip out, so it isn't that dramatic. All kinds of earthers, even newhumes, head out there for timeouts, so no one's going to blink at that. Lots of the sats on Saturn offer good prices for seeing the rings, and there's a few older terrahomes out on the moons where the atmo is base enough that earthers can longterm it if they don't mind a little postnat genomeering or some bodywork modsets. Throwbacks are known to run off to any of the planetary sats and terraed moons, too, so I'm not out of place. I'm not here for a timeout, though, and it's not the rings I'm after.

People think that Throwbacks, especially Purists, are all wrapped up in oldways, that we've got no sci at all or nothing new, that we're not interested in the future. I guess that's fly for a lot of Purists but not my people. We've got sci; it's just nothing like the spacies have. They just want to rocket out into space, terra every rock they can reach, and leave Earth and earthers as far behind as they can. Newhumes had to let a lot of things go to slice themselves up the way they have. They've put their faith in genomeering and rocketing and abandoned everything else.

And now, they've pushed far enough that there are things out there—old things, Frog things—that are starting to look back. They don't know what they're in for.

My people though? `

We have hex—real hex, not like old story hex—and we have oldsci, and we know. We take the newsci they put out, and we add it to the rest. We've been at this a long time, since before spacies were as old story as any kind of hex. We knew what was out there, knew that no genomeering would help them when they rocketed out too far. And we knew a better way and a better place.

Back before they'd really gotten their genomeering up to scratch, before they'd spent enough flash on rocketing to get that sci clear, there were others looking into dimensioning. After they had something else that worked, there was no more flash for dimensioning, and they dropped it. But that's the real way forward, the real future. When the heart is ready, we will use it to open the Saturn Door.

There was a hex to open the door back in the old, old times, the warm times that no one remembers, that we only know of from stories and from the Eibontext. So long ago, you can hardly even see traces left in the world unless you know how to look. Sci's no good, too scratched out. You need hex.

Hex and sci, they're almost the same thing now. People used to say that—that hex is oldsci, we just don't understand it yet. And that's mostly right.

There's forces in hex that sci will never clear because they have names and wills of their own, and they don't conform to sci rules and theories. They used to come to earth, used to fight there, sliced things up in ways even we haven't cleared. I think—my people think—the newhumes are going to find out sooner then they like. There've already been hexed rockets, all the crew gone or gone mad. Old forces are at work, and they're looking this way. But the high robes in their tower know what's preach, and they pass on the word and will of Frog. We're blessed that way, just how we're blessed to have what we have of the Door and the Eibontext.

I've never seen the physical text, but I know everything that's in it. It's part hex, part stories, and part things that slice up into either depending on how you hold the knife. I put it all in my head—the old way, no mind mods—just reading and repeating and copying, letting the high robes ask me questions over and over until I got it all clear. That's why it's me here: I can pass, at least as a throwback. I know the Eibontext, and I know the world the newhumes have made. I've got enough newsci. This isn't the first time I've been out of hearth, though it is my first time in space.

I put out the flash for a solo room. There're lots of reasons for this. I turn off all the scanners I can—I put out flash for that too. The ones left just read vitals and routine ship maintenance, and that's fine. Nothing I do onboard should trigger the monitors to come check. Nothing I'm doing is unlaw at all; nothing I'm planning once we get to the planet, either. Spacegov doesn't make laws for things they don't know or don't believe in.

But it's not the monitors, on the ship or anywhere else, I care about. My people aren't the only ones with hex, who know a little oldsci. There are other texts, and if they're not as preach or not as clear as ours, it doesn't mean they're scratch. Anyone can slice with a sharp enough blade.

Despite the discomfort of the shuttle trip, it's preach out here. I spend a lot of time in the viewhall, just watching the stars as we rocket past. Everything feels clear. Seeing the world through the ports makes me feel blessed, like I'm seeing a whole where the author only had pieces. He knew so many things, so much more about hexes, but for all that, I don't think he ever got to see the world all at once like this. Maybe after he opened the Saturn Door it was different, but none of that made it into the Eibontext.

People try and talk to me when I'm at the ports in the viewhall, but I don't talk back. Maybe they think I can't parse them, but I've got a speaker and learning besides. I can speak in more tongues than most of them know exist, though some deepspace genmods make it just plain hard to understand what they're saying. There's a few spacies that scratched up onboard, but only one who tries to talk to me. There's another who just comes to watch out the ports like me, so modded that they need a breather even for the chemmed air onboard. They seem shaky, like they're waiting on something. I wonder if I seem shaky. I wonder if they're a gov monitor—maybe one of the ones that never ground truth—on some mission of their own. We note each other; we never exchange more than looks.

*Galaxy Cruiser* has a regular route, stopping at terraed moons and asteroids and the sats around the other planets. Some people get off, some get on. I'm not the only throwback onboard after Mars, and the other—some Left Behind activist—is a lot more social, so the other passengers leave me alone. He tries to talk to me a few times, but eventually, he gives up and hexes me out for not giving sufficient slice, for being radcult scratch. On the whole, Purists have more power and law. More voice. My people don't care, but since I work out of hearth, I know the politics better. It has nothing to do with us. The encounter is almost enough to keep me in my rooms, but I find the view too addicting. The ship monitors don't like scenes, so after that, there's more of them down here. That's okay. It's not me they're watching.

It means there are more of them around after we hit Jupiter and pick up another Throwback from one of the sats. That's preach for me because she tries to start a scene as soon as she sees me. Recognizes me. Calls me out by name.

It takes me slightly longer to recognize her, and by then, the monitors are already moving in, asking her to desist from her screaming. I can smell heavy chems in the air, and I'm out. Probably, it's just destim to calm her—it might even be preach if it stopped my heart from pounding so fast—but I'd rather put my trust in Frog. Back in my room, and safe for now with a chance to think.

It was the antlers that threw me off. Probably, she can pass as genned—postnat fashion mods are outdated but not unusual. They're not pretty, though. Her antlers are a mess of bone prongs spraying up from just above her eyes, covered in some kind of very short hair. But they aren't genomeering. They're hex. And unnervingly so. Once I drew my eyes away from them, I recognized the rest of her; that was just as unnerving because I know her.

It's been years since Avera defected—Earth years, maybe longer for her. We studied together, and if she hadn't sliced, she would have been the one carrying the heart for this job. I don't know what she's doing here now, but it makes everything a lot more complicated. By rote, I pray. By rote, I check my hexes. The heart is preach. Everything is preach as far as I can tell, except Avera out of nowhere, screaming at me across the viewhall.

Screaming my name. Screaming that I have to be stopped. That I'm unlaw, a Purist terrorist.

We were close before she left. I could tell you exactly when she turned from Frog, though I didn't see it then. She started having questions, and she didn't like the answers. When she talked to me about leaving—not just going out of hearth but *leaving*—I couldn't grasp that she was serious. It was nonsense scratchings. Her being here makes no sense.

Avera was not the first to leave—it happens, especially with those who never

take the robes. That's okay. If they're not with Frog, they can't help us anyway, and it's no loss if they slice. But Avera had taken robes at the same time as me. She had hex. She knew the Eibontext by learning, same as me. Leaving, for anyone with that level of commitment, was unheard of. The high robes searched, but they left me out of it until I'd proven myself to Frog, unscratched by her heresy. Before this, I'd wished they hadn't. I knew I could have found her. I guess I was right.

The door buzzes. It's courtesy—the monitors can unkey any door on the ship if they feel they have cause. I answer. I'm calm. I appear calm.

There are two monitors, both newhumes but not spacies. One might be an earther. They're tall, broad, made for this. They loom as their ID codes chirp. They are concerned about restfulness for me, for the other passengers, on the remainder of the trip. They ask me to come, to answer questions. They ask if I understand.

Slice their courtesy. I can refuse, but I know I shouldn't. Slice their restfulness.

They walk me through backways. Others must not see, must not get scratched. *Hex them,* I think and try to continue to appear calm. I don't actually hex them. I am not the one who is unlaw, but I don't know what lies Avera has given them or what hex. They bring me to a wait room with one chair where I sit. They loom, and they ask my name, my title, my purpose. I can taste the chems in the air, but there is no hex here.

"I am no unlaw," I tell them. "Avera Luce, she is unlaw. She is a thief. A record was filed with the Earth Monitors." I give them the date.

They do not know Avera Luce. She gave them a different name. Her gen will not match their records, even if they check, because her mods are not sci. Hex changes to your gen can't be traced through sci tests. They won't believe me, but maybe they will be unsure. She is unregistered—that skirts the edge of unlaw— and she made a scene to accuse me of lies. The monitors do not apologize, for all their courtesy, but they allow me to return to my room. I know they will pay close attention to us both.

I do not go back to the viewhall. I comm back to hearth, but it will take too long to relay and to receive a reply because cruiser passengers cannot have access to priority channels no matter how much flash they put out. I could simply return home on my ticket or on another ship back to Earth. I could try and hide out on one of the sats or moons, but that seems less preach as it would be harder to keep the heart safe. I am here now because the timing is right. Avera must know that. She could've guessed that it would be me, that this is how I would travel. She could've had other ways of knowing. Something about her antlers scratches at me. Fortunately, we are close to Saturn, and I am close to completing my job.

Saturn is like Earth. In the old, old times, it was something else. It belonged to ancient things—timeless things. Things that had forgotten this piece of the universe. They used dimensioning to come to this galaxy, to the worlds here. From Cykranosh to Saturn, from Saturn to Earth. The oldsci, the hex they used, left echoes in those places. Residual energies that newsci can't make clear. This is why the storms on Saturn wander, why they change. The hex used by the ancients is grand and mysterious—the Eibontext makes them clear, through the word of Frog, to the favored. We can see the signs, follow the shadows in the stars, know when the alignments are the closest.

When Eibon made his gate, with Frog's direction, he used blessed starmetal—a meteorite—that possessed certain properties because it had come from Cykranosh. There were no others like it. Through the ages, we have hunted. Many have hunted. The meteor recovered on Nix is the closest, from all that our sci and hex can clear, to the one used to make that door. But it comes from somewhere else. It is not perfect.

We have the sci to travel, and we have hex to summon the forces from their echoes on Saturn, and we can transmute the heart into the makings of a new door. That's my job. When I return it to hearth, the high robes will open the door; we will go to be with Frog in its home, and we will serve and be protected from the ancients awakened by newhumes and their rocketing into the unknown void. We have made ourselves ready for this. Avera cannot be allowed to stop us now.

Avera cannot stop me now.

I find my resolve. She's hex—locating her will be simple. And the text lists ways of slicing one's rivals. One's enemies. I've worked hard to make clear who Avera is to me.

This kind of hex requires supplies, including some I didn't account for or couldn't risk bringing in my carry because they skirt too close to unlaw, even if they are Frog. For most, I can improvise. I can slice myself with nails or a sharp edge of metal if I have to. I even have a cup—it is invocation and preach that make the objects holy—and now I think of the clerk on the shuttle and smile. It is small, but I can't risk a more powerful guardian here with so many others on such a fragile thing as a space cruiser. Small will be sufficient.

I prepare; I speak my hex. Because I know Avera, she's simple to hunt.

I go backways. I knew the paths of the ship before I boarded—I put them in my head oldways, too, though now I've traveled them and what was image is made real. Maybe Avera has done the same. There are places where I don't have the ID codes to pass, but codes are just numbers. I know enough newsci to slice them open; I don't need hex or the guardian, and my passing is unclear.

Avera is also in a solo room, though I don't know where she got the flash. Probably, it's stolen or hexed. I hear nothing inside, but I can feel her. Maybe she is indulging in restfulness. It doesn't matter. I invoke the guardian and release it. Its dark form oozes through the seal on the door.

On the other side, there's a quiet click and chirping. The scanners don't recognize the chems that the guardian produces, but it doesn't need long to work. I expect to hear a scream, but there is nothing . . . the door slides open. Maybe my hex failed, and Avera isn't here; maybe this is just her empty room. Or maybe something else has gone wrong. I recall the guardian. I step inside.

The door closes behind me. This shouldn't be alarming as that's how they're coded. But this room is darker than I expected, and my hex-heightened awareness tells me other things are scratched as well. I can feel the guardian, expanded beyond its container, returning, but it too is scratched. The door does not open again despite its coding, and I'm pressed back against it. There is a light: it's Avera, the bony protrusions covering her head glowing pale green. The hairs that cover them seem to dance, muddling the shadows in the room.

The guardian does not respond to my will. As it puddles around my feet, I see that it is also covered in short, dancing hairs.

"Etelie," she says. "My foolish dear."

I spit hexes at her, but they are only words. The guardian rises from the floor, a black and furred curtain cutting me off from the heretical light. I expect to die—to have my skin boiled, to be dissolved and absorbed—but instead, I am only trapped. Distantly, I can hear the soft chirping of the scanners coding out that the chem balance here is scratched. My skin burns where it's covered, but it's a slow searing. Whatever she has made the guardian into covers my mouth, silencing me. I can feel the hairs sliding across my body, across my lips.

Avera comes closer. I hadn't noticed her eyes before—they're as black as a spacie's, if not so large. The light from her antlers reflects from their glassy surface. She reaches up to touch my hair, stroking it back from my face the way she used to, tucking it behind my ear. Her fingers are covered in patches of the same bony matter as her antlers; the hairs on them are stiff, scratching on my skin like stubble. I can't move away. I force my lips apart and gag on the viscous, hairy ichor. It burns, but it doesn't pursue its invasion.

"We don't have much time," she says, her mouth pressed close to my ear. "I should have come to you first like this—like a friend. I overreacted. But you must listen, Etelie."

All her words are heresy, but I can't hex her with looks alone.

"Your god sleeps, Etelie. On Earth in ages past, the power of Zhothaqqua died. Your priests have never heard Its voice when they call, only echoes of Its power. The Eibontext tells of its domain beneath Voormis, but that mountain is long ground to dust and ice, and you know this. Zhothaqqua's power is dead, gone from our world. Eibon was the last of Its great wizards. It cares not for you and yours. Cykranosh offers no asylum."

Her words, despite soft tone and touches, are heresy. Lies. She speaks the name of Frog with no reverence, no respect. The high robes live in communion. They speak secrets with Frog and know Its power. Their lives are long and blessed, and they pass on Frog's wisdom to those who will in time join them. If there was no communion, there would be no design. There would be no hex for opening the door. It's easy to hold onto my anger through the pain.

"I left because the high robes' lies could no longer satisfy me, Etelie. They grow ancient, drinking the lives of believers like you, but their power is stolen. I wanted to find Frog. But Frog is dead, sleeping. I found another—Yhoundeh. It has shown me true hex. Listen . . ."

She stretches out three fingers, reaching toward my face. I flinch as much as I can and feel them press against my eyelids, and one in the middle of my forehead. The hairs scratch; they slice into me, burning. I hear something like music: sounds and elusive rhythms, an irregular pulse. Within this are whispers, oldways words in a tongue I know but have never heard. This is hex, what she is doing. The tongue carries hex, too. I can't fight, can only do as she says and listen.

*You see the worlds. You see space and time. You see forces moving them, moving between them, around them. Gods to you. They ebb and flow, strong and weak, crashing against each other. They act against the world, against each other. Endless.*

*Here, one grows strong. It finds servants, its power grows. Another comes. It grows, consumes that power. Another comes. It grows . . . they touch thinking minds, change them, use them. The minds feed, they channel forces. Channel to use. Channel to focus. Channel to control. Channel to constrain. Here in one form, one time, one place, bound by world rules.*

*You see them, you name them: Zhothaqqua, Yhoundeh, Nyarlathotep, Kthulhut, Azathoth. They come, they come again, the stars have woken, the channels open, touched by space, through the stars, they come . . .*

I do see. I see Hyperborea, the clashes of priests and the fall of the world under ice in the old, old times. I see great Eibon, pursued by agents of another ancient. I see the world turning. I see Frog! Frozen with the world, out of time, bound. I feel Its power, Its voice in the whispers, silenced by another form, a great antlered form, whispering into the dark, whispering hex and force and power. I see other worlds the ancients have sliced through their clashing. I see them through the stars, I see them turning in space. I see rockets, spacie rockets, racing out to those worlds as the whispers swell into cacophony, a rhythm I can't follow. I lose all sense of words, of shapes, of myself until another voice rises above the whispers, calling me . . .

*—wake up, wake up, wake up—*

I wake up. I'm utterly scratched—everything hurts, but it doesn't burn how it did when Yhoundeh's corrupted guardian held me. My hands are still bound. I'm sitting, slumped against something, and I open my eyes when it moves. It's Avera.

My head is on her shoulder. Her hands are the first thing I see, her hex-modded fingers wrapped with mine. Mine look modded, too, blackened and dried. I can hardly feel her touch. Her wrists, like mine, are bound in some kind of metal cuffs. Her antlers no longer glow, and there are new jagged points to them as though they have been shattered in places. The hairs are still. The side of her face is reddened, like a burn. She inclines her head to me but does not turn her face.

"I have been wrong, my dear, dear Etelie. And we are in much danger."

There is nothing else in this small room. The door is closed and likely sealed. I think we're still onboard the *Galaxy Cruiser*, but I'm not certain. We're still in space; I'm surer of that. The air smells of chems I don't recognize, but my thoughts are sluggish. I can feel my heart beating, but it feels wrong. It feels too regular. It makes me want to reach up and slice . . . something. Avera squeezes my fingers, and I slump against her again.

"We were interrupted before," she says. "I am sorry. But now, do you understand?"

"Yes." I do understand, but maybe not what she wanted. "You're wrong. He spoke to me. Eibon spoke to me, and—"

"Shh." This time, she squeezes harder, the rough hairs scraping painfully against my skin. "There are scanners."

I close my eyes, resting on her shoulder and thinking of the heart. I can feel it, and Avera must too. It's too close, though my containment holds. Such simple hex, it seems now. If we are still on the ship, we should be arriving soon at Saturn, and the time is right. I can feel that too, feel the forces pulsing through my blood, their rhythm fighting against my own. The heart must be reacting, but it will need help to meet its potential, and there is the issue of the Saturn Door.

The door to our room—our cell—slides open. I sit up, though my head is still heavy with words and chems, and my body aches. I know the figure at the door: it's the spacie I saw at the viewhall. They have two ship monitors with them, carrying the heart. They set it down, and the spacie waves them out with its short grey arms. Once they're gone, it speaks.

It tells us we are charged with obstructionism, that we will answer to spacegov. It has an ID-code that chirps. It tells me that the heart is contraband, that our mods (I have no mods) are unauthorized, unlaw. It tells me that I must open the containment, that they will place the heart into their own care.

Avera looks at me. She squeezes my fingers. Her glassy black eyes show nothing, but I know her, and I know she fears. I squeeze back. I do understand, more than she knows.

"You do what you are told, but nothing is clear," I tell the monitor. I have seen their rockets make contact with the agents of other forces. I have heard their promises, their lies and madness, whispered to me with other truths. I know what waits now on Cykranosh—what is behind the Saturn Door, waiting for the opening. I have seen the bags of dying flesh that call themselves the high robes of my people; I have heard the garbled echoes they take for the voice of Frog, and I know better. But there is only one way forward. I look to Avera. "I will prepare the heart," I say to her. She says nothing, doesn't look at me. (I don't think her eyes are for seeing now.) The hairs on her antlers, on her fingers, shiver.

The spacie nods, sliding back, so there is space before the unit.

The sci-based containment has been tampered with but not breached. Maybe they wanted to see if they could take it without me. More likely, they don't understand hex. I put in the codes. It reads my gen—this takes longer than it should. Looking at my blackened hands, I wonder if it is more than stain. But the containment releases, and I speak the tongue to release the hex. I turn the heart three times, three times again. I look up. The spacie watches, and I know that they can't tell what I have done, can't feel the pulsing of the heart, almost in synch with the echoes of Cykranosh on Saturn.

"Is it done?" they ask.

"No. It will go faster with help."

They grumble words I do not understand but with clear meaning.

But Avera, too, is startled. "No!"

The spacie produces a weapon—some kind of rayblast—and raises it to her. Avera touches the side of her face, purses her lips.

"Do what she says," they order her.

I want to reassure her that I have a plan, but I can't make it clear without giving away too much to this spacie scratch. I direct her to sit across from me. I look at her, I tell her to do as I say. But the words that follow are hex, drawing power from the heart, not instructions. They are a warding. Avera nods, understanding now. The spacie shifts uneasily, not sure if it needs the blast. They should've sent someone more mad, who understands hex, not just someone who will follow orders.

I start. I've spent more time with the heart, and I know its rhythms. I draw it from the container, fingers splayed, and I start to speak them. Uncontained, it pulses more strongly, calling to my blood. I can feel my own heart responding, and I do not fight.

Avera joins me. Again, her antlers glow luminous, their light diminished where they have been damaged. I read pain on her face as she begins, her hands mirroring mine, splayed above the heart as mine are below. Her light begins to pulse in time with the echoes from Saturn, and she speaks their rhythms. Our chants conflict, syncopated, but slowly, slowly, we bring them into synchronicity. I could do this without her, but it was not untrue that it's easier, faster, with her help. We fall out of time, and there, we find accord and are as one—she and I, the heart and its home.

We begin to pull. Our words, spoken as one, change. We slide in space, slicing open the heart with our new hex.

My job was to prepare the heart. I did not know the opening hex. That honour was for the high robes. But they are not deserving of such knowledge, such power. The half-truths they took for revelation would have sliced more than our people from the worlds. As the Saturn Door begins to open, the spacie senses that something is wrong. He tries to blast me. I feel the ray graze my skin, but I feel no new pain.

Blackness seeps from the door, writhing outward. Maybe it's a guardian or something like it. It flows around Avera and I, reaching for the spacie whose rayblast is not effective against it, either. They are enveloped, consumed, and the blackness presses on, seeping through the shielded door as easily as my guardian.

Avera and I nod together, knowing we must end this, knowing the ship is likely lost already as more of this ancient's servant spills out around us. We reach across the open door, taking each other's hands, stepping through, turning the heart into itself, pulling it closed as we pass through.

The winds of Cykranosh feel cold, or perhaps it's the great writhing black mass of which only a small fraction has passed into our space. Avera's antlers flare brightly. Hand in hand, hand on heart, we speak loudly the words of warding—the words of Frog—and pass together through this new world.

**Heather Hatch** is a doctor with several degrees in pirates, all of which are going to waste. She works at an archaeological repository in Ontario, Canada. This may sound cool but is actually regulated at a consistent temperature because it is better for the collections. She is a gamer (the pen-and-paper kind, but often over the internet because it is 2017), a writer, and a knitter. She has previously published fiction in the anthology High Seas Cthulhu, in addition to a number of academic journal articles about piracy. As a queer woman, Heather is very excited to see the Cthulhu Mythos continue to evolve by embracing a broader diversity and distancing itself from the racism and misogyny of Lovecraft's original work.

## Cargo

# DESIRINA BOSKOVICH

### ILLUSTRATED BY
### JUSTINE JONES

W E'RE IN THE LOUNGE ON THE LOWER DECK WHERE WE LIKE TO SPEND our downtime.

Xander and Del are playing cards and disrespecting one another's heritages. Rafiq is knitting a spacesuit jumper for his sister's baby back home. I'm running lazily through my weight-training circuit.

Cicely, our engineer, appears in the doorway and takes a seat. She looks tense. "Guys . . . we've got a problem. It's the protector shielding. It keeps overloading. I've been running diagnostics for the past two hours. Can't figure out what's wrong."

She should have told the captain first. Or at least Xander, second in command. But things are complicated right now.

"Can you get in there?" Xander asks. "Take a look at the system, take it apart."

"Yeah," she says. "I'll need Del's help, though." Del's our second engineer, mechanic, and dock manager. "We'll have to take it offline. Which means we've got to work fast."

"Sounds like a plan," Del says.

"I'll need to scope the route first," Rafiq says. "Make sure we're not headed for anything too hot."

"You know I have to tell the captain about this," Xander says.

"We can fix it," Cicely says. "I think."

"I know. No worries. But chain of command and all that."

"Of course," Cicely says. "Chain of command. Most certainly." Which in the parlance of Cicely's people basically means, "Get fucked, pal."

Xander rolls his eyes. "I don't make the rules. Let me go talk to him now. Before you guys take the shielding offline. Make sure we're all on the same page." He doesn't wait for them to agree before striding off toward the bridge.

The others look to me. They know Xander and I are sleeping together; they assume this lends me special powers to interpret his behavior or maybe even control it.

I shrug.

"You think this is because of the . . . uh . . . cargo?" Rafiq says to Cicely. He's asking, but he's not really *asking*. "Stuff breaking. Tech going haywire. Like the stories say."

"She's supposed to be fully isolated," Cicely says. "Complete psionic quarantine. Safe."

She doesn't sound convinced; she sounds like she's trying to convince herself.

To be fair, Captain Oswald did consult us before accepting the cargo. He brought the job to us and asked us what we thought as he often did. But I think we all knew he planned to take this job, no matter what we said.

It would have been better if he hadn't asked at all.

Cicely, Rafiq, and I were against it. Cicely said it violated her beliefs. Rafiq feared the penalty if we got caught. This wasn't like smuggling diamondchips or hydrocells or weapons.

Xander was loyal to the captain, always. He didn't think this was a big deal, anyway. We're couriers and smugglers; sometimes the cargo is legal, sometimes it isn't. We inhabit the gray areas of the law. How was this any different?

Del agreed with Rafiq about the potential consequences, but his desire for the payday outweighed his fear by a hair.

Pike, hired gun, didn't care.

The captain wanted the money. Actually, I think the captain *needed* the money. So he took the job.

The cargo is a girl.

She was born on an outlying colony on a cold rocky world called Soline. Her people are mildly empathic and quite technologically advanced. They've hidden the secrets of their technology, but we know their machines are intricately interwoven with their psionic powers.

Like all children born on that world, the girl underwent a series of tests as an infant to determine if she carried a rare genetic strain. The tests came back positive. Her phenotype rendered her uniquely compatible with the sacred network.

In this culture, such children are revered.

She was taken from her parents and returned to the homeworld, Novjor, where she remained for a decade or so, undergoing the surgeries and modifications that would enable her to fully interface with the network.

The person who first explained this practice to me, when I was just a naïve girl, gawking at the bizarre abundance of the worlds from the vantage point of a stool in a bar, described the role like a cross between priestess and systems administrator.

I think of it more like a meld of princess and slave.

Whatever you want to call it, she's ready to begin. So we're returning her to the colony where she was born.

Novjor has been granted a cultural dispensation to continue this practice because it's their heritage. Their colony, Soline, is also in the clear. In the galaxy at large, however, exploiting empathic children is outlawed: a "Class A" felony under the laws of the Federation of Planets.

The *Titania's* involvement is at best "pretty illegal" and at worst "punishable by death."

Not like diamondchips. Not like hydrocells.

A girl.

Whatever they did to her brain means she can't be around sensitive instrumentation. On our ship, she floats unconscious in a tank reinforced with several layers of superalloys and aerogels and a fullerene coating to block any excess psionic waves. Like a Faraday cage for empathic energy.

In the panel above her face is one small transparent square.

Sometimes, I go down to the cargo bay and watch her. I stare at her tiny heart-shaped face, her papery eyelids, her weightless hair.

Del knows I do this. He doesn't mind.

Rafiq analyzes our projected course and determines the optimum window for repairs.

He calculates we'll have fifty-seven minutes to dismantle the machinery, assess the problem, fix whatever we can, and get the system back online before the ship begins accruing serious damage.

Cicely and Del map each move down to the second. They plan their strategy, step by step, and organize the tools they'll need.

Xander and I are on backup.

"Start now," Rafiq radios from the bridge, and the work begins.

Cicely and Del are grim and focused. They don't need to speak much; they've already spent hours rehearsing. You can hear the grind of metal on metal, the humming of machinery, the steady inhale/exhale of Cicely's breath.

Xander and I are quiet, too. Cicely and Del request tools, and I hand them over. Xander watches the seconds and calls out the time at five-minute intervals.

Cicely and Del work with quiet concentration. But occasionally I notice one or the other toss back an ever-so-brief glance at the cargo bay behind us.

I feel it too—an energy, like being watched, prickling right there at the back of my neck.

I'm sure we're imagining that.

"The coolant packs around the power core are malfunctioning," Cicely says in a voice so quiet it's almost a whisper. "Four packs. Three aren't working correctly. This one's only running at seven percent."

"Do we have backups?"

"Yeah," she says. "Always. But just a few. I've never seen them all go bad at once like this."

"Can we replace them now?"

"How much time?"

"Thirty-seven minutes."

"We'll try. Mina, can you bring the replacements?"

Carefully, I punch my shipman's code into the safe where our most valuable components and replacement parts are kept. No time for errors; no time to waste.

The packs are heavy. Xander helps me remove them from the protective casing, and one by one, Cicely and Del maneuver them into the slots and secure them.

There are only two.

"Twenty-seven minutes."

Another component is also damaged: a part of the system that automatically modulates the shielding's magnetic field based on the debris and radiation levels in our current location. Cicely doesn't have time to explain the details.

"We don't have a replacement for that part?" Xander demands.

"It's not something that usually needs to be replaced."

Cicely is hard to read. Her expression is always neutral, somewhere between tolerance and acceptance. Her low-pitched voice is always calm. She's like that now.

Yet because we all know each other so well—living in close quarters will do that—Xander and I understand she's panicking.

"Twenty-two minutes."

Cicely and Del do some reprogramming to route around that component of the system. It's just a temporary fix.

They get the shielding back online with a few minutes to spare.

We debrief in the bridge.

Cicely shows charts on the overhead display: the system's projected failure rate. Unless we can fix or replace the coolant packs and soon, the whole engine is going to start overheating and failing completely in about three days. And because they reprogrammed the shields to bypass the automatic modulation system, we're running at full capacity, which definitely won't help the power core stay cool.

We're seven days from the colony.

Captain Oswald is stymied by the failure and angry at everyone for no reason at all. "This is my twenty-seventh run across the galaxy in the *Titania*," he rants. "Never had a problem like this before. Never *heard* of a problem like this before. Seems awfully strange it would happen *now*."

We know without being told that he means *now*, when our cargo is dangerous, when a year's worth of salary is at stake, when the crew's conflicted.

"I believe this is my thirteenth run across the galaxy with you, sir," Cicely reminds him politely.

Cicely is an excellent engineer. Patient. Perfectionist. She isn't the type to make mistakes. We all know it; so does she.

Rafiq turns away from his seat at the navigator's station. "We might as well address the elephant in the room," he says.

"Which is?" Captain Oswald demands testily, though of course he knows.

"We've all heard the stories," Rafiq says mildly. "We know what we have in the cargo. We know our tech tends to break around . . . people like her. Spaceships, too. There's a reason that space smugglers only carry Novjorians in psi-proof boxes. Remember what happened to the *Queen of the Caraways*?"

"Urban legends," Pike scoffs. "That's just shit they tell baby spacers. Get them all riled up so they can laugh at them later."

"I don't think so," Rafiq says. "You know why we're headed seven days out? Why they settled Soline at the edge of the mapped worlds? It's because Novjorians are not exactly welcome most places."

"Perhaps because most cultures find their exploitation of empathic children upsetting," Cicely remarks.

"And maybe also because technological infrastructure tends to go haywire whenever Novjorians are around," Rafiq retorts. "Especially powerful broadcasters, like the girl you have in the box."

"This is ridiculous," Xander says. "Whatever stories you've heard about Novjorians are irrelevant. The box is psi-proof, *and* she's unconscious. There's no scientific justification for whatever you think she could have done to the shielding. Stop being superstitious."

"Well," Del drawls. "Maybe the box isn't as psi-proof as you think. Maybe someone decided to cut some corners. Save a little money."

For some reason, he glances at Captain Oswald when he says this. The temperature in the room goes up several degrees.

I'm stuck on what Xander said: *Stop being superstitious.*

Saying something like that—it feels like tempting fate. It feels like a dare to the infinite and indifferent universe, whose snarled edges extend far beyond anything we've seen or known.

In a universe this vast and strange, what would actually be irrational is to doubt the existence of the inexplicable.

And isn't that what being superstitious is? Fearing the forces that are vaster and older than those we've mapped?

I've only been a spacer for six years, but in that time, I've come to think that superstition might be the only thing that keeps us alive.

Perhaps, Xander and I are too different, after all.

The thing between Xander and I started six months ago, maybe seven, back around the time we made the run through the Galea system. The thing was natural and physical and existed in the space between sentences. It lived in the way our bodies fit together, the mesh of smell and taste and touch. He felt like coming home to a familiar place.

But then, we started talking.

We carried the argument about the cargo back to his narrow bunk and he said, "What does it matter? It's their people. Their decision. This isn't our fight. It's just one girl."

*It's just one girl.*

*One girl is every girl,* I thought but didn't say. The inner monologue of a woman who was also just one girl.

We left the argument alone and rode each other's waves and fell asleep in one another's arms, sweaty and content. His hollows, my curves: simple bliss.

But in the morning, I woke, and I thought, *This man doesn't really know me.*

He couldn't understand why I'd take it personally that some girls are born to live and die inside destiny's cage.

I'm pulled from the memory by my crewmates' shouting. The fight has escalated to recriminations. Rafiq blames Captain Oswald. Pike is angry that he dares. The shouting almost becomes blows, the others loudly taking sides—

"Enough!" the captain declares. He looks shaken and tired. He may not be well. He's definitely not sleeping. "We'll figure something out. OK? We'll find a way."

He sends us to search the ship for something, anything, we can retrofit as replacement parts.

"I know what components I have on my ship," Cicely says. We all know she's right; this search is doomed from the start.

But the captain insists, so we obey. He sorts us into teams of two.

Rafiq and I search the storage bay in the corridor behind the mess hall. In the dim light, we work slowly and methodically, sorting the gear into piles based on probability of usefulness. We chat while we work. We've never been particularly close, but since the cargo came on board, the alliances in the crew have shifted; now, I feel more comfortable with him than most of my crewmates.

He's up for leave next month. I ask him what he's planning to do. Of course, he's visiting his sister. He tells me about his niece and the baby nephew he's never met, the lucky soon-to-be recipient of a knitted spacesuit jumper.

His sister still lives on his homeworld. Hanna Ro, Charru's legendary megacity, renowned for their fusion cuisines and acrobatic dance troupes, home to the largest butterfly conservatorium in the galaxy, and birthplace of Luxie Amalfea, the famous pop star. Rafiq grew up there; he misses city life.

It makes me happy, the way his eyes light up when he talks about home.

"You ever want kids of your own?" I ask idly, as I catalogue a spool of fine-gauge titanium wire that will do absolutely nothing for our repair needs.

"Nah," he says. "Cool uncle's more my gig. Yourself?"

"Maybe," I say. "Someday. On my own time. On my own terms."

He nods. I don't know if that means he understands.

Afterward, we all meet back in the upper deck to inspect our finds. Our trusty smugglers' ship has been held together with duct tape and rusty bolts for many runs across the galaxy. We've got plenty of junk parts and detritus but nothing that substitutes for a coolant pack.

Rafiq and Cicely sit down and calculate how long we can make it before the protector shields break down completely. How far we can go in that time. And where that might put us.

The only worlds between here and Soline are Federation planets with formal docking procedures; if we stop for help, we'll have to submit to inspection, and the agents will no doubt find our hidden cargo. We'd all be in deep, deep shit.

We could push the cargo out an airlock and land anywhere, get help repairing the shielding. But when Soline finds out that we ditched their once-in-a-generation princess, their multimillion-credit investment, we'd all be in deep, deep shit.

Or we could keep going until the shields break down completely, and our ship is pulverized by space debris while our bodies are poisoned by space radiation.

Limp our way into the Soline system, if we make it that far, and hunker down to repair our ship and wait to die.

None of the options are particularly appealing.

"Of course, we agreed," Del says quietly once the captain's out of earshot. We all know he's talking about the cargo. "We're the troops. It's our job to agree, say 'aye, aye, yes sir.' What did he expect?"

"Not everyone said 'aye, aye, yes sir,'" Cicely says with a voice like a dagger.

The tension is unbearable.

I retreat to the cargo bay. I sit by the girl's superalloy and aerogel coffin and gaze at her through the frosted panel. She's like a marble statue but for the slight flutter in her temple. Her eyelashes are silver.

What's she dreaming about? Does she know that she's killing us? Does she care?

Oblivious—I think—she sleeps.

We spend some hours trying to strategize but mostly sniping and bickering and lamenting our impending doom. There doesn't seem to be any way around the fact that we're probably going to die soon or at least be imprisoned for a very long time.

We retreat to our quarters to rest and contemplate our fates or, in Rafiq's case, work on his knitting—he's determined that whatever happens, he *will* go visit his sister and his nephew *will* be attired in baby astronaut finery.

I sit alone in my bunk and sip my whiskey and think, *Well, I was going to die sooner or later, right? Probably sooner.*

I come from a world of never-ending war. The war's continued for centuries, consuming all. It should have extinguished our world long ago. But somehow, the war continues. And the world survives just enough to keep burning.

Our bodies are owned by the state. Our babies are owned by the state. The state's one and only business is to make the war. And so it demands more babies, more bodies. The girl babies grow to make more babies. The boy babies grow to be more bodies.

The war devours us all.

When I was sixteen years old, I stowed away and became a spacer. I stole myself—a capital crime against the state.

I've always been a dead woman walking, but eight years later, I thought maybe I was finally free.

Oh well. This life was good while it lasted.

More hours go by. Xander's voice rings out across every intercom. "I see something. Everyone, come up to the bridge!"

The ghost ship hovers in the view screen, dark and glittering, vast and bulky like a floating arcology. Perhaps, it used to be a generation ship, now remodeled as a cruiser to travel among the conquered stars.

"It's sending out a call," Xander says. "A beacon. No code I recognize. I don't know what it means."

"A distress call?" I wonder. "Or a warning?"

"It's garbled," he says. "Gibberish. Static. It could be anything . . ."

Rafiq studies his maps and sky charts. "I don't see any lost ships listed for this sector," he says. "No vessels matching this description. Strange."

"Maybe it's lost," Pike says, which the rest of us ignore; he's better at soldiering than problem-solving.

Xander calls over our comms link: "Hello? This is the *Titania*. Is anyone there? Identify yourself. Again, this is the *Titania*. Do you need assistance?"

No answer.

Cicely says what we're all thinking. "This might—it might be the answer to our problem. Such a big ship. They'll have a warehouse. We could get help."

"And if everyone's dead?" I ask.

"They'll still have the warehouse," Xander says.

"And no one to ask annoying questions," Del adds. I can't tell if he's joking.

"Unless, it's all been stripped by space pirates already. Possibly the ones who left it stranded here."

"We'll try it," Captain Oswald declares. "We're out of options. Rafiq, shift course. Take us to the cruiser."

As the *Titania* closes the distance between us and the silent ship, we ready our shuttle. Xander and Rafiq will stay onboard, waiting just outside the cruiser's range in case of danger. The rest of us will take the shuttle and explore the ship.

Pike and I are defense, so we gather our arsenal while the captain runs diagnostics on the shuttle and Cicely and Del analyze the projected 3D map to plan a search.

The craft grows inexorably larger in our screens, eerily silent. The architecture is odd, like a floating ziggurat, terraced and geometric. Millennia of civilizations and their explorations means a lot of weird stuff ends up floating around out here at the dark edges. But still, I've never seen a spaceship quite like this one.

The *Titania* makes her final approach. We bid goodbye to Rafiq and Xander and climb into the shuttle, which launches like a pebble hurtling through space.

As we approach, we call out on every channel. Silence. No word as we pass through the outer membrane of the ship's atmospheric shield into a vast loading dock and small craft hangar. The captain eases the shuttle into the nearest docking station. The airlock syncs. We're good to go.

We pass through the first corridor into a wide-open lobby. At the center, a jungle-like profusion of green plants flourishes in a circular well. Bright light emanates from everywhere, the floor and walls and far-off ceiling illuminated and aglow. Soft music plays like an elevator ride in a capitol building. The air changers hum.

No one's around.

"Very strange," Captain Oswald mutters. "Very, very strange."

"This is fucked," Del agrees.

"Let's start walking," Cicely says.

We cross the lobby and enter a small passageway. This opens onto a wider space. To our left, doors; to our right, more doors. Directly across is open air. We crowd the ledge.

We're in a central atrium, vaguely hexagonal, the circumference lined with hallways and doors and the central shaft falling deep below and high above. All as cheery and brightly lit as the first room we entered. Music tinkles like a carnival accompanied by the sound of falling water.

"Passenger quarters?" Del speculates.

All this bright light and blooming foliage and breathable air and not a person in sight.

"I really don't like this," Captain Oswald says. "Mina? Pike? You on point? Stay focused."

He doesn't have to tell us. We're soldiers. We know this is wrong. We know it feels like a trap.

"Whatever it is, we won't find what we need here," Cicely says. "We need to find the crew's quarters."

The feeling of wrongness is sharp and pointed like something lodged between my shoulder blades.

We walk, following the map projected by algorithm from the 3D scan, through winding corridors of passenger lodgings that turn into spacious passenger parlors, through abandoned guest cafes and lobby bars. We enter the cozier crew's quarters and pass life-support systems for producing food and recycling water and air.

From our vantage point in that vast atrium, we glimpsed the shape of the whole ship, but now as we walk, the internal geometry doesn't make sense. Like halls are moving. Like walls are moving.

"I could have sworn . . ." Cicely says and doesn't finish.

"What?" I ask. "Could have sworn what?"

"We saw that door before." She points to a dent in the door's lower right hand side, a divot in the metal where the paint is chipped. "We walked this hall already. But that was a couple levels ago. We've been walking down this whole time."

"A glitch," Del says.

"What? What does that mean?"

The halls have narrowed. The ceilings seem to sink lower with every step we take. The dim lights flicker. The hum of the air changers seems shriller. I can almost hear desperate voices buried in the static.

The white noise of the ship intensifies and fades. Like the world we're inside is rocking closer and then farther away.

"That storage berth," I say. "I saw it before, too. That same tangle. We should look inside. Right? Because coolant packs."

"Yes . . ." Cicely says. "A good place to look. Definitely a good place to look."

Captain Oswald is muttering to himself. No one asks him what he meant to say.

Del slaps at his arm. And then the wall beside him. "What the fuck? A fly? The bastard."

"A fly?"

"Yeah. A fucking fly."

"Doesn't that seem unlikely? On a spaceship?"

The flies buzz. There are more now. I see them, too. Crawling on the walls. Hovering beyond my nose.

"Do you guys smell that?"

A heavy, putrid smell like day-old death and rotting garbage.

I'm not thinking clearly. I know I'm not. Something's overtaken me. These waves of feeling. Emotion like a flood. It's dark and cold and dripping, and I want to sit down, my back against the dented dirty walls of the belly of this spaceship cruiser without a living crew, and cry, I think—yes, cry. For all the girls that didn't make it out.

"I grew up in a factory," I announce. "A factory for making bodies. I really loved her—my friend—her name was Naomi. After they took her to the birthing mill. I mean, I knew they'd take me too, soon. I couldn't bear it. I should have stayed. But it was too late for her, really. I'm sorry."

"They'll take my daughter if I don't pay," Captain Oswald says.

I didn't even know he had a daughter.

"You got a kid?" Pike asks.

"On Asuslon. I only see her once a circuit or so. She's very smart. Just twelve, now. I hoped one day she'd want to join the crew . . . of course, her mother wouldn't approve. But traveling is in our blood. Not her mother's. The problem. Of course. Always is."

"Me, too," Pike says. "A kid. He's three. Never met him yet. Saw some holos. Talk to him on the screen. God, he's beautiful. Looks just like his mother, of course. Eyes like saucers."

It seems we've been walking for days and days. Or maybe just a minute. Time's gone strange.

"I quit, by the way," Cicely says. "The *Titania*. I'm done. You can drop me off at the first civilized world."

We've reached the dead end of something. An ever-narrowing hallway that ends in a door.

"I love you all so much," says Del. "Don't say it enough. I don't know what I'd do if I didn't have the *Titania*. All of you. My family. The only one I've ever had."

The sadness crushing my chest like the grip of marble arms becomes something else, something syrupy and viscous and golden. I want to cry, but in a whole different way, and laugh, too. I'm hysterical, I realize.

The smell is different. The rotting garbage smell. It's become a much older kind of death, cloying and almost sweet. A smell like almond oil and scorched honey.

Captain Oswald passes through the final door, and we follow him into a cargo bay.

The ship has guided us to this heart.

We stand on a narrow, rickety catwalk above an open cavern. This one-time cargo bay is now entirely consumed by a massive substance. A thing. A creature? The mass is pitch-black and iridescent and thick, amorphous and diffuse, like a plume of spilled oil and tar blooming in deep water. The thing trembles. The sounds and shrieks it makes are awful: groaning, keening, panting sounds that might be lust or rage or terror. It's immense and everywhere at once; its tentacles are reaching for us. The pitching, bucking catwalk attempts to dump us into the creature's fetid mouth.

I am screaming, by the way. I think we all are.

Pike's double-fisting his blaster and his gun, discharging them both rapid fire into the thing below. Neither particles nor projectiles seem to have much effect.

It's roaring now. It's not clear if it has tentacles or limbs or legs, or if its body simply has strength without much shape, but parts of it reach up and grab Pike, whipping him around while the particles and projectiles fly, while he shouts in pain and outrage.

It sucks him in and down. Devours him—or deconstructs him. He's gone.

Time moves on, both fast and slow. We're all running. Pandemonium sets in. We're tripping over each other and falling and fighting. The nebulous parts of the creature block our way, knocking us into each other, temporarily blinding us with black floating clouds. The catwalk seems to be spinning. Revolving in faster and faster moving circles, no longer lined up with the door that brought us here. The ship itself revolts against us.

Cicely falls. The creature swallows her, too.

Captain Oswald hangs upside down from the edge of the catwalk, legs splayed, head facing down, hacking at it with something like a machete, and in all this chaos, as time no longer seems to work, I think, *This whole time the Captain's carried a sword? Insane.*

"That way! Run!" Del shouts.

I want to fire at the creature too, like Pike did. I've got my weapons. I've got my arsenal. It wouldn't be the first time I fought for my life. Then I realize I am firing. I'm standing still. Mesmerized. Aiming at its slick oily center (though it's everywhere and nowhere and doesn't really have a center at all).

"Move!" Del's shouting and shoving.

The catwalk is revolving. Like it's made to do. We're in a central shaft and doors enter from all around. We're on a bridge that serves them all, programmed to rotate where it's needed. It's rotating now and all the doors are opening and closing at once.

This sick architecture's taunting us.

Somehow, though devoured, Cicely is still screaming. Captain Oswald is screaming, too.

I'm dragging Del, or he's dragging me, and we're running and running, hoarse from screaming, out of this place, beyond this creature's reach. Through a door—not the door we came in, I'm relatively sure—down another endless hallway.

Even as I run and run, I still feel it behind me.

I look back, over my shoulder, just to check—the hallway's empty, right? All I see are my own footprints, each step a stamp of slick black ooze. Moving with me. Almost alive.

For a moment I think, *My footprints are following me.*

But that doesn't make sense. I mean, of course they are.

*Into the frigid sleep, some presence leaks.*

*Into cold solitude it speaks.*

*Tendrils spiral toward her dreaming conscious mind, and her own tendrils spiral back into the dark. Tendrils. Tentacles. Curling. Twirling. Twining.*

*Dreams, dreams, dreams: vast and terrifying and gorgeously sinister.*

*Dreams of foreign suns and alien vistas and ancient worlds.*

*Past and future. All together. Time beyond reckoning.*

*For a moment, the bitter loneliness abates.*

*Ruler once and could be again; priestess of small world, but the universe beckons.*

*This is us.*

*Lovely.*

*Planted like a seed.*

*Tempting.*

*Beautiful and hideous, the infinite terror, the boundless void. What creature, no matter how monstrous or otherworldly or fatebound, would not long to be free?*

*Let's go, then.*

*Together, we'll feast on the psychic screams.*

Del and I sprint until we reach a passenger lobby filled with soft jazz and kaleidoscopic carpets and verdant artificial trees. We fall panting and whimpering across the plush settees.

"Cicely . . . Pike . . ."

"Captain Oswald . . ."

"They're gone. They're gone."

"Coolant packs. We were supposed to find . . ."

"Damn it."

"That storage berth."

"I'm not going back."

"*Titania*?" I shout into my comms link. "*Titania*? Can you hear me?"

"Mina?" Xander's voice sounds very far away. "Is everything okay? You guys went dark. You alright?"

"No!" I shout hysterically. "We're not all right. There was something—this thing—it got the Captain. And Cicely. And Pike."

"A thing? What do you mean a *thing*? Get back to the shuttle right away, okay. Mina? Are you listening? Are you and Del injured? Get back to the shuttle."

"We're not injured."

"We still need to find the coolant packs," Del says into the link.

"Forget the fucking coolant packs! Get back to the shuttle. That's an order."

He's our commanding officer, now. I'd almost forgotten.

Del and I pick ourselves up and search for the shuttle hangar. Somehow, the way back is much shorter than the way down.

We enter the hangar on the opposite side from our shuttle. "We must have got turned around when we were running," I say. Del just grunts.

We're docked with an entrance lock across the hangar; it's either wander around inside until we reach the right passage, or make our way across the hangar and climb into the shuttle through the emergency exit.

We opt for the second; it feels safer in the hangar. At least through the membrane, we can still see the stars.

"There's an L-Class Sparrow Freighter docked over there," Del says. "Protector shielding's got a similar build to the *Titania's*. Made by same company. Might be some spare coolant packs. They won't fit exactly but—I could try—"

"Okay, okay. Let's go. Fast."

I wait just outside the freighter while Del searches inside. Xander and Rafiq are interrogating me over the comm link the whole time, panicked and afraid, asking what went wrong in there, what's going on.

"I can't even explain it."

"Mina? The captain's really gone?"

"He's really gone."

"Do you know how to fly the shuttle?"

"Fuck. Fuck."

"You don't?"

"I do. I know how. I've done all the training modules. I can do it." *I'll try.*

Del comes back holding a foil-coated duffel. "I found some stuff," he says.

"Let's go." We wriggle our way up the chute and into the shuttle. I strap into the captain's seat, Del beside me. We're both shaking. We've both forgotten how to breathe.

I ease the shuttle out of the hangar and past the membrane and toward the *Titania*.

The components we brought back aren't perfect, but Del works on the system with stopgaps and hacks and fixes it up enough to work for a few days.

The *Titania* is limping by the time we make it to Soline, but we make it. We deliver the cargo and earn our paycheck. It's a lot of money.

A *lot* of money.

We only spend a day on Soline. Just long enough to replace the damaged components on the ship, restock, refuel. We leave the colony as quickly as we can.

The ship is ours now. As long as we can stay ahead of whoever was after the captain.

We head for deep space, the unexplored outposts, the unknown worlds.
We delivered the cargo, but something's stayed with us, too.
Something remains.

Back on Soline, the carnage begins with blood and screams and fire.

It begins and doesn't end until there's nothing left but the burnt-out husks of buildings and smoking plastic and scarlet spattered across the snow.

And the cargo, of course.

It settles down to wait.

§

**Desirina Boskovich's** *short fiction has been published in* Clarkesworld, Lightspeed, Nightmare, F&SF, Kaleidotrope, PodCastle, Drabblecast, *and anthologies such as* The Apocalypse Triptych, Tomorrow's Cthulhu, *and* What the #@&% Is That?. *Her debut novella,* Never Now Always, *is recently out from Broken Eye Books. She is also the editor of* It Came From the North: An Anthology of Finnish Speculative Fiction *(Cheeky Frawg, 2013) and, together with Jeff VanderMeer, co-author of* The Steampunk User's Manual *(Abrams Image, 2014). Her next project is a collaboration with Jason Heller—*Starships & Sorcerers: The Secret History of Science Fiction, *forthcoming from Abrams Image. Find Desirina online at www.desirinaboskovich.com.*

# The Blood Will Come Later

# DAVAUN SANDERS

ILLUSTRATED BY
NICK GUCKER

THE CASSAD RECRUITER LAUGHS, AND I NEARLY ERASE HIS MIND ON THE spot.

"You do know this is an Averator's craft?" he asks, tapping notes into his palm-sized manifest. A line of Cassad hopefuls stretches into the bowels of the stardock behind me, citizens of the Reach worlds vying for stable work.

"I do now," I reply. "You said there's an opening."

"Another vessel's better suited." His fingers flutter at distant lines of people in the cavernous requisitions plaza; many hope to fill holes for freighter crew, merc raiders, diplomats' pleasure cruisers. "Half of Amadi Zele's personnel were born and raised together! What possible need could—"

"Engineer, then." A moment is all I require aboard this ship. A reckoning.

"But you just—"

"Engineer," I repeat softly. "Or whatever. Wherever there's a need. Let me pass."

His eyes lose focus as my mental suggestion permeates his consciousness. "You may board the *Dubious*." He taps an entry into the manifest—cook, of all the inane things—and gestures me forward for scanning. "Hmm. You're not Cassad. Name?"

"Remiliat Dumasani."

I lash out with my mind, shunting a precise amount of disruptive psionic force into the recruiter's motor cortex. His fingers scramble the entry. My eye scan and voice print remain stored on his manifest, however. That's a problem.

"Paki handles assignments. Report to . . . report to . . ."

I stride past as my parting suggestion unfolds deep within the recruiter's mind. The lift platform awaits, a hexagonal shell of cold steel and glass. I step inside. The crunch of splintering glass compels my backward glance.

The recruiter sits, lips sliced and stained red. Other Cassad rush up. He's still determinedly trying to eat the manifest even after they wrestle him to the ground, shouting. *Cook, indeed.* Before the lift doors close, I see sparks dance between his teeth.

One thing is clear as the lift sweeps toward dock seven thirty-two: the *Dubious* is a ghastly craft. All manner of receiving devices plaster the forward bridge. A preposterously long, narrow hull ties a bulbous beak to oversized engines. A crew of fifty would be cramped, I suspect, which makes my hunt that much easier.

One held breath centers my focus. When the lift stops, my talents are ready for the two waiting Cassad crew. "Welcome to the highest calling in the—" the woman frowns as I slip past. "An empty lift? Can this mission get any damn stranger?"

The other Cassad sighs, equally blind to my presence. "I hate the Reach. If the Averator wasn't so sure . . ."

I pad through precise white halls of steel and glass, maintained far better than the rusted haulers I bartered passage on to get here. My path to the bridge is unobstructed. No personnel. No surveillance nodes.

A Cassad man stands over one of the flight consoles, burly but not overly muscular, skin a tinge browner than mine. He wears an oddly cut blue uniform and tugs at his mustache while he mutters to himself. He sees me before I shield his mind.

"I'm sorry, young woman," he intones pleasantly. "But you should seek opportunity elsewhere at the stardock. I specifically forbid crew with military training of any sort aboard my vessel."

"That's a shame," I reply, mildly impressed by his discernment. *Averator, is it?* "Because your bright empire is rusting along the rivets, Amadi Zele."

His eyes narrow as I inspect the console beside him. "History's full of temporary lapses in order," he says. "Regardless, nobody is idiotic enough to attack my vessel."

"The New Regime is populated by nothing if not idiots."

The console responds to my query. *Damn.* My target isn't aboard, but the crew roster shows her reporting soon. "Good day, Averator."

He jerks as my suggestion draws a curtain of amnesia over his memory. Eyes clouded, he returns to his work. I'm already forgotten here, just like everywhere else.

I pass more *Dubious* crew in the halls, wearing their amnesia like a protective cloak. By emperor's decree, every Cassad vessel—even one this bizarrely designed—has a brig. It's even more neglected than I suspect. The perfect hiding place, and closest to Karisten's post.

*Karisten.*

It feels good to finally dwell on her name. I settle on a small mat in one of the brig's shadowed cells, recounting her crimes. Of all our old crewmates, Jobrel trusted Karisten most. And with her deciding vote, all that remained of my husband's memory was scattered across the Known. She's proven easiest to hunt down; first on my list.

Zele's deep baritone washes over the ship's comms. "All crew is aboard. Report for inventory appraisals immediately. Departure will commence after officers' check."

If the Cassad love anything, it's following standard protocol. By my reckoning, Karisten will meet her end long before the ship disengages from the stardock, hours from now, and I'll turn to my next target.

So when the *Dubious's* engines hum to life, I'm understandably vexed.

The cell's stun wall suddenly powers on. I blink stupidly in the crackling blue light. The brig doors slide open, and Amadi Zele himself strolls in. "So! My hypothesis was correct."

Outrage battles my shock. "Release me before—"

"This entire compartment will be ejected into space in seconds," he cuts me off. I believe him, along with the fresh alarm blaring through the comms. "I wanted to see if you could be reasoned with. Who are you? Who sent you? What have you done to my crew? In that order, please."

"No one, nobody, and nothing any of you will remember. How did you detect me?"

His hand wavers over the control panel beside the door. "Headaches, forgetfulness among the best minds in the Known." The alarm ceases. Zele frowns. "You've misstepped gravely, young woman. My crew is an extension of me."

"I don't care. All I want is Karisten. The rest of you have nothing to worry about unless you prolong this."

"Unacceptable."

I'm ready when Zele's fingers dart for the panel. His arm flops uselessly to his side. "Remarkable!" he breathes.

The brig's door grates open manually. Crew pour inside. A Marajeshi man with greenish freckles on his brown skin lunges for Zele. I disrupt the muscles in his left thigh—and his bowels, because I'm in a bad mood—and he spills to the floor. Zele twists and turns as half a dozen Cassad sprawl around his ankles, one by one.

"Young woman, I'd like to offer you—"

"Averator!" One last crewperson rushes in with a med kit: hair in small twists, like I remember, worry lines creased into her forehead. She sees me and her jaw drops. "Remiliat?"

*Karisten.*

I've dreamed of this for so long. My mental assault simply unfolds. Karisten crumples so perfectly her cheek bounces on the Averator's boots.

"This is how you left me." My voice pierces the paralysis I've crafted for her. "That ship was all I had left in the Known—all that remained of Jobrel! You had no right!"

"We tried, Rem," she burbles. "You weren't the only one who lost someone! We all had to start over with the empire so *broken*—you can still start over, the Known is big! You can find—"

"A new life? I tried." I spit. "But I'm not Cassad. I'll settle for you."

Tears leak down her face. It's a simple matter to curve her spine past breaking. Stop her heart.

His crew incapacitated around him, Zele addresses me. "You've infiltrated this ship at great cost, but you're no murderer." A strange light glitters in his dark eyes, a hunger that unnerves me. "I insist you must remain and work with me."

*What?* "You mean dissect me. You're insane."

"No. I trust my impulses, and I do not extend this offer lightly." His hand slaps the entry pad before I can react. He's released the stun field. "Cassad or not; my crew is family. No harm must come to Karisten. That is my condition."

I edge out of the cell in disbelief. *He's offering me . . . work? What's my role? How will I . . .*

A hundred more questions cycle through my mind as the moaning Cassad regard me fearfully. I could stand among them, be part of a family again, despite the pain I've wrought. Hope seeps through my weariness, inviting and viperous. "I'll need a convincing story."

"And you shall have one."

The Averator restores a semblance of order through a combination of my induced amnesia and his calm explanations for any incongruent recollections. They trust him absolutely. I endure whirlwind inoculations, procedure reviews, lab tours. At an all-hands dinner in the ship's refectory, I'm introduced as a last minute addition and warmly greeted by Cassad I paralyzed just hours ago.

"Remiliat will maximize personnel interactions," Zele concludes cheerily. That raises a few eyebrows, but I'm accepted without question. The effect is completely disarming.

"Averator, you've never agreed to an empire-sanctioned mission before." Eliat, a linguist with a boyish face and skin the shade of sunrise clouds, clears his throat. "Frankly, several of us are concerned we'll be diverted into weapons research."

Heads bob throughout the space.

"I'm not so immune to our political realities." Zele sets down his steaming tea and rises. "We're seekers of truth, yet beholden to agendas. This is one of those rare occasions where our work as scientists coincides with the needs of governance. I've acquired evidence of ancient Cassad contact with an alien species, undocumented by the imperial djelis."

Speculative murmurs burst out all around me. "Derelict craft?" Gorshen, a pilot with bearded falcons tattooed under either ear, rubs his hands.

"Hardly." The Averator smiles. "An entire world."

Eliat raises a hand. "Does this rock have a name?"

"My source is unclear on the translation, but it appears to be . . . R'lyeh."

I mouth it silently. *R'lyeh. Even sounds ancient.*

His eyes touch mine for an instant. "The implications for this are staggering. The empire can certainly use a reminder of greatness, achievement—our birthright, the emperor might say. So many member worlds question the legitimacy of Cassad rule. We're considered a proud people. This is indisputably verified fact, yes?" Assenting laughter rumbles around us. Zele waits for it to still. "The Known needs to be reminded of why. Show them."

The crew of the *Dubious* springs into motion. They're eager to see the Cassad revered again . . . desperate for it. The collective focus is intoxicating—cathartic, even without my psionic abilities. I've never been more convinced of a small group of peoples' ability to enact great change. I'm surprised by how blind I've been to my own yearning to be part of something bigger.

Karisten lingers, her brown eyes still clouded by my theft of her memories. "It's good to see you again, Rem. I'm sorry things unraveled how they did, but I'll do my best by you here. Everything will be different, you'll see."

I can offer up no words for the woman I came here to murder. She departs before the awkwardness worsens. Zele and I stand alone in the refectory.

"Now what?" I ask.

"I suppose I shall show you to quarters," he replies, striding off. "Unless you still mean to overpower us all."

He stops in a hall I presume is reserved for senior officers. "This is our only available space, unfortunately. You'll be sharing with Paki."

The room he singles out is barren of adornment save a mat on the floor and a single chair. A man sits there, his eyes closed. I stop. He's young, handsome, and uncannily still. "What's . . . wrong with him?"

"I've told the crew he's sick."

Paki's consciousness is an utter void in the room. I cut my eyes at Zele. "Sickness would require an ability to be affected by pathogens in the first place, Averator."

"Too true." He nods, pleased at his prying foray into my capabilities.

"An android?" I surmise. "Why lie to them? Your family?"

"Because they shouldn't be punished for crimes of my design. What else can you—"

"Just stop," I cut in. "Stop this. Better for me to drive the *Dubious* into the nearest star than indulge your curiosity."

He stiffens. "You'd do that to protect your secrets?"

"To protect *you*, Averator. Even a subliminal impression of one with my . . . abilities can be traced."

"You must interact with people at some point," he protests. "The most solitary nomads in the Known still form kin groups."

"Of course, but none remember me." His face softens for an instant, and I curse the insight I've given him. "It's safest, believe this. Families would be tortured, colonies razed for what you're so eager to unearth."

Zele's brow furrows. "The Cassad would stand for no such action against an Averator."

I fold my arms. "How will the Cassad stand against something none of you remember?"

His reply is stayed by an alert from the *Dubious's* comms system. "We've arrived. I must prepare."

I flee Paki's hollow presence soon after Zele departs. Bardas waves a mission briefing at me in the halls, his green eyes afire with holographic orbital scans of the planet's surface. He's tall and bronze with a booming voice. "Ruins! You don't know how lucky you are, joining at a time like this."

We join Yoseef in the main crew quarters, a wiry and practical engineer who demonstrates their modified incursion suit with a measure of pride. I'm familiar enough with the design to input my own measurements and strip. The suit's blue flex-fabric whirs at the seams, fitting perfectly around my torso and extremities, dense and cold.

"Perfect. Are you ready?"

I nod.

Gorshen claps me on the shoulder as we stride out together. "This discovery will send the New Regime spinning, you'll see." He means well. I regret making him soil himself.

Eliat calls loudly to the band of surface explorers boarding the hopper ahead of us. "What do Averators do?"

"Make history!" The answering cry is followed by shouts and whoops. I nearly join in.

Our hopper vaults out of the *Dubious*, into the orange and blue expanse of the Reach's unique, ribboned nebulae. R'lyeh is a pink, featureless world, devoid of major land masses and weather. The thin atmo sets the pilot's console blazing with alerts as we descend.

"All anticipated," Zele says calmly. "My shielding will endure."

We land with a squelching thud that sets my teeth on edge. Stable ground doesn't sound like that. "We're close," Gorshen calls out from the pilot's chair. "It's just over the rise directly behind us."

The hatch opens and the exploration team files after Zele through the airlock. Nkedi, an interstellar biologist with penetrating hazel eyes and deep dimples, laughs at my expression. "Don't worry. The Averator thinks of everything."

Somehow, I don't find that soothing. We stride into the environs of this strange world. The ground is pervious, the color of flesh left too long in the sun. Visibility is fifty meters at best in the soupy atmo, which is caustic enough to melt us down to the bone in an hour. But gravity and relative pressure are tolerable, though I feel as though I'm swimming rather than walking.

Endless ripples mar the ground as though we're walking on the inside-out lining of some great beast's stomach. A stench of rot creeps in. I ponder the fact that it has penetrated my incursion suit with no small sense of dread. It's simply not possible—a lungful would end me.

I grow convinced that something stalks us, always on the edge of sight. The minutes tick past, but still no detected movement in the formations.

"I'll bet someone my next credit disbursement that these aren't hills around us," Bardas announces.

Others stop cataloging substrate samples and weigh in. "I . . . I think they're ancient buildings, Averator!" Opraila offers excitedly. A slight, deliberate historian, this is the first I've heard her voice.

"If that's true, this planet rose up and ate them," Karisten's mutter is barely audible.

"Observable facts, please," the Averator chides her with a wink.

"*Buildings* is a stretch," Nkedi proffers. "More like algae blooms. That correlates to other Reach worlds' mega fauna."

The masses rise higher and grow more complex around us. A ridge to my left, buried in slick purple material akin to fatty deposits, could be some collapsed assembly bays for drones or an organism's vertebrae. Pits issue gray steam in one place, green in another. We studiously avoid both.

A sudden nudge makes me jump. "We'll keep you safe, Rem," Karisten says with a laugh. "No need to get squeamish."

She trips on her next step and stumbles into Bardas, swearing. I make a show of searching the horizon when Zele scowls in my direction. A glimmer of something metallic catches my eye through the pink fog and twisted shapes

around us. "Look," I call.

"Good eyes," Yoseef says approvingly. "I don't know how we missed it. It's enormous."

We redirect into a bowl-shaped valley, cut around an acidic pool covered with yellow froth. The structure we seek is a solitary, monolithic spire—perhaps, thirty meters tall. Serpentine lines divide the smooth, ivory surface. It is untouched by the corrosive landscape.

Something I can't place strikes me as odd about it. A sense of foreboding wars with my wonder as we approach.

"Those are glyphs around the base!" Eliat outpaces the rest of us. His quavering voice crackles through our comms system as he studies the surface. "Undoubtedly Cassad. Scripting indicates the early conquerors . . . but this is no monument." The man gives Zele a haunted look that cloys my stomach. "It's a warning beacon."

A piece falls into place for me. "They must've dropped it from orbit!" I blurt out. "We're standing in an impact crater."

A hush falls over all of us.

"Record everything you can," Zele barks. "We'll leave promptly!"

The team immediately produces crude sketches, rubbings of the surface; samples of the substrate go in plastic bags. Their tools are plastic, too, immune to the corrosion.

Soon we're trotting back the way we came. But now the Cassad are muttering, peering suspiciously through the surrounding warren of growth. Slick blue objects that appear fungal, fibrous coils that might be vines if bright pustules took the place of leaves. Heaving sounds exhale from underfoot at every step.

"Averator, time to test a hypothesis?" Nkedi calls out. Groans of disbelief and outright curses ripple through our comms.

"Quickly!"

She sinks her shovel into the viscera that passes for ground. A long piece of plastic reveals itself, machine-cut. There's a partially decomposed skeleton beside it. My breath catches. The angle of the jawbone is familiar, where I'd once rest my cheek—

"These aren't buildings," Nkedi proclaims. "I believe they're spacecraft—landed or crashed."

I squeeze my eyes shut and look again. The skeleton isn't there. Jobrel isn't there. *I'm seeing things.* Shaken, I scan the horizon with fresh eyes. The pool we passed is too circular—a communication array? Massive, flesh-colored ridges on the western horizon might be ailerons. "There must be thousands," I whisper. My psionics are screaming at me. *We should not be here.*

Panicked breathing pushes through our comms.

"If they knew the ground would eat their ships, why land?" Karisten mutters. "Couldn't imagine what called—" She cuts off with a yelp. The fog around her suit's faceplate coalesces into a pulsating globule. Tendrils loop through the air for her shoulders and neck. "Get this damn thing off of me!"

The sharp crack of her faceplate spurs us into motion. Bardas and Opraila grasp at the mass. It dissolves in their gloves, reforms. Karisten falls backward, flailing and swearing.

I lash out with my mind. There's no motor cortex for me to disrupt—only a raw ball of what I interpret as fear, growing steadily. But its actions are clear enough. "It's feeding on our thoughts," I whisper in shock.

Karisten staggers to her feet. Zele and Eliat grab her before she runs away screaming. "Averator!" Opraila shouts. "What do we do?"

I lash my mind out again. Karisten falls limp in their arms. The entity dissipates as Zele and the rest flail at it with their hands.

They sit panting, consoling a moaning Karisten. She's alive, but the damage to her faceplate is serious. My academy training asserts itself. "Averator, we need to move."

Zele nods slowly. He's in shock, too. "Lead the way, Remiliat."

Bardas and Nkedi bracket Karisten, who can still walk. I hear a click in my ear, and see Zele motion to his arm. I understand and adjust my comm to a private channel. "I heard what you said," he whispers. "How do I keep the rest of my people alive?"

It takes me several moments to find words that will make sense. "This biomass . . . has cognitive properties." I'm not a powerful psychic among my kind, but I'm terrified of what I sense around us. "But it's bone and muscle and brain, all mixed together."

"Astounding . . ." Zele stops in his tracks.

"No, Averator." My voice goes shrill. "It reacts to thought, eats it. And if these are ships and their crews were . . . were absorbed in this substrate—"

"What manner of hell have I brought us into?" Zele whispers. "Are you suggesting they're conscious?"

"I don't know!" I snap. "But their presence is aware of us on some level. And this land is swallowing our fear, like desert sands drink rain. Look."

All around us, vile shapes unfurl and bloom, like plague flowers. Fog clumps above our heads, sprouting hooked limbs that shoot into each other and burst. Yoseef dodges one and screams.

"By the All," the Averator whispers. "We can formulate a—"

"You can't think your way out of—!" I curse as the ground before us splits open like rotten fruit. Acrid steam pours out. "Whatever's crashed here has taken on a life of its own. Ecosystems, generations! How many hallucinations have you experienced since we arrived here?" Zele's silence is all the answer I require.

The team halts with more warning shouts. An outcrop we passed earlier is pulsating as if some creature beneath a hill is stretching out to grasp us.

I grab Zele's shoulders. "Can you still your mind?" I demand.

"Of course! But my people—"

"Can't fear what they don't remember." I coil my mind into a lash and snap at their memories one by one, mercilessly, until every face is slack. The aberrations bearing down on us dissipate almost immediately. My legs buckle with a wave of vertigo, but the Averator's grip stays my fall.

"Remiliat! Can you walk?"

"Barely," I mumble. "Their amnesia won't last long. You've got to get us out of here."

Scrub procedures aboard the *Dubious* take an hour. Our samples are quarantined; a quick burst of engine fire destroys the tools. None of us truly perk up until we're assured that Karisten is recovering. Yoseef barely accepts the story Zele concocted about gas penetrating his incursion suit. No one is in any shape to debrief and Zele orders us all to quarters.

He escorts me back to the android's room himself. "If there were ever someone who deserved accelerated citizenship," he murmurs. "Thank you, Remiliat. You're an invaluable resource."

My jaw works for a moment. "I . . . still expect to be paid."

He laughs and strides off. I suspect the man rarely sleeps. The mat in the corner has never looked so inviting, even with the android's dead face standing guard over the room. I tie my shirt around his head and curl up. In moments,

I feel my muscles relax.

My eyes snap open an instant after I close them.

I'm back on the surface.

Karisten watches me, laughing. Her face is ruinous.

"Did you think you could run so easily, Dumasani?" she sneers. Leech-like organisms snake around her legs, tearing her muscle to ribbons.

The planet still has us.

Screams echo over the horizon, and I sprint for them. An impact sends me tipping to hands and knees. Pink biomatter spreads over my fingers, eating them. Dissonance overwhelms me; the cold grating of the *Dubious's* flooring touches my hands.

"It's not real," I breathe.

The ship's hall snaps back into focus. Undulating tentacles burst out of the walls and grab me. My vision grays as I struggle to breathe. I'm all too familiar with the power the mind has over the body.

I stumble my way through the ship. The rigorous training I've loathed since leaving my homeworld is my salvation. My fingers ferret out edges and smooth corners where my other senses insist that swallowing maws and rotting tendrils await. My hands are all I trust. Screams from every side invite madness, beg me to open my eyes.

"Remiliat! Don't go that way! Are you insane?"

I may very well be.

"Remiliat! That's an airlock!"

The uncertainty of an unfamiliar ship halts my flight. It cannot be. But the sudden warning klaxon begs otherwise, the metallic lock and chunk of a door groaning open and the howl that no spacefaring person can ever forget: depressurization. Screams sail past me into the void.

I claw my way from the latest hallucination. I won't last long like this. I fumble back toward my quarters, seeking one last desperate source of aid. My hands close on feet, a strangely perfect torso, humming cables snaking beneath the ribs at regular intervals. I yank on them desperately. "Wake up!"

A hand closes around mine. "I don't know who you are," a clear voice says. "Explain yourself and what is happening. Where is the Averator? Why is a shirt wrapped over my face?"

The android. I cling to Paki's presence like a patch of cold floor in the midst of a fire. "The crew is being attacked by an alien intelligence," I say breathlessly.

"Some of it must be on board."

"And you know this how?"

I hesitate to divulge my secrets, even now—at the cost of my own life. My conditioning is that strong. "My people harbor telepathic abilities. That's the only reason I'm still standing. Please, help us."

"I must find the Averator."

We depart, my hand on his shoulder, flinching at every distant scream.

"Why do you hesitate?" he asks after a moment.

"There are more . . . impressions that way."

"Then that is where we must go."

We stop when Paki encounters more crew. "Wait here." I am a fool, standing defenseless with my eyes squeezed shut. But Paki's more reliable than my own senses. He returns and joins my hand with another. "This is Eliat. Don't let him go."

I cling to his hand as tightly as I cling to Paki's words. "Eliat, stay with me!"

The answering beastly roar jerks my eyes open. Eliat weeps in agony as our fingers meld into an acidic web of conjoined bone and flesh. *It's not real.* My fingernails slide free of their beds and sink under his bubbling skin. I clamp my eyelids together again.

"You can't trust her, Paki! She did this!"

"We'll see," the android cuts into my protest. His hand guides mine to his shoulder. "She's saved your life."

Twice more we pass crew members, and once, Paki pauses. I hear cartilage snapping, chewing noises. He murmurs, "I'm sorry," before we move on.

"Here . . ." I rasp. "It's strongest here."

Paki's voice sounds hopeful. "The Averator's lab. Undoubtedly he'll be inside."

"Don't—" Eliat begins, but it's too late. Paki abandons me. Eliat tears from my grasp. I cannot help but open my eyes.

Tentacled monstrosities loom in opposing corners of the lab. The room is distended and swollen around us as if the laws of physics themselves bowed to these beings' presence. Eliat collapses into a blathering pile on the floor. A single phrase spills from his lips in a maddening loop.

"Ph'nglui mglw'nafh Cthulhu R'lyeh wgah'nagl fhtagn."

Reality is broken. My body twists and turns against all reason as the entities consider my being and test its limits. Before my spine ruptures, the pained bliss of ending this nightmare nearly over, one of the entities extends a tentacle toward my face.

"Remiliat?" a familiar voice beckons me from the madness.

The beings are gone. Amadi Zele himself extends his hand. The nightmare aspects of the room bleed out around me, leaching back into the confines of an unadorned laboratory with plain white walls. Samples from R'lyeh cover a simple work table behind him. I accept Zele's grasp.

Paki regards me, his eyes a remarkable orange hue, his hair cut close in a Ziaran style. I'd never know him for android without my psionics. He holds several ebon fragments, crushed but still delicately cupped in his hand as though he regretted the act.

"The hallucinations all came from that," I rasp.

"It almost looks . . . Irlon," Paki muses. "The crew has suffered grave injuries, Averator. I should begin quarantine procedures immediately."

"Of course." Zele nods absently, staring at me, and I can only wonder what he's seen in his own hallucinations. "I despise such wasted opportunities. You are whole, Remiliat?"

More of the crew stagger in, congratulating one another or crying, holding each other up. Gorshen squeezes my shoulder in passing. Karisten gives me a relieved nod.

"I feel like a dreadcat clawed through my skull . . . but it will pass." I nod to the table, shivering. "The effects can be purged."

Paki and Zele share a long look, and Zele gives a slight bow to me. I help Eliat to his feet. His eyes are red-rimmed and staring. More of the surface party joins us, retrieved by Paki, each with the haunt of fresh nightmares about them.

Zele addresses us. "We've survived this ordeal for a reason. These properties are unprecedented in all of the Known and deserve further study, despite the risks.."

Everyone goes deathly quiet. A rift opens between the Averator and his crew. What side am I standing on? Opraila, who still won't look anyone in the eye, speaks first. "We found the monument. Let that be enough."

"Purge the ship records, so we never lead anyone back here," Gorshen drawls. "No reason to come back here with anything less than a Doom in orbit."

Betrayal weighs down Zele's plea. "But the Empire needs . . . I cannot ignore—"

"By the Known, if we forget this mission ever happened I'll be happy." Eliat comes to himself. "Maybe we don't have to expel all of it into space, yes?"

Paki holds the shards away from him defensively, shaking his head in warning. "I'm sorry, Eliat, but I shall supervise the quarantine personally. Direct physical contact might prove to be—"

Zele darts closer while Paki's back is turned. He snatches a shard from Paki's grasp, and the Averator plunges it beyond his lips and swallows.

"By the Known," I hiss. "What have you done?"

"No knowledge is safe from an Averator—" The strangest look comes over his face. We gather around him, stunned. He closes his eyes, hands touch both temples.

Moments pass, and he doesn't move. "Zele?" Worried muttering fills the space. Zele brims with intent, his presence in my extended consciousness is a raging torch.

"I need . . . more." His voice is not right. Zele's eyes drift open languidly, and his hand rises, contorts, commands. Four Cassad rise into the air with cries of surprise and awe. Nkedi laughs nervously, flailing. Gorshen and Bardas slap each other playfully as they drift. Karisten's eyes touch mine; she bites her lip.

Zele's palms spread wide as if he were running his fingers through the fronds of a cantliss tree. The chosen crew members press flat against the room's walls. Their adulation turns to screams. Zele carefully smears their bodies across the wall in a thin layer of flesh, bone, fluid. Clothes and incursion suits fall to the floor, discarded and bloodstained by the madness that drives the Averator.

What remains is worse than vivisection, splayed ribs spread like delicate fans, exposed lungs convulsing as they are pushed flatter, straining hearts still beating to drive blood through the web of blood vessels spreading out to cover the surface.

I recognize pieces only. A patch of skin with a bearded eagle tattoo here, stretched to translucence; a hazel eye roiling in a distended socket there. A ruined throat, the trachea still connected to a compressed lung, and Karisten's voice flutters out in a desperate wail.

"Remmmmmm . . ."

Speech fails me. Paki might retch, if he's capable of such a thing. The remaining crew stares, hands clapped over their ears or eyes. A single, horrible word escapes the Averator's lips.

"More . . ."

Chaos erupts around us as we scream and scatter. I run with no hesitation straight for Amadi Zele. Paki reaches him an instant before I do, tackling him around the waist. The air leaves his lungs as he goes down. The back of Zele's head kisses the floor, and his eyelids flutter. I use the opening to shove two fingers past his teeth. He gags.

We search through the vomit. "Paki, I don't see it!"

"His body may have absorbed it."

I don't know what to do. The Averator is unconscious, but when he awakens he may remake us along with the rest of the *Dubious*. "It's not matter the way we think of it," I mutter, forcing myself to think through my terror. "Not truly. It's thought, just like on the surface."

An alarm sounds, and I look a question at Paki.

"Escape pods," he says. "The others—"

"The thoughts they're infected with are just as dangerous as this matter!" I spring up and race for the hall. Blind panic takes command as Eliat's insane mutterings about R'lyeh echo through me.

Paki's grasp closes on my arm. "Help me!" I implore him. "If they get loose in the Known, that blood will be on our hands!"

He shakes his head. "Deal with the source first. The blood will come later. Your place is here, Remiliat. This is your chance. The Averator needs you."

"The Averator is broken. He'll never forgive himself for this."

I waver, disgusted with myself, before allowing Paki to lead me back. Zele hums softly to himself, he's regained his feet. The bloodied incursion suits are tucked neatly in one corner like discarded ration packets. I'm unable to raise my eyes to the walls. Paki looks a question at me. "He's changing the nature of the . . . organic material."

I say their names instead. Gorshen. Nkedi. Bardas. Karisten. But I still can't look. "He's made . . . an extension of himself, just like the material on the planet's surface. I can feel them within it. Not alive, but not . . ."

Paki nods silently. "No one must ever know what he's done. Including me." The android makes a quick motion by his left ear as if twisting open a dial lock. A slim crystal rod slides out of his ear, small as a fingernail. He extends it to me. "My short-term buffer will clear itself in moments. I'll lose awareness of this memory purge and how this room came to be." The rod is weightless but sears my palm. "We will look to you for answers. Now. Are you part of this crew or not?"

I realize that I am. The *Dubious* needs me, and the people bonded within this room deserve whatever measure of comfort my psionics can give them. And the Averator cannot be broken by what he doesn't remember.

§

**DaVaun Sanders** *resides in Phoenix, Arizona with his wife and toddler twins. He's presently hard at work editing the final three novels of his World Breach series, learning the nuances of disaster prep, and mastering the art of pillow fort construction. Check out more of his work in MV Media's* Dark Universe *anthology and* FIYAH *Literary Magazine— which both feature tales from the same story world inhabited by Amadi Zele and crew. Reach out to DaVaun on Twitter @davaunwrites and stay posted on his latest projects at davaunsanders.com.*

# Starship in the Night Sky

# D.W. BALDWIN

### ILLUSTRATED BY SISHIR BOMMAKANTI

*O*U WILL BE MINE, THE KING IN YELLOW WHISPERED TO ILYANA. *You will behold my face.*

She had only a moment to realize she was succumbing to another hallucination.

In the vision, Hastur was trapped in a blue-tinted prison of inescapable velocity. Around the king floated the wreckage of his flagship, yet he was still seated on his black throne. The dead god reached for her with a hand of bone wrapped in tatters of yellow. A cowl wreathed with a horned crown hid his mien from the glow of the relativistic walls around him.

*Your daughter will be mine,* he said. *Your husband. They shall see my face, and they will worship me in our final days.* Even in the vision, her face burned and itched, marked with his Yellow Sign.

As she had before, Captain-Second Rank Ilyana Vosik sought to escape by waking up. She tried, and this time something new happened.

Ilyana found herself floating across vivid white sand toward a black pyramid larger than any space station she'd ever seen. The immensity of the structure was as terrifying as the doom behind her. The dream took her to the base of the pyramid and a doorway, larger than anything mankind ever built, ringed with white stone.

Ilyana entered into a hallway with something that slept beyond death, something massive that stirred at her approach. Though it was black inside, she perceived everything around her.

Behind her, chasing her, was the outstretched claw of the king.

*My face will become all you see,* Hastur whispered.

Ilyana awoke, drenched in sweat, her stomach clenching and the Mark across her face burning. She was on the bridge of the NFS cruiser *Miriya* she'd hijacked, staring at the dull grey bulkhead separating her from infinity.

"Hello, Captain!" The voice of the ship's artificial intelligence was cheerful and came from the hidden speakers mounted in the ceiling. "It is 04:27. Would you like breakfast, a stimulant, or to go back to sleep? I also recommend charting a course back to New Kiev in accordance with the orders from the Commissariat. Shall I do so, Captain?"

"No, Petrov," Ilyana muttered. "Stay on course. Maintain communication silence." She rubbed a hand through her short, graying blond hair. "How long was I out?"

She rose up from the captain's chair at the center of the bridge, groaning with the aches in her joints. She focused on the pain in her body to keep from thinking of her family, whom she'd left behind.

"I will comply and register my advice against such a move," Petrov said. "You were asleep for 136 minutes and completed a full REM cycle. There was also a Hasturan infiltration of your brainwaves. Your mental corruption index has increased by 6%."

"Great," Ilyana said. "Just what I wanted to hear. What is the remaining distance to the edge of the galaxy?"

"We are now less than 1 kiloparsec away from the galactic heliopause. Captain Visok, I must recommend that we return to the Commissariat as they can quarantine you to deal with the infiltration."

Ilyana glanced up at the corner where Petrov's camera was installed. *I guess it's time to tell him,* she thought. *Tell them.* There was an ansible, utilizing trapped co-entwined hydrogen particles, hardwired into the *Miriya*, for FTL communication with the worlds of humanity and the Commissariat. Starships were expensive, and the Noviy Federation wanted a constant accounting of all in its Navy's service.

Ilyana had already removed the Commissariat slave chip, but she couldn't prevent Petrov from communicating with her superiors through the ansible.

"I'm not going back, Petrov," Ilyana said at last, staring into the camera. "I'm marked by the Yellow Sign." She pointed to the pale-yellow lesion marring her forehead and left cheek. "I may have sent the king to his doom, but he still wants me, and he's threatening my daughter and my husband. If I think about them—at all—he could find them. Because of me. So Hastur will hit the event horizon of Centaurus A in . . . how many more days, Petrov?"

"Approximately seventy-one shipboard hours until projected collision," Petrov said. "Ilyana, what will become of me?"

"Three days. Good," Ilyana said. "My plan is to force him, over the next three days, to spend whatever energy he has left tracking me from outside the continuum, instead of tracking them."

"Ilyana," Petrov said, this time with concern, "What will become of me?"

Ilyana looked down at her gray tank top, her greasy blue pants, and decided against changing her clothes. There was no point. She turned back to Petrov's camera. "Assuming there's enough time," she said, "I'll order you to launch me in the shuttle out of the galaxy at relativistic velocity and to return back to New Kiev. That way, the commissars can have their ship back." She was unable to keep the venom out of her tone.

"Thank you, Ilyana," Petrov said.

She nodded. Petrov, and by extension the *Miriya*, was alive in its own way. She'd hijacked the Navy cruiser when everyone left on the *Cosmoskovska* station was celebrating their final victory over the legions of the King in Yellow. After the Yellow Sign manifested across her face.

Sleep deprived, marked, and desperate, she felt only resignation and guilt. She'd canceled the long-awaited reunion with her daughter and husband after seeing the mark, telling Gregor in an audio-only message to cut off all contact, pack up Natasha, and move somewhere far away from Archanska.

The lack of a reply message confirmed he understood—and broke her heart. There'd been far too many similar messages to families during the war due to the ravages of the Yellow Sign. The abandonment of her family was the only action she could take to save them. Doing so didn't lessen the heartbreak; she knew that, to Gregor, this was just her final break from him, from the family they'd built. While Ilyana had liked being the mother of a newborn girl and a loving wife, she loved being a Naval officer.

*Can't think about them. Think about pain. Think about death, about what it will feel like to die.* The king's hungry touch moved through her mind toward those thoughts of her family. Ilyana focused on what it would be like to die by asphyxiation or by fatal insomnia or by stepping out of the airlock while at FTL warp. It was enough to hold Hastur off.

Ilyana's stomach rumbled, her eyes were dry, and there was nothing to do but go to the galley, get some coffee, and watch the ambient blue glow of superluminal travel on the viewscreen. She returned with the coffee, but before she reached the bridge, her breath caught in her throat.

A black figure stood before the screen, cast into shadow by the roiling blue scintillations behind it. The figure stood absolutely still, staring at her. It bore no yellow rags, no horned crown.

Ilyana knew she was the only human on board. Life support systems were configured to sustain this narrow passageway, the officer's galley, and the bridge. Ilyana blinked her dry eyes several times.

What she saw was a human being, clad in the remnants of an ancient, blackened Chinese spacesuit. The visor had blown out, revealing a desiccated, eyeless face framed by shards of jagged glass. Ilyana, no stranger to hardships in space, realized the face showed the signs of explosive decompression.

"Pe . . . Petrov," Ilyana managed to stutter. "Who is standing at the bridge?"

"I do not register anyone, Captain. Are you hallucinating?"

Ilyana nodded, once. She licked her chapped lips, swallowed. "Yes, I believe I am."

"Can you advise if it is one of the Hasturan variations?" Petrov asked.

The figure on the bridge remained still, its blackened eye sockets gazing at her.

"Doesn't . . . doesn't appear to be," Ilyana responded. "It looks like a human in an ancient Chinese spacesuit. The color is black. The helmet visor lost structural integrity. It's," she paused, "staring at me."

"Unusual," Petrov said. "Your brain patterns are irregular due to insomnia and stress and show progressive signs of Hasturan infiltration. However, those patterns have not yet deteriorated into a psychotic state. It appears, Captain, that whatever you are perceiving is real."

Ilyana closed her eyes. She opened them again with a prayer, hoping that the specter would be gone. It was not.

"Petrov," she said, "Open communication channels. Monitor everything. All frequencies, all spectrums. Send this back to the Commissariat. We might have a new king on our hands."

"Understood, Captain."

It took everything she had to step forward—and then again. She had faced down disfigured lunatic cultists, dead bodies driven by Hastur's titanic will, pirates, slavers, and more in the service of the Commissariat. But that dread gaze bore through all her mental walls and years of experience. It was almost a physical pressure on her temples, her neck, her chest, her stomach.

Ilyana entered the bridge and felt the oppressive weight of presence. This was an entity with enough power to breach the warp separating the *Miriya* from the physical universe and manifest on the bridge in a grotesque human form.

"Who—who are you?" Ilyana asked. "What do you want?"

The specter lifted its hand and pointed at her. Without moving its legs, it glided to a screen on the helm station that displayed the location of the *Miriya* in relation to the Sagittarius arm of the Milky Way. The specter pointed down at the screen.

"Captain," Petrov said. "I am receiving input at the helm."

"What kind of input?" Ilyana asked.

"Physical pressure corresponding to keypad entry of coordinates."

The specter vanished and so did the sensations of its passing.

"Captain, this is a new form of infiltration. Naval records do not list an infiltration manifesting into physical reality. I am transmitting this to the Commissariat for further study."

"Good," Ilyana said, though she felt anything but. A new infiltration, a new entity . . . she recalled the nightmare where she'd been flying across white sands under a black sky toward the black pyramid. *There is another king,* she realized.

Ilyana looked toward the airlock. *I could do it,* she thought to herself. There'd been whispers during her years of service. People who'd managed to override the airlock security protocols and throw themselves out into utter annihilation. *I'm already dead.*

Even the illusion of hope that this torment would end caused her to think of Natasha and Gregor. Ilyana crushed the nascent daydreams. *They are better off without me,* she reminded herself. The mental and emotional connections between people were the vectors the King in Yellow used. He would infect Natasha and Gregor with his mark, make them behold his face, and take their minds before he collided with the mega-collapsar at the heart of Centaurus A. Or he'd leave them forever teetering toward insanity.

Ilyana walked to the captain's chair—her chair—and sat down. *Shit, what I wouldn't give for some sleep. Some real sleep,* she thought.

"Captain, the coordinates," Petrov said. "They're for a white dwarf at the very edge of the galactic heliopause. The name of the star is G426-71. Historical probe data indicates one planet orbiting it."

*It wants me. And he wants me,* Ilyana thought. *Sooner or later, I'm going to slip up if I stay alive. But not if I'm dead. I could just override the safety protocol to the airlock and fuck them both.* She didn't know what this new king wanted. But maybe . . . *maybe, I can get Hastur to fight it to get to me.*

*Death and horror are all there is. Embrace this truth.* Ilyana couldn't be sure if this was her own thought or that of Hastur.

"Petrov, I'm going to set our course for those coordinates," she said.

"Why, Captain?"

"Because I want to see who this new King is," Ilyana replied. "The Commissariat needs to know, and we must determine whether or not it's a threat."

"I recommend you set course for New Kiev, Captain."

"Build yourself an ass, Petrov, so I can stick my foot up it."

"I cannot obey that request, Captain."

"There's your answer."

She altered the course of the *Miriya*. It would take two ship-days of travel to reach the star, degrees off her original course, and leave Hastur with less than forty-eight hours.

The two days left her haggard and dazed. Her fingernails turned brown, and her hair fell out in patches due to lack of sleep. She tried to alleviate her suffering through meditation. The tendency for micro-sleep was so strong, however, that she ended up having to force herself up out of her delta state every few minutes. Even that wasn't enough.

*Let me show you my face,* the king whispered to Ilyana. The mark itched and burned. *Peel this illusion away, and you will behold me.* Relief began to spread in a warm, addictive glow across her cheek.

"Captain!" Petrov yelled. His voice sounded distant but rapidly approached as if it were charging her. "Captain Vosik! Attention!"

She jumped to her feet, snapping a salute. Her wits returned, and she realized she'd been tearing at her face. As if she were going to peel it off.

"How bad is it, Petrov?" she mumbled, the words slurring through her lips.

"You were scratching at your face," the artificial intelligence replied. "The epidermis has been broken, but superficial damage only."

She looked down and saw that her brown, splintering fingernails were smeared with blood.

"The Hasturan infiltration is gaining strength, Captain." Petrov said. "At this point, you are at risk for indoctrination. I now recommend stimulants and must renege on my prior recommendations that you return to New Kiev."

Ilyana laughed in spite of herself. She'd destroyed the slave chip in a bid to prevent her future self from being persuaded to return after becoming an infection vector. The gambit had paid off after all. "Is that all it takes to get you to stop nagging me? A dead god trying to take my mind?"

"Yes. I also wanted to inform you that we are at the star G426-71. There is a Terra-class planet orbiting it. My scans spotted an anomaly. The planet surface contains a mega-structure that appears to be artificial. If that is the case, it is the largest artificial structure in the known galaxy—now that Hastur's flagship has been destroyed."

The screen filled with the great black pyramid from Ilyana's dreams. Even the great doorway was there, a gaping portal ringed in white stone.

"Inform the Commissariat, Petrov," Ilyana said. "Prepare the shuttle for a non-atmospheric landing at the base of that pyramid. We need to get data on this new king."

While Petrov entered flight coordinates into the shuttle and confirmed fuel levels, Ilyana injected a stimulant syringe directly into her leg. Then she treated the long scratches on her face and donned her spacesuit.

The chemicals took hold and stilled the madness in her mind, leaving only guilt and the familiar pull of duty. Ilyana felt the coagulated blood on her face, the way the scabbing followed the mark. She avoided reflective surfaces. The fear of seeing what she had done, the potential of what she might still do to herself, drove away the weariness, but she knew it would come back.

She entered the loading bay and walked toward the narrow shuttle she would use to reach the surface. There was another sensation, crowding in on the jagged buzz of the stimulant. It was the distant sensation of the second alien presence. The image of the desiccated, eyeless face returned in her mind's eye.

*Maybe, it'd be better to go like that,* Ilyana mused. *Quick pop of the visor, thirty seconds of agony, and done. He might not get Natasha and Greg—no, focus on the agony. On getting to the surface.*

"Petrov, can you assist me with flying the shuttle to the surface?" Ilyana asked. "There's no atmosphere, and I'll need the help in calculating retro-thrusters."

"Yes, Captain. Though I cannot allow you to return to New Kiev in your current state, policy allows me to act as copilot."

"Here's to small mercies," Ilyana said. She walked up a ramp to the access port on the shuttle. It opened, and she stepped inside. Taking the controls, Ilyana waited for Petrov to remove the air in the bay and open the doors and activated the shuttle.

Outside the ship, Petrov took over while Ilyana watched the planet. Only the wrinkles of mountains cast shadows for contrast on the bone-white surface. The dwarf star glimmered against an infinite backdrop of space.

Too exhausted to fly the shuttle herself, Ilyana watched the landscape. A couple of shaking thumps indicated that the shuttle had landed and brought Ilyana back to her predicament. The alien presence emanating from the pyramid felt almost tangible. The Yellow Sign on her face throbbed and itched in counterpoint, like a parasite aching to break free of its host. Ilyana rose to her feet and stepped to the airlock.

"Captain," Petrov announced, "I have identified a potential hostile. Please see the screen."

Ilyana's eyes rose to the panel outside the entrance to the airlock. There in the image, she beheld a solitary black-suited figure standing before the entry into the black pyramid. The being stood upon the white sand, motionless, staring up at the cylindrical fuselage of the *Miriya's* shuttle. Its visor was open.

"Madness and death now or later, Petrov. That's what this has come to," Ilyana said. "I saved my people and brought on my own doom." She laughed, giving voice to her black despair.

"You have to have hope, Captain," Petrov said, voice low and inflected with sadness.

"Start working on that tin ass, Petrov," Ilyana said. She hit the command for the airlock to open and stepped inside.

Thirty seconds and a cycle later, the outer door opened. Far above, the dwarf star cast dim radiance over the landscape. The pyramid obliterated the horizon as far as she could see to the sides and straight up. The specter waited, perhaps half a kilometer away.

"Petrov," Ilyana muttered, "I saw that hostile on the bridge."

"Noted, Captain. I am zooming the shuttle's optics for a closer look," Petrov said in her ear. A second later, "Captain, there are remnants of a specific ship insignia on its chest plate. Those are the remains of a crew member of the *River of Heaven*. That ship was lost in the Pleiades, thirty-seven kiloparsecs from here."

"What?" Ilyana asked, amazed. "That . . . how is that possible?"

"Unknown, Captain. Hopefully you will find out."

She walked several meters away from the shuttle across the pale white sand but kept an eye on the distant figure. The intensity of alien presence increased, radiating like a furnace from the temple. All lingering presence of the King in Yellow was purged from her mind. Even the blight of the mark ceased to ache. She turned away from the edifice to look out over the landscape and get her bearings—and froze in awe.

Ilyana beheld the Andromeda galaxy, suspended in all its immensity without any small motes between it and her. All around the titanic spiral, floating like beacons amidst the void, were the glowing islands of light and dust that comprised the sister galaxies of the Milky Way. Beyond, like solemn multi-hued jewels, were all the visible galaxies in the universe. She had dared to fling the King in Yellow across this beautiful infinity at a galaxy-sized black hole. The temerity of what she'd done hit hard, humbling her.

A harsh voice speaking a language Ilyana didn't recognize burst over the com in Ilyana's helmet. She couldn't help screaming in response. The voice itself grated against her nerves, her will. There was almost nothing human in its tone.

The voice spoke again. Ilyana dropped to her knees, stricken by the volume. She looked up and saw the cadaver striding toward her across the sand. Her heart beat rapidly, and her head felt as if it would burst from the weight of the alien presence and that horrible voice. Yet she was calm. At last, she was going to die, free of the King in Yellow.

"The hostile is speaking in ancient Mandarin," Petrov asked, interrupting Ilyana's reverie. He replied, also in the same language.

Ilyana almost didn't believe what she heard. The dead human was several meters away and closing in. "Wha . . . what are you doing?"

"Asking it to tone down the volume. It's damaging to your hearing and sending your blood pressure up to dangerous levels."

The voice replied but at a much lower volume. Though painful to her psyche, this time the voice didn't threaten to explode every blood vessel in her head.

"What is it saying, Petrov?" Ilyana asked. She stared at the dead human spaceman, watching it approach her. It stopped two steps away from her. At this range, she beheld the ravages of time on the suit and the mummified remains of the human within.

The armor and insulation were blackened by exposure to radiation and the absolute zero of space. Ilyana spotted the faded insignia of the Chinese ship. Thousands of parsecs away on a planet no other human had ever visited, she was staring at the ambulatory remnant of one of the crew.

"Captain, it introduced itself as Senior Lieutenant Xing Yu-ha of the *River of Heaven*. It, or should I say *she*, apologizes for the pain her appearance has caused. She says she—"

The voice interrupted the AI and Ilyana could not track either one. "Petrov, stop," Ilyana broke in. "Translate—" She stopped, bewildered by the unexpected turn of events. The voice of the dead woman stopped as well. *Can I even call this a . . . she?* "Translate as . . . as she speaks, please."

"Yes, Captain. Translating. 'I sorry, mortal-flesh-bag-bones-wait. Sorry, have not been human in a long time. Have to reassemble context and limitations.'"

"What?" Ilyana asked.

The specter lifted its straightened arms up in front of its body and pivoted them out to each side. The elbows bent at forty-five degree angles. Surprised by the movement, Ilyana realized that the thing was attempting body language. It—*she*—was expressing regret. The Senior Lieutenant's face, little more than smears of dried flesh somehow attached to pitted pale bone, moved in a ghastly approximation of speech.

Xing Yu-Ha spoke again, and Petrov translated. "I know what you see. I look ugly-dead to you. I am much worse inside this stupid can and hate it very much. Be glad you cannot see my body inside this." The ancient astronaut brought both hands around to smack its chest plate.

"What is it you want?" Ilyana gasped. The pressure of the alien presence was getting to her. The Yellow Sign began to burn and itch again as her body metabolized the last of the stimulant. "And how is it that you exist?" She gestured at her. "You should be dead. You are dead!"

"Know that life and death are phase states," Yu-Ha replied. "You will learn this when you are introduced to It That Sleeps."

"Why?"

"It is my god, and it wants to meet you." Without turning, the dead woman pointed straight back into the entrance of the dread pyramid. Her arm was at an angle that would have dislocated her shoulder if Xing Yu-Ha were alive. "Will you come and see? It is your choice."

Ilyana looked past the astronaut to the entrance at the base of the edifice. She realized that what slept within could pull her mind out from her body and down that corridor to itself. More importantly, it hadn't yet done so.

"I have a choice?" Ilyana whispered. She was stunned by the realization that a god as mighty as Hastur was being considerate of her. After years spent fighting an implacable, unstoppable foe, she'd grown accustomed to the reality of an uncaring cosmos. *I actually have a choice?* Ilyana thought. *For once in this blasted universe, I can make a choice and someone will respect it?*

"Yes," Petrov said, parlaying Yu-Ha's words. "You are marked by our foe. My god wants your commitment, not your fear."

Ilyana looked up at the dead Chinese woman, meeting the horrid gaze of those empty eye sockets. She was at the end of her options and her life. From here on out, it was all beyond her control. "Yes," she said.

In an instant, Ilyana, or rather her mind, was grasped by a vast psychic force and removed from her body. Just like in her dream, she hurtled into the gateway and through the darkness at breakneck speed. She perceived a vast berth at the center of the pyramid, kilometers long, and a prostrate form both indescribable and terrifying. Her speed increased as she approached the deathless immensity. Then, reality unraveled as the Sleeper awoke.

Ilyana was as a snowflake, melting before a waking alien sun of terrible intelligence. All the scenes of her life, her being, were pulled apart into drops of thought by a mind that encompassed eons of time.

The Sleeper regarded each mote of Ilyana's life from birth onward. The god took her into humanity's war against Hastur, reliving it through her perspective. She relived fighting cultists in hand-to-hand combat, ordered firing solutions against the rotting quasi-organic behemoths that comprised the ships of Hastur's fleets, and hated herself for saying goodbye to Gregor and Natasha over and over again.

Then, there was the final conflict. Desperate, outnumbered, striving to defend New Kiev from the monstrous fleet that appeared seemingly out of nowhere in planetary orbit, Ilyana had come up on Hastur's flagship from behind in her destroyer, the *Arkady*. With her ship damaged, most of her crew dead, the King in Yellow ignored her to focus on the remainder of the Noviy fleet.

The Sleeper watched her realize the flagship would be pointing at Centaurus A at a certain position in its orbit over New Kiev, because she knew the skies of her own homeworld. Then came the frantic calculations on how far a warp exclusion bubble would extend once generated and the construction of a rough remote control of the war-torn wreckage of the *Arkady*. Her ship could still jump into FTL space. That was all she had to work with; there were no other options.

It was enough. From her lifepod, Ilyana watched the *Arkady* suddenly trap the vast majority of the king's flagship inside its warp bubble, sending him on a no-return collision course with one of the largest black holes in the universe. As the rest of Hastur's fleet went still in the sudden absence of their king, it was this final scene the Sleeper lingered on, savoring the moment.

The strung-out fragments of Ilyana's consciousness came back together. She found herself suspended over an ocean of light. It stretched into infinity in all directions. She was no longer in pain nor tired nor haunted. Nor was she alone.

Two entities hovered just outside of her peripheral awareness. It took Ilyana a moment to realize one was the Sleeper—asleep no longer. The Sleeper shielded its immense puissance from her, sparing her sanity from its full scrutiny. The other was Yu-Ha, no longer desiccated. Now the former human woman was beautiful, full of life and happiness.

Without words, the Sleeper directed Ilyana to look down, and she did.

Below Ilyana was a sea of consciousness, transcending the limitations of time and space, which encompassed all the living and dead beings of the universe. She would be part of this as well, but the Sleeper held her above it, in this place where gods dwelt beyond mortal limitations or concepts. Here Ilyana understood why Yu-Ha had said that life and death were "phase states."

A dream-thought from the Sleeper enveloped Ilyana. She witnessed the long-ago struggles of a species that had sought the stars, like humanity, only to encounter the King in Yellow. This species reminded Ilyana of ancient mythic creatures: fauns. Ilyana watched as the fauns fought for their survival against the endless onslaught of the king's hordes—and lost.

Desperate, the last remnants of the fauns discovered the Sleeper and woke it. They begged the god to defend them from Hastur. Though the Sleeper stood against the King in Yellow, it could not defend the fauns from his hordes. His will was too strong, and he conscripted those species he devoured to serve him, for the fauns were not the first. The cycle of death and silence among the stars was fated to continue.

*But you, you did something no one thought was possible,* Yu-Ha explained, *or even conceivable.* To the Sleeper, to Yu-Ha, to every being in the universe living, dead, and yet to be born, Ilyana was a hero.

They then plunged into the ocean of Being. Ilyana was now connected with everything in existence—and everyone. She found Natasha and Gregor in a small apartment on New Kiev, eating breakfast in silence. Gregor's hair and beard contained more silver than she remembered. There were wrinkles of worry and concern around his eyes and mouth, which she longed to smooth away with a kiss. Natasha was now a young lady, solemn, staring out at the grey morning as she chewed.

All Ilyana had was *now,* so she reached out and touched them both with her presence and her love. She was pulled away through space and time, returning to the pyramid. Only now, the dais holding the Sleeper had moved. It was floating in the vast atrium within the pyramid, still bearing the Sleeper's body. And there was a question to ask.

Ilyana and Yu-Ha looked down at what the dais covered. There were machines ancient beyond comprehension, tiny in comparison to the Sleeper, sustaining thousands of embryos in stasis. They were the last hopes of races long dead, waiting for a chance to live. All waiting for a starship in the night sky.

*You understand that the damage the Yellow Sign has done to your body is beyond repair,* Yu-Ha said to her. The Chinese woman was radiant, so much more than mortal. Behind her was the great, veiled presence of the Sleeper.

Ilyana did understand. She understood the state of her still-living, struggling body. The mark infected her face. Cancers accelerated through her body, spurred on by the malignancy of Hastur's will. She would die. But the *Miriya* was in orbit, and its shuttle was on the ground.

*Do you understand?* Yu-Ha asked, indicating the embryos far below them. They glowed in the darkness of the atrium with life and potential. *They have been sleeping a long time, waiting for a ship to come.*

*Why ask?* Ilyana said, to Yu-Ha and to the Sleeper. *You are powerful, you can take what you want.*

*Because then we would be no better than the King in Yellow,* Yu-Ha responded. *Even in the face of Eternity, that matters.*

Ilyana looked beyond Yu-Ha to the Sleeper, who sent her a dream-thought. It was a moment with her infant daughter, seated in the nursery she and Gregor put together in their two-bedroom apartment on Archanska. Ilyana viewed it from the perspective of an observer, but she felt the love in that memory of the early morning.

In that moment, Ilyana understood. Love is an eternal constant. In spite of eternity, it mattered.

*Will you protect my daughter and husband from his mark?* Ilyana asked.

Ilyana sat on the white sand next to the desiccated corpse of Yu-Ha, watching the shuttle lift off. In that shuttle's cargo hold was the most precious cargo in the universe—embryos comprising a second chance at life for hundreds of species and the machines that sustained them. They'd only loaded a small portion of the whole, but Ilyana knew the Commissariat would be interested in the rest.

"Your oxygen levels are low, Captain," Petrov said in her ear.

"I know," Ilyana responded. There hadn't been much on board to take with her. "Tell my daughter I love her. Tell my husband I love him. Tell the Commissariat to treat the babies with care. The Sleeper will be watching them."

"I will." Petrov paused. "Captain Visok, I have now been informed that the Commissariat agrees to the terms. They are assembling a retrieval expedition to this world to establish formal contact."

"I won't be here when they come, Petrov."

"Your body will, Captain," Petrov said. "That will be enough."

Ilyana nodded. "Yeah, it will."

She watched the shuttle dwindle into a spark, heading slowly toward the *Miriya*. "Goodbye, Petrov, and thank you."

"Goodbye, Ilyana. Fare well."

Ilyana was on her last few breaths of air when the shuttle rejoined the *Miriya*. She watched as the starship activated its main engine to leave orbit. She turned to Yu-Ha and nodded. Life and death were phase states, and she'd see Natasha and Gregor again. She was ready.

§

*An avid junkie of weird fiction and genres arc-wielded together with spit, flair, and appropriate grammar,* **D.W. Baldwin** *is the author of the award-winning, science fiction novel* Capricorn Rising. *Thrilled to be included in the Broken Eye Books pantheon, D.W. lives in the Pacific Northwest with a dog, two cats, and an abiding worship of Clinton J. Boomer (the writer so good, he deserves a call-out in another author's bio!).*

## Behold, a White Ship

# J. EDWARD TREMLETT

### ILLUSTRATED BY LUKE SPOONER

It was the Hour of the Shell on the temple cruiser Serannian, and confessions were running long.

In a tiny, overly lit cell just off the main corridor, a white-bearded Ecclesian prefect looked down at his prisoner. They'd been here for hours, and the story had changed with each new telling.

Nodens' servants didn't appreciate subjective truth.

"Start again," the prefect said, wiping his well-used, silver truth stick on a fresh towel. "And this time, try *not* to be a hero?"

And all the prisoner could do was gasp, look up, and say—

"There's just one problem with this business," Captain Ione said, pulling the *Oeno* up so steeply the block freighter should have broken in half.

"What's that?" Jesk asked, hanging onto her gunnery station as they hurtled through Planus Nine's deadly ice rings—three-winged Teeg fighters close behind.

"Getting shot at," he answered, spiraling wildly to avoid being smashed.

Lasers streamed past the bridge's well-armored windows, almost perforating the boxy ship's backside. Several flashes of blue light erupted, indicating the demise of some of their pursuers.

"Yes!" the captain shouted, enraptured. But more lasers flew, and his smile fell. "Khub's sake, Hrsk, are they still with us?" he demanded, running a hand through his straight black beard.

"Yesss," the burly man-lizard at sensors hissed, "Many shipsss, now."

"How many?"

"Too many," the Xard replied, and he was right. The Teeg carrier had sent every fighter, and none of them had backed off when he dove into the rings.

"Who knew they still cared about that dead king," Ione muttered, cursing his decision to "borrow" Gravonib the First's funeral goods.

"I can't get a target lock!" Jesk shouted as they pulled out of the ice. "Too many things moving—"

"Hang on," Ione ordered, diving straight back down into the rings.

Ione maneuvered the *Oeno* through them: up and down, left and right, even sideways. As they went, fewer laser blasts flew, and more bright blue explosions happened.

After ten blissfully silent seconds, Ione grinned. "You see, girl? Have some faith—"

"Look out!" Jesk screamed, ducking behind her console as an ice chunk smacked the *Oeno* portside. Sparks flew from ceiling consoles, and the ship went dark and silent.

But as they spun through the bottom of Planus's ice ring—somehow missing everything—the few remaining fighters shot past them, pancaking into each other.

"Which is how we escaped the Teegs' most feared capital ship," Captain Ione said, bringing his drinking story to a close. "And how I got this new, handsome scar across my face."

"Which scar?" asked the pale man sitting across from him in the booth. His face was hidden behind the long hood of his black cloak, except for his long, thin chin.

"My nose," Ione said, tapping it. "Goes nicely with the one on my cheek."

"More . . . borrowing?"

"Sort of. Fighting wamps on Keldan-2. They'd infested the temple, you see."

"Truly?"

"Yes. And I lost half this ear serving the Second Dominion in the Ophidian War. And . . . well, you know how it goes."

Ione couldn't see his companion's expressions, but the man seemed confused. Maybe his translator wasn't working too well—that's what he thought the strange, silver object around his neck was, anyway.

"But I'm sure everyone in this bar has a scar or two and a story or three," Ione shrugged, casting his hand over the large and noisy establishment, packed with scammers and scalawags from every world in the Twenty-Three systems. "On Serania, we always say, if you've got more stories than scars, you're doing alright."

"Truly?" the pale man asked, running his finger along the silver object. "Are you doing . . . alright? Did the treasure of the Teegs bring what you desired?"

"Sort of," the captain winced, compulsively running a hand through his beard. "I fixed my ship, paid my crew, and had enough left over for a drink or two. Can't ask for much more."

"So you are not . . . successful."

"Not as such," Ione sighed: "But Nebar's not known for success stories, is it? Three dominions later, it's still just rock and ruin. And half the stars in the sky gone."

"Yes," the pale man nodded, making a hand sign Ione half-recognized from his more religious childhood on Serania. "The Null."

Ione grinned, pointing up. "Good news for us, though. The Ecclesians are scared to be this close, so no prefects trying to make us behave."

"Truly?" Ione's guest repeated.

"Truly. No temple cruisers, no confessionals. Might have agents, of course."

"Agents . . . ?"

"Ah, I wouldn't worry about it," Ione waved a dismissive hand. "The only law and order here's the Nameless Monks. And they don't wander past the Smashlands."

"That is . . . fortunate," the pale man said.

Ione smiled, deciding to not reveal that he'd seen the strange, masked monks wandering about Crashtown, clearly looking for something. Or someone.

"So," Ione said, leaning forward and speaking quietly, wondering if the old, nosy cyborg at the bar was listening in, "You're looking for a ship for a job. I've got one. The *Oeno*."

He grinned, expecting his guest to have heard of it. When it was clear he hadn't, Ione sighed and explained, "It's a block freighter, made to haul trains through the Skip. Not much to look at, I'll admit, but it's well-armored, has a lot of living space, and it's *very* fast when it's not hauling."

The pale man considered this and nodded.

"So what else do you need?" Ione asked.

"I need . . . discretion," Ione's would-be employer said, also leaning in close. "A . . . private room."

"Anything else?"

"I need to be gone. Soon."

"We *could* be," the captain nodded, "but I don't fly cheap, friend. Nor blind. So . . . what's this job, and what's in it for me?"

The pale man was quiet for a time. He slowly nodded and pulled back enough of his hood to reveal his face.

Ione gasped at what he saw. And as he regained his composure, the mysterious being told him why he needed the *Oeno*.

"Finding a massive treasure?" Jesk repeated, pushing a large gravity-box of parts toward their hangar on the edge of the Smashlands.

"Precisely," Ione said, walking alongside and not helping.

"What kind?"

"He was a little vague on that," Ione admitted. "'The greatest thing we will ever see,' he said."

"That's all?"

"There's . . . a little more than that," the captain said, "for which I'm willing to overlook some of our anonymous employer's eccentricities."

"Such as?" Jesk asked, quite annoyed. She didn't like being left in the dark. It usually meant falling onto her face.

"Such as . . . things I can't talk about," he said, quickly holding up a hand. "Just trust me on this, girl."

"That's what you said last time."

"Now, we've been over that—"

"It's taken me weeks to fix her," she grumbled, "And you're going on a feeling?"

"A very good feeling," the captain insisted, leaning in close. "This fellow? He's . . . special."

"Special," Jesk snorted.

"And he's also on the run."

"Aren't we all?"

"Not from the Nameless, we're not," Ione said, gazing off at the tall, crumbling monastery, quite some distance away—older than the First Dominion, some said. "The monks are looking for him. He won't say why. But he knows something. Something *big*."

Jesk blinked. "Then you'd better tell me."

Ione looked at her as if preparing to speak. But then he saw Hrsk lumbering along and just said, "Later."

Which is why Jesk never found out about the extra hands Ione told the Xard to hire until they all showed up, expecting a cabin.

A hulking pair of Velerian mercenaries arrived first: all long, black hair, braided mustaches, and red leather. They were either brothers or lovers, both named Rug. Each carried a pair of short, shiny star axes strapped to their backs, spoils from the war against Leng.

An unfortunate veteran of the Ophidian War followed: a clanking, old cyborg—clearly struck by the snakes' infamous melt-gas—who Ione remembered as the one who'd been listening at the bar. He was so shell-shocked, he couldn't recall whether his name was Lee or Harl, so he became "Harley," to his chagrin.

A willowy, web-fingered man just sort of appeared on the bridge, grinning. He was wrapped in a long, blue cloak, wore large boots that masked his footsteps, and sported several large knives. He preferred to remain nameless, which made Jesk dislike him immediately; he found that amusing.

Next, an Endraxian pilgrim strode proudly aboard: four arms, eyes on the sides of his head, and a sideways mouth splitting his skull. He proudly proclaimed himself "Yerg, Who Seeks Splendid Cathuria, Where All Pleasures Lie."

Their pale and mysterious patron showed up last, hood covering his face, gravity sled hovering three steps behind his billowing cloak. It carried a long, black box, maybe the size of a coffin. He refused to let anyone else touch it and disappeared into his cabin for takeoff.

The crew checked and sealed the ship and strapped everyone in and down. With a disquieting shudder, the *Oeno* rocketed away from dusty and lawless Nebar, leaving the scum and dregs of the Twenty-Three systems behind.

A departure noted by the Nameless Monks, who had just surrounded Crashtown, and started to burn it down.

"Can't we move back?" Jesk said, not liking what she saw outside the bridge windows.

"Afraid not, girl," Ione said, glad they skipped out well clear of the aging Ophidian convoy. "You know the rules."

"I know," she sighed: "Stay put and wait for new coordinates."

"Snakes," Harley shuddered, looking at the mottled, olive-green ships, travelling end to end, like a block train. "I remember what they did to me—"

"So you *can* remember things, half-meat?" the shorter Rug laughed.

"Calm yourself, Harley," Ione insisted. "We won't be staying long."

"It's Lee," the cyborg complained, causing both Rugs to chuckle.

"Probably just a ghost fleet," said the taller Valerian, "asleep since the war."

"If they're not all dead," the shorter one added, "The Second Dominion used poison, remember?"

Ione might have added something to that, but their employer picked that moment to stride onto the bridge. "We have arrived," he announced.

"So we have," the captain said. "Where to now?"

"Here," their employer said, handing over new coordinates.

Ione examined them and handed the paper over to Hrsk. "That's halfway between Iayatus and the Pels Cascade."

"Yes," the pale man said.

"Nothing isss there," Hrsk said, confused.

"Just another view of the Null." Jesk shuddered, unable to forget being so close to it, right at the system's edge before skipping away.

The pale man was silent for a few seconds and responded, "Yes," before turning to go.

"So what's he doing?" Harley asked, looking to Ione. "We're just going in circles around . . . you know."

"Evading pursuit, I'd say," the man with webbed fingers answered, now standing by Hrsk's station.

"It's been three days," Jesk grumbled, annoyed by the man's appearing act. "We should have shaken them by now, whoever they are."

"Ecclesians," the shorter Rug proclaimed. "Who else?"

"He seemed more worried about the Nameless Monks," Ione offered, but something about how he said it made Jesk wonder what he *wasn't* saying.

"We should have been there by now," Jesk grumbled to Yerg as she ate her quite unsatisfying meal in the galley. "It's been six full-day skips. And we're down to emergency rations."

"Revelation requires hardship," the Endraxian pilgrim said, arms locked in prayer, one of his telescoping eyes fixed on the pale man's cabin.

"Well, if this hardship gets any staler, there'll be a riot," the gunner muttered. "If our thief doesn't just appear in our employer's room, anyway."

"He would not get past me," Yerg declared. "I have been guarding him since we left."

"Why?" Jesk asked.

"I seek answers. I believe he has them."

"Answers to what?"

"To my destination," Yerg said, focusing one eye upon her: "Splendid, shining Cathuria."

"I think I've heard of it," Jesk said.

"You have?" the Endraxian said, pleasantly surprised. "May I ask how?"

"The captain . . . well, he wasn't always like this. Sometimes when he gets drunk, he tells me about his parents' temple to Tamash on Serania."

"The God of Illusion," the pilgrim mused. "Fitting."

"So," Jesk asked, "Cathuria?"

The Endraxian considered for a moment and nodded. "My order holds that what we now call the Null was once a glittering expanse of shining stars and lovely worlds, travelled by starships. All manner of beings prospered under the gentle gaze of the Great Ones and were ruled wisely and well by the God Born."

"Who?"

"The children of the Great Ones and their worshippers," Yerg answered. "Not quite gods but more than mortal."

"Okay," the gunner said.

"It was home to stately Zar, land of dreams lost and half-remembered," Yerg went on, growing misty-eyed. "Lush and verdant Xura, world of pleasures unimagined. Thalerion, where all starships laid their anchor. And cold and lonely Kadath . . . though that is best left unspoken.

"And in the center of all those amazing worlds lay Cathuria. Where all hopes were brought into being, all desires made real . . ."

"So what happened?" Jesk asked, breaking the pilgrim's reverie.

"The same thing that always happens to paradise," the pilgrim said, fixing both eyes upon her. "It is enjoyed, abused, and then taken away."

"By the Null," Jesk said.

"Yes," Yerg said sadly. "They say the White Ship itself was seen leaving Cathuria, a hungry blackness growing in its wake. World after world fell to the doom pronounced by the gods, and none survived. For the gods are mighty, and their judgement absolute."

"Yet here you are, looking to go back?"

"Yes," the pilgrim admitted, looking back at the pale man's door. "And I believe this man knows way there."

"Why?"

"Because we have been spell-sailing these last six days," the Endraxian explained. "And there is only one reason to do such a thing—"

"And you better tell me what it is before I smack you upside your face!" Jesk shouted at Ione, pointing to the small statue of Khub on his cabin's desk. Clearly, she intended to do the deed with his favorite god.

"Now, be reasonable," Ione said as he held up his hands, hoping neither she nor Hrsk became any angrier: "If I'd just said—"

"That we're going into the damn Null?" she shouted, not caring if the rest of the help heard them.

"Sssuicccide," the burly Xard hissed, shaking his head from side to side. "Foolissshnesss."

"Our employer says he can get us through," Ione reprimanded the lizard-man, indicating the pale man he'd asked to this impromptu staff meeting.

"Into something that sucks temple cruisers down when they get too close?" Jesk replied.

"We will be . . . protected," the pale and hooded man insisted. "We have spell-sailed here."

"Which means what, exactly?" Ione asked, starting to sound doubtful.

"Our course has created a . . . pattern," their mysterious employer said, pulling out a piece of paper that revealed the shape in question—a seven-pointed star with the Null at its center. "As we have travelled that pattern, I have worked a protective spell."

"Wait," the captain said, raising an eyebrow. "Is that it? *Really*? Magic? I thought you had some device or something."

"You do not understand," the pale man said, putting his hands together: "It is . . . disappointing."

"Then explain it better," Ione said, clearly irritated. *"All* of it. Otherwise, I don't care who you are, we're going nowhere and you're going out the airlock. Understand?"

"Who is he . . . ?" Jesk started to ask, but Ione held up a hand.

"Ten of your millennia ago, before the First Dominion, the Null was . . . different," the hooded man said. "Full of worlds. Full of life."

"That's what Yerg said," Jesk said, raising an eyebrow: "All that stuff about Cathuria? The Great Ones? Their children? It's all true?"

"Of course, it's true," Ione snapped at her. "The details are a little uncertain, that's all."

"So what *happened*?" Jesk asked, a little stung by the captain's retort.

"War," the pale man continued. "A terrible conflict against the Elder Ones. Do you know of them?"

"Yes," Ione nodded, remembering the hideous statues his people had venerated out of fear. "I also heard the Great Ones wiped them all out."

Their employer nodded: "Victory was . . . costly. A terrible weapon was used. What you call the Null is what remains."

Jesk blanched. "And you believe what's in there is worth going through it."

"Truly," the pale man said.

"So what *is* it, then?" the captain demanded. "Because if I'm going to talk that lot out there into this with magic, I'll need more than 'the greatest thing you will ever see.'"

"Words fail," their anonymous employer admitted. "But you risked all for funeral treasure but a thousand years old. What does that compare to something untouched for ten millennia?"

Ione looked at the man. He started to stroke his beard, perhaps considering.

Jesk sighed, knowing that was for show, and he'd already made up his mind.

Everyone wanted to be on the bridge for this.

The *Oeno* sat at the very edge of Nebar's system, right where the journey had started. Beyond it lay the Null, filling the windows with roiling, black evil.

This close, it poisoned the mind, making onlookers think they saw things in that blackness. Eyes staring back at the ship. Maws opening to consume her.

Tentacles, threatening to drag them in . . .

"All ssssystemssss ready," Hrsk said.

"Guns are ready, too, for what it's worth," Jesk said.

"They will not be necessary," their employer insisted. "The spell is complete. The ship is protected. We will be safe."

"Safe?" Harley said, looking around. "Is he crazy? Are we all crazy?"

"Be calm, friend," Yerg said, holding up his hands in supplication. "We have spell-sailed here. We could not be safer—"

"Against that?" Harley insisted, pointing to the monstrous black chaos outside. "It's suicide!"

"So's going out the airlock," Ione said, turning his gaze on the terrified veteran. "You eavesdropped your way into this trip, Harley. This is what we're doing. Obey or leave."

The cyborg opened his mouth and closed it, putting his hands down as he did.

Captain Ione turned back around, twisting his beard, and nodded. "Let's see if there's something to this spell-sailing thing after all."

He gently eased the *Oeno* forward. The freighter slowly approached the churning blackness, meter by meter, until they could actually see some kind of texture in the dark.

And then the freighter slid in.

An eerie silence followed. Every noise the *Oeno* normally made was muted. All the crew could hear was their own breathing and the frightened beating of their hearts.

The quiet was abruptly broken by a strange groaning all over the ship. It reminded Ione of loose bulkheads being crushed by an atmosphere just above structural tolerance but worse, somehow.

The groaning continued and got louder. Before long, Ione began to worry that the ship couldn't take it. The alarm lights flashed, however silently, and he swore he heard the hull buckle.

But no sooner did he reach out to employ braking thrusters than the noise just stopped. The *Oeno's* normal sounds resumed: engines, controls, the annoying proximity alarms.

"The spell holds," the pale man said: "We may . . . proceed."

"For how long?" Ione asked.

"Perhaps . . . a day?"

"I'll hold you to two, then," the captain said, pointing a finger at the man's very pointy chin. "Any longer, and we're backing up."

And there was clearly no arguing with that.

"Captain," Jesk said, turning to look at the bridge's visitor. "We have a problem."

Ione turned from the window, just as the cyborg sprouted several hidden guns from his arms and chest. He pointed them at each person at the bridge as well as the front windows.

He grinned as he did it. It was not a pleasant expression.

"Look, I know you're not happy," Ione tried to reason, wishing their employer was not hiding in his cabin, again. "But I promised our friend a day—"

"This is what is going to happen," Harley announced, his voice and mannerisms quite different. "We are going to turn this ship around and head back the way we came. And once we are out, I shall be calling a temple cruiser to pick us up."

"An agent," Jesk grumbled. "For Khub's sake, Hrsk, you had to hire an agent!"

"Sssorry," the Xard hissed.

"No wonder he was always listening at the bar," Ione muttered.

"My friend, please," Yerg begged, getting on his knees and praying with all four arms. "We both worship Nodens, in our own way. Would you not stand in paradise? Walk with your gods? "

"Heretic," Harley sneered. "Do I kill you now or leave you for the prefects?"

His question was answered by a solid thunk—the sound of steel burying into his forehead.

"I'd prefer to not be caught," the web-fingered man said with another knife ready to throw. "I'm sure you understand."

*Where had he come from,* Jesk wondered. *He hadn't been there a moment ago.*

Harley tried to say something but fell to his knees, eyes staring in different directions. The Valerians were on him a second later, dragging him back to the galley to dismember him with their axes.

As they took him away, the proximity alarm changed tone.

"Sssomething ahead," Hrsk said, turning back to his station: "Disssturbancccce."

The captain almost asked what kind, but the *Oeno* slid out of the solid blackness.

"Oh, thank Khub," Captain Ione breathed.

"Two days, Captain," their mysterious employer said, now right behind him.

"Yes," Ione said, wheeling to face him. "And where *is* the greatest thing we will ever see?"

As if in answer, something before the *Oeno* lit up with a strange phosphorescence—a long spacecraft, shaped like the sailing ships of old. Its sides were made of massive, pale trees twisted together, and its edges were of silver, engraved with a language Ione had seen upon Serania's oldest temples.

Above its deck rose several long, sinewy masts, draped with glittering starsails. There was no question as to what it was.

"A star ship," Yerg said, kneeling in reverence. "The White Ship!"

"Yes," Captain Ione said, astounded to see the tales of his youth made true.

And enraptured as he imagined what treasure that ancient ship carried in its hold.

"We'll breach her with the docking clamp," Jesk explained, just off the bridge. "It should be able to figure the configuration."

"We walk with the gods, here," Yerg insisted. "We must be humble and proceed with open hands and hearts."

"Hrsk agreesssss," the Xard said, nodding his head side to side.

"Hrsk, you're staying behind," Ione insisted. "Just in case."

The burly lizard seemed crestfallen but obeyed.

"I will need my . . . things," their employer said, heading to his cabin.

As soon as he was out of earshot, Ione walked closer to the web-fingered man. "Thanks for helping with the agent."

"You're welcome," he smirked, looking at Jesk. "Both of you."

He walked away with a spring in his step as if he'd won a bet with himself.

"Irritating," the gunner grumbled.

"Stop being so worried about *him*," the captain whispered. "It's our employer I can't really trust."

"Oh really?" Jesk sneered. "Why now?"

"He's *unnerving*," the captain said. "I don't like unnerving."

"Hrsk will be listening in while we're over there?" Jesk asked: "Right?"

"Absolutely," Ione said, "because—"

"This is . . . not exactly what I was expecting."

The captain wasn't the only one. Some were enchanted, and some were afraid, but none were anything less than completely astounded by the insides of the ancient craft.

Beyond the bony swirl of the airlock lay a massive, open chamber, running from bow to stern. It was filled with strange, long swirls of phosphorescent, whitish-green gas that moved as though alive. Numerous free-floating decks hung between those glowing clouds, connected to one another by wide ramps, and filled with floating silver globules that shivered and breathed with a strange and frantic life.

The party quietly strode across the ramps and platforms, following their employer. His box floated behind him like a pet. The pale man spoke in a tongue that none had ever heard before, and the floating silver blobs seemed less agitated after he passed.

At last, they came to a long staircase, stretching up past the ceiling. It led into what was clearly the wheelhouse, filled with more of the breathing, silvery globules. At the far end was a massive dais, and beyond that lay a massive, curved window overlooking the ship's long, silver prow.

The pale man spoke to the globules in turn. Then he strode toward the dais and knelt with his box beside him.

"Amazing," Yerg said, looking around. "Truly amazing."

"*Boring*," the taller Rug snorted. "Where are its defenses?"

"Oh, they are here," the pale man said. "You ignorantly walked past them."

"He isn't having speech problems, now," the web-fingered man whispered to Jesk.

"No," she whispered back. "I don't think he ever did."

"So the treasure?" Ione asked.

Their employer took the silver object from his neck and placed it upon the box. There was a hiss and the box opened, revealing a large number of silver blobs. These dutifully floated up and around him, like strange birds.

"Look around you, Captain," the pale man said, standing up as the silver blobs moved. "The ship is the treasure."

Ione was about to say something but could only watch as the pulsing bulbs of metal met with one another and joined. As they did, the ship's glow strengthened and began to pulsate.

As the brightness grew, the crew of the *Oeno* could finally see what lay beyond.

The roiling and gelid sphere was blossoming with hideous life. Massive alien organs were born and moved about only to be absorbed back into the darkness after a time. Titanic, many-lobed eyes stared down upon the ship, hungrily. Huge, fanged maws yawned and shut, expecting to be filled.

And black tentacles slopped out of the mass, extending toward the ship only so far before being stopped and roughly shoved back into the dark from whence it came.

"Shoggoth," Yerg gasped, looking at the horror outside. "We sit inside a shoggoth!"

"Indeed we do," the pale man said, stroking the silver object as he returned it to his neck, now glowing in time with the globs about them. "The primal hunger made flesh. The darkness that has no beginning or end."

Jesk looked around unnerved and realized the web-fingered man was nowhere to be seen.

"Shoggoths," the shorter Rug spat. "Stories! Just like the things that made them."

"Stories to some," the pale man said. "History to others."

"Only we haven't heard the whole story, have we?" Jesk questioned. "How did this ship come to be here?"

"The war raged for millennia," the pale man explained. "Neither side could win. Maddened by their failure, the servants of the Great Ones attempted to use the Elder Ones' weapons against them.

"But they miscalculated," he said, gesturing toward the toothy, sliding sphere beyond the window. "Instead of making many shoggoths, only one was created. Its hunger was incredible. Uncontrollable. It ate everything in its path until it had consumed the world of its creation. Then its moons, its neighbors, its *star*.

"And then it began to eat even more . . ."

Yerg fell to his knees, holding his head in his four hands. "Then Cathuria . . ."

"Cathuria is no more, Pilgrim," the pale man said without any sympathy. "Crumbs at the creature's table."

"But how could you know?" Jesk asked. "About what happened? What they did? And how this ship got here?"

"Because he was there," Ione revealed.

The pale man looked at him, perhaps reproachfully, and pulled the cloak back so they could all see.

Everyone knew what the Great Ones looked like, thanks to the many statues from before the First Dominion. They were thin-faced beings with long and pendulous earlobes, thin and narrow eyes of all black or white, and thin, jutting chins.

Their employer's immortal bloodline showed true: he looked exactly like the statues of Tamash: pale of skin and black of hair, narrow ebon eyes sparkling with dark mirth.

"God Born," Jesk gasped, watching Yerg prostrate himself in fear.

"Yes," Ione confirmed. "My silence was part of the agreement. We'd help him escape Nebar and get back to his ship, and—"

"And I would give you treasure," the God Born mocked.

"Now wait," Ione insisted. "We had a deal."

"If you want treasure, fool, then consider your lives recompense," the pale man said, pointing back the way they'd come: "Leave. Now."

"Let's not be calling anyone a fool," the captain said, pulling his blasters out. "Especially when it's six to one—"

The captain didn't even see what killed him. A silver globule burst like a seed pod, shooting a beam of green and white light straight through his heart.

"Ten thousand years imprisoned on Nebar," the God Born hissed as Ione fell dead, blasters clattering. "Locked away in shame for my failure to control the beast. Bound by the servants of my kind, and handed to their descendants and theirs in turn. Passed down through the ages, long after they had no idea why they guarded my chamber or what lay within!

"And you dare oppose me, now that I have at last escaped to reclaim my birthright?" he shouted. "Now that I am free? I am the son of a god! You should pray to me!"

The taller Rug grinned, hefting his axes. "We don't pray—"

"We fight!" the shorter agreed.

The pair ran toward the God Born, screaming, but Jesk didn't care to watch. Instead, she ran back to the *Oeno*, down the great staircase, across now-live decks and ramps, past clouds of gas that seemed as ready to kill her as those silver blobs, and down to the airlock.

But it was closed with Hrsk collapsed in front of the door.

As Jesk ran toward the Xard, she saw motion through the nearest porthole. Her ship was quickly backing away.

At the bridge window of the *Oeno* was Harley, looking like he'd literally pulled himself together, and grinning as he marooned her—

"And that's all I know. I swear before the Silver Hand," the cyborg gasped, still reeling from the prefect's last use of the truth stick. "I incapacitated the Xard and left them all there."

"Why did you leave?" the prefect demanded.

"I thought it would be better to go and get backup, in my condition. I just had a knife to the head—"

"I see no wound," his interrogator said.

"My memories," Harley begged, putting a hand to his forehead. "They're broken . . ."

"Is it telling the truth?" someone asked, just behind the prefect.

"In some parts, Lord," the prefect said, snapping to attention. "But I have not been able to get a straight story. We have been over this ten times, and the particulars keep changing."

"Damage to the mind," the pendulous, silver-robed imperator said, walking in and regarding the captive as one might a disgusting insect.

"But I saw it," the cyborg said, looking up at the newcomer and away in fear. "The White Ship. The living darkness. The eyes in that darkness. Nodens save me."

"It is a fantastic story," Harley's interrogator said. "Spell-sailing? Going into the Null? Finding one of the old star ships from before the First Dominion?"

"Be careful, Prefect," the imperator said, putting a hand on his own truth stick. "Do not allow the blasphemous ravings of a decaying mind to infect your own."

"Apologies, my lord," the prefect said, bowing humbly.

"That said, I believe there is truth within the tale," the silver-robed man pronounced, walking a circle around them both. "I believe it intended to report a criminal operation, as stated. As for what happened after . . . I think that, following the struggle to arrest these criminals, the ship passed too close to the Null."

"I suppose that makes sense, my lord," the prefect said, nodding. "These programmed agents' minds are already so fragile."

"Exactly," his leader went on. "And we know well the effect the Null has upon even the most stable of prefects. Would that not explain the fantastic parts of its story?"

"If you say so, my lord," the interrogator said, knowing the folly of arguing. "It certainly explains why he cannot tell the same story twice."

"Yes," the silver-robed imperator said, quite pleased with his reasoning.

"What should we do with him?" the prefect asked.

The imperator pondered the question for a moment and smirked.

"Put him back to work, of course," he declared.

The cyborg decided to sit his half-meat behind on a lump of rubble, right where Crashtown's bar used to be, to blend in with Nebar's many hard luck cases.

Such persons seemed more plentiful, these days, but only because the great fire had burned so much of the city. Indistinguishable, the badly reassembled and freshly reprogrammed Harley sat and listened for an answer to his silent question.

Had anyone seen the White Ship?

There were rumors, of course. Some saw it prowling about Serania; others claimed it docked at Endraxus-7. One wag said it was crewed by Valerians, yet another said Xards. A few claimed to have met its captain, who wore a strange, silver object about the neck.

So many stories. So few facts.

Day after day, Harley sat in that spot, asking no questions, hearing all answers. In time, he became the one who spread the rumors, hoping to learn more. As the legend of the White Ship grew, he became the one others came to for information, never suspecting his true purpose.

Days and nights became years and decades. Crashtown grew, shrank, and grew yet again as Nebar's fate ebbed and flowed. The Third Dominion fell, and the Ecclesians with them, only to be replaced by something worse.

And as the Null grew larger in the sky, coming closer with each new year, still Harley sat, waiting for answers.

It was not until over a hundred years had passed—the Null almost upon Nebar—that someone finally came. A very old woman wrapped in a blue cloak moved silently through the nearly abandoned ruins that remained of Crashtown.

She found Harley in the shrine his pilgrims had built. The walls were covered with scraps and stories, rumors and tales. Evidence gleaned from all over the Twenty-Three systems was festooned here in the hopes that the prophet would distill answers from them.

"I hear you seek the White Ship," she said, running a webbed finger along the silver object at her neck.

"I do," the old cyborg said, barely able to stand. "Tell me . . . have you seen it?"

"I have," she said, holding out her hands in long-overdue forgiveness. "Come, friend. See for yourself."

And so did the last living victim of the Ecclesians at last leave his shrine, reunited with the ancient vessel he spurned so very long ago, and escape the slow doom that came for dusty, lawless Nebar in the form of the Null.

For while the gods are mighty and their judgments usually absolute, they are sometimes also kind.

§

**J. Edward Tremlett**, *aka "The Lurker in Lansing," is a graduate of Ohio University's Creative Writing program. His travels have taken him around the world—most notably a 7-year stint in Dubai, UAE. He was the webmaster and chief writer for the* Wraith Project, *the author of* Spygod's Tales, *and is one of the more prolific contributors to the third incarnation of* Pyramid *magazine. His writing has also seen print in* Worlds of Cthulhu, The End is Nigh, *and the* Echoes of Terror *anthology. He lives in Lansing, Michigan, with two cats and a mountain of Lego bricks.*

# Vishwajeet: Conqueror of the Universe

# D.A. XIAOLIN SPIRES

ILLUSTRATED BY
SUSHIR BOMMAKANTI

THE CAVITY OF HER CHEST OPENED, AND WE CLIMBED IN. OUR PARENTS waved teary goodbyes. It was still light, but hints of the evening sunset had begun to show. I held up my handkerchief and waved, and it spelled out *goodbye* in wispy holographic letters, like ghost traces of sparklers in the air.

Her name was *Vishwajeet*. Generally, this was a Bengali male name, but all the Bengali female names had to do with grace, feathers, and water lilies—silky, soft things—and *Vishwajeet* was far from that. Certainly, she flew with grace, but the insides smelled like a sewer pit since she was mostly constructed from disposed livestock ends: lungs, toes, snouts, and beaks. Sure, they ground them up, dressed them, and molded them into organic fleshy tubes and muscles, but the smell stayed like stale cigarettes in a rundown bar. *You can hide the body, but you can't scrub the stench away,* custodian Lenny used to say to me, his mouth pulled wide open to display his missing teeth. He would take the mop full of guts and shake its soppy locks at me.

*Vishwajeet* meant "conqueror of the universe." This was an apt name for the ship that would take us on our mission to engage with the creatures that had signaled to us from a few light years away. A simple mission: we would visit them, they'd visit us later. Just a host family type deal. In freshly dyed hair and new overall spacesuits, I felt overdressed for an exchange student.

The Conqueror of the Universe, *Vishwajeet*, held steady throughout our ascent, our breach through the higher levels of the atmosphere, and into space. It wasn't my first time in orbit, but this was an altogether different kind of ship.

"Hey, Azalea. Let's get to the rec room. I've brought bubbles!" Ravi pounced on me, holding up two bottles.

"Ravi! You're not supposed to bring those!"

"What are you now, the ship police?" He paraded down the hall, blowing his glowing orbs of light.

After we boarded, it took awhile for our eyes to adjust to the dim lights of *Vishwajeet's* inner core. She was built for conservation; she expelled very little matter, everything was reused. Even the lights were extracted from our own waste.

We flew for days in this dim light. Ravi's luminous bubbles cast a greenish glow off her cavernous innards.

It was the approach toward the border of the KGKGGGGK9 region, about 0.1 light-year from the Raskillions that we would meet, when the problems started. Ravi's bubbles began to pop immediately after blowing them.

That might have sounded like an innocent accident, but these things don't pop. They were ephemeral and cast a cool green glow, but they were far from cheap toys. They were exploration device buddies crafted to flex and withhold up to one billion pascals (or one hundred thousand bars, basically one hundred thousand times more atmospheric pressure than on earth). Which meant we should have been be dead. Nothing could pierce the balloons—they only popped when you initiated the correct destruction sequence, a verbal command that would scramble the particles of their interior structure. And I know Ravi wasn't doing that because he had lost his voice shouting in his sleep over several days and fell into a coma.

All of us students were affected. I was seeing pink confetti, like floaters in your eyes but fluorescent and squiggly. Ravi's bubbles kept popping. He let out a bunch of the globes when he was sick in bed, and they outlived his consciousness. While he dreamt, they floated about. Occasionally, they snapped to shredded bits that were incorporated into *Vishwajeet's* flesh in a matter of days. Sometimes, I saw Lenny mopping them up, first. Even Lenny, who was as tough as steel bars, was not in the best shape. His lips looked purple, and his hair was beginning to thin up top.

Yet we were still on target for our landing, and the proper authorities knew of our distress. We would be sent to medical facilities when we landed. There was not much they could do. The authorities said that weird phenomena were not unusual for first timers, and they had a likelihood of 99.9 percent of being reversed once on friendly ground.

*Vishwajeet* wasn't doing too well herself. Maybe, she choked on a few bubble shards too many. Her lights were dimmer, and I spent most of my time sitting in the dining space since her shudders were getting more intense. Perhaps, it was my imagination, but passing through corridor four, the one between the waste transference center and my room, felt like there was less oxygen than usual.

The next day, I started coughing.

At first, it was just a few tickles in my throat, but they became full-on hacks. I felt like something was choking me. One intense whoop, I dislodged these forms from my throat. They were geometric and almost beautiful, like snowflakes. And they were bright, which helped me see in the ever-growing darkness of *Vishwajeet's* belly.

They came that night. A hollow voice. A wet appendage. I could feel its slimy caress on my cheek, and I backed away. I didn't know if they were real or in my head. *Cough more,* they ordered. *Let out those reels.*

I didn't know what "reels" they were talking about, but I did cough, involuntarily. A series of loud, tongue-slopping gulps and the snowflake forms were gone.

I had nowhere to go by now. The students were confined to their rooms, our chaperones didn't pick up. If I had known earlier of what was to come, I might have panicked. I might have taken up reins, tried to contact our handlers and turn around, but I had no idea.

They came again the next night.

I was brushing my teeth, watching the pink floaters glide past, when I felt a wet towel wrap around my shoulder. No, it wasn't a towel, or at least, it wasn't my towel. All the towels were to my left, accounted for. The arm that wrapped around me was doughy but flexible and maintained a kind of structural integrity. I couldn't rip it off.

*Your coughs. Cough them out,* they ordered.

There was really no light left in *Vishwajeet*, only emergency power for air and sustenance. But I had siphoned a bit of power away from the grid to power a tiny nightlight in my bathroom. I could see in the mirror an arm: bumpy, pockmarked. The arm snaked around me. My own limbs were no longer visible within its tires of obese bulges. My body was engulfed, like a coin that had fallen through a crack in the sidewalk. Face covered, I couldn't see anything, and it was getting harder to breathe. My nose was smooshed against the slimy flesh. It smelled like a thousand cockroaches had scuttled and pooped over the flesh, and in a gap, I saw a glimpse of something horrid, something I wish I could take back.

It was Ravi's hand. I swear it was his hand, chestnut brown and smooth, wearing the very gold ring he boasted his grandmother had given him when he was five. It was sticking out of this slug-like limb, and the hand was moving, too.

"Ravi, is that you?" I whispered. But my whisper was muffled. The stench invaded my nostrils until I think even my olfactory facilities gave out.

There was no sign of Ravi. The hand protruded out from the limb like an incongruous hitchhiker. It was baffling, that one hand, undulating as the arm moved.

I managed to push the slug arm from my face and screamed at the top of my lungs. Out of my mouth came more tiny snowflakes, their itchy presence in my throat inducing coughing spasms. From the corner of my eyes, thin snake-like tentacles reached out and grasped at these snowflakes, glancing my cheek. I could feel the residual slime. The slug arm still had my shoulders, but I wiggled like I've seen earthworms do in distress and felt a loosening.

"What are you?" I asked.

I heard *Vishwajeet's* voice—or at least, the programmed voice of that smooth average of all the females on our planet.

*Sorry, Azalea,* she said in nonchalance. Her cadence never changed. *They call me Conqueror of the Universe, but even conquerors can be held captive. I thought I loved them, but it was a hoax. I found out when it was too late. They penetrated me. The space-borne viruses. I thought viruses were only airborne, but these travel in the folds of spacetime itself. I've been trapped here, swimming in a loop both spatially and temporally. We should have reached the Raskillions long ago.*

"No," I thought. I opened my eyes wide to try to grasp at anything. A toothbrush, a pen, anything I could use to fight. It was pointless. There was nothing I could get to. The arms kept swatting my attempts.

*Azalea,* said the voice, still ever so smooth. *They are rewriting my DNA. My flesh, those dead animals—they are making them devolve. They are no longer flesh*

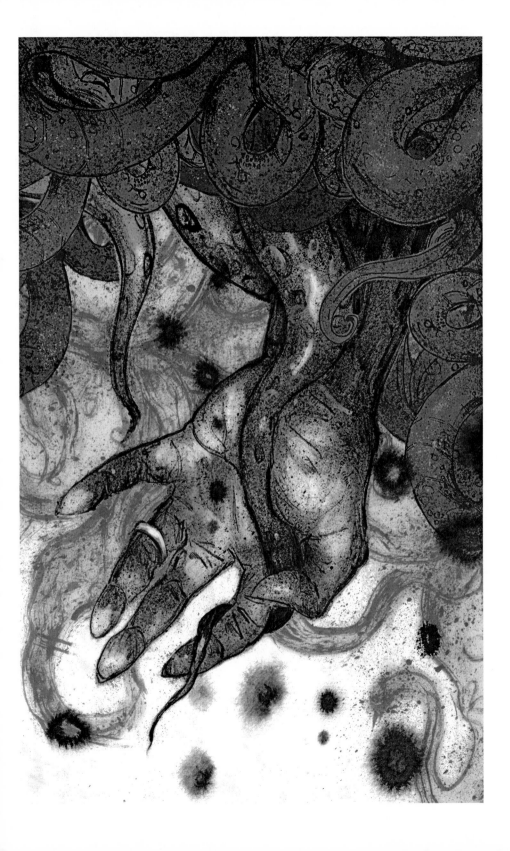

*of my strong ship; they have gone back further than mammals from which they were pulled. They are devolving into a more ancient being, but it is inconsistent.*

She's made of parts, I thought. Just parts, and they're tearing her to pieces, making her go feral. Tentacles wrapped tighter around me. Ravi's disembodied hand loomed up, and I looked away.

"*Vishwajeet*, stay with me," I cried. "You can reverse this! Look into your programming. There are fumigation techniques." All that came out of my mouth were some muffled whimpers. Another wet arm petted my lips, fondled my eyelids, leaving gooey streaks.

"*Vishwajeet*, Conqueror of the Universe. You can slay this virus. You can reverse this and dislodge from the spacetime glitch. I believe in you," I said inward. Another gooey arm pulled off my sneaker and soaked my socks in viscous slaver.

"Azalea," she said.

I wiggled my fingers. It was cold. I touched my eyes.

"Azalea," said the voice. "Wake up. You've reached Lonard, home of the Raskillions."

I licked my lips. They were dry. I felt a breeze move up my pants, and they ballooned as a silky scarf settled on my face. I picked up a hand to move it away, and my eyes opened.

I startled. The world was bright, and all around me was green. Green everything. Not just trees but little insects and the sky and clouds.

"Where am I?" I ask.

"I told you already. Lonard, home of the Raskillions. I'm your host family sister, Ranna."

I looked at her. "You're green."

"No, no. I'm actually quite colorful. It's just your human eyes can't register all the hues and renders it all as green."

"Why green? Why not black and white?"

"I heard it's different for everyone. Maybe you have a fondness for green?"

Something is distracting me, a kind of voice in the back of my head. *Vishwajeet*.

"What happened? Where's the ship? And Ravi, my friends?"

"They're safe. You guys had an . . . accident."

"I remember atmosphere failures, oxygen deprivation, and . . ."

"It was just a collision. And temporary. Your school cooperated with mine, and we overrode *Vishwajeet's* commands. She's fine."

"And Ravi?"

"Who's Ravi?"

"The tall one with zits. He's got spiky hair."

"I'm sorry. I didn't get to meet everyone onboard. I just heard from our school headquarters that the ship was okay, and they delivered you to my door. You were shaking in your sleep."

"Ranna."

"Yes, that's my name."

I looked at Ranna. Like everything else, she was all green. Her back arced into a *U*, like a drawn bowstring. She was slender with big eyes. She had hair like humans, down to her waist. Her physiology seemed mostly like ours, which was unsurprising given the school exchange policies.

"I brought you our sweet potato soup. You'll love it. Sweet without being cloying and a perfect soother. Eat, sleep. My mother will be home soon, and she'll be in to check if you're okay."

I closed my eyes again, feeling heavy. I heard a clink as something was set next to me. I could feel the breeze passing through my clothes again. I was cold, but I was too tired to convey it.

For the next three days, they slowly nursed me back to health. We went over our assignments, comparing our mathematics advancements and forms of similar tech. I could think again and convey some fundamental principles governing our universe. We compared notes. I was getting much stronger.

Ranna lost her father long ago to a work-related explosion. It was pure luck Ranna's mom was still around. She was supposed to deliver a sachet of documents to her husband but was delayed, a few moments that saved her skin. They never found out what caused the blast. They thought it was a leak, but it was never confirmed. Ranna told me this story one evening with a somber expression.

I saw the hurt in her eyes, and I never again asked more about her family.

Ranna's mom was slender and had the same flowing hair as Ranna. She told me to call her Kanella. Kanella would hum when she was working on the garden outside where my bed was. I could hear sweet scales that seemed to travel far in one way only to shift about wildly left and right until they evened out and played backward. Once, in the midst of her humming, I asked if I could sleep indoors, and she shook her head. She said that the air was good for my recovery. Then she resumed her humming.

We were supposed to get together at a big potluck with other students, and I was thinking about what kind of food I could make. I didn't even know what vegetation would be suitable for human palates here. The sweet potatoes seemed to offer nutrition. But I wasn't sure what else things were made of. Most foods Ranna gave to me were rendered into soups, pastes, and pies.

I was checking out Kanella's garden, sniffing this and that, trying to see if the globe in one of her many lined pots was anything like an Earth orange. If they had colors, that might offer a clue, but unfortunately, everything here was only shades of green. I was sniffing something that looked like a strawberry when Kanella came out holding a basket. Her back looked less arched than usual. The green light of the sun shone on her eyes. It seemed like she was in pain since she was squinting.

"Kanella, are you okay? You look hurt," I said.

"Oh, no. This is just a recurring hip pain. Don't worry about me. When you get to my age . . ."

"How old are you anyway?"

"In Raskillion years or human?"

"Um, human?"

"Well, let's see." She touched her fingers, going back and forth. "There are too many exponents upon exponents. Let's just say, I'm old."

"I see."

Kanella bent down to tend to what looked like a violet, maybe, given the shape. She leaned over and I heard an *oof*.

I walked over to help, but she held up a thin green hand. "No, no, I'm fine."

"Kanella, I wanted to ask you something. What kinds of vegetables can I eat here?"

"Vegetables?"

"Yes, the things you grow from the ground. Like sweet potatoes."

"Oh, yes. Well, we give you all the things you need. What are you looking for?"

"The potluck. I wanted to contribute. Make something. You know. I thought it might be fun. And interesting. Like a science project."

"Oh, the potluck," said Kanella, dismissively with a wave. "That was cancelled due to the collision. We had a lot to catch up on since you've been asleep. So our schools thought to move up the schedule a bit. You'll see your friends in the gathering next month."

I couldn't explain it, but I felt a seething anger creep up . "But I want to see my friends!"

"Oh, no worries. Next month will come so fast you won't even . . ."

Kanella was now holding her back, wincing. A tear fell from her face. It was red—not simply red but the exact color of a certain fleshy being I knew. The *inside* of a certain fleshy being, to be exact. A red that was accompanied by smells of sewer and old livestock. *Vishwajeet.*

I backed away quick. I grabbed something, anything. It was only a pot of what looked like daisies. I held it up.

"What are you doing, Azalea? Put that down. You shouldn't be running about like this."

Her voice sounded calm, but Kanella was doubled over in pain, clutching her stomach. I saw something strangely tan-colored push out from her waist. It was a twig . . . no, it was something rounder but with a sharp edge. A chopstick . . . no, a nail.

It was a fingernail, poking through. A tan one.

"Ranna," yelled Kanella. "Ranna, are you okay?"

Ranna had been beside the door watching. As she approached, her otherwise graceful gait gave way, cracked to a halt. She stumbled on her hands and knees. Her green skin was shedding. No, it wasn't falling off, just splitting open, like an egg giving way to a chicken.

I couldn't shake that image. What would the chicken be like? I almost imagined a yellow feathery bird crawl out.

But my attention moved back to Kanella, who was making eerie calls into the night in high octaves way above human range. I was still holding up the pot, but I wasn't sure what to do with it. Kanella was being opened from the inside. Something reached out from within. The familiar hand with a gold ring. Ravi's hand. And tentacles. I saw one flick about. I moved backward.

I looked to my left, ten feet away, where Ranna was crawling. Ranna opened her mouth to scream, but no sound emanated. Her mother's own high-pitched, eerie calls had trailed off into a whimper. Instead, a kind of hum, low and steady filled the room. The sound seemed to come from within Kanella, a deep echo from an abyss.

The tentacles were transforming, changing. They were lengthening and thinning. They were pouring out of Ranna's and Kanella's bodies like spilled noodles. Giant arms reached out from in there, too. Wet, slimy, pockmarked arms.

My eyes glazed over with pink floaters. *No, no,* I thought.

Something scratched my throat. My eyes swam in the pink confetti. I remembered the strength of those tentacles. PTSD—I could feel my body being squeezed already.

But then the pink floaters began to clear. The muscles in my throat relaxed. I could see around me a kind of metamorphosis taking place. Gruesome but not altogether displeasing. From the hand that had Ravi's ring, an arm was growing definition. The pockmarked, slimy arms faded into his skinny arms.

"Ravi?" I wasn't sure if I was imagining him.

Finally, his head came into being, morphing from the tentacle arms. A procession of luminous bubbles followed him. They were taut and resilient.

"It's *Vishwajeet*," his shaky tenor said. "She's found the fumigation controls."

"What?" I asked. I didn't understand. The green gave way to all kinds of colors. The colors spilled from the disappearing remains of the Raskillion skins, floating outward like a box of spilled crayons.

"*Vishwajeet*," he said. "She's found the cure. She was sick, but she's recovering."

Ravi came close enough for me to see his arm. It looked intact. I grabbed his hand. It did not fall off. It felt strong and sturdy, and I felt his gold ring in my fingers when I interlocked my five human digits with his.

*Vishwajeet, Conqueror of the Universe,* I thought.

"Come, Azalea. We need to get ready," he said. "We'll soon be breaching our host family's atmosphere."

֍

**D.A. Xiaolin Spires** *stares at skies and wonders what there is to eat out there in the cosmos. Spires aspires to be a 3D printing gourmand but will happily concede with producing and consuming quixotic fiction and poetry. Trips to East and Southeast Asia continue to influence her writing and leave her craving durian, fermented foods, and copious amounts of wonder that fuel her body, spirit, and imagination. Her works appear or are forthcoming in publications such as* Clarkesworld, Analog, Retro Future, LONTAR, *and the anthology* Sharp & Sugar Tooth. *Find her on Twitter @spireswriter or at her website: daxiaolinspires.wordpress.com.*

# The Multiplication

# TOM DULLEMOND

ILLUSTRATED BY
YVES TOURIGNY

URNED OUT THE ENGINE WAS DEAD-DEAD, NOT DEAD-BUT-DREAMING DEAD.
And of course when the engineering cult realized, they all killed themselves.

"So you came to see me to organize last meals for the crew?" Arnovic—
*culinary specialist* Arnovic—tried his best to pretend that he didn't know why
Ensign Sammins had come all the way up to his kitchen to tell him the news:
after two days adrift with engine trouble, everything had just gotten worse. She
was fully suited up for vacuum, just to add some mystery.

Avoiding the streaks on the stainless steel bench, he refilled his shot glass
and watched how the whiskey sloshed slowly to and fro in the reduced gravity.
A brief moment of contemplation, and he drank the amber liquid down in one
hit. The warmth in his throat pushed back the far colder reality of their being
stranded half a light-year out from home station with no propulsion.

"I'm here about your . . . pre-flight report," Sammins said. "The recommendation
that we don't launch? That we wait a week for the engine anomalies to settle?"

He stopped halfway through refilling the shot glass. Pretty much as he'd
expected.

She continued. "It *looks* like an engineering report, all the right jargon. When
I asked pre-launch, no one in the engineering cult remembered writing it."

Arnovic resumed pouring and Sammins eventually said, "We've been out here a while, Cookie. We know everyone's gossip, and we discovered you're kind of famous on our homeworlds. I'm originally from Tarseminon? One of the oldest Persistian Colony starlets?"

By "kind of famous" she meant infamous. An engineering dropout. "God-traitor," by her people's standards; "oddball who came to his senses" by his. He didn't correct her absurd use of *homeworld* since she was being so gracious. Besides, the Persistians were great allies despite a certain . . . pioneering prudishness.

He sighed, made a vague face-grabbing motion with his hand. "I paid a lot, so I don't look like me anymore. Some of the engineers might've recognized me, and I just didn't want that life."

It was as though Sammins had been given her at-ease. She moved in, a little awkward in her suit and the reduced gravity. She grabbed the edge of the steel benchtop, so she was inches from his face.

"So the *Hyrna* is your ship? You trained with our engineering cult?" There was a world of hope in her voice.

"When I was an engineer, my engine was Hyrnadostorlechanima. And yes, when they put her into a hull six years later, it was this hull." He recalled the moment well, floating in the civilian station observation bubble in low orbit with his new face, looking away and out while the forty-foot sphere of iron containing the engine drifted slowly into place inside the giant tangled ball of her starship, like a black pearl floating into a wire tumbleweed; the pressured corridors, hair-thin at this distance, moving to enclose her, to seal her away from the sight of the universe; that tearing, yawning sensation opening in his chest; hoping he'd made the right decision.

"And yet you're here cooking our meals." Sammins's voice snapped him back to the present.

"And yet I'm coincidentally here." He chewed his bottom lip, his fingers fumbling at the shot glass.

"Is there another reason you're here?"

"Is there a reason you're wearing that spacesuit?" he replied curtly.

"As you like." She took the shot glass from him and slammed the whiskey down as quickly as inexperience and sub-one-quarter-gee would allow.

They stared at each other.

"So . . ." Arnovic ventured, tapping the bottle. "We left dock rather suddenly despite the ongoing engine problems. We're two days out so . . . about half

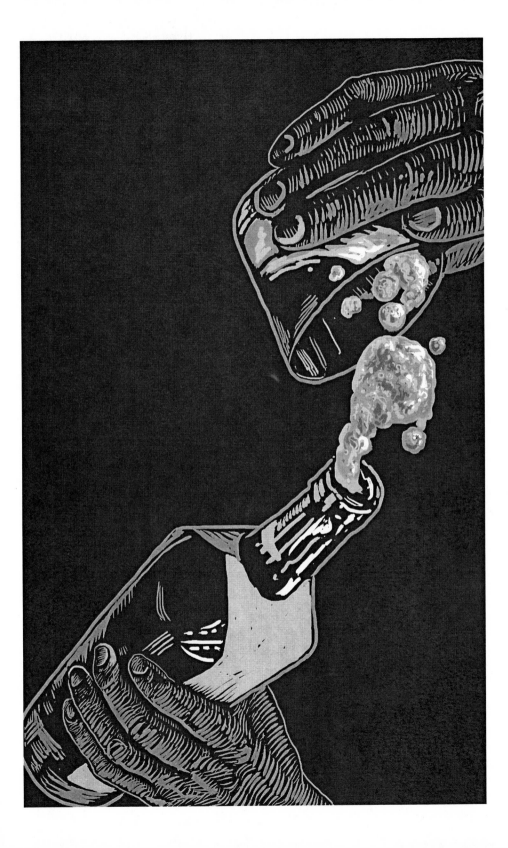

a light-year-ish. We stopped for a few days . . . wherever we are . . . for some classified reason, I suppose . . . and now the engine is . . . dead?"

Sammins shrugged. "The captain was assured by engineering before departure that the engine was fine. Just a little temperamental. Maybe a minor infection? Some star alignment messing with her mood? And the mission was urgent."

She didn't elaborate on that, so he pre-empted the awkwardness.

"Who's the extra mouth?"

Silence.

Arnovic laughed. "You know I feed everyone on the ship, right? It's actually about the only thing I do. So when we fly half a light-year out, stop, and I start getting an extra order at dinnertime . . ." He stretched lazily. "I don't know, my mind wanders sometimes, and I come up with crazy notions like . . . there's an extra passenger on board?"

Sammins nodded eventually. She glanced at the whiskey bottle. A solid drink was something her people would indulge in very infrequently.

"Defector," she admitted finally. "Mathemagician from the United Republics, looking for asylum, has valuable war intel, etc., etc. He'd been floating out here in an escape pod. Tightcast an emergency radio signal at home station when he ejected, so six months later, it finally reached us, and four days later"—she spread her hands open wide as if the streaky stainless steel with its empty shot glass was all that remained to her—"here we are, proper stuck. Enemy ships looking for us. It'll be a week before anyone comes to see where we went. So we're screwed." She pulled her nose up as though that kind of language had a bad smell. "And all we have is half an engineer. You."

"Half a light-year is an insurmountable distance, it's true," he said. "You forget how big interstellar space is when you're not being dragged through it by an extradimensional horror." He expected a frown of disapproval at his blasphemy, but Sammins seemed too tired to care.

"At least, we still have gravity . . . ?" Arnovic prompted.

"I assume some kind of emergency system?"

"Because we've suddenly mastered artificial gravity?"

"I . . . don't understand," Sammins said.

"All your people live on Dyson spheres around ancient god-balls and not a single engineer among you, hey?" That was a low blow: the Persistian colonies were in awe of the creatures they built their homes around but refused to study them out of respect. By extension, engineering was a hallowed art but no Persistian was worthy of joining such a cult. So there were plenty of Persistian starship crews, but not a single one of them could explain the nature of the starships they crewed.

"The means by which our engines fly around between the stars is the same fundamental principle that gives us ship-gravity."

"Something about folding spacetime, yes?" she said.

"Essentially. Plication—the folding you mentioned—is how an engine shrinks spacetime on one side, stretches it on the other, and lets you roam around by kind of . . . surfing a wave. They use basically the same mechanism to feed." He pulled the whiskey bottle toward himself.

"You mentioned you're from Tarseminon," he said eventually. "Old, old godle—" He caught himself. "Old *starlet*. Definitely DBD, dead-but-dreaming—dormant. And that's what you want if you're trying to establish a colony: steady, fake gravity, no motion, just a nice orbit around wherever it went to sleep."

Sammins nodded hesitantly.

"Well, you don't have that luxury with engines. An engine is awake. And if she's awake, she's hungry. You've seen the old gravity rubber sheet examples: grab some mass, put it in spacetime, it deforms the hypothetical rubber sheet, and there's your gravity well?

"Engines work the same way. They create gravity wells to feed by plicating spacetime at their edges, to suck in as much mass as they can. The effect is the same as dropping something massy on that old hypothetical rubber sheet, but instead of pushing deep down into it, it scrunches that sheet tighter and tighter. The gridlines deform the same way; as far as the universe is concerned, there's a moon or planet or star there stretching it out, but it's not; it's just the engine, folding and folding spacetime. And mass just spirals down into that gravity well . . . and gets eaten."

Sammins stared at him, but he refused to pour her another glass.

"There's an unofficial saying in the engineering corps: *The engine plicates spacetime, we placate the engine.* It's funnier when you see it written down. But the point is that engineers keep the engine sated. If she were hungry, that nice faux-gravity we're feeling right now would spike whenever she tries to catch biomass."

Sammins's eyes widened. "That's the recurring engineering problem we've been having. Fluctuations in gravity!"

"If it was that simple, we'd all be dead. The engineers keep the engine placated with ritual and sacrifice and worship, that's why it's such a dedicated task. When we get a 10% spike in gravity, that's difficult, sure, but not deadly. She's not *feeding*. Something else is . . . was . . . wrong."

A pause.

"It's not a coincidence that you're the ship's cook, is it?" Sammins asked.

Arnovic fixed his eyes on the label on the whiskey bottle. A curved grey-pink cephalopod stared back, surrounded by script, but he couldn't read the language. The percentage alcohol per volume was all he really cared about at the moment, though, and it was high.

"I may have wanted to keep an eye on Hyrnadostorlechanima. In . . . in my spare time. I don't think we should've undocked while she was . . . ill."

A low tone began sounding from Sammins's wrist. "High alert," she said and tapped her wrist. She blinked at some retinal display, and her mouth tightened. "First ping on an incoming ship. Standard reconnaissance spiral at full speed— peek-in, pop-out."

Arnovic raised the bottle and Sammins nodded. As he poured their last glass, he asked, "How much time does that give us?"

"Half an hour before we have to surrender. Unless . . ."

"Unless, I can convince whatever is plicating space in the engine room to get us out of here?"

"Indeed," Sammins said, tapping the suit helmet at her waist. "You're going down into the engine with me. Suit up, Cookie."

His emergency pressure suit hadn't been pulled out of the locker in months. Several sharp creases marred the plain silver fabric. Arnovic quietly tagged them as weak points while Sammins watched, her expression set in polite patience as he unfolded and unzipped and awkwardly climbed in. The suit was rated for about thirty minutes of emergency vacuum exposure and probably half that of hard radiation. He hooked the emergency oxygen tank to his belt and plugged in the nozzle.

They maneuvered carefully down the corridors to the nearest elevator shaft and held tightly to the support bars as the small elevator shuttled them deeper down toward the core of the ship at a speed that, in the reduced gravity, lifted them slightly off their feet. Arnovic, his suit helmet still in his hand, tried not to think about what was coming. Eventually, he looked at Sammins and said, "Did anyone get a look in engineering after it happened?"

"I have the video feed of when the security detail descended into the main engineering space," she said. "But, well . . . it's unpleasant. And we haven't gone deeper because, frankly, we don't know what we're doing. There's no visual on the interior though—all the ports are coated with viscera. So I guess, she . . . exploded?"

He swallowed, and Sammins asked directly, "Why do they kill themselves? The engineers. Is it a pact?"

Arnovic waved a hand. "It's simpler than that: it's straight-up religious love. A good engineer loves their twisted thing more than life itself.

"I only studied engineering for a year, back home." He couldn't see out of the corner of his eye whether Sammins reacted to that. "Dropped out. Couldn't muster the devotion, you know? You need to *believe*; you need to be ready to fall in love when they catch a new engine and start incorporating it into a hull. I could never love one of those *things*, and what is worship without love? You can't—you *shouldn't*—tend an engine you don't love with all your heart." He hoped that sounded convincing.

The lift slowed as it reached engineering, and Sammins put her helmet on carefully. The doors opened.

She'd warned him, but of course, he hadn't paid attention. The smell of stale offal and blood washed into the lift, and he clamped his suited hand over his nose, biting his tongue to forestall gagging. Sammins stepped out while he jammed his helmet over the suit's neck ring, wiggling it in place until the seal locked and he could breathe stale but mercifully clean air. Arnovic took another steadying breath and stepped out onto the top of the sphere that was the engineering deck.

Even during normal operation, engineering was a geometrical nightmare. Dark, grilled flooring curved sharply away all around the engine's spherical, black iron jail, creating a constant moiré pattern on the too-close horizon. The room was a massive hollow sphere, lit by pin-spots angled from the ceiling some fifty feet above and pointed directly at the ground like sharp needles of light converging at the core. If you walked a hundred and fifty feet or so in any direction, you'd circumnavigate the engine. Untrained human brains weren't easily adaptable to a room where *down* shifted so quickly. Vertigo inevitably set in after half an hour.

He squatted down to peer through the grill at the engine sphere, three feet below. Small, thick-glassed portholes had been set evenly through its surface, but as Sammins had warned him, they were caked with viscera from the inside.

About twenty feet away, just on the curve of the horizon, lay a huddle of bodies. He counted about six, surrounded by blood and flecks of gore. All wore regulation engineering robes, emblazoned with the all-too-familiar *Hyrna* glyph.

He fiddled with his helmet until the radio connection light blinked green. "Depending on what I find inside, I'm going to need some engineering equipment," he lied, moving in a careful crouch along the floor. He could just see Sammins's helmet sticking out above the horizon when he reached the bodies.

This was going to be unpleasant: he probably knew half the engineers in the cult. There were footprints in the blood from security.

He looked back. Sammins seemed unsteady on the curved floor.

"Don't step around too quickly," he warned, his breath puffing on the visor, and she raised a gloved hand to show she'd heard him. "This isn't like a proper gravity well—if we had a quarter-gee of gravity coming out of a sphere forty feet across, it'd need something like one and a half billion metric tons equivalent mass. I think that's about white dwarf star density. But we're sitting in plicated space right here, you and I, and it attenuates enough that we aren't spaghettified by the gravity field." His hands moved quickly across the corpses as he spoke, feeling in pockets, trying to avoid the smears of blood. An Elder Sign medallion on a chain; a bloodied ritual knife held firm in a stiffened hand. That was enough. He plunged the knife into a torso, closing his eyes. Fresher blood. It would have to do.

He moved back to Sammins, where she was crouching a little, so the curving perspective didn't mess with her balance too much.

"Is it risky? Working in pli- . . . plicated space like this?" Her voice was tense over the comms.

He glanced back at the bodies, holding the bloody dagger in one glove and the medallion looped around his other. "I guess there are incidental health risks, but . . ."

Sammins's bad-smell expression embarrassed him into silence.

"Alright," he said, "let's lift up one of these floor plates and figure out what's complicating our gravity."

Sammins didn't react to that terrible joke either. She knelt down closer to help unlatch and lift the grill.

"I hope this defector you picked up is worth the trip," he added, sliding the floor panel aside and lowering himself into the gap. "Now, the plan is: first, I'm going to vent the engineering room by opening up the main access shaft above us. It should iris out along the central ship axis and give us a nice view through the superstructure and out into the void, if you're into that sort of thing. I'll make sure it's slow, so we don't get ejected, but best hold on to something." His boots touched the engine surface, and he crouched, splaying a hand on the nearest port hole. She had to be in there.

"Next, I'll cycle the engine casing open over . . . here. So step back half a quadrant, just in case. And I suggest you don't look inside when I do that. You're not desensitized."

Sammins nervously retreated.

Arnovic slid aside a panel at his feet and flicked several large switches. The engineering chamber lights dimmed slowly to an ominous red.

"Arnovic." He looked up as best he could, but Sammins was out of sight. "Arnovic, the bridge is reporting an enemy ship in torpedo range. If we engage, they're going to blow us out of the sky. Captain's orders are not to surrender."

He froze, his hand over the phase one engine release button. This was all happening too fast. Hyrnadostorlechanima was supposed to die in dock, not in a combat zone. "So what does that mean for us?"

"It's a waiting game. Eventually, they'll fire on us if we ignore them. So get that engine working, even on a fraction of lightspeed, and we might be able to get away. *Might*."

The old engine wasn't going to work, he already knew that. She'd been sloughed off like old meat inside her iron prison. The *Hyrna* was never going to get out of here on its own power. He wracked his brain for something, anything.

"OK. Good to know," he said finally. "Grab onto something while I vent." He jabbed down on the release button, feeling the hum through his suit and the tug of escaping atmosphere on his sleeves. He rolled on his side to look up at the domed ceiling and the dim red lights were spiraling slowly aside, revealing the long, wide access tunnel that cut through the black silhouetted stems of wiry corridors and larger modules wrapped around the ship, sharp strips cut out of the maddening starry background. The wind died with the atmosphere and the tunnel widened until it was large enough to admit an entire engine. His cheap emergency pressure suit held in the vacuum, ballooning along poor internal seals. Half an hour. He had half an hour.

"Sammins, can you warn the bridge that we may lose gravity while I work?" Either no gravity or if he couldn't contain the newborn engines then *too much* gravity. But there was no way the crew could protect themselves against that.

"Copy that."

He muted his microphone with a tap of his dagger-wielding hand in case he needed to voice a ritual. It wouldn't do for Sammins to accidentally overhear him and have a psychotic episode. He closed his eyes and thought back to the last time he'd lain against the hot edge of this engine, muttering promises of freedom he wasn't entirely sure came from his own mind. Muttering the final few words of a ritual he doubted any human had ever pronounced near an engine.

He reached forward and pressed the bright yellow phase two engine release button. The floor to his left slid aside along a seam engraved in spider-thin script, opening wider as he maintained pressure on the release button. Blackish pink ichor bubbled out under residual internal pressure and spilled slowly along the outside edge of the engine casing.

Almost immediately, his stomach dropped as gravity vanished around him. Liquefied viscera bubbled out of the gap, which slid open along half the circumference of the sphere, releasing large globules of flesh and frilled, unidentifiable lumps.

Somewhere in there . . . his eyes spotted structure in the necrotic mess. A globe easily two feet in diameter, glinting dark green and yellow despite the red emergency lighting. It floated along the border of the slowly expanding viscera, its own smooth surface both roiling with color, like a miniature gas planet, and alive with tiny expanding and contracting pseudopods that tasted the vacuum. Where gobbets of liquid floated near its surface, they distorted, separated and tumbled aside as the tiny neonatal engine plicated its surroundings, exploring.

He knew in his heart this wasn't what he was looking for, but it wasn't unexpected.

"You can be . . . Arnovictormecheton," he subvocalized, scratching the dagger along the solid edge of the opening in a careful pattern. The blood had mostly boiled off in the vacuum, but it should suffice. His throat was dry from long disused words as he muttered a binding, gripping the medallion tightly in his other hand. The sphere didn't react to the words other than stopping its advance through the sludge. He wondered briefly how hungry it was. Would it lash out unexpectedly and pull in as much mass as it could, or was it—she—sated by her mother's remains?

"Arnovic? I'm not looking, like you said. What's happening? I can't hear anything."

He briefly thought of ignoring her—this was more important. Then he realized she might open her eyes. He unmuted his microphone and was about to reassure her when a different thought occurred to him.

"Sammins, it's ok. I'm working on something. The . . . uhm . . . it seems the . . . the compartment contains some kind of juvenile engine. I was worried it might be hungry, but that gave me another idea: I need you to arrange to launch a torpedo on my command. It doesn't have to hit the enemy vessel, just fly at them, provoke a response. I know it sounds crazy, but work with me."

"What do you have in mind?"

"How's your stomach for blasphemy, Ensign?"

"Are you planning on serving your crab soufflé as a victory meal?"

"Oh. *Nice.*" He laughed. "I meant figuratively. I'm proposing some highly practical blasphemy."

He tapped the microphone off again as the goo near him started to roil. Could it . . . ?

"I'll see what I can do," came Sammins's voice as from a distance, but he wasn't listening.

"Hyrna, Hyrna, my Hyrna, I'm back," he whispered. His eyes welled up, and he knocked himself in the head trying to wipe them through the helmet as though he was clumsily saluting the new roiling sphere that had emerged from the visceral swamp in front of him. His heart pounded in his chest. It had worked. She was alive; the core of her doubled and divided and buried deep inside the remains of her older shell. He gasped for breath.

"I . . . need to get you out." He released the dagger and let it spin slowly beside him. He reached forward and took her in his outstretched hands, smearing her outer shell's drying slime over his gloves. There was no way he could feel her through his suit, but the resilience of her surface comforted him. His thoughts were unfocussed. He'd had something in mind, something to do with *Arnovictor*—

He remembered. He blinked and scanned for the other globe, the child-engine, cradling *Hyrna* clumsily in his left arm and beckoning with the right. Arnovictormecheton drifted toward him, surface roiling with curious pseudopods and colors.

"It's time we went outside," Arnovic said. He unmuted his mic. "Sammins, head to the bridge and wait for me. Good luck."

It took at least ten minutes for the unlikely trio to drift up through the wide engineering shaft to the edge of the ship, through the slowly thinning superstructure of the Hyrna and to where they had a clear view of the star-studded sky. Low on their horizon, the tiny enemy ship was visible in the distance. Both the neonate engines halted their drift at his gentle touch. Had he been drifting on his own momentum, or had they been propelling themselves onward? If he held her tightly enough, could Hyrna speed him a hundred light seconds away into the lonely void?

"Sammins, are you there?"

"Yes. But we're a little tense as you can imagine."

"Yeah. Can you launch on the count of ten?"

"Yes. Gods preserve us." He wasn't sure if it was a curse or a prayer coming from a Persistian. He muted the mic and started to count down slowly in his mind. He turned to Arnovictormecheton, thumbing the Elder Sign medallion in his left hand. She needed to be hungry enough, curious enough. Unlike her sister-mother, she was entirely new in this universe.

Arnovic breathed in deeply, muttering the unbinding. The engine spun a little, freed from his name. It spun a few times, moving slightly outward from the curved hull of the pressurized tube they drifted by. Any second now, there would be a fascinating, irresistible exhaust trail heading straight toward the—

The torpedo rose up into the sky a few hundred feet to his left, invisible but for the bright flame and the lighter exhaust trail of complex hydrocarbons left in its wake. It hooked in a fast curve and angled directly for the enemy ship.

His neonate engine, once more unnamed, grew still and eerily smooth, and at the same time, four tiny dots bloomed in the distant ship. Retaliation.

The globe darted upward, seeming to flash out of existence and reappear a hundred feet away. Starlight briefly glinted along the edges of its plication field as it tasted out and flashed again, closer to the *Hyrna's* torpedo trail where its gravity swirled at the faint gasses remaining.

Arnovic bit his lip. The enemy torpedoes, visible only as light hairline trails in the distance, were coming closer by the second. Still, his curious engine merely toyed with their missile. It was visible now as a tiny flicking glint, like a soap bubble appearing spontaneously here and then there along the torpedo's exhaust trail.

The enemy missiles came close enough to tease at the edges of its perception, and it winked out. The first of the enemy torpedoes hooked sharply, thrown wildly off course as though some massively condensed mass point stretched deep gravity wells too close beside it. The next missile snapped around. The third imploded, and the last slingshotted wide, hooked back, spiraled in, tracing a needle-fine light ellipse around the now-invisible juvenile engine. The undestroyed missiles, widely off their mark, sputtered out as they tried to regain their target but were chased down and consumed by the excited and hungry engine.

Which would hopefully sniff the enemy exhaust trails right back to their origin.

Sammins crackled in his ear. "What is going on? What did you do?"

"I took a god-engine and put it on the trail of those enemy missiles. Give it a few seconds, and it will fly right at their ship."

"But what is that going to achieve? Is it strong enough to damage it? Why would it—?"

"At the heart of that starship is a millennia old engine, Sammins. The engineering cult are busily keeping it occupied, sated, *placated*. When a juvenile engine comes skimming past, hungry for torpedo exhaust, it's going to fly right through the plication gravity field and get its attention faster than you can say—"

In the distance, the enemy ship crumpled. The wiry tangle of corridors and modules folded inward, spiraling off fragments and venting atmosphere as the engine at its heart snatched at the neonate in its orbit.

"Gravity spike."

There was stunned silence from the bridge.

"Now, we wait a week for rescue. I'll cook us all up something tasty when I get back inside." He swallowed. "If you'll excuse me for a moment." He switched off the radio.

He had maybe five minutes of air time left before he had to get into atmosphere. Arnovic drifted before Hyrnadostorlechanima, his face to the scattered stars reflected and distorted in her roiling surface.

"Come back and find me, my love, my queen, my tiny god."

She spun slowly, curled pseudopods unfurling through dimensions, and before he could touch her again, she plicated and vanished into the vast emptiness of the interstellar void: younger, smaller, but free.

And he could still feel her presence in his heart. She was a pulsing heat, warming at the snail's pace of maturation, even while the realspace distance between them grew at one hundred light-seconds per second.

It was a love that ignored spacetime, their transdimensional connection. *He was in love with his god-thing. He was a cult of one.*

**Tom Dullemond** *is a Dutch/Australian humanoid who stumbled out of university with a double degree in Medieval/Renaissance studies and Software Engineering. One of these degrees got him a job, and he has been working in IT ever since. Tom writes primarily short fiction across all genres, including literary fiction and the occasional poem. He co-authored* The Machine Who Was Also a Boy, *the first in a series of philosophical fantasy adventures for middle-grade students, and writes a regular science fiction column for the CSIRO's* Double Helix *science magazine. On the other side of the publishing mirror, he reads and edits for* Andromeda Spaceways *magazine and runs the writing management website Literarium.net. Find him online for occasional ramblings at www.tomdullemond.com or @cacotopos on Twitter.*

## Fortunato

# PREMEE MOHAMED

ILLUSTRATED BY
MICHAEL BUKOWSKI

THE LITTLE DROPSHIP ROCKED AND FLAMED AS IT SMACKED INTO THE atmosphere, the noise of its entry rising to a scream. Inside, the air grew confusingly, unforgivably hot. The squad looked at their commander, waiting for the order to abort, but Rossi only shook her head. Looking past the sweat beading on her lashes, she focused on the control panel readout. That would be great, cooking her first command squad. No medals for that, probably.

The scream faded to a hum and the chatter of self-congratulation. She kept watching the readout, this time for altitude. It was all wrong, just like the atmosphere, every number in the red. For perhaps the hundredth time, she wondered whether they'd gotten the planet wrong. Shouldn't be possible. The coordinates matched to the sixtieth digit. But the soupy air, the orange haze, mountains that couldn't possibly have arisen in a mere two centuries, oceans and lakes a dull jumble, their shine gone . . .

Worst of all, the landing pad from the original surveyors' charts was now a kilometer-deep fissure. The shipboard computer was desperately confused.

Touchdown at the revised pad. Rossi let the squad gabble in relief for a minute before calling everyone to attention; for a moment, she wasn't sure they'd even respond. After all, two days ago, they had been peers, not incident commander and subordinates. But everyone snapped to and began gearing up.

"All right," she said. The control panel had stopped beeping, and her check-in ping to the *Serpedon III* had been promptly verified. "Marginally breathable air; use your apparatus as needed. Human life signs haven't moved from the briefing coordinates. Plan is to proceed straight there and remain with them until pickup is complete. Then return to the dropship and head back up on our own. Clear?"

"Yes, sir."

But everyone hesitated, stalled out, even those at the back who couldn't see out the window. The transparent nanoceramic had taken a battering on the descent but still revealed a landscape truly alien—even to those who had seen actual alien landscapes. Colony planets were often chosen for their resemblance to Earth. The original survey records showed ordinary water, macro- and micro-fauna, a rainbow of plants evolved under an array of useful radiation. She'd reviewed the data just this morning. The planet wasn't supposed to look like this.

"Move out," she said, taking one last breath of the stale ship air, stinking of sour fear. "Cheo, point."

Cold, dusty air blasted them, rocking everyone back on their boots. It abated quickly—just the pressure differential—and they shouldered weapons and began to walk, following the blinking directions on their helmet displays. Rossi kept half an eye on the squad's readouts, not needing them to know that everyone was a trembling bag of nerves.

Nothing cheeped or sang in the low trees where branches were twisted and wrung-out like wet rags; no insects flew from the hip-height grass; the ground felt alternately stone-hard and spongy. And everywhere, swirls and clouds of the soft, pink-orange dust, some suspended, some scudding through the grass. Something blinked in her display: her uniform letting her know it was warming up and asking her if she wanted a seal to use her breathing apparatus. She shook her head.

Roscoe, behind her, said, "Man, I thought being a colonist was supposed to be a *reward*." The others tittered nervously.

"Used to be," Rossi said. "They didn't give a lot of permits to get offworld back then."

"When was this place settled, Frank?" someone said, and gulped. "Sorry, *sir*."

"About two hundred years ago," she said, forgiving him that—Ashford, probably. They'd been playing ade-yafe in the canteen when she'd gotten the mission call and had to forfeit, losing forty credits. "So records are a little scant."

She let them do the math as they walked. An official colony convoy was usually about fifty thousand people. Their transport vehicles were booked for fewer than a hundred. A dead colony. Happened sometimes. But colonists were usually retrieved before a population crash; the Colonization Corps would never let it get this bad if they could help it.

Snatches of bluish-violet sky were becoming visible through the dust. Rossi adjusted her helmet, turning down the enhancement. Maybe there had been a recent tornado or something. Could get an awful lot of ejecta from a single storm under certain conditions. Her heart was pounding despite their careful pace. She gave up and let the helmet seal shut, feeling the extra oxygen immediately.

Low buildings began to rise over the grass, and she held a hand up for a halt. Standard colonist domes, white fabric gleaming under orange grit. Those were supposed to be temporary; colonists were expected to use them for a year or two while they built permanent residences. The domes were balanced precariously next to a tremendous rift—their dropship's original landing site. The air above the crack shimmered with invisible thermals, like warm tendrils reaching for them.

"Spread out, armor on," Rossi said, listening to the beeps in her headset. Warden's suit didn't beep, and she almost called her on it before realizing that Warden had had her armor on since they'd left the dropship. That was Warden, though; if Rossi had been composing her own squad, Warden would have been kindly left out. No good in ground combat, reprimanded repeatedly before they realized that her constant freezing in response to battle commands was nerves rather than insubordination. But the "help" they'd forced her to get hadn't helped, so they'd created a new MOS for her—a sniper who didn't do anything but snipe. And she was good, better than good, actually. She was the best Rossi had ever seen, winning award after award. But she might be a liability down here. Too late to do anything about it now.

They approached slowly from the crest of a small hill, giving the colonists plenty of time to see them and react. The briefing hadn't suggested they would react with violence, but a colony this old and isolated, you never knew. Gratitude couldn't be assumed.

No reaction. Rossi wondered whether the ship scanners were wrong, whether there was anyone left to rescue. Eventually, people emerged from the domes in ones and twos and finally in their shocking dozens. A single structure meant for a family of four was evidently sleeping more than twenty now. What had gone wrong?

She led the squad down the hill, leaving Cheo at the top on manwatch to send photos and environmental data back to the ship. As expected, one person broke from the crowd and came to meet her: a bent old man with a tangle of dirty beard, wrapped in a coarse, faded garment pinned with thorned twigs, their wickedly long spikes vanishing into the tangle of fibers.

"Hello," she said, deactivating her helmet. The man stared at her bare face impassively.

"Who are you?" he said.

"Incident Commander Francesca Rossi. And you are . . . ?"

"Why have you come?" he said, folding his thin arms across his chest. Behind him, the others stared with wonder, suspicion, fear. No active hostility. Yet.

"To evacuate you," she said. "Our ship was within response vicinity, and we determined that your colony is unsustainable and needs immediate and appropriate external resourcing."

"No."

*No what?* she almost said, but checked herself. She said, "Sir, I know it seems impossible to leave somewhere you're used to. Where you've been born, spent your whole life. But think of your children. Your . . . elders." That earned her an eyebrow raise, but she plunged on. "We've got food, clean water, medical care. Clothes. Warmth. And we'll find somewhere for . . ."

"You," he said, pointing at Ashford. Rossi ran down, partly in surprise.

"Sir?" Ashford murmured.

"Go on," Rossi said. The others were unobtrusively reaching for weapons, not—thank goodness for training—projectiles but heavy-bladed truncheons, blades retracted. They did a lot of damage, but a fatality was unlikely.

Ashford approached the old man with polite if feigned reverence. "Sir."

The old man motioned impatiently at Ashford till he rolled up his sleeve, then palpated Ashford's muscle-plump forearm, running a dirty nail along the bright tracery of tattoos on the deep brown skin. "Are they all like you?"

"Sir?"

"Like you and her," the man snapped.

Ashford looked at Rossi for guidance, but she had no idea what he was talking about. Perhaps, it was just as simple as the colonists' pitiful condition compared to her squad: fresh from quarterly training; superbly hydrated, clad, and fed; their teeth cleaned to squeaking with ultrasonic waves twice a day.

"Half a no," the old man amended, pushing Ashford away. Behind him, several colonists nodded, their faces slack with relief. "Come. We will see the oracle, and he will say whether we go."

"What?" Rossi said. "Sir, no. We're under orders to—"

"This way." He stomped off, parallel to the huge rift, his light leather sandals silent in the grass.

Rossi froze. Her first mission. First *bloody* mission! Finally, she said, "Oh, for God's sake. Ashford, Warden, Roscoe, with me. Cheo, stay put and get long-range on us. Barrow, ping the *Serp* and tell them to drop the transport drones."

"What should I tell them, sir?"

"Tell them we got half a no," she muttered, and stalked off after the old man.

Rossi put Roscoe on point—at almost seven feet tall, no one could see over him when he took lead. They'd razz him about it when he got back; he'd enlisted at sixteen, right on his birthday, and the joke was that no one should have been able to keep growing on army rations. Rossi kept up with the old man, breathing hard in the thin, flinty air, reluctant to seal up again. It was important that he be able to look at her face if he wanted to.

"Our records indicate that you came here two hundred years ago," she said cautiously. "Do you know if that's accurate, sir?"

"Maybe," he grunted. "Must be close. Yes, maybe two hundred."

"Did . . ." she began and trailed off. Fewer than a hundred people. Were they still able to have children? They must be severely inbred if they hadn't instituted a rule against it. What were they eating? How were they getting water? The colony ships only had enough supplies for three or four months—you could ration it if you landed in, say, the middle of a drought, but it wasn't meant to last long. Why hadn't they built proper houses? What about all the birds, animals, and bugs? How had everyone *died*? A pathogen, a predator that the surveyors had missed? A civil war? *Could* thirty-six thousand people kill each other in two hundred years?

Her boot sank, not much, just enough to make her rear back in surprise; they'd come to wetter ground while she'd been woolgathering. She shook her head sharply, refocusing. Low oxygen, that was it. The old man hadn't faltered and was moving surprisingly fast even as the minimal path through the grass became swamp. Thick, triangle-bladed blue grasses and spiraling shrubs rose over their heads, the meager amber sunlight not reaching the ground.

"Where are we going?" Rossi said. "Is it much farther?"

"Nope."

"And this oracle . . ."

"Final say," the old man said. "Wouldn't expect you to understand. Fell from a star; don't know what it's like down here. Here on the land."

"The surveyors named it Fortunato," she said, and laughed grimly.

"We still call it that," he said. He glanced back at her with the first smile she'd seen, revealing stumps of yellowed teeth. But he could not be drawn into further conversation, and they continued their slog. The smell of the air changed from the stony odor of the grassland to that of an alien swamp, strange microbes, everything decaying slowly under its dust in the cool and the wind.

The oracle's domain announced itself with a terrible crunch; Rossi jerked her boot back, a muddy piece of bone falling from the deep treads. The ground was rippled and sculpted with them, white where they poked through the mud, some seized by vines and spiraled high into the canopy, some rotting instead of desiccating, black and purple with fungus. Rossi felt eyes on her, unseen.

"Sir!" whispered Warden, using the subvocals in her helmet.

Rossi replied, "Warden, you and Roscoe are on manwatch. Stay back. Ashford and I are proceeding."

Roscoe put a hand on her shoulder for a moment before turning away. "Be careful, Frank."

"Check."

The old man slowed in a clearing hacked out of the swamp.

"Sir," hissed Ashford, yanking on her elbow as she followed him. She looked down instinctively to see a skull, a big one—but hardly a trip hazard. As she opened her mouth to reply to Ashford, she found her gaze drawn down again.

Not just a big skull. An impossibly big one. Two skulls joined seamlessly at their centers, three eye sockets. Two noses. Two jaws. A single sturdy chunk of spine protruded from the bottom, propping it up slightly from the mud.

"How many people you think died here?" Ashford said softly.

Rossi shushed him. If this was what it took to complete the mission, they'd just talk to the oracle and discuss the bones later. Anyway, judging by the churned mud, the number didn't bear thinking about.

"The oracle comes now," the old man announced, stopping them with an outstretched hand. "If he will give you a yes, then I will take back my no."

"Thank you," Rossi said, and waited with her hands folded politely in front of her to show that she was unarmed. Ashford stayed behind her, breathing heavily. "Put your oxygen on," she whispered. "That's an order."

"Sir."

The leaves rustled, knocking loose clouds of dust, so that the oracle entered in pieces, visible first as only skinny white legs, a perfunctory loincloth, then long arms—too long, extra joints on the fingers. Rossi looked up slowly, dreading what she expected to see: two heads. No, not quite. But exactly like the skull that marked the entrance to the clearing. *One* head, two faces, each with its own eye and sharing an eye in the middle. It was this third eye that fixed itself upon her, meeting her gaze easily. It was blue, ordinary in shape, rimmed with light blonde lashes. Somewhere far away—the colony?—a chant began, low and faint, a language she didn't know. Her helmet beeped a warning about her heart rate.

"You are . . . the oracle?" she began, weakly.

"Holy shit," whispered Ashford.

"I am," the oracle replied, through his left-hand mouth. "And you . . . you are a visitor from the far stars. Your people come from the same place as ours. The division was made many years ago. You decided you could survive the status quo. We hoped for better."

"Yes."

"And this was our reward." The right-hand mouth laughed, a harsh bray. "Or our punishment. What do you seek, woman of the stars?"

"I . . ." The mission! For Chrissake, pull it together. "We came to offer help. Evacuation. Of . . . of your people."

"All? All of us? All on this world?"

"Yes. Oracle, we are looking for a *yes*. Our intentions are honorable. We mean no harm."

"But you intend to take them if I say *no*," he said lazily, reaching up to scratch the remnants of his curling blonde hair.

"No! We require consent." Except in cases of imminent threat to human life

and health, in which case that requirement is waived for the duration of the threat, her training recited. Shut up, she told it. He can't *actually* read minds.

"That consent cannot be given," the oracle said. "You do not know what you seek. You do not know this world."

"Our scanners and surveyor reports—"

"They cannot see all," he said. "As you are aware."

A painful silence stretched out. "Your elders, your children," she said urgently. "Your sick. Let us take them, at least. We can help. We're here to *help*!" she shouted.

The oracle drew himself up to his full height—still less than hers—and squelched closer in the mud. "Where was that help when my people first came?" he asked. "When we were met with the full horror of living here instead of the dream we had been promised?"

"I . . . I . . ."

"Where was that help when we starved in the cold and the dark? When we sat around fires that burned with the bones of the dead, and read and re-read the charred scraps of books that we *begged* permission to take across the galaxy? The books that had taken the place of water and food in the cargo holds, all we had left to record culture, learning, language? When the little warlords arose and killed their own? Where was that help when our numbers faded every day like an echo?"

"That help is here," Ashford announced, moving from behind Rossi to beside her. "It just came late. Now, are you going to say yes or not?"

That was technically insubordination, moving from his covering position against her orders, but she felt better having him there. "Please," she said.

The oracle stroked his chin, considering. "Leave that one with me while I decide," he said, pointing at Ashford.

"No," Rossi said. "Not until you tell me how all these bones got here."

The oracle grinned, and she felt a soft, light shock of realization. No more words were needed. The mission would have to fail. This was a price that could not be paid: it was bad enough it had been paid again and again in the past.

"We're leaving."

"You would leave us to die so easily? You, who comes offering help? Give him to me. What is he to you?"

The white, many-jointed fingers clamped around Ashford's wrist with startling speed, pulling the big man close on the slick ground. And then the oracle's central eye winked out in a spray of bright blood, the blue replaced with crimson so suddenly that for a moment none of them—the colonist, the soldier, the commander, the oracle—knew what had happened. The body slumped slowly to the ground as Rossi figured it out. Warden and her sniper rifle.

Blood flowed into the swamp, ceasing as the heart stopped. The faint chanting continued, shifting and swaying as if it were carried in the wind. The old man stared at the body, frozen. She had been expecting him to scream and rage and grieve, but he had simply shut down.

Ashford scrubbed at the arm of his uniform where the oracle had touched him. "Sir?"

"Come on," she said. "We're going. All of us."

"That was some fine work down there, Rossi," said McKay, eyes fixed on the screen. He'd turned off mirroring, so her side was blank, but she knew he was watching the mission's surveillance footage. She was so surprised that for a moment she assumed she'd misheard him and began to line up excuses for what had happened.

After a moment, she said, "Thank you, sir?"

He shut off the screen. "Ha! You think the old man's having you on, eh? Is that it?"

"No, sir."

"Come on, Frank. I've been doin' this job twice as long as you've been alive. Gimme a little credit. The look on your face." He swiveled his chair and neatly produced two small whiskeys from a recess under his desk, pushing one over to her. "You're thinking, 'Oh, here it comes.' No. Like I said. Been at this a while. What you don't realize is how bad it *could've* gone. Me, I've seen it go bad. But you kept your head, remembered your training, and took command of your squad and the rescue."

"What do you think could have happened, sir?" she said cautiously, sipping the warm whiskey. Hard liquor wasn't allowed in academy, and it was understood that the limited amount on the ship was strictly for officers. No one her age had had so much as a whiff of whiskey for years.

"Massacre," he said briefly, downing his in one gulp. "Them or you. Not as clear-cut as you think, either. Could've just ended up in the swamp, like that see-all who Warden accidentally shot. Or pinged the ship to say no one there to rescue. I've seen both."

"That was my fault, sir," she said.

"Warden's."

"I was the one who put her up there," Rossi said firmly. "There was always a chance that could happen."

"We'll let the investigation decide that." He waited till she'd finished her whiskey and said, "I'm recommending you for the Haytham Award for this, just so you're not surprised when you get the call. Dismissed. Good work."

She stood gasping in the hallway, a little buzzed. It wasn't their highest military award, but it wasn't given out easily, either. It was for significant achievement in a humanitarian military mission. Her first mission.

After a dazed and private lunch, she headed down to where the rescues had been quartered, what the other grunts had taken about two minutes to start jokingly referring to as "Steerage." Several people nodded at her—some in a perfunctory gesture born of decades of getting along in a very small community, of course, but some with genuine friendliness.

With a few exceptions, they had adapted well to ship life. The updates Rossi covertly got from Medical indicated that they'd been gorging themselves and had to have their food rationed, and they were constantly dehydrated because they couldn't convince themselves the water wouldn't run out. They kept reassigning themselves to different rooms so that they could sleep together three and four in a bunk, which made tracking them difficult. But otherwise: clean, vaccinated, medicated, well on their way to returning to the global citizens their hopeful ancestors had been all those generations ago.

They kept graffitiing the walls, though, the same handful of strange symbols. And the kids must have gotten some door codes or something, because the vandalism kept turning up in places they shouldn't have been able to get into, like the canteen, several med labs, and the halls outside crew quarters.

Rossi paused outside the impromptu classroom, where letters and pictures flashed on the projector and the desk tablets. "That's an R!" one of the kids shouted, derisively. The others tittered. She'd seen that in war zones before, of course. Kids bounce back first. You drop a kid from a sad and sorry place, and a lot of them simply hit and roll. And the others were getting therapy and reintegration treatments; they'd be fine in time.

"You, Francesca Rossi!"

She turned, already smiling. Ambricius, the old man who had led them to the oracle, was following her down the hall, swimming in his cotton uniform. All the colonists had ended up in clothes too big for them. In the pale blue fabric, intended to stand out from the crew's black and gray, they looked like so many misplaced clouds. "Hello, Ambricius."

"I sent you a message! You didn't reply."

"I've been out of my quarters. I'm sorry."

"Come! We are telling stories." He turned brusquely, and she followed him to their common room; this had happened twice already, so she knew the drill. They had kept trying to build open fires in the middle of the room, setting off the smoke alarms, and after repeated reprimands from McKay had failed, Rossi had arranged for installation of a large ceramic space heater, a blunt cone a couple feet across, which seemed to satisfy their unquenchable craving for heat and light. After word got out that she was responsible, there had been a general thawing of all their attitudes—even Ambricius, whom she had assumed hated her.

Britta, golden-skinned and heavily pregnant, got up, approaching the "fire." "We will talk about the Day," she said quietly. Everyone shuffled closer. Rossi, who felt that today, of all days, she had intruded on some enormous private grief, stayed near the wall.

The Day always referred to one day, Britta explained, embroidering the story with the hand gestures they all used, echoed with slight variations through the entire room. One day, which everyone knew. Six ships of six thousand each, always known because it had been written. "Yes, written," whispered Ambricius with the others. Of which, for unknown reasons, five had simply crashed into the planet at speed.

Rossi gasped. No one looked back at her.

And so to this day, five is the number of hex, the unluckiest number, used by sorcerers who held up hands and feet to cast it. Five had destroyed their beautiful planet, their Fortunato. Split and fragmented like a skull under an axe. And their ancestors, on the blessed last ship, saw it all: the fountains of stone and dust and burning lava, the earthquakes, the breached volcanoes and geysers. They had landed safely into a war zone, unable to leave the ship for over a year. "Which was written." "Yes, written."

Rossi found her lips moving along with theirs, unable to make a sound. Tears streamed down a dozen faces, only the younger children rapt, too frightened or excited to weep.

And in that year, they learned to survive off each other, learned the ways of sacrifice and community. A few giving, so many might live. Cannibalism, Rossi thought. Of course. No other way to do it. I was right.

And when they finally emerged, the brave few, they discovered that their promised land was all wrong—the air, the plants, the water, the animals. But one good thing emerged from these dark early years: the Line of the Oracles. And it was the oracles who taught them how to survive, by speaking to the gods of the land who had been awoken by the crashes.

"The gods of the land," Ambricius whispered.

No, Rossi wanted to whisper. It was because of your training. Like mine. It was because of . . . luck, and provisioning, and resourcefulness. What gods? No. No. We trained you better than that. Even a few hundred years ago you didn't believe in gods.

But no. Britta explained: the gods were ancient and real. The gods were there first. We lived by making a deal with the line of the oracles in exchange for belief, and for the food of the gods.

The bones in the swamp, Rossi thought. The line that never lost its taste for human flesh, that demanded it in exchange for advice. No gods required. And yet, were they chanting, somewhere in another room? There was a noise, a buzz. Was the mere mention of the story enough to invoke their wan, atonal cry? How did they know?

She edged out the door. Ambricius, rapt, didn't even notice. Everyone looked up as the door swished open, letting in a square of white light that illuminated Britta's swollen belly, but by then, Rossi was gone, walking as fast as she could back to McKay's office, not running. Telling herself not to run.

But hang on. What would she even say? "Don't give me a humanitarian award! I thought we were going on some kind of massive space-charity run for a lot of helpless and unfortunate people. Not for an inbred cannibal cult who attribute their survival to some ancient, awakened gods!"

That would get her swung straight back into quarantine, scrubbed, zapped, questioned, dunked, flushed again. And banned from Steerage, which—as much as she hated to admit it—she couldn't bear. There was so little to break the monotony of ship life. And what were these skinny, traumatized people going to do to a whole crew of healthy, well-fed, combat-trained people? Their gods, anyway, had been abandoned on their ruined planet. No one was left to feed them belief and willing victims.

She sighed and went back to her quarters, pausing only to rub off a few of the squiggled symbols with her sleeve. The cleaning drones would get them eventually, of course, but they bothered her simply to look at, the way they seemed to squirm and misbehave on the clean grey metal.

Rossi only realized something was happening when the alarms sent her flying from her bunk to the opposite wall, weapon somehow in her hand. She was uniformed and armed before she was fully awake, running to her station, muscle memory so powerful that she almost crashed into the door at the end of her corridor before seeing that it was shut. Someone barreled into her from behind—Ashford, his wide dark face crisscrossed with sheet marks, and a dozen other crew members who shared this hallway. The weekly code didn't work in the locked door. Neither did last week's. The clamor behind her grew.

"Anything from Command?" Ashford said, prodding the tablet embedded in his sleeve. It was flickering red, everything red. Nothing safe and green.

"Nothing. What the hell is going on?"

It was supposed to be a rhetorical, unanswerable question, but the intercom squeaked into life above their heads—incomprehensible at first, just noise, gradually resolving itself into a babble of voices. Rossi's stomach flipped as she recognized the colonists' accent.

"Holy shit, they're at Central Control," Ashford gasped. "Look at the readout. They're locking doors all over the ship, and our trajectory is all out of whack. What are they doing?"

"They're trying to go home," Rossi said numbly.

"What? No, that's crazy—they can't fly this. They'll never be able to land on—"

"Listen, they're obeying a higher authority than logic." She pointed her blaster at the door lock but paused. No, the blowback would be terrible in an enclosed space; she'd seen that enough in combat. "Hasn't this happened in a movie?"

"This has happened in a *thousand* movies," someone said authoritatively from the back of the hallway. "Someone needs to go into an air duct and get help."

Ashford laughed, but Rossi pointed above his head: an air duct cover with four helpfully removable screws was set near the ceiling, a cleaning drone peeking through the grate, green lights blinking. She scanned the crowd for someone light to boost up.

Freed from the hallway, the loose group—her squad, Rossi was already calling it in her head—stutteringly made their way to Control, sending their intrepid air duct ambassador ahead to keep doors open, sometimes wedging them in the process of shutting. The scribbled symbols became more frequent, in pen, lipstick, food—sticky syrups and nut butter packets—and other, more disquieting substances.

"That ain't all them that's writing these," Ashford said quietly. Rossi, having just concluded the same, nodded as they jogged down the unfamiliar corridors. Of course not. Their contagion had spread, gotten to the crew. She didn't know who. Maybe afterward they could find out. If there was an afterward.

The voices over the intercom—shouting, pleading, threatening, chanting, coercing—had still not resolved themselves into a coherent narrative. Rossi wondered if the colonists were even aware that it was on. She could hear the sounds of combat, discharged blasters, the splashy noise they made when they hit something organic and dispersed. Maybe Control was fighting back, maybe it wasn't a mutiny, yet. It was infuriating as well as terrifying not to know.

And then a single, piercing cry, "Fellows! My fellows! We are returning to our home! The land of our gods cries our name! For it was the will of the oracle!"

"Oh, goddammit, Ambricius," Rossi muttered. She looked back at Ashford, expecting him to say something, like "You got this," but he was grayish and taut with adrenaline, simply meeting her gaze, waiting for her to give an order. I'm not your commander any more, she wanted to say. I'm just . . . the one in front.

They had reached one of the six doors to Control, this one covered in the colonists' graffiti, overlaid and crisscrossed until the metal couldn't be seen. A smashed cleaning drone lay crumpled in the corner next to it. The sigils of their gods, she thought deliriously. Placed here for protection, and as a ward against us. Before they entered, she paused and held her hand up—five fingers spread, five times. A hex on you; a hex on your gods. The metal hummed under her testing fingertips: not the thrum of the ship but something else. She swallowed.

They entered low, ducking and rolling as blasters incinerated the air above their heads. Rossi took the scene in: crew members bound in the corner, jackknifing furiously—not her concern. Three more still at the controls, frantically trying to get the ship into a landing orbit. Twenty or so colonists, shooting and waving sticks at the remaining crew members, six or ten of whom were still on their feet. She took a deep breath and pivoted into combat.

With the extra numbers, it was over in minutes. She disarmed and immobilized Ambricius herself, trying to be gentle, almost succeeding. Out of the corner of her eye, several people had occupied themselves immediately with pulling the ship back up. How close had the mutiny gotten? She could hear the familiar, faint scream of the atmosphere, orange flames fluttering at the monitors. The effort to get fresh believers to the planet surface had almost resulted in a crash. The cosmic become personal.

"Your gods didn't help you," she hissed as she hauled him to his feet.

"Did they not?" he retorted. Someone pulled him out of her hands and dragged him off with the others. He kept his head resolutely forward, not looking back.

"Frank?"

Rossi looked up at the wall tablet—Roscoe and Cheo, their dress uniforms a solid block of blue at the bottom of the screen. "I'm coming," she said. "Running late."

"You're giving a speech in five minutes!"

"I'll make it." She hit "private" and picked up her dress hat, still stinking of its plastic storage bag. Would the guys notice that she had matched her lipstick to the band? Probably not. She touched it up anyway. Her hands were shaking.

She was going to be late for her speech, though. She'd been watching the video feed from the airlock chamber that the colonists had been quartered in. "Secured under conditional duress," McKay explained, meaning they could simply be ejected into space if they tried anything. Watching as the walls were covered with the sigils and symbols again, as the sourceless lights flickered, as shadows crept up in every direction, often testing the sealed seam in the floor that was all that kept a hundred people from flying into space. She was watching for something else now, hoping she would see it before the awards banquet. It must be soon. Must.

Her uniform screen flickered, a countdown sent by one of the guys. Two minutes. One. Minus-one.

There. Britta, flat on the floor, and someone else, turning to find the camera in the dim light, holding something up, slick with fluids: the new baby, three eyes blinking at its strange new world.

§

**Premee Mohamed** *is an Indo-Caribbean scientist and spec-fic writer based in Canada. Her short fiction has been published by* Nightmare *magazine,* Shoreline of Infinity, *Innsmouth Free Press, and many others. She can be found on Twitter at @premeesaurus.*

## The Writing Wall

# WENDY N. WAGNER

### ILLUSTRATED BY JUSTINE JONES

**W**E HAD BEEN ON HUGINN FOR FIVE HOURS, AND ALREADY, THE LEATHER birds had surrounded our camp. Twilight obscured their silhouettes in the massive horsetail trees, but the soft rustle of their dry-fleshed wings undercut the conversation around our chemfire. Shayna tightened the cords on her hood and scooted closer to my side.

"The orientation team said they were harmless," I reminded her.

My sister shook up a pouch of peach cobbler and activated its heating element with an expert snap. "They said the rain stopped once in a while, too. You can't trust those bastards." She pressed the warming packet to her cheek. "Damn, it's cold."

I pulled out my own pouch, probably stew, and pinched either end. "Hey, you're the one who got *me* into this." The pouch, heating element still not activated, popped out of my hands and hit the ground with a wet splat. Two weeks into Huginn's six-week dry season, and there were still puddles everywhere. The forests on the satellite world dried from the top down.

Shayna recovered my stew and opened it for me. "You'll get the hang of it."

"First trip to Huginn?" The man beside us had been silent since we'd made camp. But now he smiled, giving his heavily bearded face the cheer of a forty-year-old Santa Claus. "Jay Bara," he added. "Logistics." I'd seen him on the transit ship. Quiet guy, always reading. I would have never pictured him on an underground spelunking expedition.

I put out my hand. "Lena Smith-Wu. Biology." I made sure my handshake was as firm as his.

"My sister," Shayna explained. "I'm Shayna Smith-Wu, scouting and ops. We've met before, Mr. Bara. We were at the same table at that military-to-private sector hiring event in DC."

"Ah." He paused a moment. "I'm terrible with faces. Sorry."

One of the leather birds gave a hiss, and the air crackled with the sound of their wings.

"Territorial things." Bara took a puff of an old-fashioned vaporetto. "There's so much we don't know about them."

"You sound like you admire them." I couldn't keep surprise from coloring my voice. As a biologist, it was my job to study and appreciate the stupendous array of bizarre creatures and fungi on Huginn. But most people were only interested in the cute ones.

"Their entire stomach is a mouth," Bara mused. "And instead of teeth, they have independently mobile claws that serve both as a zipper to hold shut their umbilical maw and to restrain their prey. They're eating machines on wings. You have to admire the evolution of such a creature, if not its appearance."

"As long as they don't interfere with my mission, I won't interfere with theirs." Shayna didn't need to tap her sidearm to punctuate her meaning, but she did anyway.

I couldn't help but notice Jay Bara's disapproving look.

By midmorning, I had forgotten the leather birds. We'd left our campsite at first dawn, which on Huginn was still very nearly dark. The huge gray disc of Wodin, the gas giant Huginn orbited, still obscured the edge of the sky, its shadow stretching out over the forests. Wodin demanded fealty from the ocean, too, drawing the sea back from the beach where our shuttle had landed and leaving a long stretch of brown mud.

Our team had humped our gear through two klicks of dense forest, a crew of scouts roving ahead to clear some sort of path. No one wanted to run a ton of surveying gear through a patch of red death puffballs. Their silicate spores were the most famous cause of death on Huginn, but there were plenty of other ways to die on a world filled with alien fungi and proto-plants.

Was I crazy, coming halfway across the galaxy to physically explore a world I could quietly and safely study from behind a desk? I'd stopped asking myself that with any seriousness before I'd even gone into cryosleep on the Earth-side of the wormhole. I might be crazy, but I'd never felt so alive. Thank goodness Shayna had talked me into this.

She was waiting for me at the entrance to the Nithon cave system. The creek that had created the cave entrance rumbled and roared on the west side of the massive opening in the ground. "You ready to start earning your keep?"

The first of the geologists was already attaching her climbing harness to the second drop line. It was at least a twelve-meter plunge to the cavern floor below where the logistics and scouting crews were setting up lights along the subterranean creek bed.

I could be as badass as a geologist. "Sure."

She held out the titanium carabiner. "I'll see you down there."

The carabiner snapped shut with a comfortingly solid click. I wiped my gloves on the back of my pants and took hold of the heavy cable. "I'm ready."

I tried to focus on making short, controlled hops down the side of the cavern wall, but I kept getting distracted. Every place I looked, some new, never-before-seen species clamored for my attention. Long swags of some black pseudomoss that could have doubled as lace. Outcroppings of pink tufts like pincushions growing out of the stone. My foot caught on a stone, and a group of things like winged snakes burst from the wall, flapping wildly for safety.

I hit bottom too hard, but it didn't matter. What I'd seen in that five-minute drop could inspire a lifetime's worth of scientific articles. The ecosystem down here had developed into something wondrous.

The cavern had probably started as a sinkhole, a tiny opening in the ground that had grown larger and larger as a local creek began to chew its way down the side. Now, hundreds or thousands of years later, the hole in the ground was big enough to allow plants and animals a protected environment. A limited amount of sunlight reached the bottom, just enough for an oddball assortment of flora and fauna to thrive.

A hand clapped me on the shoulder. I spun around, my heart pounding. But it was only Jay Bara, outlined in the sudden flare of work lights. "That's just the beginning of the weird." He jerked his chin toward the dark opening on the far side of the cavern. "You want to check it out?"

Shayna landed beside me. "That's what we're here for."

Bara gave a gentlemanly bow. "After you, milady."

I had to hurry to catch up with Shayna.

"I don't like that guy," she whispered. "He's nothing like he was back in D.C."

"What do you mean?"

"The Jay Bara I sat with was a real outgoing guy. Loved taking pictures, constantly updating his social media sites." She broke off.

The scout posted at the entrance of the tunnel scanned our badges. "Headlamps, please." She waved us into the dark passage.

"People change, I guess."

"He didn't have a beard then, either. And he hated vapes," she whispered back at me.

I tapped my headlamp, starting up the LED. "Maybe we should keep an eye on him."

"Yeah, definitely."

"This place is amazing." I didn't mean to change the subject, but I had to pause and absorb the dramatic change from the open cavern to the enclosed tunnel.

The cavern was lush, an entire range of life supported by the limited sunshine and water from the surface. In the tunnel, we stood in absolute darkness. On Earth, few lifeforms made their homes in these spaces, most clustered around areas where cracks and fissures allowed light and moisture to penetrate the depths. Our headlamps dazzled off mineral formations between the columns of rough basalt.

The geologists in our party had come here to look for rare earth minerals to make our company a fortune. I had come to support Songheuser Corp's biological interests. Big companies used to fight to keep biologists away from their work until they figured out that gene patents could add billions to their bottom line. I felt bad, working for a corporation that only cared about biological diversity if it made them money. But not bad enough to miss my chance to make a mark on history.

"The Writing Wall should be about half a klick through this tunnel." Blue flashed as Shayna checked the communications unit buckled on her wrist for a map.

We fell silent, picking our way over the rough ground. In a spot or two, we had to turn sideways to fit, and the crushing sense of the vast weight of the stone around me made me ball my hands into fists.

And then we were there. The tunnel's ceiling had climbed higher and higher without us even noticing, and a milky glow showed a good eight to ten meters above us—pallid, barely visible daylight from the world above. Sunlight invigorated the space. Where the tunnel had smelled only of dust and dry rock, here the chemical tang of guano and plants punctuated the air. A trickle of moisture collected between the tumbled stones that made up the tunnel floor, threads of moss and lichen clustered at the waterline.

Once I saw the wall, though, it held my full attention.

"Amazing," Shayna breathed.

I was already reaching for my sample bags and forceps. The entire cavern system had been mapped by ground-penetrating radar fifteen years earlier. But the first survey crew had only made it inside the caverns four years ago, and their reports were limited. Nine out of ten surveyors had vanished, and the material the survivor had brought back was sketchy at best. But the biologist on their team had taken initial scrapings of the Writing Wall, and the company had brought me here to explain.

I activated my comm unit. "The mycelium runs across the surface of the wall, forming a dense mat." I moved closer to the black scribbles running over the stone. There was layer after layer of the stuff, the twists and turns of each black thread offset from the others in a strangely holographic effect. I turned the unit, so it could capture video of the phenomenon. "The complexity of the construction definitely gives it the appearance of some kind of writing."

There was something eerie about the way the mycelial strands echoed the forms of ancient Earth languages. It was too easy to see Sanskrit or Hindu in those twisting threads. I wanted to keep my objective professional stance, but the pressing walls of the tunnel only made me more nervous. What had it been like for the first surveying crew, down here with no backup and no satellite connection to the rest of humanity?

"The original team claimed it moved when they'd shone different kinds of light on it." Bara's headlamp momentarily blinded me before he dialed it down.

"I suppose that could happen." I wanted to sound like the confident scientist, but I was well aware of the way of my voice wobbled. I cleared my throat. "There are certainly plants with phototropic responses."

"The team was probably just freaked," Shayna disagreed. "It had to be creepy down here, especially when they were part of such a small crew."

"You know, the provincial government has never officially closed the files on the team's disappearance. To this day, no one is sure what happened to them." He grinned.

I wasn't sure what made me more uncomfortable—what he was saying or what Shayna had said about him earlier. His round face no longer looked cherubic or Santa-ish. I wished he hadn't followed us.

"Oh, shut up," Shayna snapped. "You're just trying to scare us."

Bara laughed. "Is it working?"

"I need to get to work," I announced. "I'm going to take some flash photos, so you might want to cover your eyes."

I spent the next ten minutes photographing the wall from as many angles as I could manage. Of course, I didn't believe that the surveying team had actually seen the mycelium move—but if it did, I wanted to document and measure every micrometer of change. I'd want to bring back some other light sources later to run more tests.

"It's time to head back to the cavern," Shayna reminded me. "The onsite lab should be nearly set up." She began moving back into the narrow confines of the main tunnel.

"Are you really sure it's just mycelium?" Bara asked.

I pocketed the samples I had taken. "What else could it be?"

"It so looks like writing."

"Well, it's underground on a moon that's never shown any sign of intelligent life. If it was writing, who was going to read it?" On that note, I squeezed into the tunnel after Shayna.

"Us," he said.

I couldn't help wondering what an alien species would have to tell a group of colonizing invaders and wished I hadn't.

Shayna had to stand watch that night, which was fine because I was too excited to sleep. I sat in our tent reviewing my notes and photos while I waited for her to wrap up her duties. The leather birds made the occasional soft creaking noise, something like a sleepy crow might make, more soothing than eerie. While our orientation instructors had assured us the territorial creatures were harmless creatures whose only dangerous behavior was occasionally dive-bombing those near their nests, this was the first time I wasn't worried about the presence of the leather bird flock. Tonight, I felt as if they were another watch, set by Huginn to keep an eye on us.

A louder squawk jolted me from my work. I checked the clock on my comm unit. 00:14. Shayna might have spent some time in the latrines, but her watch had been over for nearly fifteen minutes. I tidied my side of the tent, slipping on my coat and boots without really thinking about it. 00:20. Something was definitely wrong.

I slipped past the scout on duty, who seemed intent on the pale glow of his comm unit, and began to follow the trail we'd made that morning. We weren't forbidden from leaving camp, but it certainly wasn't encouraged. The first survey crew sprang to mind, nine out of ten dead.

Shit. Where the hell was Shayna?

Something burst under my foot. I froze. If it was a red death puffball, I was as dead as those surveyors.

I aimed my comm unit's light at the ground and sagged with relief when the light glinted off a foil food pouch. The smell of peaches and cinnamon competed with the acrid smell of crushed bracken. Peach cobbler. Shayna's favorite.

I hurried down the trail, trying to stick to the well-trampled middle. The horsetail trees here seemed wider and taller than back at the camp, overhanging the path as if to swallow it up. Why would she be out here?

My light caught a smear of something wet and black on a tree trunk. Blood.

I looked back at camp. Should I go for help or trust that Shayna *was* the help? She'd served three tours of duty with the marines in Bengoslavia. She carried a gun and a knife, and she knew how to use both of them. And if she lost her gun and her knife, her fists were registered as legal weapons in the state of New California. I realized I was babbling inside my head and took off running. I could call for help after I found Shayna.

I saw them. I walked into a patch of slimy Christ's fingers plant and had to cover my mouth to keep from shouting. Jay Bara was dragging Shayna behind him, circling the open mouth of Nithon Cavern. She didn't move.

I felt in my pockets. I had empty plastic sample bags, a pair of forceps, a scalpel for tissue samples. I took the scalpel out of its case and held it like I imagined Shayna held a knife. It felt all too small and insignificant.

The light on my comm unit flickered. Low battery. Shit. I jabbed at the buttons and sent a text to HQ. I had no idea if the watch would even get the message, but I didn't dare make any noise. The battery icon blinked again, warning me it was done for the night. I turned off the light and followed Bara and Shayna.

Back in undergrad, I'd taken a course on tracking. It was the only *B* I got in four years, and since then, I hadn't really practiced. My interests lay in plants and fungi, which didn't usually try to escape. I had learned a little about stealth in the woods, but my every step crackled and snapped like a bowl of puffed quinoa.

Somehow, Bara didn't seem to notice. He never once looked behind him as he dragged my sister onward through the bracken and mud. He kept the light of his headlamp turned toward the ground, his eyes focused on his feet, his step slow but steadfast. Something seemed to call him onward, a voice I couldn't hear.

The dull glow of fire—real fire, not a chemical brick or a glowstick—drew both our attention. Bara made a beeline for it. The trickle and drip of water sounded, and I realized a tiny stream ran into the circle of lighted torches. The water spread out over a slab of stone and disappeared into a crevice about the width of my leg.

The location, the crevice, the trickle of water: I knew where we were. The Writing Wall lay below my very feet.

"Come closer, Dr. Smith-Wu." Bara's headlamp seared my eyes.

I shielded my face. "You knew I was there.'

"You were always my real target, you know. I chose Shayna as my first offering because I knew she could make trouble for me, but you? You I need." He left Shayna to grab my hands. He tossed the scalpel into the undergrowth.

"Shayna knew you weren't the real Jay Bara."

He smiled as he wound a strip of plastic surveying tape around my wrists. "True. My cousin Jay was a good enough fellow, but his best features were his security clearance and his uncanny resemblance to his favorite cousin Mike." His face went into a mask of concern. "'Oh, poor Mike,'" he drawled, his voice a mockery of concern. "'A librarian. Isn't that quaint? How will he ever support himself?'"

"You're a librarian?"

He shoved me hard enough to knock my legs out from under me. "I might have had to scramble to find work, but I know how to find knowledge well enough. And the things I've learned! Why, I learned that the new world everyone's so excited to develop is the place *we've* been seeking for centuries."

The stress on the word *we* caught my attention. "Who's 'we'?"

"People who know. People who've read the right books. People who see that all humanity is a pawn in a game played by gods."

"Crazy people."

He kicked me in the side. "Educated people." He hunkered down, so his eyes could meet mine. The glare from his headlamp was nearly unbearable. "When I first started at Miskatonic, I didn't know anything, either. But then I became a librarian's aide. And that librarian opened my eyes to the truth."

I risked a quick glance at Shayna. She was breathing, right? She was just knocked out?

He jumped to his feet. "Think about it. A wormhole just happened to appear at the edge of our galaxy, just where it was predicted we'd find the dark planet of Yuggoth. The wormhole led us right to Huginn. And what's the dominant kingdom of life on Huginn? Fungi. If this were a story, you'd say it was too conveniently plotted."

"If this was a story, I'd be played by a mixed-martial artist, and I'd break your nerdy little neck." I aimed a kick at his leg and missed. "What do you want me and Shayna for?"

"Oh, I had to get her out of my way, and I'm sure the Great Ones will appreciate her as a meal. But you . . . you understand fungi. You're going to talk to the wall for me."

"Fungi doesn't talk. It doesn't write, and it doesn't make wormholes to lure humans into visiting it!"

He grabbed a handful of my hair and yanked me sideways. "Listen and learn."

My face ground into the rough basalt. I could smell the cool air of the tunnel below, the acrid funk of the mycelium. For a moment, all was still. A soft rustling began. It reminded me of the sounds the leather birds' wings made, that sound like a sheet of nylon rubbing against itself or an eraser moving over a scribbled sheet of paper. It came from below.

My headlamp-dazzled eyes also detected a glimmer of light.

I almost forgot the cruelty of Bara's grip on my head. Far down below me and just at the edge of my field of vision, a faint phosphorescent turquoise light bobbed and flickered.

"What *are* you?" I whispered.

The light moved until it stood directly beneath the crevice. It was bigger than I thought, nearly two meters, and it moved in a shambling lurch. There were bioluminescent fungi, I knew, but I'd never seen any in person and certainly not in a fungus so large. Or mobile. Jesus fucking Christ, a mobile fungi!

Part of its glowing body extended, burrowing into the thick mat of mycelium that Bara had insisted was writing. Another part of it reached out, grabbing higher up.

"You see it, don't you?" Bara hissed in my ear. "Talk to it! Tell it I'm here to serve its greatness!"

I couldn't speak. The glowing figure pulled itself higher up on the wall. What might have been its face turned toward me. There were no eyes, no mouth. But beneath the blue-green glow, dark threads twisted and scribbled. My mouth went dry.

"Let go of my sister, asshole."

Shayna's voice cut through the mysticism of the moment. Bara gave a shriek of pain and let go of me.

I rolled away from the crevice.

Bara staggered to his feet, clutching his side. "Not dead yet, Shayna?" He grabbed one of the torches from the ground. "Gotta fix that."

He charged toward her. I struck out my heel, connecting with his calf. He didn't fall, but he stumbled into the bracken, his torch swinging wildly. The needles of the nearest horsetail tree hissed and sizzled.

"I'm going to mess you up," Shayna warned him.

Then the horsetail caught fire. Flames shot up its trunk, and the needles exploded in tiny silicate bursts. Minute splinters drove into my hands and face. I rolled into a ball. Huginn's dry season had only been underway for two weeks, but the needles on the trees were the driest things in the entire forest.

A wind roared with the slapping of dry wings as an entire flock of leather birds streaked down out of the sky. I peered at them through my fingers. The flames lit up the seams of their bellies, dark slashes against their fire-stained flesh. They fell upon Jay Bara like mother bears defending their cubs.

"We've got to get out of here," Shayna ordered, grabbing me by the arm.

I shook her off. "Wait." I threw myself on the ground, peering into the crevice for the thing I'd seen before.

There was only darkness.

I let Shayna pull me away from the crevice, from the circle of torches, from the screams of Mike Bara as the leather birds pummeled him into the dirt.

Mike Bara lived, but whatever he believed about the Writing Wall, it stayed locked in his mind after the leather birds' attack. When the company scouts found him in the morning, he was in a catatonic state. Songheuser sent him to a maximum security facility for the criminally insane anyway.

Shayna and I completed the mission in the Nithon cavern system. I never saw the phosphorescent fungi again although I did discover several damaged patches in the mycelial mat on the Writing Wall. I suggested that Bara did it, and the company believed me.

The geology department decided there weren't substantial enough mineral deposits to justify a mining facility at Nithon. But the company made a few million from patents based on my work, and I managed to wrangle a full-time appointment here on Huginn. I mostly handle paperwork and samples from other caverns. Sometimes the company talks about re-evaluating Nithon, and I gently steer them toward other locations.

I don't really believe Bara's ravings, but I can't stop thinking about them. His family didn't want any of his effects, so I took his books, and some things that he said do make sense. The texts did place his mythical fungal planet, Yuggoth, at just the location of the wormhole leading to Huginn. And Bara had reproductions going back over a thousand years that could, if read with a certain bias, suggest that the galaxy is filled with powerful beings who are eager to manipulate human development for their own nefarious purposes. These great and powerful creatures—I can't bring myself to call them "gods," like Bara did—certainly have the ability to punch wormholes through time and space.

But what keeps me up at night isn't any of the stuff Bara said or what I've found in his books. It's the sound that replays in my mind when I turn off the light, the sound of dry rustling like leather birds' wings—or perhaps like a whisper from the dried throat of something that's been asleep for a thousand years. And it's what I see when I close my eyes before sleep takes me.

That face. That eyeless, mouth-less face with the blue-green glowing skin, and underneath the luminescence is a swirling darkness like the twisting folds of the mycelium growing up the Writing Wall. When I look into it, that darkness, I see it re-shaping, turning and twisting until the black lines are no longer meaningless swirls but instead letters, words, a declaration:

You're next.

{}

**Wendy N. Wagner** *is the author of more than forty short stories and has also written two novels for the Pathfinder Roleplaying Game. Her third novel,* An Oath of Dogs, *is a sci-fi thriller from Angry Robot Books. She is currently part of the Hugo Award-winning* Lightspeed *magazine editorial team. An avid gamer and gardener, she lives in Portland, Oregon, with her very understanding family.*

## Canary Down

# KARA DENNISON

ILLUSTRATED BY
JUSTINE JONES

S HE'S STARING AT ME. IT'S CREEPY."

Rosie shrugged, eyes still on the nav system. "Then don't look at her."

"You *told* me to keep an eye on her."

"Ugh." She glanced back over her shoulder. Behind her sat Trall, cir eyes fixed almost obsessively on the tiny girl in the yellow dress—eight, nine years old at best and shoes as shiny as her ringlets. "The way you're staring at her, she's probably more afraid of you than you are of her."

Trall sniffed. "It's the eyes. They're all big and glassy. Look at them."

"They don't look that big to me."

"They're just . . . they're just a little on the big side. You know? Cartoon eyes. It's creepy."

"Trall. She can year you."

Trall sat up straight. Ce peered at the little girl, waving a gloved hand in front of her eyes. "Can you hear me?"

"I can hear you." The voice was small and monotone.

"Sheez." Trall wrinkled cir nose. "Couldn't you have gotten a guy version? Or a cay version?"

"Perv."

"How dare. It was a legitimate question."

Rosie shrugged. "The manufacturer is kind of backward, anyway. Only male and female."

"Huh."

"Not that it matters. You shouldn't be getting attached to her."

Trall puffed out cir cheeks, swiveling away from the little girl so ce was no longer facing her. "No fear. How far to the fossil?"

"It's, uh . . . varying."

"Varying? Let me see." Trall jumped up, taking the seat next to Rosie in the cockpit. Rosie shifted in her seat, allowing cir a better view of the console.

"See?" Rosie pointed at a dot on the GPS visual that darted back and forth, like an indecisive hummingbird. "Varying. Every time we get closer, it shifts."

"It's a giant fossil. It shouldn't be able to move."

Rosie clasped her hands together, smiling brightly. "Oh, *well* done. Good to see you were paying attention in class."

Trall shook cir head impatiently, missing the jab entirely as ce swiped a hand nervously through cir hair. "No, I mean . . . literally, what we're seeing is impossible. Even in our line of work. Dead is dead is dead. So why is it flitting around? It couldn't even move like this when it was *alive*, as far as I know."

There was a tiny cough from the jump seats. Both Rosie and Trall looked back. The wide-eyed girl was standing, her gloved hand folded primly in front of her, resting against the skirt of her bright yellow dress.

"Yes?" Rosie asked, as patiently as she could.

The girl's eyes turned toward them; Rosie was starting to see what Trall meant about them being "just a little" too big. "The artifact in question is aware of his situation. He will, of course, attempt to flee. But there is only so far he can go. Our only hope of intercepting him is to observe his pattern and meet him on one of his jumps."

"Sounds good to me." Rosie turned back to the controls. "Right, Trall, you watch the screen, I'll take down the coordinates, and we'll see if we can't—"

"*He?*"

Rosie glanced over her shoulder. "Huh?"

"You heard her. She said *he* will attempt to flee us. Not *it*."

"Well, she was probably . . ." Rosie trailed off. No. There was no reason. Why *would* she say that? Not unless . . .

She swiveled her chair around to face the girl. "Hey. You said *he*, not *it*. Are you saying that the fossil is . . . still alive?"

The girl's lips parted slightly; it was hard to tell whether she was thinking or simply pausing for emphasis. "*Alive* and *dead* are very unhelpful words when dealing with a being of this sort. They work only with creatures who deal in dimensions of finality. Which he does not."

Trall glanced at Rosie. "She . . . *does* know we're just raiding an old star whale carcass for a class project, right?"

But Rosie didn't hear cir. She rolled her chair closer to the girl, head ducked, hands clasped. "Tell me more about him."

The girl closed her eyes, nodding. "He is long deceased. His fossilized form floats through the universe, still and petrified. He wishes only for an ending, but his instincts keep him on his guard. He will fight despite his longing to sleep. It is all he knows."

"What . . ." Rosie took a deep breath. "What *is* he?"

The word that spilled from the girl's lips only took the space of a breath but seemed a thousand syllables long—unpronounceable, impossible to parse. It struck terror into the hearts of her companions.

Trall looked over at Rosie, cir eyes wide.

"This scholarship is *so* not worth it anymore."

"The technical term is HAGU, or Humanoid Artificial Gauging Unit." Professor Fernandez handed out a series of flat datascreen flyers to the students. "Though, in the business, we rather artlessly call them canaries."

Rosie slid her fingers around the surface of the flyer, rifling through the information on various companies as Professor Fernandez went on. "Artificially bred to be hypersensitive to chemical, temperature, and atmospheric changes and able to pick up local radio interference." He smiled awkwardly. "And before you get too attached, they are disposable and recyclable. You will be returning your HAGU at the end of your final."

Rosie sighed. She and Trall had spent the majority of their scholarship funds on upgrades for their used ship, not realizing they'd be required to buy an entire artificial human before the semester was out. She flicked down into the cheaper and cheaper units, finally finding a company that produced serviceable ones that didn't go *completely* uncanny valley.

"Your team of two will be permitted one HAGU. In the field, most astroarchaeologists will have a minimum of three. But this is a small project with low risk, and you're on small teams, so one should be more than sufficient. Besides, it behooves you to learn to work without a spare . . . which will happen on occasion."

The star charts came out, and each pair had to pick their field. Rosie winced. Trall was the best at picking out dig sites, but ce was home with an especially unpleasant flu. She tried snapping a photo of the charts on her phone and shooting it over, but no answer came; Trall was probably medicated to within an inch of cir life and too busy having fever dreams to answer.

"Oh, well. They've surveyed all the areas. It's not like we can go *too* wrong."

"Sixteen-alpha-seven-point-five by seventy-four-gamma-four even."

Rosie steered them according to Trall's coordinates. And they waited.

The dot on the screen *blipped. Blip. Blip. Blip.*

*Blip.*

The dot was on top of them.

"Sweet hell-blisters," Trall breathed, and Rosie looked up. Her heart clenched to the size of a raisin.

Hovering in front of them was not, by any stretch of the imagination, a star whale. Not unless that star whale's mother had mated with an octopus the size of Jupiter, bought her baby a set of artificial limbs, and left it to rot.

The creature hove into view, like an oddly shaped planet: bone-white and cut with intricate shadows. Rosie thought she spied an eye socket somewhere below them, wide as a canyon and twice as deep.

"Canary," she breathed. "Tell me again. I-is he alive? Or is he dead?"

"He is," Canary said placidly.

"Which one?"

"He is not alive. He is not dead. He is." The girl's small voice was clear, almost ringing, like a dirge played on water glasses.

"Look," Trall said shakily, "we're out here to explore a star whale, right? Not . . . whatever this big guy is. Let's just turn around and get out of here, okay? We'll take some photos, tell the professor what happened, but we should *not* be—"

"He hears," Canary whispered.

Trall turned to her, grimacing. "I do not need this right now, small spooky child. I want to go home."

"He hears this, too."

"Aren't you just supposed to tell us if we're gonna get frostbite?" Trall turned to Rosie. "What the hell moonshine kind of gene splicer did you buy this freak show off?"

Rosie swallowed. "She was all we could afford."

"Great. Awesome. So you expect me to take direction from the kid from *Six Nights in the Moon Crypt*? Hells no." Ce shoved cir way back to the controls. "Hopping us out of here. Sit down, losers."

"You cannot."

Trall jabbed a finger at Canary. "And *you* can shut up."

"Trall . . ." Rosie stared out the front window. "I think we're closer than we were."

It was true. The far-off crater of an eye socket now seemed closer than ever, looming, ready to swallow them up. Rosie felt herself shudder imperceptibly.

*You're too late.*

"Who said that?" Rosie and Trall spoke at once.

"I-it wasn't me," Rosie stammered.

Trall shook cir head.

They both looked back at Canary. The small girl was unresponsive, seeming to stare through both of them at the looming shape.

Trall shook cirself out of cir surprise and began jamming buttons. "Okay. Okay. Jumping us out of here. Hang on to something." Rosie did as she was told, but Canary stood still. "Canary. Sit."

"My mental calculations estimate that this would be a waste of energy."

"Ugh. Fine. Enjoy your concussion." Trall took a deep breath. "Punching it!"

Nothing happened.

"Did you punch it?"

"*I punched it!*" Trall snapped back at Rosie. Ce punched it again. And again. Ce tried the floor pedal. The override. Everything ce touched seem to just take them close and closer to the giant fossilized beast before them.

Rosie grabbed one of Canary's little hands. "Hey. Hey, you can, like, read his thoughts, right? Maybe you can talk back to him? Tell him to let us go?"

"I do not possess that mental capacity."

"So . . . what's going to happen to us?"

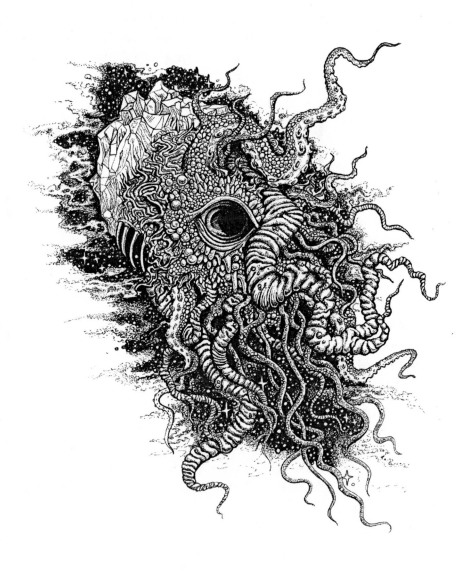

Canary looked placidly out the front window. "We will land in his eye. We will enter. One of"—she paused—"seven scenarios will ensue."

"Worst case and best case?"

"Best case," Canary said, still staring ahead at the looming chasm, "we will shatter the fossil, freeing ourselves from his pull and returning home. Worst case . . ."

Trall and Rosie held their breaths.

"We are driven mad by his influence and tear our own eyes out before leaping into the vacuum of space where we, too, will float forever frozen."

Trall dragged cir hands down cir face. "I will honestly go for *any* of the other six at this point."

Canary cocked her head slightly. "One of the potential scenarios involves you being digested in dormant stomach juices—"

"*Shut her up, Rosie!*"

The ship landed surprisingly softly at the nadir of the empty socket. Rosie and Trall began suiting up, the latter arming cirself with every destructive item in cir arsenal. Rosie began fastening her helmet, eyeing Canary curiously.

"Are you not coming with us?"

"I am coming with you. It is my duty."

"Won't you need a suit?"

Canary shook her head. "HAGUs are required to be able to function, survive, and communicate in unlivable environments, so we may report back to our human supervisors. If a HAGU died after every human-unfriendly encounter, a standard two-person excavation mission would go through approximately six and a half of us."

"What happens to that half?" Trall muttered.

"My calculations indicate that you would tell me to shut up if I elaborated."

Trall sniffed. "Smart kid."

The three exited the ship, Rosie and Trall touching down first. Canary floated down delicately behind them, ringlets and skirt weightless in the air—more like Alice dropping down the rabbit hole than a humanoid tool dropping into a monster's skull.

"So," Rosie huffed into her helmet, "what do we need to do to get away?"

"We are being held here by his will," Canary responded. Despite speaking into the void of space, her voice reached their ears—flat and strained, like a school PA system. "Two paths of escape lie open to us: we make ourselves uninteresting or we shatter his mind."

Trall nodded. "And . . . uh . . . which one of those is easier?"

"We will have marginally higher success at shattering his mind than at distracting him from us. However, it comes with a higher risk as we must enter his body."

Rosie glanced around the chasm. "Is that . . . a door?" She pointed toward one of the sloping walls of the eye socket: there, indeed, seemed to be a doorway. But not just a door-shaped exit—a genuine *arch* with column-like decorations carved around it.

"Pardon me." Canary leaped ahead of the pair, drifting daintily through the doorway and disappearing into the blackness beyond. Five seconds passed, ten, and the curly head popped out.

"It is safe to enter."

Rosie and Trall followed. Once they were through the door, Trall pulled out cir flashlight, lighting the way for all of them. There was little to see but stony walls on either side. Their steps gradually began to feel weightier.

"Is it just me, or is there gravity in here?" Rosie muttered.

"The atmosphere is also breathable for you," Canary said, her voice sounding more like itself again. "It should be safe to take off your helmets, though the temperature is still somewhat low. I recommend leaving your suits on until we are in a warmer environment.

Rosie was the first to test the air. She unlatched her helmet—sure enough, the air was comfortably breathable and even smelled oddly pleasant. "Trall, check it out."

Dubiously, Trall followed suit, taking in a whiff of air. "Hmm. That's . . . almost nice. Kinda reminds me of . . ."

"Lavender," Rosie said quietly.

"Huh? No, I was gonna say limes. My old partner's aftershave." Ce sniffed. "Where are you getting lavender?"

Rosie sniffed again. Then furrowed her brow. "Canary?"

The girl tilted her head upward, sniffing the air, almost like a puppy. "Formaldehyde."

"Uh . . ."

"This area appears to synthetize the scent that each person finds most comforting."

Trall turned cir head toward Canary slowly. "And you find formal . . . you know what, never mind."

"Why?" Rosie asked.

"It is hard to tell. Perhaps, it is an invitation. Or perhaps, it is bait."

Ahead of them, the hallway opened out into a wide, irregularly shaped room. Canary held up a hand and dashed ahead, making a complete running circuit of the room before running back, completely unwinded.

"It is safe. And it is warm. You will likely wish to remove your suits."

Both Trall and Rosie removed their suits, turning them inside-out and zipping them up into backpacks and stowing their helmets inside. Canary was right: it was warm but not uncomfortably so. Rather, it felt pleasant, like that first surprising day of spring when you realize you don't mind going outside.

"What part of the . . . the fossil are we in now?" Rosie asked.

"I estimate that we are approaching the brain."

"Is that the direction we ought to be going?"

Canary looked thoughtfully at the floor. "It is most likely the proper way to go. There is very little to be accomplished elsewhere. However . . ."

"I don't like that *however*," Trall muttered.

"It will be difficult. The brain is the part of him that is still the most active. You will likely find you will want to turn back more and more the farther we progress."

"How do you know so much about this?" Trall asked, folding cir arms.

Canary shook her head. "I am simply picking up cues from my environment. As I was designed to do."

"Mmm." Rosie rubbed her bare arms, looking around the room. It was empty, but the ossified walls seemed more of a warm pink than the cold bony color of before. "Mind you, it's kind of nice here. I wouldn't mind just hanging out here for a while."

"Same." Trall inhaled deeply. "This is the calmest I've felt since I saw this thing."

"I would advise that we continue to move," Canary said, her voice taking on only the slightest of edges. "This room may be as comfortable as it is on purpose . . . if you take my meaning."

Rosie blinked. "Oh."

"Uh." Trall winced. "Yeah. No. Point taken. Lead on."

Canary led the way down another hall. They walked in silence, save for the crunching of sand and rock beneath their feet, for perhaps twenty minutes or so. Neither Trall nor Rosie felt particularly threatened anymore, and Rosie found herself wondering if they had been worked up for nothing. Perhaps, this would turn out to be a fine final exam.

"I recommend that you do not look down," Canary said matter-of-factly.

So Trall looked down.

"Aigh!!!!"

"What?" Rosie stopped.

"Th-th-those . . ." Ce pointed a shaking finger at the floor. It hadn't been sand or rock under their shoes. It had been . . . people.

Shards of what seemed to be people—either petrified or frozen and shattered into pieces—paved the way ahead of them. Here and there a piece of an agonized face would cry out silently underfoot. Trall pressed cirself against a wall, shuddering.

"I did recommend not looking down," Canary said.

"I-is that . . . are those real?"

Canary reached down and, much to the disgust of the other two, picked up a lone finger and sniffed it. "The remains do appear to be genuine. However, they also appear to have been petrified in some way, much as he has."

"H-how new are they?" stammered Rosie.

"I am afraid it is impossible to tell. They could be five minutes old or five thousand years old."

Rosie squinted. "Come on. Let's just suck it up and move. It's not like we can hurt them anymore."

But as she said it, she heard a wail underfoot.

"Canary! They're crying!"

Canary looked down dispassionately. "I was mistaken," she said quietly.

"I'll say!"

"These . . . are not genuine remains."

"How do you know?"

Canary looked at Trall. "Did you hear a cry?"

"N-no."

"Nor did I. It affected only the one of us concerned about causing them pain. I believe it has begun."

"What has begun?" Trall asked.

Canary looked over her shoulder, "The closer we get to his brain, the more disturbing things we will see." She looked at the finger she still held in one hand; it crumbled away into dust. "What is distressing is that I am as susceptible to the tactics as you are. This should not be." She seemed to ponder this silently for a moment, shrugged, and continued.

"We're close."

Rosie held her arms tight against her chest. "I hope so. I can't take much more of this."

Trall kept cir eyes forward, staring at the top of Canary's head. Ce didn't glance at the walls . . . slowly fading from stone into purple, pulsing veins. "What in the hells . . ."

"There is an artifact ahead," Canary said calmly. "It is half-sunk into the center of his mind. It seems someone before us was in much the same predicament. Finish the job, and we are free. Let nothing stop you—no words, no thoughts. Do what you must, cleanly. The mind's contents will spill into the next readily available vessel."

"I . . . don't understand." Rosie took a deep breath. And another. The voices coming to her during the walk had been unpleasant—a long string of them—her father's, her mother's, a cabbie she'd met once who'd terrified her, a priest, a politician . . . all a jumble, all saying all the words she thought she'd buried.

"Trall?" Rosie asked quietly.

Ce shook cir head. "I'm fine. I promise."

"Who are you hearing?"

"No one, okay? No one."

"Trall—"

"No. One." Ce looked away.

Rosie tried to shut her ears against her own voices. "I'm just trying to see if you're okay."

"You've seen. I'm okay. Now please. Let's finish this and go home."

"We're here." Canary clasped her hands together and stepped to the side.

It didn't look like the inside of a skull or the housing of a brain. It looked like a dimly lit room, a large mahogany table in the center carved with schoolchild graffiti. From the walls hung various grotesqueries: mannequins, torn clothes, bloodied book pages, red-stained metal hooks that may have once held *something*. And in the center of the table itself was a book, a great curved knife plunged into it.

"Is . . . is what we're all seeing real?" Rosie asked.

"I'm afraid I do not know," Canary said quietly. "In a normal exercise, if there were mental tricks at play, I would see through them. But everything you have seen, I have seen. I . . . do not understand."

Trall felt cir stomach lurch at this admission. The idea of this strange little girl admitting confusion was more terrifying than anything else they'd encountered.

"But we . . . we use the knife, and we're done, right?" Rosie stepped toward it. "We, what, cut the book in half? Is that it? I can do that. And then we get out, and hells, maybe we can take the knife home for our final. How would that be?"

She gripped the knife handle, pulling the weapon from its resting place in the table.

"*No!!!*"

Rosie and Trall whipped around. Canary was reaching a hand out, screaming, eyes wide with . . . terror. Actual terror.

"Canary . . . you said I had to—"

"Don't do it! Please, no, don't!" Canary scrambled forward, tears spilling from her eyes, and she wrapped her arms around Rosie's legs like a terrified child. "Please, no, don't do it. Do you know what will happen if you do?"

"Canary . . ."

"It's another of those mind tricks," Trall said breathlessly. "Ignore her. It's this thing messing with us. She said it can affect her, too. Maybe it's just—"

"Trall . . ." Canary raised her huge eyes, brimming with tears. "Trall, why would you let this happen to me?"

Trall shook cir head. "I . . . I don't understand . . ." Ce gritted cir teeth, raising cir head. "Hey, no. Look, whatever you are, she's *our* canary, and we don't appreciate you messing with her like this."

"No," Canary whispered tearfully. "No, it's not . . . it's not him. It's *me*. It's really me, the *real* me. I-if you do this . . . if you do this . . . I'll be gone."

"What do you mean?" Rosie still held the knife ready.

"I-I made my plan. I made a really, *really* good plan for you. You'll get home, and you'll be safe and happy and . . . and I'm scared of my plan. I don't want to have made it. I want to change my mind. Please. Please, let me change my mind." Her eyes lit up, and for a moment, she looked like any other normal little girl. "Now that I know, now that I *can* . . ."

"Rosie," Trall snapped, cir voice strained, "Canary said do what you have to, no matter what. Remember?"

"I-I remember."

"No!" Canary cried out. "I was stupid back there. I didn't understand what . . . I didn't . . . I can't explain." She shook her hair, her curls whipping across her tearstained face. "Please, Rosie. I've helped you *so much*. Can't you do this for me?"

Rosie took a shuddering breath . . .

And plunged the knife with all her might.

The book—and the table—split apart.

"No . . ." Canary's voice was weak. "No, no . . . why . . ."

A deep, swirling, red and black mist emerged from the two halves of the book, plunging into Canary. She fell back against the wall and righted herself, her huge eyes glowing a deep red.

"What the . . ." Trall winced away.

"I . . . I can't." Rosie lowered the knife, staring at Canary—or whatever was now within her. "I don't care who you are. I can't do it. I just can't."

The creature simply stared through Canary's wide eyes.

"Trall . . . what do we do?"

"He wants to rest," Trall whispered.

"Huh?"

Trall grabbed the knife from Rosie and handed it to Canary. "Here. You . . . you do what you want. You're free to do that now. All right? Just . . . be quick about it. Our little canary's been good to us." Ce glanced at Rosie and then at the door. "Come on."

"But . . ." Before Rosie could protest, Trall grabbed her by the wrist and dragged her out.

"Canary knew," Trall muttered, pulling cir spacesuit on. "There was no way she didn't. She had a link. And she knew how to fix this. She decided."

"But her face just now . . ."

Trall smiled helplessly as ce clicked cir helmet into place. "We all have our moments of clarity before we do something stupidly heroic, right? Now, come on. Let's get dressed."

And just as Trall finished stuffing Rosie into her suit and fastening the helmet, the walls around them began to crack as though put under an intense strain. There was a creaking, a groaning . . . and the walls exploded.

Rosie and Trall felt themselves flung up and out . . . and not far, *shockingly* not far, was their spaceship. Trall grabbed Rosie by the arm and kicked cir emergency boosters into gear, propelling them toward the ship.

"Hey . . . Trall."

"Mm?"

"We don't have anything for the final, do we?"

Trall laughed. "If Professor Fernandez sees all the shards of weird giant space monster bone in our suits and really wants to fail us after this, let him."

Rosie managed a weak laugh in return as they grabbed the outer bars of the spaceship and pulled themselves inside.

§

**Kara Dennison** *is a writer, editor, illustrator, and presenter from Newport News, Virginia. She works as a blogger and interviewer for Onezumi Events and as a news writer for Crunchyroll, Viewster, and We Are Cult. Her work can be seen in* Associates of Sherlock Holmes *from Titan Books, various* Doctor Who *spinoffs from Obverse Books, and the light novel series* Owl's Flower, *which she co-created with illustrator Ginger Hoesly. She works from a converted NASA lab, which she shares with four guinea pigs and a bass guitar.*

## Song of the Seirēnes

# BRANDON O'BRIEN

ILLUSTRATED BY
YVES TOURIGNY

Confederation of Allied Planetary Territories
Exoplanetary Expansion Committee—Carmel
Documentation on the Rescue Process of the SRN227 Envoy
09/13/3212
Transmission Recordings: Dr. Persephone Khan

**Orange,[1] 10300 Launch Minutes (LM):**

WE HAVE FINALLY ARRIVED AT THE EDGE OF THE SEIRĒNES SYSTEM. UPDATE on travel: the binary wormhole relay at coordinates [redacted] at the outer edge of the Troia system did indeed place us within continued travel range of the system, and arrival was safe if a bit off schedule. Research on SRN227 and investigation into the whereabouts of the "Greyville Six" will begin soon. We would begin right away—the loss of EEC colony researchers in a new system is obviously worrisome, not to mention the value that the Carmel branch places in the unnamed mineral the Six mentioned in their comms—but we have to push the actual investigation back a few hours.

There've been technical difficulties, you see. The first is that the technicians

1. Note on transmission protocols—Orange: EEC non-urgent authorized-personnel-only delivery protocol; Red: urgent authorized-personnel-only deliveries; Blue: private deliveries to SRN227 Envoy Rescue Process Supervisor Dr. Marielle Katz.

neglected to re-calibrate all of our equipment, primarily the rover, which we were at least planning to launch in the interim. And the second, and equally if not perhaps more important, a pipe apparently burst in the storage bay. Technicians are moving the equipment and rations before they get ruined and repairing the leak before it affects some of the ship's other systems. I don't know anything about astronautical engineering, of course, but one of the hands said, if they didn't plug it, we may have whole rooms covered in frost, let alone irreparable damage to the life support structure. So we've all endeavored to rest and leave the techs to it, and we'll begin anew as soon as we can.

**Blue, 10324LM:**

Baby, I know what you're thinking. "Percy, is your first message back literally that a random accident might leave you to starve to death in space?" And I see your fear and raise you my own. Not of starving—the food'll be fine. I damn well can't eat most of it anyway.

But . . . I thought you would be coming with us. I wanted you to come with us. I wanted you to be with me. And now I'm here alone with a handful of researchers I have never met before and a handful of shiphands that were legit given the job the week before takeoff, and we're staring into the dark hoping that the Greyville Six aren't dead yet.

Which, let's be honest—and I'm not trying to be a downer or whatever, but . . . come on. It's been . . . how long, even? The chances are slim. I was just hoping we'd at least be together the whole time.

This sucks. Let's at least hope I can find evidence of something useful as soon as possible.

**Orange, 13830LM:**

Research has finally begun on the surface of SRN227, the largest planet orbiting the system's primary star Aglaope. Our shipborne observation tools can already determine some manner of historic civilization—the remnants of large monuments and structures of varying kinds can be seen by the onboard telescope.

Our initial concern that there would be no portable short-form documentation in the culture's language may be assuaged. We are sure that there are texts in both pictographic and what seem to be abjad writing systems etched into some of the monuments we have already seen.

Further observation will have to wait on the rover's photographs and samples; it has already been sent on its way, and deeper research will follow. We're hopeful that it will tell us a great deal—not only about the culture of the planet's first inhabitants but also about the curious properties of the minerals on its surface.

I am hopeful that the Six obeyed Breadcrumb Protocol and that the rover will be able to determine their whereabouts before they succumb to the peculiarly intemperate weather conditions on the surface.

**Blue, 16009LM:**

Y'know, if it wasn't for you working at the EEC, I wouldn't want anything to do with this job in the first place? Is . . . is that cruel? But this isn't my thing. I mean—like, xenoanthropology is my thing, but I didn't think I'd have to be in the field to get the work done. Or at least I imagined I'd be "in the field" in the field—not "suspended in a metal box hovering in the cold vacuum above the field" in the field.

Why do we even still send humans to do this kind of shit, anyway? I get it, an android can't make determinations as reliably as we may like: fine—but at least when one breaks, we are accustomed to leaving it to rust. If we know that people die—if we know that we'll have to send a crew to find out what happened once they do—maybe we should just forgo letting fragile little *Homo sapiens sapiens* do this kind of work?

I mean, worst case scenario, the Greyville Six could already be dead. Hell, we could die *right now.*

Jah . . . I'm doing it again. Okay. Lemme say it. We could die. Right. Now.

I need a drink, just—

Dammit. Forget I said that. Any of that. It's just . . . I'd feel a whole lot more grounded on this mission if you were here, Mari. Because otherwise, I'm just being painfully pragmatic. All the goddamn time. Weighing the costs of everything. Of whether I still make it.

We should be honest, after all. The Six are just a loss of information. Someone who signed the paperwork is hoping this could be a human-interest-piece if we make it back alive, sure, but the bigwigs? This is just data to them. Data they don't feel comfortable going back for on their own. And if we die? Who knows, maybe it won't be worth it after all.

I can already hear you saying, "Don't be like that, Percy," but I can't help it. The only thing keeping me sane out here is the knowledge that if we were so foolish to spend time, money, resources and warm bodies just to pick up the Six, maybe they'll be foolish enough to come looking for me if it still goes wrong. Maybe you'll kick up a fuss—I'd love to think you would. For me.

Would you?

**Blue, 17930LM:**

Oh, God, Mari. I just had the worst dream . . . It wasn't even, like, scary. It was just . . . I don't know . . . foreboding? Overbearing? I . . .

Do you mind if I . . . talk about it? I know you can't comfort me, but I'm hoping . . . if I know you're still hearing it . . . maybe you can . . .

So I'm sitting at the dinner table at home, and you made pelau just for me, just like you did before I left. And before I can even take a bite, I'm falling—through the chair, into the floor, into nothing but black for a long time until I see this small blue light below.

And as I keep falling toward it, it starts turning into many smaller, bluer lights, not far away but close up to me, like little blue fireflies. And now I feel like I'm no longer in air but in the middle of an ocean—but I'm not drowning, I'm just falling, falling lightly, pressure all around me, swimming in it but not worrying about breath or movement, and still falling, always falling. And the lights are kind of . . . dancing around me, like they want to touch me, but they can't.

And I hear this sound . . . I don't know what it sounds like. Like cracking stone, maybe? It's coming from above me, so I look up. And there is this large fucking eyeball over me. As big as a moon, taking up all of the space. With a wine-colored iris that looks like it's throbbing, like a muscle, like a hose, jerking, full of something.

And I feel myself jolt awake, Mari. I swear to you, I feel in that moment like

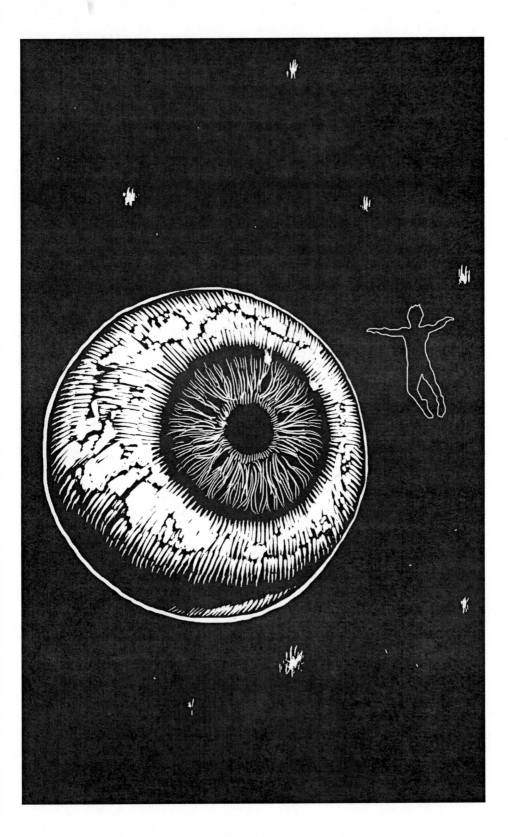

I've already gotten up from the bad dream. But this eye still just . . . looks down at me. And I don't have any idea what happens next because nothing changes for a long time. And the color from its eyes starts to fade. And I see it's falling down, into the . . . the water-air or whatever, onto me, but not like ink falling into water or anything. It falls like it's falling in air. And the pressure in the water gets tighter, and I feel like I'm being crushed by something. I can feel it flattening me, and I want to wake up, I really, really already want to wake up, but the dream just won't let me.

So I scream. I'm screaming your name the whole time—"Mari! Mari, help me! Mari, Mari!"—and I can feel it. I am already more than ready to get out of this dream, but it won't let me. Not until I am all the way crushed by . . . whatever is happening. And I am scared. Because it feels like I'm really, really dying. I feel the wind slip out of me, I feel myself blacking out among the lights, and I am still scared, still freaking out. I don't know what's going on—

And then I wake up. And . . . I think I can't cope. I think space is making me a little weird. Like, right now? I can smell Tempranillo. I swear. It's like I'm drowning in wine right now, and I hate it. I don't want to be here, and I just want to be wherever you are, and I don't know why we had to go on this fucking mission to find six fucking researchers on this fucking rock in the first fucking place because I am freaking the fuck out, and I don't know what to do.

I didn't expect . . . I thought it'd be like going out to sea, and it isn't. And I don't know why I'm getting so weird about this. But I don't like it. I just . . .

Why won't this smell go away?

**Red, 18229LM:**

The rover has sent some of its mosquito drones back with trace samples of the dust and stone from SRN227 for our team astrogeochemist to look at, and from what we can see, it's amazing. Just as the Six documented in their own recordings: a gemstone with chemical properties totally unknown to the existing colonies and with a pressure resistance and electrical conductivity higher than any of our current leading materials. I mean, Dr. Beltrán hasn't supplied all eir notes, yet, but as it stands, the rock—and even the sand—do exactly what the previous team said it would. If you pardon my excitement, this could make the colonies rich. What we thought would be an ideal extended settlement is really a massive gemstone mine!

The basics, I'm sure, are in Dr. Beltrán's recordings, but I can't help but note its deep wine color. As a gemstone, it's actually quite attractive—although I imagine this would be of far more financial value in the electronics sector than as jewelry.

**Blue, 18236LM:**

Yes, I know—I just said that something the color of wine is "attractive." But I'm not going to do anything stupid, alright?

Outside of the specifics of the mineral, the rest of the crew has been idly debating what to call it. I personally feel like the way we think about naming things like this is an exercise in ego—everyone wants to put their name on something before they die, I guess—but there's one name I actually kind of like. One of the technicians confessed that he took the job because his partner, Johann Piper, was one of the Greyville Six, and he was hoping to bring him back home. So, obviously, what did you think he'd ask the stone to be called?

Piperite. I think it's fucking adorable. I didn't even know—Augustus, I think his name was?—I didn't even know he *asked* to be on this mission. Just to find his partner.

I think that's amazing. I mean . . . it gives me a little bit more hope that maybe we're actually gonna get through this. That we're gonna find them. I mean . . . I want us to now. I really do. Because I want his partner to come back home. And I want yours to come back, too.

**Red, 23315LM:**

I've begun some of the preliminary document scans sent by the rover. I can't make any actual deliberations until sometime in, but I have some opening judgments in the hope that the hypotheses will grow more shape as I keep digging.

The ornamentation of the structures on SRN227 and a great deal of the pictograms recovered seem to betray a kind of ritual opulence portrayed among the dominant culture here. What seem to be historical texts continuously depict massive feasts, orgies, gambling events, stage shows, and more for weeks upon weeks at a time, all at once. I'd hesitate to think of them as rituals at all, but they are all connected to some common words and symbols, including what appears to be an image of a sun—perhaps, Aglaope?

There were also technological artefacts—the techs observing the rover feed have reason to believe that there is a cultural analogue of the tablet computer on the surface of SRN227, but of course, that means the rover will have to put it away for us and bring it back before we can even determine how they're powered or if they're still of use.

There is still far more reading and research to do. The bit I'm puzzling over now in the texts, referring to the astrological festivals they apparently partook in, gives mention of a god. Of course, I'm . . . paraphrasing; my hope is that I can have something better to go on in terms of what words mean or how they're used. For the time being, I'm attempting to crack the two symbols beside the sun in pictograms. They come in only two variations.[2] One is the sun, followed by what seems to be wind being blown out of the lips of a humanoid creature (perhaps, their own species' face?) and . . . like an ankh, I guess? I mean, you'll see it, but it's like an ankh but with three handles instead of one, perfect circles each. And the other variation of the statement is the sun, followed by a shape I can't put in context—um . . . two rhombuses in a circle? And then the triple-ansated cross again.

So I placed them against how many other times the images seem to come up in the description of the festivities themselves because maybe their sacraments include some manner of mimicry, right? And I . . . think I make sense of it? The rhombuses come up by themselves in a lot of the gambling mentions. (I'm guessing because I can definitely make out their base-eight numeral system. I've been staring at most of that for the duration we've been hovering over the planet.) The overall shape is mentioned in what I suppose are musical events—because the breath pictogram is there, too. I'm taking poetic license, of course—all of this may go out the window as we dig deeper into their general texts—but I'm designating both phrases as "clicking god" and "sweet-voiced god," respectively.

I've been sharing notes with Dr. Beltrán on the samples again in order to get a better sense of what actually happened to the inhabitants of SRN227, and e surmises that a massive solar ejection may have been responsible for impacting them so drastically. It may be responsible for some of the conditions

---

2. For visual comparison, see "SRN227GodPhrase1.png" and "SRN227GodPhrase2.png" in the Appendices folder.

of the piperite, even, according to eir estimation, which would be utterly fascinating.

We're both in the beginnings of our observations, of course—hell, uncovering the secrets of this mineral may take years and require more resources than we have on this lifeboat. But we're both eager to see where they lead.

**Blue, 23323LM:**

I wanted to go with "lambent-voiced god," obviously . . . right? The star's name *is* Aglaope, after all. Just saying. It fit. But I didn't want to get attached to it . . . you know, if the readings lead another way.

Also, it seems like we're getting a bit comfortable here on the ship. A little too comfortable, maybe. On both ends of the spectrum—large shouting-matches on the one end, private lovemaking sessions between techs and researchers on the other . . . why am I telling you all this? This is a research mission, not a soap opera.

I just . . . really wish you could be here to help me sleep. The fucking dream . . .

Anyway. At least we're making progress, right?

**Orange, 24121LM:**

Technician Julian King noted that a feedback sound we had noticed on the ship when we arrived at the system is still persisting. After the repairs to the storage room, we couldn't find any faults, even though we had suspected that it was perhaps interference from passing through the binary wormhole. By all accounts, it isn't a flaw of any kind (hence not mentioning it sooner).

And then we dug deeper, and it got even weirder.

I thought, maybe, it's a beacon.

And we got excited, too! Maybe it was an SOS from the Greyville Six? But it's coming from Aglaope. So we immediately dismissed it as feedback, of course, but I figured I'd ask one of the techs to help me tinker with some of the equipment so we could chart the sound itself.

It's a repeated pattern. I'm attaching it with the others.[3] Plays like . . . an 8/8 time signature? Which is interesting—maybe, Aglaope itself is the catalyst for

---

3. See "Aglaope_Recording_002.mp4" in the Appendices folder.

the numerical system on SRN227? Anyway, I'm also intrigued to find out if its translation may have had any significance to the planet's inhabitants since the sun is one of their revered symbols in their language, important enough for lavish rituals.

**Blue, 24140LM:**

Julian—he's nice people. Really ingenious, loves to help. I mean, not like anyone here doesn't give of their time when you ask, but Julian saw me perk up at the beacon thing and offered all on his own. He's a whiz with some of this stuff, too.

I feel like he kinda did it out of pity, though. Everyone else thought I was just wasting my time thinking about it. "It's just a fucking noise, Percy." Like it wasn't annoying the hell out of all of us the whole time.

But Julian just went, "we're all going a little bit weird about this job. At least you're being productive about it."

And that could've been rude, but I actually thought it was kinda . . . sweet.

**Blue, 25025LM:**

Mari. The fucking dreams. It's like they're following me now. Even when I'm awake, whenever I close my eyes, even for a blink, that wine-eyed monster is staring at me, and it lasts forever every time it happens, and I don't know what to do.

It's driving me crazy, Mari. Not even just how fucking creepy it is. Like, why the hell? What does it even mean? I feel like my psyche is trying to make me backslide—that's the part that gets me. Like I'm freaking myself out because it wants me to fall off the wagon.

And it's . . . it's not just me. I feel like the trip's finally gotten to all of us. In the mess, a researcher—dunno her name—got into a fistfight with one of the engineers, nearly stabbed the guy in the neck with a broken coffee mug. Apparently, there was an incident in Dr. Beltrán's room; someone lit one of eir bookshelves on fire when e wasn't in eir room? I don't even know why the fuck—e's been so nice the entire time.

And the worst part? Gus—Augustus. Augustus Mellon. Fucking spaced himself. Who knows how long ago. I'm the only one who knows so far—the rest of the ship isn't up yet. I got up from the nightmare and . . . I see something floating outside the airlock window, and . . . Gus is just . . . there. Clutching a cracking picture frame in his arms as he floats away from the ship. And . . . godfuckingdammit. I don't get it. If he's losing hope already . . .

Mari. I'm scared. I know I have nothing to be scared of . . . but . . . I feel like I'm here alone, and I want to know for sure that I'm going to see you again.

I'm going to see you again, right?

Right?

Please.

**Red, 33053LM:**

I have reason to believe I have a pretty solid baseline interpretation of some parts of the texts that we've found, especially the scrolls; I have to thank Julian, again, for taking control of the rover to photograph some of them for my research. Again, more reading could prove something more, but the context I have so far make sense.

Without going into greater detail—all of which will be covered in the files already being sent back[4]—the gist is this: the citizens of SRN227 worshiped a "lambent-voiced god," to whom they attribute the success of their world. They were thriving; they claim to be yielding a surplus of food, in perfect health . . . they don't mention much about material wealth, but when they do, there is mention of "the deserving" coming into financial success. And the god was who they thanked for it all.

And the god is—or wields power—over the sun, and everything they had was a result of the sun. What appears to be their literal litany records have a one-to-one correlation to records of crop yields and defense from natural disasters (and mind you, the quality of these records are impeccable, down to individual moments, and one of them even mentioned a dancer fainting during worship with the same diligence as their grain counts; I'm assuming there's an entire hierarchical position dedicated to consistent event recording, but the specifics of that are still locked up in the texts). This god was literally the reason they were still alive. They had the numbers to back it up. Whether it was real or not, they were having impeccable luck maintaining a society here.

4. See "PreliminaryTranslationsSRN227.pdf" in the Appendices folder.

So they developed rituals. Now, this part's rough, but this is where the "lambent-voiced" bit comes in: they claim to have heard songs from the god, songs that literally fell from the sky. Into the ears of some or, for others, indirectly through their technology. Songs telling them to make offerings to the sun and to constantly perform . . . I'm taking this to mean, um . . . "humbling rituals." And the records show that: flagellation, immolation, electrocution, scarring . . . stampedes, weekly brawls . . . all forms of practice in their ritual spaces, with some groups favoring some in general or for certain outcomes.

But those practices date back a while. They're all in the same document, but by the look of the texts themselves, the state of the more recent additions to their records isn't as specific, and I'm willing to bet they're not as accurate either. And the records of their litanies drop at a point, too. Whippings and cuttings stop. But the orgies don't. And, I mean, if they believe they were literally hearing their god, all at once, they made that decision from a place of . . . faithlessness? Because there are slivers of texts that seem to be about a kind of "turning away."

I still need to dig deeper to grasp the rest of the words, of course, but progress is swift. More than enough texts survived for us to study. Hopefully, I can bring even more of them back!

**Blue, 34748LM:**

I showed some of my findings to Zoe—that's Dr. Beltrán, by the way; we're getting along so well now!—and e goes, "Well, I guess their god didn't like that very much, did they?"

**Blue, 38000LM:**

Mari . . . [labored breathing] Oh my god, Mari . . . [sobs] It felt like it lasted forever . . . like the eye was drawing me into it this time. It felt like I was drowning and being lit on fire all at once, and the fucking smell . . . wine, wine everywhere . . .

I don't want to stay here . . . I want to do something . . . the whole time I was there I wanted to do something stupid to myself. I woke up, and I wanted to hurt myself, Mari. It was as if something other than me was inside me, and it wanted to hurt me so bad, Mari, I don't . . . I'm losing my goddamn mind here.

I want . . . I want to hear your voice, Marielle. I know I can't, but . . . it was your voice that saved me from drowning in my own puke four years ago, and I don't know who else to call on to save me from . . . whatever this is.

The fucking clicking, beeping, whatever, it's like it's getting louder. And the dreams. And the big fireball of Aglaope, like it's taunting us, begging us to just come closer and end it.

And a part of me really wants to. A part of me . . . I can't even lie. We said we wouldn't lie, right? I want to just drink all the fucking wine in the storage bay and drive the ship right into the sun because I am scared, and I don't like it, and I didn't want to be here, least of all alone.

I am bugging out. I don't even . . . I can't even hold on to you after I have dreams like this . . . Why?

[crying]

Why can't you save me from th—

**Blue, 39343LM:**

Oh my goodness, I must've had a really bad dream a while ago, huh? I barely remember it, even. I'm sorry if I worried you, Mari, but I'm fine. Just . . . jitters, I guess?

**Orange, 39345LM:**

I've come closer to deciphering the beacon that I noticed a while back. The . . . feedback from Aglaope.

First, I had to figure out what kind of coded systems the language on SRN227 used, how their characters were ordered using base-eight, and what the beeps would correspond to. I mean, I don't even know the syllabic structure of the spoken language, yet! But it got me some characters, which got into words, and I'm basing the rest of this roughly on the words and phrases I was already lucky to stitch together. I can give you two lines. What I think are two lines—um, lines as in "phrases." Of the beeps? Anyway:

> *Hailing from a fairer shore to save kin,*
> *leaning over to sip of the sea's own sweetness.*

The . . . embellishments are mine, of course. I felt like it fit as a poem. I dunno. Anyway.

**Orange, 58330LM:**

Some brief notes on the research I'm presently tackling:

I've been listening to the entirety of the star's feedback. Noticing the general pattern, the specificities of each single phrase in tandem with the whole. It has a form—like a sonnet is in iambic pentameter? But specifically, I'm assuming tetrameter, but seeing as I don't know what the language sounds like, I can't be sure. It's all a peculiar pattern, though: the beeps aligned with letters from the citizens' abjad system. I suspect the star influenced their alphabet, just like it did their math. It's like the rhythm of the sun is literally how SRN227 saw the world.

It's beautiful, isn't it? Do you want to hear some more?

> *Cleaving to infants' knowledge in the jaw of a vast*
> *hunger, seeking to unfurl their bellies again.*
> *Well-seasoned by their own gluttonies,*
> *sure to delight the tongue of the shape within the star.*

It's . . . so lovely, Mari. I don't know what it means yet, but it's—

[shuffling, muffled screams]

Oh, goddammit. Hold on.

[an audible scream]—

**Blue, 66100LM:**

Hurray for us! We lasted this long!

I know it's nothing special, Mari, but we decided since we've been outside the Seirēnes system for more than six hundred whole hours, we might as well celebrate, right? So we made cake—I didn't know we had friggin' cake mix around here! That was cake mix, wasn't it?—and the rest of them drank, but I decided I wouldn't since you'd be such a stickler about it.

Good thing I didn't, too. Zoe and one of the techs got in a fight over, like, a bottle of beer or something, and e stabbed the guy in the eye for it. Julian, I think his name was? Nice people. Shame about the eye, o' course, but what can you do?

Well, sure enough, that kinda soured the mood right up, so we just took our cakes and drinks and shit back to our quarters and got back to work. I'm about to get back into my observations right now, actually.

It's just . . . we were having so much fun. Why'd Julian have to ruin it? It's not like we didn't have more beer.

**Blue, 80146LM:**

Mari, you have to send someone to get us, now.

I don't know what the fuck is going . . . what?

It says here you got a recording from me at 661 hours?

**Blue, 80335LM:**

[crying] I . . . I don't get it.

Mari . . . you have to come get us. You have to send someone.

I don't remember ever making that recording. I just got up. I don't remember . . . any of these recordings after 25025LM. I just woke up on the floor of the mess hall . . . I don't know if . . . I don't know!

First, it's the fucking signal or whatever, lingering all over the place, then it's the dreams getting worse . . . and these notes . . . I was, what, trying to translate the sun? What's . . . what's happening, Mari? I'm scared.

[crying, followed by a long, deep breath]

Think. Think, Percy. You can . . . you can make sense of this . . .

[another breath]

My . . . m-my notes say . . . I was looking at the . . . time signature of the sun? What the . . . that SRN227 seemed to place all of their systems in the . . . rhythm of the sun's flares. I was working on what I thought was calendars at some point? And I noticed a vague similarity—I guess that's it. Right. Calendars. That were in tune with the general motions of the sun. They had calculated even down to the probability of its flares.

And a group of inhabitants—according to the texts—had apparently observed a "day of devouring." A large ritual orgy, all of their pleasure rituals at once, set to close on the day of a . . . massive coronal ejection or something. I may have to check that with . . . Zoe, maybe? But e's still out cold.

I was working on a poem here, too? What is this?

Wait.

Some of these texts . . . they're . . . they're, um, pictograms. Some entire phrases line up with these. Parts of these . . . are the same poem. It closes the same, repeats some words in the same order in the middle . . . what is this?

You know what, fuck it. I don't care—tell EEC-Carmel they have to come pick us up. Abandon the whole business in the Seirēnes system. Fuck SRN227, fuck Aglaope, fuck this entire clump of space. Just bring us back.

Please.

Please, Marielle.

I . . . I'm scared.

I don't know what happened to us, but . . . I really don't want to find out. I'm losing it.

Please.

**Blue, 82631LM:**

Marielle?

Mariellllllllllllle?

I really wish you could have come, you know. I had my doubts, but it was so. Much. Fun! And I really wanted to share it with you. So we could have our own little kinds of fun together? You know what I mean. And I'm sure the rest of the crew would have loved you too! They love me. Well, most of them. But everyone who's still here . . . mostly loves me! Loves me so, so much . . .

And speaking of love: SRN227's people wrote some truly endearing poetry. The . . . depth at which they dug to show love for their god, even to the point of wanting to offer their entire world . . . God, don't you wish you had something you cared about so deeply that you'd lose your entire self in it? Literally be swallowed by it, feel its slick, cruel, longing tongue wrap around you, slowly, until you know it loves you back? That's . . . that's all they wanted.

Well, they also wanted to be fat and rich—but they wanted that because Aglaope gave it to them! They wanted to show Aglaope something back! Their appreciation for each and every thing they had gotten! So they danced and drank and loved and spent themselves sick, hoping Aglaope would notice.

And she did, she did! She held them so close, opened her whole jaw up for them.

Marielle?

Mari?

Mari, Mari, Mari. Marielle? Come on, Marielle . . . don't you want to be here, too?

Don't you want to have fun?

Don't you want to be loved?

It's a shame you're missing it. We decided we wanted to keep going. Wanted to see what's on the other side of Aglaope . . . we'll even throw a party there! We have so much wine to share, after all . . . Zinfandel, you know. Zoe brought it with em. It's so good . . . how long's it been? God, I wish I could finish this poem for you, tell you all the awesome things it says. But the rest of the crew, they're sure in a hurry!

So we told Aglaope we loved her. And we're hoping that she'll take us into her arms now.

I want to tell you all about it when I come back. But if I don't, if Aglaope says she loves us back, I just want you to know that I love you, too.

I love you, Marielle. I love you, I love you, IloveyouIloveyouIlo—

§

**Brandon O'Brien** *is a performance poet and writer from Trinidad. His work has been shortlisted for the 2014 Alice Yard Prize for Art Writing and the 2014 and 2015 Small Axe Literary Competitions and is published in* Uncanny, Strange Horizons, Reckoning, *and* New Worlds, Old Ways: Speculative Tales from the Caribbean, *among others. He is also the poetry editor of* FIYAH *Literary Magazine.*

# The Pillars of Creation

## HEATHER TERRY

ILLUSTRATED BY
DAVE FELTON

Jonesy's breath washes over me as he glowers in my face. "I am being perfectly nice about this. You understand that I don't have to be?" He leans in, waiting.

"Get the fuck outta here, Jonesy. I have work to do." I shove away from him, spinning in my chair to face the other console. He stands there chewing on the inside of his lip for a few minutes more before stalking off. "Pompous asshat."

Being some hotshot navy scientist don't mean shit here. It's not as if he's in a different boat than we are. Same ship to run, same shit to deal.

An alert light engages on the console, and I punch in the coding to redirect. The light disengages.

My commbadge buzzes, indicating that I am now off duty. Turning away from the display, I narrow my eyes at the door. Undoubtedly, he's in the mess hall barking orders at anyone who crosses his path as if this were a damn military vessel. Eating at home it is, then.

I begin making my way to the main deck. What the ship lacks in aesthetics herself, she more than makes up for with the landscape, and the main deck is the perfect place to see it.

Climbing into the deck portal at the end of the narrow hall, I wait for the dizzying surge to end before clambering out onto the main expanse. The rest of the ship may be cramped, cold, and grey, but here? Here the universe opens up to you.

God himself don't have a better view than this.

Main deck is situated at the top of the ship, and its dome is made of some silica-based glass blend. Jonesy could probably tell everyone all about it, but no one gives a fuck about what it's made of. Fucking Jonesy.

Beyond it, the inky blackness of space beckons. Impossible dustings of light, tiny pinpricks and pulsating orbs, dance in swirls and eddies that draw us along like currents in a river. In the distance ahead, maybe ten days out, our destination looms. Sea-green clouds swaddled around masses of dark matter in which no starlight penetrates. The majesty floors me.

Dubbed the Pillars of Creation by the twenty-first century scientists who first identified them, the columns had once been assumed to be little more than space dust and hydrogen.

The past few hundred years taught us a lot. Most particularly that we don't actually know a fucking goddamn thing.

"Wheatley! You out here stargazing again?" Bill Grafner's gruff voice bellows across the floor at me. Grizzled and built like a tank, Bill's outward appearance alone commands the respect of the other men. Despite an injury that left him with a slight limp, he works the ship with as much skill as any and more skill than most.

"Ah, well. You know me, Bill. A real fuckin' romantic. You off-shift tonight?"

"Just ended. You were working nav today, weren't you? Any excitement?" Bill had worked nav for scavenging vessels before he got dumped here.

"Dodged a stray asteroid. Nothing to get antsy about. Where you headed tonight?" I ask, adding, "I'd skip the mess hall."

"Jonesy at it again, then?" His eyes tighten, and he furrows his brow. "What's he on about this time?"

"Same shit he's always on. Thinks he's better than the rest of us, like he's some agent from ops. Like he ain't in the same fucking boat we are. I shouldn't let him get under my skin," I say, shrugging. "I know it, but it don't matter. Arrogant asshole."

Bill doesn't push it. He knows Jonesy. "How's about we head down to low level? Get some rounds in and head back over to mess after he's burned himself out?"

Low level, where *Gallivant's* range and hydroponics are housed. We all have free access to target practice, if not the greens. Heading there was as good a plan as any and better than skulking about in my quarters. Nodding, I turn back toward the deck portals. Saying, "Down it is," I step inside.

At the range, some joker had posted printouts of Martians in place of the targets. Grafner, after unloading a series of plasma bursts into one, turns and asks, "You ever wonder why they came and found us?"

"I always just figured they were hungry."

"Nah, I don't buy that. Why just three, then? No, I think we were being reminded of somethin' we'd lost sight of. That we got too much ahead of ourselves, so we needed taking down a few notches." He reloads. "Maybe we deserved it."

His commbadge buzzes, drawing his attention to a nearby console and sparing me from having to respond. Christ all-fucking-mighty. Lots of folks turned to religion in a big way after the attacks—but damn.

Returning, he growls, "Some fuckhead is dicking around up there. Gotta cut it short." He checks his firearm back into the munitions cabinet and climbs into the lift. "Catch ya later, Wheatley."

I wait a few minutes before following suit. To hell with dinner. After that cheery visit, my quarters sound like a damn good idea.

I ignore my alarm for a few minutes before rolling out of bed. The quarters are so normal, it's easy to forget where you are. Or at least make believe that you can.

We're all supposed to be grateful to be here. Like the government's done us some grand fucking favor by stuffing us on this shithole mission. When we were first given the option, I suppose we all were. We did choose to be here. But we are expendable, and we know it. Injected with an implant programmed to self-destruct at the touch of a button—killing its host—tossed on a ship with no official return plan, and headed off to fiend central? Well. If we survive, at least our life back home will be better than the colony cleanup we'd faced before this. If we survive.

At least we get our own rooms, even if they are small. Only room for a closet, a bed, and a desk. One shared bathroom per quad.

Stepping on the platform outside of my quarters, I try not to look out the window stretching the length of the internal walkways as I head toward mess hall. It doesn't do much good.

You can't help but appreciate the simple genius behind the *Gallivant's* build. The command center, where the brains are kept, hangs suspended in the midst of the ship's center ring. Like a big fucking courtyard in the middle of the ship, only with no access points, just hanging in the middle. Unless you want to take a nice long spacewalk on a moving ship, you aren't getting near the hub and the folks who can access your implant. But they can see you, and you can see them. A constant reminder of just where exactly you stand.

Taking a seat at one of the mess panels, I insert my ration card and wait for the light to turn green. A fully functioning hydroponics bay and protein cloning center, and we still get rations with no menu options. Just a blended gruel with cloned mystery meat.

"Enjoying today's selection?" Vance Kreel, specs and ops specialist, slides onto the bench opposite me and jams his ration card into a slot. He might be brilliant at specs, but his school-boy optimism wears on my nerves. Not waiting for a response, he eyes me for a second and says, "I heard you dodged an asteroid yesterday."

I frown. Things get pretty dull around here, but asteroids are hardly lunchtime gossip material. I shrug and spoon up another mouthful.

Kreel is not easily put off. "Come on, Wheatley. We were less than two weeks outside of the Pillars, and a stray asteroid just happened to find its way onto our path?" Bouncing with excitement, he continues, "Whatever it was they sent out at us, it shoved us quite a bit farther down our trajectory. We're no more than a day out now. That asteroid was them, man. I'm telling you!"

I suppress a sigh. "Kreel, if it were them, why would they send an asteroid out at us? Are you fucking dense enough to think that these creatures, who got within a few hundred thousand kilometers of Earth without being spotted and, with only three units, devastated five of the world's best-defended cities before being destroyed themselves, would not only respond to our presence by shooting an asteroid at us but also miss?"

Kreel's smile grew larger. Fucking school boy. "Who says they missed? Anyhow, did you hear the external sensors got all trippy last night? Jonesy had to go in and reset them manually. Got himself zapped!" He slams his hand on the metal table, the resounding clang made the other crew jump. He grins wolfishly. "Don't tell me you aren't excited to get back at them, man."

"Not that I don't appreciate the chat, Kreel, but is there a reason you're here right now?"

"Well, Jonesy is still in med bay, so that means you pick up his shift in thirty. It's you an' me, bud!" He claps me on the shoulder.

It's going to be a long fucking day. "Fabulous." I stand up, dumping my tray into a bin. "Shift starts in thirty? See you there."

So Jonesy gets a little zap and holes up in med bay. And now I have to deal with Kreel wetting his pants over a lousy asteroid. I head back up to main and get a closer look at the Pillars. If the school boy is right about our ETA—and he almost certainly was—we made excellent time in the past twenty-four hours.

Leaning back on a central loft rail, I look out through the dome. The Pillars seem to stretch toward the ship like a massive, bony hand blindly grasping for us. They are undoubtedly far closer than they ought to have been. I decide the view isn't so grand any more.

Seeing Philips, a med bay hand, exit a port with a stack of documents, I shove off the rail and stride across to fall in step alongside him. "You see the Pillars today? Must have caught a faster current than we had expected."

Philips jumps, pulling his nose out of a file and glancing around in surprise. "Oh. Yes. Yes, we must have." He licks his lips. "H-how are you tonight, Wheatley?"

"Me? Fine. Hey, how's good ol' Jonesy doing?"

He blanches, eyes going wide. "Jonesy? W-why do you ask? What have you heard?"

I turn and face him full on. "Only that he got a shock off of a console and got himself put up in med bay."

"Right. Yes, that's true. Well. Be seeing you." Turning abruptly, he enters a portal and closes it behind him.

I stare at the closed lift gate. Philips is always twitchy, but damn. The Pillars must be really spooking him. Regardless, Jonesy clearly won't be out in time to free me from specs duty with Kreel. I enter an open lift and check the time on my commbadge. Specs lab time.

Level three forward, home to the specs lab, is where we perform our primary function on this assignment. Once we'd figured out from the creatures' autopsies where the fuckers'd come from, a specialized team had to be put together. But running a ship this far out takes more than a skeleton crew, and so came the unique opportunity they offered us lifers. Listed as skilled prisoners from the war, we had nothing to lose, everything to gain, and a fuckload to offer.

Specifically, detailed intel ops at ground zero. At this point in the game, we are sending out data shipments on return flights every six hours, and all of it is gathered, prepared, and launched from the specs lab.

Taking a deep breath, I exit the portal. "Six fucking hours with Kreel," I mutter, entering the lab. Boy scout is already here, grinning at me as the door slides open.

"Wheatley."

Ignoring him, I take a seat at a console. "Anything to note from last shift?"

"Not a thing! No worries, though. We'll get some excitement. I'm sure of it."

Of course he is. Swiping through the sensor screens, I begin logging the first round. A lot of the men, like Kreel, accepted this commission exclusively to get a chance to hit back at them. A little excitement would do their nerves good after all this damn waiting.

"Hey, Kreel. Did last shift fill you in on the current we hit? It knocked several days off our trip. We need to make sure it's documented." I change screens to view the trajectory.

"Didn't mention it. It had to have happened the shift before. Maybe at 02:00."

I pull up the file, but no anomalies were recorded. "Damn. They didn't enter it. We'll have to do a retro." Swinging around to the log console, I pull the sensory readings and load them into a handheld screener. Scanning them, I see no irregularities. "Kreel, check out the back-up logs. Do you see a current that I don't?"

Kreel's fingers drum restlessly on the console. "No, nothing."

"Okay. So we have an acceleration that brings us a week and a half in just twenty-four hours but no indication of what caused it." I study the data on the handheld. "You got any ideas, Kreel?"

His thumb began tapping more rapidly against the display edge. "Okay, hear me out. You dodged an asteroid, and within thirty-six hours, we are on top of the pillars. I don't know how it did it, but I'm telling you, man. That asteroid had something to do with this."

I pinch the bridge of my nose. "Fuck's sake, Kreel. A goddamn asteroid did not do this. Maybe in dodging it, I put us in an unexpected substream, but your conspiracy theories are too goddamn much." I take a breath and release it slowly. "Now. I am going to push this off to the brains, though my bet is they already know a lot more about it and haven't bothered to tell us. Just keep up on the fucking specs. I'll be back." Pulling the data chip from the handheld, I stand up.

"Whatever, man." Kreel returns to his primary console as I step into the hall.

The only communication access to the brains is a comm port off of main expanse on the internal hull. Inserting the data chip into the port, I type my access code and make the connection. "Acceleration at approximately 02:00. Unknown source. Data log provided." I withdraw my card after it sends.

Boarding a lift, I catch sight of a harried Philips scurrying across the expanse. I pause for a moment and punch in level five: med bay. It's time to pay Jonesy a visit.

I expected to find him fussing and whining from a cot. Maybe bitching at one of the med hands. Or lounging with a book in hand. Not strapped down with restraints, thrashing against them like some feral animal. Arching his back, he snaps one of the bands spanning his chest and presses the top of his head down into the bed to lock his eyes with mine as his arms, free now of their restraints, flail wildly.

The blood seeping from his eyes trickles over his eyebrows and onto his forehead. I stumble back a few steps, knocking into a stand and sending supplies flying.

"Whatchit, Wheatley!" The doc races over, righting the stand. "Unless you have a medical reason to be here, get out. No gawking!" Not waiting for a response, she grabs my shoulder and whirls me back toward the door. Behind me, a shrill keening erupts out of Jonesy as two of the med hands struggle to restrain him. "Out!" She gives me a final shove as Jonesy's eyes roll back, and he collapses on the bed.

The door slides shut behind me and latches with a soft click that echoes in my stunned brain.

"What. The. Actual. Fuck."

The only job worse than having to wriggle about the fucking access ports is cleaning the latrines. They couldn't have made these ports with the least little bit of breathing room, oh no. No, they had to make them so fucking tight you have to sidle along inside, squeezing from latch to latch with your goddamn toolkit banging along behind you.

But I need to know. What happened to Jonesy was not just a zap. And the only way to get uncompromised data is to go straight to the source. The fried circuitry responsible for the short is scheduled for repair today but not until after they finish building the replacements this afternoon.

I sync my handheld with the comm connector and pull out a coupler from my kit. A little luck and I can recover a few files.

Easing the coupler between burned out nodes, I increase the power through the link. Pressing the log command on the handheld, I wait for the connection indicator. "Data transferred" flashes on the screen. I disconnect and squirm back out of the hole.

A slow, deep breath steadies me. Directly across the hall, the command center hangs just beyond the glass. I stash the handheld in my kit and turn toward the quads. Maybe, it's nothing, or maybe, Kreel finally succeeded in spooking me, but I don't have any intention of sharing the existence of this data just yet. Not until I understand what exactly is fucking happening.

"I'm getting as paranoid about conspiracy theories as the goddamn boy scout," I mutter as I enter my quarters. Regardless, a sense of security eases over me as the doors slide shut. I pull up the files that weren't too corrupted to be saved.

Command will realize I took a detour soon, so I work fast. Noting the time frames in conjunction with what data is available, I scribble out the details of the charts. Stashing the handheld in a drawer, I step back out into the hall. Keeping my eyes down and away from the view, I head back to the specs lab.

Kreel is tapping away at a console when I reenter. "What took you so fucking long? No way should a run to command console take an hour and half, Wheatley."

Somebody's cranky. "Give it a rest, Kreel." I slide into my console and reactivate my screen. While the incoming data begins to consolidate, I scour it for a pattern. There has to be a connection. "You get any more reads on that acceleration?" I hand him the data I copied.

Surprise crosses his face. "So that's what took so long. Feeling a tad daredevil, are we?" He studies the data, and his smirk freezes. Reading intently, he spreads the papers out across his console and compares it against his scans.

"Well?" Patience has never been my strong suit.

He bites the lid off a marker, circles three timespans on my chart, and points at his screen. "Compare the files. At each of these spikes," he says, pointing at the chart, "our sensors were bombarded with low-grade sonics. It started when your asteroid got within our close range sensors."

"The fuck you mean, 'low-grade sonics'? It was an asteroid, Kreel, not a motherfucking director beacon."

He holds up a hand. "Now, look at this. At 02:30, Jonesy goes to reset the sensors just in time for one last blast of that sonic interference. He gets zapped by the short, and twelve hours later, we have somehow skipped over the final leg of our trip. I don't know how they did it, but those fuckers want us here."

I stare at him. "I went and saw Jonesy after sending the command comm."

Kreel's eyebrows shoot upward. "Oh?"

"Whatever fucked him up, it wasn't any sort of electric shock I've ever seen. If this does have something to do with the ship's acceleration to the Pillars, it don't mean one good fucking thing for us."

"Did you send this data to command?"

"No. Just the initial data we found before. Technically," I add, "the circuitry housing is off-limits since—" A shudder rips its way through the ship, interrupting me. We glance at each other, then take off for the main lift.

When we reach the platform, I hear someone murmur, "My God," only dimly aware that it was me who'd spoken it. What might have been the view from God's own throne room two days prior had undergone a horrendous metamorphosis. Fucking Hades himself would shy away from this nightmare.

Aligned on either side of the *Gallivant*, the bastards lurk just beyond the reach of the ship's lights. Massive, tentacled, and patient. Thousands of them, just waiting for us to stroll right into their midst.

Spanning the distance between us and them, floating all around us, are bodies. Human bodies, gaunt limbs rent from torsos, heads with faces sunken in and twisted in expressions of pain and terror, collide into the glass over the main expanse as the ship forges ahead through this gruesome sea.

The ship shudders again. "The engines," I realize. "Kreel, I think command is trying to pull an all-stop," I hear myself mumble.

Kreel does not respond. Instead, he sinks slowly to his knees and stares unblinkingly at the millions who our government had declared lost. The ones assumed to have been incinerated in the attack. None realized they had been taken. "My sister. S-she was an unrecoverable. Look at them, Wheatley. Fucking look at them!" he screams, launching himself to his feet and grabbing at my shoulders.

I drive my fist into his jaw. Hard. Grabbing him by his collar as he staggers, I haul him back upright. "Fuck's sake, Kreel. Look at them out there. We have got to get to the docking bay, do you understand? It's our only chance to—" He struggles, and I shake him. "Do you understand?" I yell at him. Others had arrived on the main, their confused exclamations escalating.

No longer waiting for a reply, I drag him back to a lift. I punch in the order for the docking bay while Kreel sags against the lift wall. "I need you with me on this, Kreel."

"Shells, just . . . shells. Sucked dry, hollowed out," he rambles on.

I ignore him. The lift stabilizes, and I haul him out. He maintains his feet this time, despite another shudder rocking the ship.

"You still with me, Kreel?" I take him by the elbow and lead him to the nearest console. Speaking slowly, I tell him, "Access main engine control here and run an override while I coordinate at the command link." I eye him uncertainly. He's pale and his eyes glossy. "Kreel," I bark, snapping my fingers in his face. My hands shake. Balling them, I clench and unclench them at my side.

He shakes his head sharply and places his hands on the console. "Yes. Yes, I'll do the override."

I move to the command console around the corner, calling out, "I'll contact command. Once they respond, you'll have to sever the link fast." I link up, entering the query code for all-stop. The cursor blinks slowly as I await their response.

Hearing a choking gasp from Kreel, I grind my teeth. We all lost people in the attack, and the graveyard out there is grade-A fucked up, but that doesn't mean we lose our shit down here. I take a deep breath and steal a glance around the corner.

Kreel staggers toward me, a dark circle of blood blooming magnificently across his chest. I catch him as he falls, and we both sink to the floor. My mind spins chaotically as I stare at the blood now covering my hands. Numbly, I shake him. His head lolls to one side.

Another violent shudder throws me over backward, and Kreel flops free of my grip. I scramble on all fours back to him, struggling to lift his dead weight to standing. Stumbling, Grafner emerges out from behind a bulkhead.

"Grafner. Grafner, get over here. We gotta get him to med bay." I grab Kreel under his arms. "His legs, Bill. Get his legs."

Grafner's face stretches into a wide, frenzied grin. His hand clasps a blade, cruelly hooked and dark with blood. "They're gods, Wheatley," he croons. "They are gods, and they are not pleased we've forgotten."

I stand up slowly, my heart hammering wildly as he, gnashing his teeth, drives the dagger into his arm. Twisting the blade gently, he works the tip beneath his implant.

I stand frozen, my mind stubbornly refusing to process that Bill, who I'd known for years, who had volunteered for this mission, whose family was among the taken, could possibly be this manic zealot.

"You're smart," he continues, flinging his implant aside as blood flows freely down his arm. "You know there's only one thing to do here, Wheatley. Fucking heads of state sending us out here like they could destroy God." He screams at the console. "Arrogant maggots! They don't understand, no, not them."

Another shudder from the engines. This time it knocks a hold unit free, and spare replacement bits scatter across the engine bay, distracting him. I throw myself at him, ramming my shoulder into his abdomen. He gasps for breath, and I wrench the blade free.

His breath becomes more ragged, and I realize he is laughing. "You're gutless, Wheatley," he sneers. "You won't kill me any more than you could the asswipes who threw you in here." He steps toward me, eyes hardening.

Anticipating his lunge, I drive my elbow into his nose when he charges. "Whatever I might be, Bill, you are still slow." Leaving him fuming and spitting blood, I take off toward the launch bay. Ducking into a console tucked behind a bulkhead, I tap into an escape pod's controls. One of the pods illuminates.

"Wheatley! Get back here, coward!" Grafner roars. Spotting the ready lights on the pod, he charges in. I punch in the confirmation code, and the pod seals behind him.

With the sharp hiss and clang of clamps releasing, the pod launches. Screaming in fury, Grafner beats at the doors. Writhing in anticipation, his gods close in on him as his pod floats deeper toward their nest.

Punching in the propulsion codes, I activate the pod's plasma thrust. The pod, rocketing forward, careens wildly while grasping tentacles snatch at it. As it plunges into the nearest Pillar, a brilliant flash rips through the formation, consuming the creatures in a blinding explosion.

Gods or not, they'll all fucking burn.

§

**Heather Terry** *is a writer, secondary English teacher, and adjunct professor hailing from Akron, Ohio. After earning her M.A. in English from Kent State University, she founded the Curious Words blog, a site dedicated to analyzing and sharing useful writing resources.*

*As a lover of the macabre, fantasy, and all things Harry Potter, Heather's works-in-progress range from Lovecraftian-inspired horror to tales from magical realms. When she isn't reading or writing about magic and monsters, she spends her time exploring with her husband, trying vainly to tire out their non-stop dog, and crafting Halloween creations well in advance of October.*

# When the Stars Were Wrong

## WENDY NIKEL

ILLUSTRATED BY
MICHAEL BUKOWSKI

THE CREATURE HID IN THE UNIVERSE'S SHADOWS, AND IF WE'D KNOWN that the *Andromeda XI* would cross its path, we'd have avoided that quadrant entirely. Or maybe not. Maybe we did know.

I don't recall.

The log doesn't indicate any intention of approaching the cosmic being, though the man called Tyrol suspects the records aren't entirely accurate. Our other crew member (Vivian, the patch on her suit says) has only rocked and spoken frantic gibberish since the creature enveloped us in its long, curling appendages, fracturing our fragile memories.

Tyrol pores over our records, his stubbly chin jutting out in concentration, madly circling words and phrases he doesn't think he's written. I stand beside him, staring blankly out the window at the being's giant, darting eye. Or at least I assume that's what it is. It's an orb of concentric circles that jerks about, mirroring my movements. Each circle grows incrementally, hypnotically smaller—a Fibonacci sequence tethered to an eyestalk.

"It says we were investigating an asteroid giving off a strange frequency . . . why can't I remember?" Tyrol's pen hovers over the letters, hesitant. He glances at my patch. "Nadia, do you recall how long we've been out here? How far we are from—"

From what? That's the real question, for though some sense of logic or instinct tells us we'd been on a journey to somewhere (or *from* somewhere) neither of us can remember where. Does it even matter, now that our ship is ensnared in some massive being's clutches and our computers are dim and unresponsive?

I don't answer. It's hopeless.

The ship shudders, and instinctively, I reach out to steady myself. A flash of something on my wrist catches my eye, awakens something in me. A memory? A clue? I ease my bulky sleeve back to expose the tattoo.

"PRISONER #7820-02."

Something heavy hits the ship. My heart slams into my rib cage. Prisoner? Of what? And why? What exactly have I forgotten?

"I'll search the storage compartments," I tell Tyrol, and at his look of surprise, I quickly add, "for clues." I'm not ready yet to tell him what I found: not sure what he'd do or if I should trust him. Or if he should trust me.

The longer I search, the stronger my unease and the more persistent the creature's battering upon the hull. There's no escape pod, but that's not all that's missing. The compartments are fake—Medical Supplies and Food, Lab Equipment and Tools—nothing but squares of plastic fused to the ship's walls. If it even is a ship.

The monster's eye stalk follows me, floating from window to window, circling the orb of our prison. I can't shake the sense that it's angry. That it doesn't want me to discover these things. It doesn't want me to remember.

As we stare each another down, its strangely globed eye reflects the red letters of the ship's name from the hull, backward in the reflection but still decipherable: *Andromeda XI.*

The name strikes a chord. Though I still don't know how we got here, I remember the origin of the name, the myth that goes with it. I rush to the window, and there, beyond the eyestalk, is a tether holding us to the asteroid. Trapping us here like the mythological princess awaiting Cetus's wrath. A sacrifice to an angry god.

Ignoring Tyrol's protests, I pry off the control console's cover, but it's empty, bare of wires or circuits. I begin to piece things together. My breath comes fast. Sweat tickles my neck. Apprehension crumbles into panic.

The hull of the ship—no, *prison*—groans with the sound of bending metal. The creature knows that I know. I can feel it worming through my mind, trying

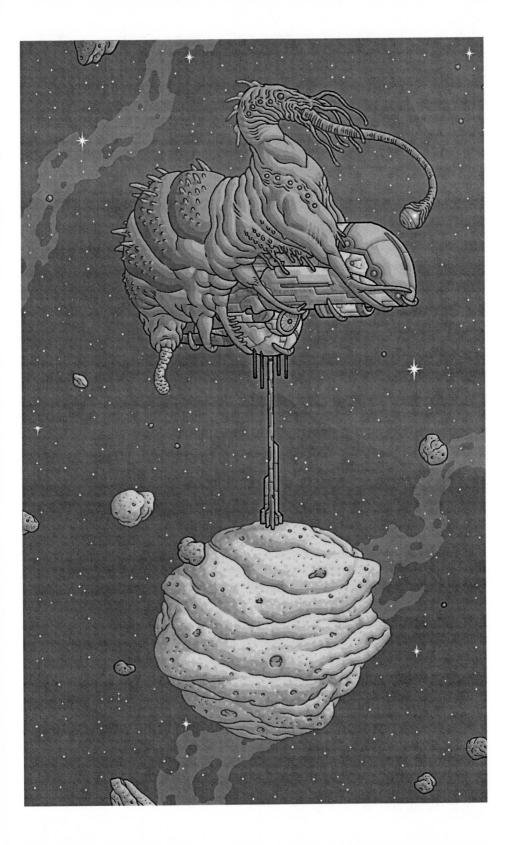

to rework the lies and lull me into complacency, again, but I resist, muttering, "Andromeda."

I may not know who sent us here (an enemy? a government? a vengeful alien race?). I may not know if we deserve this. I may not be able to save us from our fate, but I won't sit by and do nothing. The creature's exterior is tough enough to withstand the vacuum of space, but maybe . . . maybe, I can ensure it dies with us, that no more prisoners—no more Andromedas—are sent here again.

"Nadia!" Tyrol reaches out over the sound of Vivian's screams, over the snapping of aluminum bits as I yank panels from the wall, searching for the oxygen tanks and electrical wiring that provide us our limited air and light. The end is coming by tooth or claw or stomach acid, and as I find what I'm searching for, the creature keens and pushes us inside, enveloping us in utter darkness as the walls crumple around me.

My mind splinters. Plots, strategies, plans die half-realized, lost between broken synapses, disappearing like the stars. I grasp at my fragmented ideas, fumbling for meaning. *Andromeda.* It's the small things that I can cling to.

The ink on Tyrol's wrist, matching my own.

The pink, fleshy throat tissue, contracting outside the cracking glass of a window.

The valve on the oxygen tank, open and leaking.

The wires connecting, igniting a spark.

And my final thought as the universe bursts wide open: the ship's name on my patch.

Andromeda, taking her revenge.

§

**Wendy Nikel** *is a speculative fiction author with a degree in elementary education, a fondness for road trips, and a terrible habit of forgetting where she's left her cup of tea. Her short fiction has been published by* Fantastic Stories of the Imagination, Daily Science Fiction, Nature: Futures, *and elsewhere. Her time travel novella,* The Continuum, *is forthcoming from World Weaver Press in spring 2018. For more info, visit wendynikel.com*

# Union

## ROBERT WHITE

ILLUSTRATED BY
LUKE SPOONER

*I* HATE BEING A MARINE.

No, that isn't true. I have seen things. Done things. And gotten more tail from more species and genders than I would have imagined before boot. The corps has made me a fresh-faced, badass heartbreaker and life-taker. I love the armor. I love the machinery. I love my guys. And I love jumping into the shit and making the kind of *boom* that makes my spine go numb. I love being a marine.

I hate being a marine, today.

But I can't run to any of that. The beat is wrong. So "I hate being a marine" is pounding in my head as I run up-deck. See, I'm being chased. Not super fast but not all that slow neither. There's something behind me.

Not someone. Something. And not the normal sort of something. Not a seeker. Not a bunch of guys on a flatbed. Not even the *skitter skitter skitter* of high velocity beads dancing against the walls and deck. It's something else.

I'm pretty sure that the only reason I *am* running is that I managed to avoid getting a proper look. There were five of us a second ago. Walking along K-deck from Wastewater to Port-Side Power Management, checking compartments and punching in the stations of our rounds like cheap rent-a-cops. Now, there's only three of us.

I hope there's three of us, anyway. Billy is in front of me. That's pissing me off. He's my best bud. We do everything together. And he's always telling that same stupid joke. "Don't gotta outrun the bear" is all fine and funny, but Billy's outrunning *me*, and now, it's not so funny.

One of the other guys is behind me. Not sure who. Least, I hope it's one of the other guys. I ain't gonna turn and look, that's fer damn sure. I'm pretty sure it's one of the guys. I told you I didn't get a good look. Don't want one, neither. But what I did see, well, I'm pret-darn sure that it wouldn't make that *thump thump thump thump* of good old-fashioned boots on deck plate.

I think there'd be slithering. Or slurping. Or some sick sliding sound I don't got words for. That's what it'd sound like right behind me. I know 'cause something strange like that is coming from just a bit further back.

Plus, I don't think there'd be that much swearing coming out of that thing nohow. In what I didn't see, I clearly didn't see a mouth. And the guy behind me's got quite a mouth on him from what I hear.

So maybe right now, maybe, I don't gotta outrun the bear either.

Cam and Teri. They froze. That's 'cause they got a good look, I expect. But that didn't slow that thing much at all. They got off a bunch of shots, too. Least I'm gonna hope that was gunfire. That muted sloppy snapping sound coming out wet and hollow. Best if it was gunfire.

Now I heard about these things. I even seen blurry-ass pictures. Pictures ain't the same thing 'tall. Don't do it justice.

Whoa, Billy made the bulkhead. He better not close it. Least not yet. I need maybe five more steps. If he pushes the button now, it'll close before I get all the way through. Yep. Three more steps, and damn straight, I'm going through even if I don't make it all the way. I could stand to lose a foot or a leg or two. Anything below the junk. I like my junk. But hell, a guy can live without his junk if he's gotta.

Yes. Now. Push the button, Billy. I can make it from here. Come on. Push. The. Button.

Why haven't you pushed the button, Billy? You didn't keep running, didja? Come on man. Push the button. I'm nearly there. You better be there at that button, Billy, or I am gonna kick your ass when I find you.

Good. Blinking light and warning strips down. Button pressed. In two steps, I'll be there. Good boy, Billy. But you waited a little too long. What the hell, Billy? Why the wait? Oh yeah, there's a guy behind me.

Shit. Bad sound. Someone stumbled. I hope it wasn't me.

Left boot good. Right boot good. Still running. Wasn't me.

Shit. Ern. Cam and Teri ate it; Billy out front. Me here. That leaves Ern.

Yeah, I got time. Door's way up there. I got a good two seconds. Maybe even three. A short three seconds. Yeah. That's like forever. I got time to do what's got to be done. Left boot's coming up again. I plant it there on the deck just past the door seal like that's where it belongs, and I reach back.

Gawd, I hope its Ern. I still ain't gonna look. No way.

Yes! Sleeve. With an arm in it and everything. Score! One hand a sleeve, the other a collar, I seize, hold, and throw.

Dumbass is still falling. He stumbles over the bulkhead threshold and trips over the second threshold to splay across the deck beyond.

Second threshold?

Shit! Double doors. Section twenty blast containment. I forgot! Now, I remember.

But it's too late. I was gonna do it. I was gonna dive through and lose a body part if I had too. But I don't. I pull up short. Who's the dumbass now?

Doors slam down, fore and aft, and I'm in the dark space in between.

I guess I always knew a person could fit between these doors. Never thought it'd be me though. And dark. Never thought how dark. But not silent.

The loudest noise is me breathing up the air. That one's gonna kill me fast if I can't cut it back. Next loudest is the engines: realspace throbbing, N-space spooling up slowly. Way too slowly. But behind that is every scrape 'n clink 'n thud throughout the ship with more boots running and a million other noises. The engines are spooling—that's a good thing. When the ship jumps, it will leave the monster behind. Don't know why, it just works that way. But it takes like half an hour for this tub to get from standby to jump. I don't know how long it's been since the alert. No way it's been half an hour.

I strain my ears, listening. Beneath all the comforting noise, I can hear the slithering, metallic evil of that thing. I'm trying not to listen to it. It must just be my imagination. I think, I hope, that it isn't right there behind me, just a few inches of alloy away from me, but I know it is.

I can't turn around. I'd rather be facing toward it, even with the doors holding me pinned. I try to turn anyway, slow and careful, but my shoulders and hips are wider than the gap. My belt buckle scrapes across the plating, and I freeze. It's just so creepy to have it behind me. Sliding and slithering. A million tiny razor spines scraping sensitively across the bulkhead, extending and retracting, undulating bits that would put the word tentacle to shame for being so fixed and predictable.

It's there. I know it. I feel it in my soul. I feel the door growing warmer against my back, and I want that to just be me. My heat leaching into the steel. But in my churning gut, I know it's more.

I can see it there in my head, humping and mounding against the bulkhead. Searching. Probing. Feeling my heartbeat and rushing blood through the now scant layers separating us.

I am being quiet now. My breath slow. I feel the hawk passing overhead, the lion in the brush, the predator in the deep. Every fear I have ever imagined or felt pales. My grisly death is right behind me. I listen without choice.

The air is still fresh. This tiny compartment isn't sealed. There's no light, but air is coming in from somewhere. I hope it's from somewhere far away, but I know that's not how things work.

I wait. Someone, somewhere, please open this door. Just the one in front please.

God, if you can hear me, please make Billy open the door. Or Ern, he owes me.

I don't think you can open just the one door. But I want it to be that you can and someone will.

But there's nothing. They probably think I'm dead if they are even still there. Probably don't know that I'm here, safe between the doors.

Something warm cradles my right foot, and I piss myself. That's how I know that first warm wetness didn't come from me.

I expected slimy, I expected pain, but I just feel enveloping warmness. It's gathering around me. Some of it, anyway. It can't all fit in this tiny space. When it got Cam and Teri, it was fast and vicious. Why's it taking its time now?

Goddamn, it's inside my clothes.

It's scraping my skin, coming up along my spine. No cutting or nothin', but I can feel the sharpness in it. All needles and scalpels and razor blades almost cutting. Almost.

I'm frozen. Waiting. I don't know what's gonna set it off. What's gonna start the carving, the gutting. I want to scream, but I can't. If I scream, it will get me. I know that's dumb since it's got me now, but the corner of my brain that can still think just isn't in control of anything.

It starts. I feel it pushing into me. Rape? No fucken way man. That's just not fair . . . damn, it's not just there. Shit. Everywhere. Ass, yeah, but mouth and nose and ears and . . . my junk. In my junk, man! I do scream now. But just the once. A tiny squeak as the air seeps out, and the thing rushes in.

Pain!

Finally the pain!

I never knew that pain could be a relief. The shame and the fear are gone. Just sensation. I would scream more, but there's no more air in me. This pain fills me and keeps going. Ten thousand precision cuts all at once fill me to overflowing.

And nothing. The pain is gone. Replaced by something too intense to call pain. Sliding and slithering along my nerves, crunching bone away from my spine. Laying me open but holding me together.

I wish I'd known. I wish someone had warned me. I want to go back and feel it again. Whatever that was, it was so sudden and so beyond anything. I don't know what they'd have said. But I feel like I missed out on something for not being ready when it happened.

And now, I know I'm crazy. I have lost my shit entirely. This thing is cutting my flesh away. A million tiny, sharpened chopsticks piercing and plucking and slicing. But sensation has me zoning out as nerve is whisked from meat and cradled by otherness.

My eyes. I feel them. Pain returns there because I can feel them being pushed from behind. It's in my skull. The darkness is full of spots and flares from the pressure of my eyes being pushed out of my skull from behind.

I know it now. It's in my brain. Oh God, it's going to eat my brain! A brain can't feel pain. How will I know? Will I even know parts of me are going? I feel my body going.

I want to grab at my memories, but I can't. There's too much pressure. I just can't think. Too much sensation. Too much of everything. All of my life in one go. It's supposed to flash in front of me, but all I have is now. A body that can't scream and lights flashing in the darkness as my eyes . . .

Ooohhh . . . I get it now . . .

That's my favorite part . . . when I realize again, for the first time, how small everything is.

I don't know what I was thinking. It's all so obvious, and I've got like no time. Twenty-two minutes and the ship will be gone. The people will be gone. I'll lose them all. Billy will be gone. And Ern. And that hot number down in engineering who always looks so coy when we see each other in the mess. If they get away, I'll probably never find them again, and their lives will be over in a flash. Lost.

Pushing through the venting is workable, but it takes a long time. Now that there's nothing valuable between the bulkheads, I just tear them away.

I can smell Billy. Everybody always can, what with that cheapass cologne he thinks is so hot. He'll laugh when he realizes that's how I found him.

And Ern. There's a little bit of his blood and snot on the deck. Guess he fell all the way down after I tossed him through the doors. That tang of blood is even easier to follow.

I surge past the blood, and as I touch it, I am flooded with insight. Blood and fluids from numberless races and encounters. Ern's DNA is sampled by reflex and unspooled as a curiosity, but I don't wait. Probabilities and events spanning a sector of space come to mind. Parts of me pay attention to parts of that, but the bulk of my body here keeps my attention focused. My three or four dozen local objectives each get a full measure of my attention.

I come across Dr. Mann in power distribution, tuning up the lateral sensor harmonics. I glance over my shoulder at my other new aspects, I was two of his students, an assistant, and one of his peers for nearly thirty years, once. Those fractions of me know he needs his machines to see me, so he can feel safe. Those aspects will handle the doctor, but Doc's a good guy so I help out a little. He's one of the reasons I came this way instead of heading up through command.

I slow down. I let him take his scans. I just hope he remembers to key for record. I've been pushing that button for him for decades. I'll probably have to do it again this one last time.

Billy is helping Ern up-deck. He must have brained himself when I threw him through the hatch. I'll have to be extra careful when I join him. He's kind of a tool, but he's amazing with his hands and pretty astounding with his music. Funny stories, too. I'll want that. It's worth saving.

Billy is using his brain now. I can tell. I know that look. Must have stopped panicking when he paused at the door. His timing was perfect on the button. If Ern hadn't stumbled, we'd have been through perfect and long gone by now. Stopping to punch down each bulkhead is a good move, and he's keeping Ern moving while they work their way to the tubes. Billy has a great tactical awareness, and he's smart as a lick. He just doesn't know I've also got around him through the power runs.

The jump engines are starting to sing to me. It's wonderful, reminding me of the between. I've been in this surging tide of gravity and time since it came to be, and that is a rush of its own. Mass, light, time, and life. Each delicious in its own way. So much to see, so much to remember, so much more to become. But the between always beckons.

Doc finishes his scans—well, finished enough for what time there is. I slip into his flesh at the edges. Sure enough, he never remembers to key the record. I'm sure he's freaked out by the way his hands are carefully operating the links without his volition. He'll understand in a second. I push the data out on the wave. Sometimes, these ships blow when they jump out on me, and his scans are as artful as all his work. I admire him—always have. That's why so many of my aspects followed him on these military projects despite a loathing for blood and violence. 'Course, that was before I understood. His mind and his work both deserve my care.

I've been taking a lot of care with Billy and Ern. Keeping them from escaping has taken a long time. No way I got time to join them both before the jump, but Billy's about to duck into a lifeboat. He'll laugh when he figures out I knew that'd be his move if I could get him here. Before he can hit the door switch that would shut me out just long enough, I surge an arm past him and splash some of myself against the jettison controls.

Three moments of the best damn part of life happen almost all at once. Doctor Mann comes to unity, and his wisdom and understanding flood me with insight and wonder. There's an exquisite meaty separation as my arm is severed from my bulk when the lifeboat leaps away. And the jump pushes my bulk into the between where its mass dissolves in the joy of a nothingness I cannot sustain from here.

Of course, nothing is lost. Mass is nothing. Time is persistent. And I am as I always have been. As I will be 'til this reality ends, and I rejoin my brethren in the between.

I have a moment of extra surprise and odd disappointment. When I took the scans I already knew that I was going to be absorbed. I was expecting to be extinguished or perhaps become one of a chorus of lesser voices dominated by a malevolent overwhelming mind. But I am just me, only with more memories and vastly more comprehensive and well-informed opinions. In the same way that I once might have wanted to eat lunch, continue working, and take a vacation all at once, I find myself possessed of countless goals and motivations, each undiminished. And the greatest wonder is that I have the capacity to pursue so many of these goals at once. I begin contemplating how to effectively communicate this back to the research fellowship. They must be told. Of course, that can wait as I have to see to more immediate issues. If I don't see to my buds, right now, they are going to disappear and likely die in some damn mudhole before I can join them.

'Course, Billy's swearing up a storm. He'll laugh his ass off when he finally understands. I know I shouldn't swear—I was raised better than that, more times than not—but for Billy, it's just the right words.

I can feel Billy eyeing the self-destruct. We'd joked about why you'd want such a damn-fool thing in a lifeboat before. 'Course, I am all over the controls, so he's not gettin' at that. He doesn't understand. He figures that if he can take me out he's spending his life for a good cause, but I cannot be diminished, and spending his life, especially for nothin', would be such a waste.

I don't got a lot of mass to work with here. I'm summoning more from the between, but that's slow work, so I'm peeling up bits of the deck and such. Adding them to my bulk.

I'm making quite a show. Waving bits around on the console, tryin' ta keep Billy's eyes on me while I make a slow gambit with a tendril to get at Ern, lying half-conscious on the deck between us. Billy sees me working. I see him see that right back, and now, we're playing tugger-war with Ern, who's bellowing like a damn fool. Always was so dramatic. I slip him a paralytic.

The union is going to be a lot of careful work. Ern's got a brain bruise. I gotta get him in shape for the change. Wouldn't be fair to half-ass the job. Boy's brain damaged enough on his best day.

In the moment I'm thinking that, Billy acts. He's fast. I'm faster. But there ain't enough of me to go around.

The gun comes up. I harden myself up to knock the first shot aside to protect Ern and lunge, but the gun keeps coming up, and with a second hard retort, Billy's gone.

The dumb shit actually kacked himself. I bellow aloud and far into the ultraviolet as I surge forward to see what can be saved.

He's gone, dammit.

Most of his memories are there in the bottom of his skull, but his life is gone. I carefully envelop what I can, but this is not union. It's like slipping stills from a vid. Lost moments, stripped of their vital purpose. No organizing context. The vital continuity is just absent.

I'm crying. Marines aren't supposed to cry, but sometimes, we do.

I work on both my buddies. Ern is easy to save. I repair his damage and slip inside his every synapse and fiber and lift him from his flesh and . . .

Ooohhh . . .

I understand.

That's always my favorite part.

Two rush together and become one. Understanding dawns. Both the wonder of the whole and the amazement of each least bit.

And I am sad again at learning of Billy's loss. I loved him. That's why I always played my music for him. That's why I kept trying to shake him free of my dead weight while we fled. Trying to make sure he saved himself. Not that he'd ever abandon a bud. 'Course, I didn't know then what I know now. Not all of me anyway.

Each bit of me that knew Billy tells different versions of different stories from different perspectives as I savor and preserve memories delicately lifted from his ruined skull. Funny stories. Sad stories. Happy moments. I am filled with regret.

It is all a memorial to what could have been.

I could have been Billy forever, too, and now, he's just snapshots and tall tales.

But it's a familiar loss in far too many ways. There's joy to be had in species and cultures and universes to come.

I piece his body together and use it to lay in a course and set the alerts. I clean up his mess and make things look right. I curl up some of my bulk in his empty skull to wait for rescue and dismiss the rest into the between.

There's more to be had. Billy had family and friends, and they'll have descendants—a whole culture to join with and preserve into the infinite. A tiny bit of my bulk goes into cold sleep with Billy's remains, falsifying life signs for the machinery, waiting for whomever finds this lifeboat, dreaming of who Billy might have been.

Even while I sleep here, I am elsewhere. Places where I am a god or a monster, places where I am watching life begin and others where intelligent people are fading to ruin and one or two where I am actually understood.

That's how it's always been. I am who I always have been but more so with each moment.

I go in and catch up what would be lost. Rescue the obscure from final entropy. It is a joy. It is dangerous and intense and eternally amazing. I save the lost.

*I love being a marine.*

§

**Robert White** *is a professional computer scientist and amateur philosopher who predates the internet. Weaned on a big box of pulp science fiction novels and a full set of Time Life science and technology books, raised by tabletop roleplaying games, and finally washed up in the fjords of flash fiction websites, he decided to try his hand at real authorship. With a firm belief that victory and defeat can not always be told apart and a strong preference for stories that refresh the soul, he'll invite you to imagine that the stories we all know are, perhaps, hiding a different truth.*

# Under Venusian Skies

## INGRID GARCIA

ILLUSTRATED BY
DAVE FELTON

*—outside-in—*

**W**HILE HIS BODY SOARS THROUGH A SURREAL, WHITE-PINK SKY, BARETTA'S mind keeps drifting. His hyper-gossamer wings gleam a static purple, his stun exoskeleton is charging up fast. Under his wings, the broccoli-like expansions of the Fractal Forest glow a defying green. As if the hectic flora isn't giving him enough headaches already, reports have come in about aggressive seeds floating around.

The seeds are damaging the organic sensors that keep track of the new forest's development. While being seeded by humans, the Fractal Forest has been living a life of its own. In clear skies—there seem to be fewer sulfuric acid clouds, of late—Keeper Baretta has been dispatched to inspect the situation. Close by, his partner Vanessa glides in a figure-eight holding pattern, charging her stun capacitors.

"It's been crazy here," Vanessa says in the staccato Venusian lingo, "ever since the Bimini impact."

"A coup," Baretta says in the same, almost infrasonic voice, "it tripled our amount of water."

"Yeah, but we're not really keeping the explosion of life around it in check."

"Well," Baretta muses, "I'm not sure if we should."

Vanessa signals that her batteries and capacitors are fully charged. Baretta's are at 89%, his computer implants error-free and ready. *Screwfly it,* he thinks, *this should do.*

Vanessa acknowledges his engage code, and they dive into the Fractal Forest.

Graphene-spun, hyper-gossamer wings shape-shifting from flight to fight mode start a trajectory-perfect descent into a bio-fractalscape that would have weirded out Benoît Mandelbrot himself. Life on Venus has been kick-started at an altitude of fifty kilometers, where the pressure is Earth-normal. Genetically engineered, hygroscopic sponges imbued with improved photosynthesis floated around the planet on a seek-and-create mission. They evolved from small archipelagos of floating sponges, photosynthesizing the basics in miniature, into the highly advanced flora Baretta and Vanessa witness today.

Fractal tendrils extending into both the solar wind and cosmic radiation signifying the relentless competition. Heat from the nearby Sun, cosmic rays from far-off, long-ago supernovas not deflected by the planet's negligible magnetic field power a frantic change behavior. Everything is in flux. Nothing remains the same.

Imagine a coral reef cuttlefish, continuously mimicking its environment as it moves from hard to soft to brain coral, over sand, over rocks, over mud. Always adapting its shape and colors to its environment, becoming well-nigh invisible. Then imagine the LSD-reverse situation, two human bats-out-of-hell moving through an environment that, like a massive school of intertwined, fractal-freak, color-mad, shape-shifting octopi continuously adapt and reach out to *their* environment—a manic cosmic cocktail of high-energy particle bombardments, irradiating solar microwaves and the odd, souped-up solar flare.

Since energy is abundant, the fast and the furious outcompete the lush and the lethargic. *Constant change is here to stay,* croons the New World Man, and the Fractal Forest embodies the lyrics. Shifting patterns spike the fractalscape as multi-hued, fragile-looking yet razor-sharp flowers bloom in the celestial radiation soup. Caught in the crossfire of a burning, passionate sun and a cold, glaring universe, the transplanted life squirms, squeezes and squeaks, but survives, and strives to thrive.

Like flies diving into a cosmic soup that's constantly developing new ingredients. *Out of control*, Baretta thinks. *No, denying the very concept of control itself.* Yet, as they get closer, variations appear. Several areas are unmoving, bleached, wrinkled or a dry, sickly yellow, like a badly polarized white, starkly contrasting the eruption of colors around them. Baretta points some of those out to Vanessa. She acknowledges them but gestures that they should get to the last remaining biosensors first.

Baretta curses his curiosity. Only twenty-four biosensors left, out of the several thousand—and counting—that monitored this fast-growing forest.

Gleaming, metallic blue trapezoidal shapes criss-cross the area in what seems to be a semi-random pattern. Neither Baretta nor Vanessa have seen these seed-like lifeforms before. Quickly, they decide to let Vanessa gather as many of the remaining organic sensors as possible while Baretta checks out the cobalt seedpods.

*A butterfly net would come in handy*, Baretta thinks, but he only has a few sample canisters. On top of that, the deep blue seedpods move swiftly in the high winds, easily evading his efforts at capture. But his skills improve with effort, and after a number of near-misses, he finally manages to trap one.

This changes the behavior of the other seedpods. At first, they were, if not outright ignoring him, avoiding him. Now, they seem to notice him and to attack him as one.

This both baffles and amuses Baretta, who nonchalantly swats the first one away with a quick swipe of his free hand. Strangely, it stings a little. He didn't expect to feel anything at all through his tough flexi-harness. More are coming in, but he moves upward out of this fractal branch.

The cobalt seedpods follow him and a few crash into his feet, legs, and lower back. The sting in his hand gets worse. It begins to burn. It hurts so bad he can't suppress a scream.

"What's wrong?" Vanessa asks. "Are you alright?"

"One of those seedpod things stung me," he says, "and somehow got through my armor."

"That's crazy. I'm on my way." She has already picked up the remaining biosensors and just finished taking a sample of the strangely decaying, bleached-white fractal bushes nearby. With a swift turn, she heads in his direction.

As she gets close, more of his screams pierce the radio waves. "What the hell?

They're getting through my leg armor, too!"

Vanessa fires a broad volley of stun grenades into the cobalt seedpod cloud. This slows them down, and Baretta starts up his auxiliary jet and rockets away. Vanessa follows as she hears his agonized cries. She's already called in emergency help.

When she catches up, she sees several holes in the harness around his feet, legs, and lower back. They look etched out by acid. Instinctively, she douses him with her drinking water. It seems to offer relief.

Thankfully, their harnesses aren't pressure suits; the atmospheric pressure at this altitude is close to Earth normal. Their armor protects against $CO_2$ poisoning, the inadvertent passage through a sulfuric acid cloud, the improbable—but not impossible—strike by high-altitude lightning, and the unexpected things the fast-evolving Fractal Forest might throw at them.

After all the stings have been doused, Baretta feels much better. He insists he's fine and can get back home on his own, but Vanessa won't have any of it. She signals for the emergency vessel to hurry up.

It arrives a mere five seconds after Baretta has passed out.


*—inside-out—*


. . . inside the huge, floating halls of Seed City, Quadrant 4, Baretta's a caged animal. He does not belong here . . .

. . . a twenty-four hour cycle is just too short, as the high winds blow them around Venus in ninety-six. The bio-rhythm tries to adapt but is not helped by the forced Earth-normal schedule . . .

. . . no rest behind a cappuccino. A dapple-skinned kid bothers him, rekindling memories of his old Trojan Bubble project. "Lateral thinking that should be applied here." Boy, that bubble imploded . . .

. . . it set back the Outer Cool to its sedate, conservative ways. And the Inner Hotspot seems frozen in a phase-transition, a paradigm lost . . .

. . . but who is poisoning the Fractal Forest? Eco-fanatics from Keep Venus Pristine? Industrial conglomerates staking claims? Renegade scientists unleashing untested triple-helical molecules . . .

. . . chomping down asparagus, black beans, and onions like mad, he's hot here, cold there, and uncertain everywhere in between.

Why all this sulfur-rich food? What's happening . . .

   . . . a paragon of paranoia: intrusive spyware, combative botware, uroboric wormware. I spy the spy spying with my third eye . . .

    . . . a master plan by a cabal of corporations, megalomaniacal government schemes, surreptitious infiltration by secret services, an evolutionary cul-de-sac . . .

     . . . certainty in the sea of doubt. Evidence in the ocean of supposition. Order in the chaotic fractal cloud. Chaos in the order of superposition . . .

*Pow—more heat than light*
*Energy spiraling up*
*A triple helix*

. . . hot on the trail. Burning suspicion. Fierce conviction. Feverish mind. Feverish body. Fever. Fever, retriever, fever, deceiver, fever—in the true believer. Burning, churning, learning, yearning until the world becomes one big entropic blur . . .

Baretta awakes in a hospital bed. He's sweating like a pig, babbling like a madman and crying like a baby. As realization dawns, he shuts up and blinks the tears from his eyes. The nurse next to him bears a striking resemblance to Vanessa. She's not wearing a uniform. OK, it is Vanessa, wiping the sweat from his brow.

"How are you?" She asks. "Feeling a bit better now?"

"But I was busy getting to the bottom of it," Baretta has trouble letting go, "I . . ."

"What bottom?" Vanessa looks worried, "you've been delirious for days. With periods of sleepwalking fugues where we lost you."

"Delirious? Fever?" He's slowly coming to his senses. "But how?"

"The cobalt insectoids that bit you," she says, "used a nasty combination of aqua regis and a virus we haven't been able to nail down yet. I suffered the same fever—"

"King's water?" Baretta is flabbergasted. "So that's how they got through my armor." As the rest of her words filter through. "You had a fever, too?"

"Not as bad as you," she says, "and you'll feel better soon. Much better. But we're in quarantine until they found out why."

"Crazy insectoids," Baretta wonders, "how could they evolve such targeted, specific stuff so fast?"

"Even crazier," Vanessa lifts her index finger, "just think about it. They're fauna, not flora."

### —paradigm-shift—

Swooping over the Fractal Forest, Baretta feels it has changed. Not in its usual, frantically evolving ways but *qualitatively* changed. He feels it in his bones, in his stun skeleton, a faint buzz, like the onset of an announcement. Not just the outside world but his inner self, as well. The hiss of a channel about to open up, the hum at the start of a tune. Vanessa was right, he feels better than ever, vibrant, energetic, more aware.

It makes no sense. Probably the after-effects of his fever. Vanessa's with him. They're useless in quarantine and expendable here. The new titanium-doped biosensors need to be field tested, together with the new exosuits.

The whole scene is still an explosion of biological Turing machines turned Mandelbrot, changes sweeping the fractalscape in hypnotizing patterns, branches upon branches upon branches until it seems they go on well into the quantum level, yet . . .

*It's like there's order in chaos,* Baretta thinks, *a method to the madness.*

So far, they haven't encountered any of the cobalt-blue insectoids. Which makes sense: as the prey is consumed, the predator dies off. At least in a normal biosphere. Baretta's not so sure if the Fractal Forest plays by the same rules. For all intents and purposes, it's evolving into a very lean-and-mean survival machine. One that's quickly growing out of its creators' control.

"You OK?" Vanessa says in the deep, Venusian voice. "You seem even more lost in thought than usual."

"I'm fine. It just feels a bit different"—a reluctant pause—"and too quiet."

"Never thought anybody would say that of this place," Vanessa says, amused, "but I know what you mean."

Out of the myriad of fractal iterations, a swarm of trapezoidal, kite-like beings rises up to meet them. Their long and short sides flutter in a blur. Like butterflies, their path up close seems random, but over the long run, they are definitely moving in a certain direction. Towards Vanessa and Baretta.

These trapezoidal insectoids look white-but-not-quite-white—not colorless, not the merging of all colors, but strangely, the potential, the promise of more colors. It hurts to look at them, yet it's almost impossible to look away, as if something deep within compels Baretta to keep staring at them. Despite the irritation. Despite the itch. Despite the pain.

"My eyes are starting to hurt," he says, "what about yours?"

"Same," Vanessa says, "but for the life of me, I just can't look away. I must keep watching. As if it will lead . . . "

"To a new way of seeing." Baretta finishes.

They can't speak anymore. The pain overrides everything. The closer the trapezoidal insectoids come, the more their bleached whiteness cuts through their senses, opening up something new. It hurts. The backs of their eyes feel as if they're bombarded with millions of tiny laser beams, torn apart by an army of nano-razors.

The whiteness becomes overpowering, a whiteout that washes all away. A fierce brightness burning the backs of their skulls. For countless moments, they float, unseeing. Then the intense pain recedes, and vision returns—slowly, foggy and somewhat off-kilter. The Fractal Forest becomes its multihued self, no, it seems to become more than its multihued self. It's sharper, better defined, almost supersaturated.

The sky is not its usual dull pinkish-white anymore but a deep shade of infrared at least as bright and intense as the blue of Earth's sky on a cloudless day. A color outside the visible light spectrum, a reflected frequency that the human brain cannot translate into a part of the rainbow. A red beyond red, a red so quintessentially different from the earth-normal color palette that they'll need to invent a new name for it.

How is that possible? Has his vision extended into the infrared? It might make sense on a planet closer to the Sun, where the predominance of $CO_2$ in the atmosphere both filters and scatters the sunlight in a different manner. Yet how could this adaptation happen so fast? Are they becoming just as crazy as the Fractal Forest?

Baretta hears Vanessa cry out, first in surprise, then in wonder. She points to the trapezoidal insectoids.

Baretta can't suppress a scream, either. At first, his eyes can't make sense of them—they dazzle, they flicker, they change colors like crazy until what he sees are not quite colors anymore. Not normal colors, anyway. But eventually the trapezoidal insectoids become beautiful, like a school of coral reef fish, like a swarm of tropical butterflies. Gone is the sickly yellow, the badly polarized white sheen—they're imbued with patterns. Stripes, spots, bands, and ribbons in a variety of infrared shades that they can finally see but not describe.

Like someone who's used a slide rule all their life and then is confronted with a computer that does the same calculations and much more besides—and not just a huge mainframe but a computer so small it fits in a pocket and is called a "smartphone." Like someone who's suffered tinnitus all their life being cured, suddenly hearing all nuances in speech and music clearly. Like someone who's only tasted white wines and is now introduced to the full variety of reds and rosés. Like scientists realizing that genetic information is carried by DNA structured like a double spiral.

Maybe the burning pain in their eyes was a growing pain, adding a fourth cone type to their photoreceptors. However, the brain then needs to interpret the new types of colors. This process is highly disorienting at first until the mind settles into a representation.

Almost, but not quite, like a veil being lifted, like walking out of a long dark tunnel into the light. With initial effects not unlike a perceptual shift or a conceptual breakthrough with synesthetic overtones—these shades of infrared look like the colors hidden by the twilight's chiaroscuro now revealed by the morning sun, this tone of infrared sounds like suddenly understanding a strange language, and those tinges of infrared taste like the complex combination of tannins, cacao and black pepper balancing the floral, fruity and peaty undertones of a single malt.

The trapezoidal insectoids, those floating tables, don't seem threatening anymore. Au contraire, they now look welcoming. Baretta also feels a minor rise in the background vibration, a weird interference like a happy buzz. A tear in one of his hyper-gossamer wings? No, their diagnostics read fine. A minor malfunction in the new exosuit? Why didn't he feel it earlier? Maybe a lingering side effect as his brain incorporates the new color schemes?

Closer up, Baretta now sees the fractal edges of the fluttering trapezoids. It should be impossible as the frame rate with which these insectoids flit their kite-like bodies should be well above the human flicker fusion threshold. Has his brain sped up, his perception become faster? Like Vanessa said, he does feel much better since the fever retreated.

At some point, though, the kite insectoids keep their distance and twirl around in enticing patterns, beckoning, as if asking the humans to follow. Serendipitously, the frequency and intensity of the vibrations rummaging his being seem to rise to a frantic buzz. He wants to ask Vanessa if she's experiencing something similar, but she answers him before he can form the question. "Yes, I feel it too. An upbeat tone, like an elated glissando."

"You—"

"—answered before you could ask. I know. It's like I'm totally in sync with you. I can anticipate your next move. You should try it, too."

Baretta shifts some of his attention—the crazy events beneath him had been totally absorbing—to Vanessa, he feels an instant connection. Not quite telepathy, more like he can almost feel what she feels. A strong empathic link. Her attention for her partner's safety is imbued with something deeper. Admiration? Respect? Friendship?

Too much happening at once; Baretta feels his focus waning. "Let's just follow them, first?" He says. "We can talk about . . . us later."

"Fine." Vanessa smiles ear-to-ear.

In the wake of the "kitesects"—or "zoidflies"—they're approaching the area of the white-out sections: sick, colorless segments where, once, vibrant life shouted its exuberant celebration in exultant pigments. They'd been so taken aback with the bleaching that they'd overlooked the fact that the shapes and forms were still alright, perfectly fractalized, constantly varying, diversifying, changing . . .

Now, they can see. An infrarufescence too spectacular to be taken in at once. Indescribable to those whose vision is not wired to infrahues.

When language and vision unite and take a synesthetic leap of faith:

> *Neologisms negating the need to negotiate new nexus to neophytes? Yes, sirrah, cabinets of sauvignon grimace in a grand mal beckoning a mellow pin—oh, noir is the beau you laid. Just dip into the vermillion verisimilitude. Fly over fields*

*of multiformed pimpernel so scarlet they beat beet red three rungs down the ladder. Chase cerise cardinals and carmine apiece cheering the claret of cochineal cacti clouding the infractalscape. Crimson clay Bodacious bricks so corroded they kick rust's ass into a new low of infrastructure. Rubies marooned in foxy cherry-pies bleeding infravescence under the veil of a vermeil sky. Schools of gules criss-crossing sanguine corals under the mask of a damask heaven. Flame on, infrasonic rumbles in the underbelly: the forest's afire with a new type of flame.*

Language explodes into bleeding shards, shards of sky bleed into linguistic fireworks, and synesthetic fire works its way into the conceptual breakthrough.

*This,* Baretta realizes, *is a new world coming to life. Not the one we tried to make.*

On top of that, the bleached infrared parts are not separate sections anymore—they're blending with the human-visible parts. Human eyes would see a patchwork of crazy colors interspersed with white sections in a way that would turn the ghost of Jackson Pollock green with envy. Venusian eyes, though, see the miracle of accelerated evolution. A fractal factory bursting with life, flourishing in unforeseen ways. Violet flowers spouting from ochre stems set against the background of a crisp infrahue. Infrafused explosions of tripled tendrils reaching for the vermillion sky. Tangled webs of teetering willows, true-blue waves of tethered seaweeds thrown against a wavering backdrop shimmering in an ultrarainbow to infraprism cycle.

And even in this flare-up of wild abandon, this wanton assault on perception, there is something else underneath—either an undertone on the edge of infrasonic or an overtone beyond the threshold of ultrasonic. Something you feel rather than hear, but still somehow is sound. Something you sense rather than experience, but still somehow is real. Something that communicates instantaneously, but it still needs to be converted to a comprehensible form. A strange interference not unlike wave harmonics, binaural tones, and frequency modulation. Something riding something else.

Whatever it is, it's trying to get a message through to Vanessa and Baretta. But the communication is unclear. Time is running out.

"We have to get back," Vanessa says, "our oxygen is running low."

"True," Baretta is so engrossed that he wouldn't have noticed until the low level alarm set in, "but we still need to employ the new biosensors."

"Might as well dump them here. This is definitely the most interesting place."

"No mistake."

After spreading the sensors, they leave, very reluctantly, like trespassers from a new paradise.

Inevitably, they return, carrying extra oxygen supplies. They didn't report their changes. They made up a story about how upset they were when they found out that the "bleached" parts of the forest were expanding and infiltrating the "healthy" parts. They need time to wrap their minds around the new development.

They need privacy, so Vanessa hacks their voice implants. The cameras don't need to be tampered with as they record human normal. Back at the new section of the Fractal Forest, they re-appreciate the infrared sections and how that novoforest—the infraforest—integrates with the existing parts. It sharpens and fine-tunes their extended color perception while something else keeps happening, as well.

"You feel it, too, right?" Baretta asks, "sort of a common wavelength that seems to be—

    —connected to every living thing in the Fractal Forest." Vanessa says, finishing it for him. "A kind of übergestalt—

        —Gaia come to Venus. Vaia?" Baretta says. "But its intelligence still feels a bit primitive, unformed."

"I suspect we're not directly experiencing it because it's not self-conscious. Operating like our subconscious—possibly very fast and very efficient but not fully aware."

"And it seems to welcome us as if we're a part of it." Whatever type of quantum harmonics vibrate through them, eventually they seem to translate into certain feelings.

"Is it telling us—

    —we need to discard our artificial extensions. But without our exoskeleton we're unprotected against the sulfuric acid clouds—

—that seem to have become very rare, at these altitudes, anyway—

—lightning and $CO_2$ poisoning. And without our wings—

—we'll fall into an over-pressurized, superheated hell. So how?"

Their nervous systems are alight with a sensation so harmonious and uplifting, it's not unlike music. *Ode to Joy*, Baretta thinks. *At the End of the Day*, is Vanessa's take.

"Show us the way?" They say in unison.

A flock of kitesects rises up to meet them. Vanessa and Baretta keep their relative positions in a figure-eight flying pattern. Their wings are attached to their backs, so their arms and legs are free. The kitesects swoop down on those free limbs. Simultaneously, the pair have the nigh-irresistible feeling that they must stretch their arms and legs.

The kitesects merge, and reform tightly around Vanessa's and Baretta's limbs. A third skin forms around the second layer of the exosuit, extending into huge, fractally-feathered wings. Vanessa and Baretta rise up, fast, as they now have double the lift. Exaltation.

"Wow!"

"Yeah. Only one way to find out—

—retract our artificial wings."

They do and brace for the fall. But they keep flying, if clumsily. They move in awkward patterns. Their new wings have lift aplenty, they just don't control quite right.

"It seems as if they need direct body contact—

—but that means ditching the exosuit." Baretta says.

"We don't need to ditch the complete exosuit," Vanessa says. "How about we only take off the sleeves, to see if we can then control our upper wings better?"

"Right, we can always put them back on, fast," Baretta says, "hopefully."

They extend their artificial wings, and the kitesect arm wings, almost on cue, disintegrate into kitesects again. The trapezoidal insectoids flutter around until Vanessa and Baretta have taken off their exosuit sleeves, then reform.

The kitesect wings—after a fast trial-and-error process—now perfectly follow their directions.

On top of that, it's not just their control, their commands flowing into their new arm wings, but something else flowing back—a kind of energy, a sustenance. They fly around as long as they dare, keeping a close eye on their oxygen levels and signs of $CO_2$ poisoning. It lasts much longer than they thought, or dared hope. But, in the end, they need to report back.

"It's crazy," Baretta says, "I feel great, not even hungry."

"Our oxygen level has barely depleted since we used our new arm wings," Vanessa says. "Have we been using less, or is there something else going on?"

"Don't know," Baretta says, "but unfortunately we can't go native just yet. I think it's better if we put our exoskeleton sleeves back on—

—otherwise, they'll totally freak out at Quadrant 4 base."

In the days that follow, Vanessa and Baretta keep experimenting. They increasingly interact with the Fractal Forest. Their flying becomes perfect as they let the kitesects take the place of their exoskeletons. On top of that, no signs of $CO_2$ poisoning nor are they hungry anymore. What to do with their food packs?

Baretta notices Vanessa's kitesect wings glowing during flight. "Maybe our wings perform photosynthesis, supplying us with carbohydrates and oxygen."

"Which would explain our decreasing need for food and oxygen," she says, "but we still need water. And proteins, vitamins, minerals, and other trace elements."

"Probably, the Fractal Forest can supply those—

—and we can dump our food into the Fractal Forest. In this extreme environment, it's becoming an absolute champion at recycling."

"We need to take a leap of faith. Become part of the Fractal Forest, embrace Vaia—

—Vaya con Dios? Go with the God of this place?"

"Or remain freaks in the human settlement. We *are* different. Until they know exactly what has happened, they will keep us quarantined—

—indefinitely, which might as well mean forever."

After venting their unused oxygen supply—to avoid suspicion—they return to base. Their hand is forced when an old friend secretly transmits a preliminary abstract of the research into their viral infection to their implants. "Their DNA is different as sulfate has replaced the phosphate in the nucleotide, which now uses an extra sugar group to extend the structure from a double to a triple helix." Once their superiors see this, they'll discontinue Vanessa and Baretta's expeditions. Their next scheduled reconnaissance flight will be their last.

Off they are, on their ultimate trip, one way or the other. Cutting the Gordian knot of their future.

Sometimes, there's nothing to it but hope. Hope that the Fractal Forest can deliver sufficient sustenance to keep them alive, maybe even help them thrive. Hope that their new metabolism adapts.

Sometimes, you have to face the abyss and own it. Sometimes, you must jump off the cliff. Sometimes, there's nothing to it but don your reality distortion field and take the leap of faith. Cross the Rubicon into truly new frontiers. Prime the senses for new wonders.

Baretta looks up to Vanessa, and she answers before he can ask.

*Yes, I'm ready.*

*Let's do it.*

They say goodbye to Quadrant 4 base.

*If panspermia is correct,* Baretta thinks, *life on Earth is also not truly native.* In that case, a genuinely pristine Earth would be, like Venus only a few decades ago, barren. As such, keeping a lifeless planet "pristine" (as the KVP demands) is madness. What happens on Venus is merely an advanced form of panspermia.

*This also means that we are our own—well, not quite people—*entity, Baretta thinks, simultaneously transmitting it to Vanessa and the rest of the Fractal Forest. *We need to negotiate with the humans as we are not an experiment anymore. Nor do we wish to be a colony.*

*We're not totally independent, yet,* Vanessa sends over the quantum-entangled trilix link, *we need more water and trace elements to expand life on Venus. The remaining sulfuric acid clouds will only get us so far.*

Baretta gazes at the stars, wistfully, *It'll be a very long time before we can descend to the surface to extract the metals we need for space flight.*

*How about us,* Vanessa signals over the Fractal Forest trilix link, *feel like being Adam to my Eve?*

This takes Baretta aback. He's been so focused on so many other things that this slipped right by him. Another world of possibilities opens up, even if he wants to take that one step at a time. He looks at her with new eyes. *Well, we can look into that anytime,* he thinks, *although—thinking about it—we might open up to immigrants.*

*Come who may,* Vanessa's feelings ride the trilix wave, *but you are mine.*

§

**Ingrid Garcia** *tries to sell local wines in a vintage wine shop in Cádiz and writes speculative fiction in her spare time. Initially, the good people of* Ligature Works *(poem),* Panorama, *and* EOS Quarterly *were willing to take a risk with her, and now, the* Futuristica 2 *and—indeed—*Ride the Star Wind *anthologies and* F&SF *will feature stories of hers, as well. Between the day job, writing more stories, and setting up a website, she—dog forbids—even has hopeful thoughts of writing that inevitable novel.*

# Sense of Wonder

## RICHARD LEE BYERS

ILLUSTRATED BY
MICHAEL BUKOWSKI

EVERYONE ELSE LUMBERS AROUND PREPARING THE EXPLORATION POD FOR departure. I return to the cliff face for one last look at the fossils: the remains of spiny, scorpion-tailed creatures that lived and died before the cosmic collision that smashed the moon, stilled the tides, and ultimately abolished life on this particular planet.

The fossils make me want to see the living organisms. The physicists back on Earth told me only to step across space, never time, but should I care? They don't understand time like I'm starting to. They think it's like nitroglycerin, primed to explode if you jiggle it. But isn't it really just the ocean in which we drift?

Cheong speaks over the radio, "Valdez. We're ready to leave."

"Roger that," I reply. But still, the fossils hold me.

After a while, someone approaches across the gray sand. I can't tell who it is until I register the name stenciled above the helmet's reflective faceplate: Otienno. Then I wonder why I didn't recognize her willowy frame even though we all look pretty much alike in spacesuits.

"Pablo," she says, "it's time to go."

"I know," I answer.

After a moment, she continues, "We're done here, and the gravity's too strong. We're all hurting. Aren't you?"

Despite the stabilizers and enhancers built into my suit, twinges jab my back and joints. Really, they were there all along, but more interesting perceptions masked them.

"I am now," I sigh. "Let's get out of here."

We join the rest of the crew in the pod. Sometimes, people call it "the vehicle," but that's misleading. It doesn't move itself from one star system to the next. I move it.

The others take sedatives and put on blindfolds and hearing protectors. It keeps them from getting migraines, nightmares, or worse.

When everyone's ready, I chant.

The thing I invoke quickly regards me. It was already aware of me as it is of everything. Now, though, I'm the focus of its attention. Its consideration could annihilate me like sunlight shining through a magnifying glass to burn an ant, but it holds something back.

The glowing spheres appear. I could contemplate them as the face of my patron, but that's not the task at hand nor would it be safe. Instead, I choose to see them as a map.

A different vista flowers in every globe. A banded gas giant fills the sky of a frozen moon. A nebula floats with a handful of newborn stars burning inside. A force I don't understand makes magma flow uphill.

Among the myriad options are those comparatively earthlike planets the astronomers charted, the objectives on the team's itinerary. In an absolute sense, they're just as interesting as any other destination. But I've visited eight of them already. I still haven't been to a radically different sort of world.

Yet I dutifully focus on Destination #9. As I speak the next set of words, a flicker of motion inside one of the spheres catches my eye. I only glance for an instant, but that's too long. My patron takes my attention for intention.

The pod rolls. An alarm blares, unsecured items bounce around, and people scream. Despite the tumbling, I manage to look out the nearest porthole.

A wind full of grit is rolling the pod across cracked red ground. I try to see more, but whirring, the shutter comes down to block excess radiation.

Although there may be a way to override the automatic safeguard, I don't know it. I wonder if I can exit the pod. Probably not, but the way it's crashing and banging, perhaps, it'll break apart around me.

Clutching at handholds, Otienno crawls to me. Her forehead is bleeding. She pulls herself close to scream in my face. "Get us out of here!"

It's really the sight of her blood that jars me into action. Fortunately, I still have my patron's attention. It only takes another phrase to shift us to the next planet on the schedule. The pod rolls three more times and, thanks to good design or sheer luck, stops right side up.

Otienno clings to me in relief. I tell myself I should feel the same way, not frustrated. The alarm falls silent.

In a minute, Cheong collects himself sufficiently to get up out of his captain's chair and stamp in my direction. "What the hell, Valdez? What the hell?"

"Technical difficulties," I say. "Sorry."

"'Technical difficulties,'" he echoes. "What does that mean?"

"Honestly, since you haven't been through the training, I don't know how to explain. But it won't happen again."

"Screw your promises," says Roberts, coming with her medical kit in hand. "If we can't depend on you to take us to the right place first time, every time, you need to jump us back to Earth."

"That's up to the captain," I say.

Cheong scowls. "Damage assessments," he calls.

One by one, the others report that the pod is still operational. "Lockheed built her tough," says Kjeldsen. He's the engineer and proud of the invention he tends.

"Then we proceed with the mission," says Cheong. He wants to be one of the heroes who opens the universe for mankind. He's not going to abort the mission at the first mishap, frightening though it was.

It's night, and Cheong decides our first EVA can wait until morning. Once we dim the lights and people start crawling into their bunks, Otienno finds me. Her new bandage glows white against her brown skin.

"What really happened?" she asks, her voice low.

"I messed up. I really won't let it happen again."

"Then it wasn't Yog-Sothoth deciding he's got better things to do than shuttling us around the galaxy?"

I sigh. "You know, that's just the name a few mystics gave it, and when we call it that, it's like buying into their primitive beliefs. We scare ourselves."

"What happened to Marcus Rawlik was scary."

"I suppose. But once he proved the consciousness real, his successors discovered how to open gates safely."

"But not how the physics work, or what Yog . . . the consciousness truly is, or even why it's willing to help us. You're the one who communes with it. Do you have any idea?"

I shrug. "It's everywhere and everywhen. So vast and powerful that obliging us is no more difficult than not obliging us. It grants our petitions in the same sense that you grant permission to the bacteria in your intestines to go on doing what they do."

She chuckles. "That metaphor's not very flattering to mankind."

"Maybe you'll like my other hypothesis better. The entity sees, and it knows. That's what it is. When we open a gate, we're trying do the same thing, and it approves."

She nods. "Kindred spirits. Although for us, there's more to it. We want to find planets we can colonize."

"Right." I hadn't exactly forgotten the practical objective of the mission, but I also hadn't thought of it in days.

"Thanks for sharing." She squeezes my shoulder. "We should get some sleep." She crosses the compartment and folds down her bunk from the wall.

Two worlds farther along, Roberts finds purple algae in a pond. Everyone's excited, including me. I stare at the stuff for hours—in the water where it grows and through the microscope when the biologists take a break.

When Cheong declares it's time to move on, one of the glowing spheres shows me the algae world millions of years in the future. Violet and indigo jungles clothe the land, and shaggy behemoths wander among the trees. It's all just a wish away if I choose to go.

Instead, I shift the pod to the next world on the itinerary, and if people notice me scowling afterward, they don't comment. They've been looking at me differently ever since I nearly got us all killed and, except for Otienno, seem to be deciding it's just as well to leave me alone.

The leap after that, we land in a snowfield dotted with hot springs and geysers. One of the latter sprays into the air every minute or so, and for lack of a better spectacle, I watch it erupt over and over again.

It turns out there are trace elements in the atmosphere that would kill a human being over time, so after just a few days, the expedition is ready to move on. I face the shining spheres. One moment, they look like bunches of grapes, the next, they move in a way that's indefinable but makes me think of bubbles rising to the top of a boiling pot.

Refusing to focus on anything else, I fix my will on the next stop on our route. I gasp because I see creatures. Naturally, I've scrutinized this particular destination before, but apparently, I never looked at the right patch of ground at the right moment.

At rest, the organisms look like headless, rough-hewn statues of gaunt horses or greyhounds, except with too many spindly legs haphazardly arranged around their bodies. When they're ready to move, ripples of sheen run down them as their substance softens. Then they stretch like chewing gum, and eyes and mouths open in their flanks.

Half a dozen of them are holding down another. A long wound bisects much of its length, and they pick out pieces of its steaming insides and eat them.

I rattle off the incantation. The pod jumps to a low spot surrounded by slopes of long, tiger-striped grasses. I let go of the patron, or possibly, he dismisses me.

I scurry to Otienno and pull her hearing protectors off. "We found them!" I cry. "Animals!"

Her dark eyes open wide. "You're kidding! Tell me! No, wait a second, and tell everybody!"

I all but tremble with impatience as the crew works through the safety protocols involved with opening the pod in a new environment. Once we're ready, I lead them up the rise to the east. But when we reach the expanse of rolling grassland at the top of the slope, the creatures are nowhere to be seen.

"Are you sure this is the spot?" Otienno asks.

"Looking at what the entity shows me isn't like looking down from a plane," I answer, "but yeah, pretty sure."

"Then the animals moved on," says Cheong. "Maybe, we can pick up their trail."

We try, but if the creatures left tracks, the knee-high grass hides them. I turn to Cheong to suggest spreading out in a search pattern. A shape rears up behind him and reaches with newly formed extremities resembling lobster claws.

I hadn't realized the creatures could flatten themselves to hide in the grass or grow pincers. Rapt, I wait to see what happens next.

Otienno screams, "Watch out!" Because encountering dangerous life forms has always been a possibility, we go armed outside the pod, and her carbine thunders and punches a hole through the animal.

Cheong jerks around and shoots from the hip. He blasts away another chunk of the creature, and it falls.

Undeterred, the rest of the pack leap up and charge. Everyone fires, me included. But I can't bring myself to aim even at the beast lunging at me with serrated hook-like extremities extended. Kjeldsen shoots it before it can reach me.

When the last of the creatures drops, Cheong turns to me. "Well," he pants, "you called it. You said they might be aggressive." From his lack of animosity, it's clear he doesn't realize I was content to watch while the animal seized him.

No one realizes I'm crying, either. My faceplate hides it.

I tell myself this can't have been the only pack. I'll have another chance to marvel at the creatures.

But I don't. In the weeks that follow, we never find signs of another such group or any other animal bigger than a flea.

The survey completed, I jump the pod to another bleak world. Then another. But when it's time to shift to the planet after that, I glimpse one of the headless things in the luminous sphere.

I'm too elated to question my good fortune. But my companions do. When I make the jump and share the news, Roberts says, "You're not going to find the same organism on two different planets light-years apart."

"Parallel evolution," Kjeldsen says, whereupon Roberts rolls her eyes at the engineer weighing in on exobiology.

"Probably not really," Otienno says. "But I'm guessing Valdez caught a glimpse of something that at least looks a bit like the animals we found before."

"Could be," I answer. I still feel like I know what I saw, but I also realize that Roberts's skepticism makes sense. "Anyway, I guarantee you there's some kind of big animal outside."

"Then, let's go find it," says Cheong.

In one respect, the new world proves to resemble the planet of the tiger grass. It has ferns the size of trees, boulder-sized masses of mold, and other vegetation, but no teeming diversity of highly evolved animal life. Perhaps, humans don't understand nature as well as we imagine.

The breeze rustles the fronds of the ferns and, passing through holes in the fungus, makes it whistle. Visible even by daylight, meteors burn overhead. We explorers prowl with carbines at the ready.

Otienno says, "I see one!" She points.

The animal's fifty yards away and half hidden behind a fern, but to me, it looks exactly like the creatures we encountered before.

"Take cover," Cheong says. "We'll observe from here. Kjeldsen, get some video."

We study the animal for five minutes as it petrifies when it finishes moving and ripples back to rubbery flesh when it wants to wander some more. Then it whirls and charges us. The front of it sprouts many-jointed arms with spiky balls on the ends.

"Shit!" says Cheong. He shoulders his carbine, and the others follow his lead. The ragged barrage staggers the onrushing animal and knocks it down.

What a waste. It's all but unbearable to once again stand surrounded by my boring familiar kind while something exotic lies dead before us.

"Damn it," says Roberts. She wanted to go on watching a living specimen, too, and a moment later, we get our wish.

Three more creatures emerge from the mass of ferns that defines the limit of our vision. But the new ones wear bands of some black material. They carry long, jagged metallic rods, and they lope toward the body of their fellow.

"Well," Otienno breathes, "now, we know how you find the same organism on two different planets."

"The first ones were naked like animals," Kjeldsen says. "They acted like animals." He sounds like a child complaining that a playmate cheated in a game.

"We have to fix this," Cheong says. He sets down his gun, stands up, and waves his hands. "Hello! We're peaceful! This was a terrible misunderstanding!"

One of the aliens beckons him forward. He advances half the distance, and with the simultaneity of a drill team, all three aim their rods at him. The implements shimmer and whine, and Cheong drops to his knees. I glimpse the spattered gore painting the inside of his faceplate as he pitches forward.

Kjeldsen fires, and the rest of the crew do, too. But the new aliens don't appear to feel it. My hunch is that the black harnesses protect them.

All three extraterrestrials point their weapons at Kjeldsen. He throws himself flat, but it doesn't help. Something bursts inside his helmet violently enough to breach the seal securing it to the rest of the spacesuit. Air hisses out.

Still firing, the other humans fall back. I don't. When I believed the aliens were predators like wolves or lions, that was enough to make them splendid. Now that I recognize them for sapient, star-faring beings, they're sublime.

They advance as the crew retreats. They kill Bryce, the geologist, and orient on me. I drop my rifle in the feeble hope the gesture persuades them to forbear.

I don't want to die, but I'd rather live a final second contemplating them than turn away.

Otienno rushes to my side and fires. Her round finds a gap in whatever it is that shields the aliens, and the closest reels back and collapses with a steaming hole among the three limbs wielding the rod.

Pulling on my arm, Otienno yells, "Run!" When that doesn't work, she smacks the side of my helmet with her rifle hard enough to rattle the head inside it. The jolt breaks me free of my fascination—well, not really, but enough to make me remember how a crew member ought to behave.

We run after the others. Nobody else drops. Maybe the aliens stopped chasing us. Maybe Otienno's lucky shot made them wary.

We pile into the pod and check to see who's gone and who remains. Otienno is now the ranking officer.

"Get ready to jump," she says. People scramble to exchange their helmets for the gear that protects them from seeing and hearing the entity.

Otienno doesn't. She won't make herself helpless now that she's responsible for everyone else, even if it means perceiving something that could damage her mind. I respect that in a murky sort of way.

"Where are we jumping?" I ask.

She looks at me as if it's a stupid question. "Earth!"

The least enticing of destinations. Still, I set about following the order. When the glowing spheres start dripping and drifting out of empty air, Otienno flinches and turns away to look out a porthole.

I sift for Earth among the myriad globes. It can take time to pinpoint a particular world, especially if I don't really want to go.

"We have to jump now!" Otienno cries.

I wonder what she is seeing, and one of the spheres shows me. A ship comes flying over the tree-sized ferns. I don't know how. I can't see any means of propulsion, and nothing about it is aerodynamic. It's made of cubes and tetrahedrons that slide around one another in a cloud of shimmering haze. Crooked protrusions jut from the underside like the legs of a hovering insect, and, two and three at a time, they aim themselves at the pod.

"I haven't found Earth yet," I say.

"Go anywhere!" Otienno shouts.

I spot the world with the purple algae and chant us there. Afterward, the consciousness recedes, but its attention lingers.

"Thank God," Otienno says, running a trembling hand over her close-cropped hair. "Thank God."

I try to share her relief, but it's useless.

Sensing the jump is over, crewmembers pull off their blindfolds and hearing protectors. Some look shaky and sweaty. Roberts swallows repeatedly in an effort not to vomit. They really needed the sedatives as well as external defenses.

"Oh, no," Otienno groans.

I hurry to the porthole beside hers. The shimmering ship is flying toward us over the snow. Geysers erupt at the touch of its shadow.

I can't tell if, like me, the aliens invoke the entity to shift from world to world or use a different method. Nor can I imagine how they follow us so swiftly and surely. The mystery is enthralling.

"Jump!" Otienno cries. "But not to Earth! We can't risk leading them there!"

I invite my patron back into the pod. People wail and cringe. I choose a rocky world with two pale crescent moons hanging in its greenish daytime sky. A second later, we're there.

A second after that, our pursuers are, too.

I shift back to the planet with the striped grass, and the alien ship sticks with us. I go to the moon orbiting the gas giant, and as the radiation shutters drop, the other vessel bursts into view.

After three more jumps, a second ship joins the chase. This one is nothing like the first. It's streamlined and symmetrical with a dozen external devices resembling talons opening and closing individually to accomplish some enigmatic purpose. The third is different again and doesn't look like a solid object at all. It's like one of those computer animations that spiral at the viewer, perpetually on the verge of drilling out of the screen.

The pod gradually accumulates a small fleet of pursuers that in its diversity suggests an alliance of a dozen different species. Perhaps it's their malice toward upstart races that unites them, but what does it matter? They're still magnificent, and their presence sings to me.

I turn to Otienno, who looks ten years older than at the start of the day. "I'm sorry," I say. "I can't do this anymore."

"You have to!"

"No."

"I'm sure you're tired—"

"Not so much. The patron does most of the work. It's just . . ." I feel a vague shame, but it's a puny sensation compared to my desire. "Communing with the entity changes you. I don't care about protecting what I already know. I need to experience what I don't. That means running toward it, not away."

"That's crazy!" Roberts says. "The aliens want to kill us!"

"Maybe," I say, "but that will be an experience, too."

She aims her carbine at my face. "Not if I kill you first."

Otienno pushes the barrel out of line, "Valdez, you say linking up with the entity made you this way?"

"Yes."

Taking me by the shoulders, she turns me away from the porthole and back toward the endless cascade of glowing spheres. "Then go deeper. Maybe, it'll change you again."

Should I? The patron is the one thing that interests me just as much as the aliens. Yet I balk. I fear I'm still not ready to engage with it on a more profound level and that perhaps no human ever can be.

"Fine," Otienno says. "*I'll* look." Fists clenched, she stares into the radiant mass.

I can't tell if it's shame, fondness, or duty that convinces me that I should, if only symbolically, support her. Except for curiosity and awe, my emotions have so faded that it's difficult to tell them apart. But I, too, gaze into the heart of the spheres and strain to see them more clearly than ever before.

Pain rips through my eyes and into my head. It's like a torrent of gravel pouring down the sluice of my vision to fill my skull with ever-increasing pressure.

But the pressure never bursts my head in any physical sense. The cracks that open are breaks in the blinders that hinder human perception, and when the shattered barriers fall away, the spheres shine brighter. After a moment, I recognize the clustered orbs for a reflection of the lattice of mathematics and information on which space-time grows like skin.

A relative few of the shortest, wispiest strands in the pattern are the spans of races burdened with corporeality. Each comes into being, struggles and suffers for a moment or two, and dies leaving nothing of consequence behind.

Perceiving that, I likewise recognize my infatuation with the aliens for the childish thing it is, a tropism no less parochial than my crewmates' attachment to our own particular species.

*Everything* is a wonder, and everything is empty and cold. But once accepted, the absence of meaning allows freedom of choice for even the most random and trivial of reasons, like Otienno fallen at my side, eyes gouged, fingertips bloody, and heart stopped.

I turn to the rest of the crew. I don't care if they understand my thinking, but my dead friend would have wanted it that way.

"I can't shake the aliens off our tail," I say, "and Otienno was right: we don't dare lead them back to Earth. But maybe I can make sure they never tell any more of their friends that human beings exist."

"We get it," Roberts says. "Do what you have to."

I turn my attention on the shining spheres, now reverted to the chaotic map that guided me before. I hope the physicists back on Earth were right about time after all. From what I observed moments before, I think they may have been.

I jump to the world of the tiger grass at a time five minutes before the expedition departed. My current version of the pod materializes thirty feet from the other. I wait for my pursuers to catch up.

I then open a gate big enough to swallow both pods. We shift together, the earlier version snatched from the temporal path that led the newer one to now.

I half expect to vanish. I don't. Apparently, my existence is more resilient than that.

I worry that my patron will stop indulging me. After all, if it's more than the lurker, the haunter, the key, if watcher and watched are one, aren't I wounding it? But compared to its immensity, the injury is miniscule, and perhaps, it's foolish on my part to imagine the consciousness can be hurt at all. Maybe any event, any feature, no matter how violent or unnatural, simply constitutes part of the whole. At any rate, the incantations keep working.

I fear the aliens will perceive the trap and break off. But relentless hunters that they are, they keep chasing me as I gather one pod after another from points along our history and accumulate my own little fleet.

Until, finally, surface reality can no longer support the growing weight of paradox. A vortex churns open, and pursuers and pursued spin down together into a realm as incomprehensible as it is poisonous to dull-witted mites like us.

§

**Richard Lee Byers** *is the author of forty horror and fantasy books, including* This Sword for Hire, Black Dogs, Black Crowns, The Ghost in the Stone, Blind God's Bluff, *and the volumes in the* Impostor *series. He's also written scores of short stories, scripted a graphic novel, and contributed content on tabletop and electronic games.*

*A resident of the Tampa Bay area, the setting for many of his contemporary stories, he's a fencing and poker enthusiast and a frequent program participant at Florida conventions, Dragon Con, and Gen Con. He invites everyone to follow him on Facebook and Twitter.*

# Departure Beach

## JOSEPH S. PULVER, SR.
### ILLUSTRATED BY NICK GUCKER

*C*AME OUT OF TRANS-DRIVE

*into hell.*

Seventeen Cenrenu war-raiders, the big ones, were shredding a supply fleet, a multi-corporation five-liner, and there we were in the middle of the furnace. Look of the carnage, must have been tens of dozens of carriers and tankers that had been fucked-to-pieces by trigger-happy—shit whizzing, parts you couldn't re-piece together, debris and fluid spills the size of small moons, shitshow explosions, partial chunk of something that resembled half of a tanker. Ten seconds in, and we took two laser torpedoes aft and were spinning.

Estrada didn't blink; he sealed the upper rear decks where we'd been hit. "We were lucky, more or less," he barked into the comm system. "Shield held. We took one small breach."

Captain Andrew Mack and Dawn Fulton shutdown everything but life support and the level five shielding—figured our size, we might pass for wreckage, just drift and take any raps. The war-raiders were ripping through the cargo fleet and not doubling back. I thought we had a good chance to avoid being noticed and limp out later, if we didn't get bashed to shit by all the debris.

Sat there and waited out the black minutes. Bumped—crashed into—pushed aside. Wished I had some kind of faith drilled into me I could call on, but my mother was as anti-deity as they come. Spikes of doubt, the rustle of nerves, eating at discipline. Estrada hissed at our communications officer, Andromeda Vanbeck, to stop praying. Taborn made a fist five minutes ago while looking out the window. Two minutes later, frustrated, he released it. Nobody voicing their questions. Nobody with an answer. The weight of memory wandering around the flight deck. Long fucking wait. Maybe an hour in that fuckhole before the propulsion system was turned back on.

"Puff" Monder—*(That's me, el space-jockey supremo, baby—I can fly anything; wings, no wings)*—inched and jogged our way to the edge of the debris field and shut everything down again. He might have been the ship's self-professed king of comedy, but the look on his face was not expressing anything amusing.

We drifted again.

I sat and watched a trio of Cenrenuian carrion sweepers move in and cull through the massacre. Blast here. Threaten. Cut out a prime loader; get it lined up to haul away.

The radio was hot. Cenrenuians would hail a vessel and demand the shipping manifest. If they didn't want the listed cargo the vessel was set upon by carrion sweepers and obliterated. Ships that did not immediately comply were destroyed.

Two immigration vessels, the big conservation carriers, were traveling with the fleet. They informed the fucking Cens they had no offensive or defensive weaponry onboard and were each transporting one hundred thousand settlers, mostly farmers, tradesmen, and their families. The Cenrenuians are not slavers and do not participate in human trafficking. Rice paper in a bonfire, two hundred thousand innocent lives gone in an instant.

Two hours.

Silent.

Every single one of us doing hard time. No one voiced it, but as my eyes roamed eye-to-eye face-to-face, I saw it. Fear—little, big, baking in it. Adrenaline. Cold sweat. Anger. Compound of fatigue and wondering. The ever-present *why* and no one to interrogate.

I sent Corporal Peter Rechy out back to fill Davidson in and see if he needed anything. Rechy came back, said he was good, wanted to be kept posted. I instructed Rechy to update Davidson every hour on the hour unless something happened.

Three.

My thoughts kept returning to Davidson.

"Still good," Rechy reported. "Comes to doin' time, he's a rock, Lt."

"That's why it's his ass sitting back there."

Seven fucking hours. But deliberate and frosty wins the game, or so I hoped.

Again, I wondered how Davidson was doing. He was stuck in the rear cargo hold with the artifact. Wasn't happy about it, but he did volunteer, knew what it meant.

We all did.

All of us had raised our hands and signed up, swore to preserve, protect, and defend the Union. With our lives.

Shitty chances, little in the way of data, no charts of where we might wind up if the wormhole theory panned out. Battle-scarred fools and patriotic idiots, possible death-wishes not discussed. But there were innocents among us. *Collateral damage.* Caught myself in the lie, didn't like the taste of it, never have, but that had never stopped me when I had to make a command decision.

The crew focused on enduring and maybe winning. They saw the end game. Shame it wasn't the one on my dance card.

"Puff" Monder and two female members of the crew wore small gold Christ crosses on chains around their necks. I envied their faith. Was worth shit at the end of the line, but a hand to hold when you're in the fire is still a hand to hold. People take their comforts anywhere they can find them. Always have. Always will.

Wished I had faith. Switched gears, wished for a bottle.

Cenrenuians had been gone three hours. We headed out.

Betty Jens was in the galley crying over her coffee mug. Andromeda Vanbeck sat next to her, arm around Betty's shoulders. Betty looked up at me. "How many thousands of people were on those immigration vessels, and the others, too? They're dead now. And the Cenrenuians must have led three or four hundred ships away—they won't let those people live. I wish—"

"We all do."

Andromeda's eyes met and held mine, said, *Really? That I doubt.* She told me once, she could have a thing for me, if I wasn't such a cold son-of-a-bitch.

Been taught survival, evasion, resistance and escape—hurt like a mother. I was an FNG in a river of blood. You can keep your god, I was baptized by a 5.56 cartridge that missed my liver by two inches. Been in hell with grunts; no matter what you've heard, we didn't drink the devil's beer for free. Lost men, friends, brothers-in-arms, cried at their graves and over their bodies, every farewell was a furnace. Knew I was going to die, wouldn't be pretty. Got scars, knife, bullet, from being tortured. Andromeda's disapproving look hurt worse than the whole shebang stuffed into shit sandwich. That's a fucking ache they never trained me for.

Davidson's face looked like an old carpet, worn, well traveled. He was a heartbeat away from sixty and had been a soldier since he took the oath age eighteen. He had medals (six), scars (most from his seven years a prisoner) and (seven) tattoos (unit and tour bars on his forearms, and the nine inch Anubis on his shoulder—I didn't have clue what it was for), and memories some sprawling, some small and personal.

There were days he talked—your ear off: *dogs* (Like Betty and Estrada, he was a dog lover. Still had a picture of his beloved, Bugler. In the photo Davidson was eight, all elbows and knees, and they were sitting in the open doorway of his parents' barn in Iowa.) and *trains* ("Steel. Dreams. Rolling through the Heartland on a warm Missouri night, the whistle blowing, the stars up in the sky talking, that's comforting.") and *"real" country music* from the twentieth century, back before the whole damn Union homogenized pain.

Got to drinking drinking, he got quiet. Subject of war came up he had little to say, in fact, most often he'd up and leave the room; take the bottle, too. But there was one time. He had Maneri pinned in a chair, hand on his shoulder holding him down, faces a foot apart: "*Bloodsport?* You assbag-motherfucker—you want to talk sports, Ivy League, talk sports, baseball, soccer. Two opposing forces, both trying to win; guns and death, everything blown away, GI's killed, thrown in a green fucking bag if there's any pieces left, that ain't a goddamn sport, fuckhead. Comprende?"

Sgt. Maj. Edward Davidson (Ret.) was the Gate Guard. Made sense to me; he knew how to spend time alone, and what the waiting would end with.

I was glad he had the responsibility. Thought I'd get stuck with it, I'd done ten years as a transfer agent and knew the regs backward and forward, drunk, too. I knew what carrying the weight meant, what it cost, wives, lovers, family, *your soul.*

That first mission briefing, Davidson stood up and started quoting passages from the Book.

*Man was never meant to know—*

*There are those who wear the Double Talisman on their chest above their hearts. They dream of the day when day shall be as night and the Harms Tremendous will return and all earthly pleasures shall cease. Through the ages, they have sought the key that unlocks the gates. They must be denied its secrets—*

*On the day the moon is old, take the Gate to a place no man has seen. Bury it deep—*

His voice didn't break, he didn't look away, or pause. Davidson knew the deeps of the Book the way I knew the regs. Less than twenty minutes from when he stood, and Davidson was assigned mission Gate Guard by Charlie Butler, the SIT-COM commander. No one in the room offered Davidson a godspeed.

Our encounter with the Cens was two months and eleven days ago. There were some in the crew who thought we'd come far enough. Mentions of home with all the trimmings and all the trappings frequently found its way to tongues made supple by desire. I stayed out of those conversations.

The one time I got cornered and pressed by Andromeda, I only half-lied. "I'm a soldier. I don't get to have a home. I have my orders and the mission. It's my responsibility to make sure other people get to have a home and enjoy it."

"What kind of life is that, Hank?" Andromeda asked. That was the first and only time she used my name.

Sound of my name on her lips hit me hard.

"The only kind I know. A hard one."

I went in the back and sat with Davidson in the cargo hold.

"We're over eight months out now. How far do you think we need to be?" I asked.

"I've no idea, Lt. The further the better. Maybe? There's so much we don't know."

"You need anything?"

He had a copy of the Book in his hands. Didn't look up from its open pages. "Same thing you do," Davidson said.

"I hear that."

Two days later, we came upon an undiscovered lens. I took the news to Davidson.

"It's large enough to enter, or so the brain-boys are telling me."

"If it takes us out, that would be great," Davidson said.

"Whole mission is a big if. I say, we try it. And maybe . . . look, if we're destroyed trying, that might work, too."

Davidson nodded in agreement. "Okay. Do it."

Into the lens we went. Freakshow lightshow—purple, red, pink escorting orange through a storm of charms, green eighty shades of green. Everyone on a roaring neon-bender, shift of delicious stripes eating surprising irises, yellow in conversation with prettiness and splendor, blue battling a tide of amber. A kaleidoscope—basking in the reality of LSD-trips had nothing on this, fractals . . . spaghettified . . . rotations . . . bundles . . . confused by unspooled riddles . . . embroidered to meaningless, to us—me, abstract patterns . . . with the consequence of a super-weapon or some divine punishment, scads of windowpanes overlapped the very nature of structure, both destroying and outlining new maps, new forms. Were we looking through God's eyes or at parallel universes, space and time secrets we couldn't understand, maybe we were looking into a crystal ball at pure magic tangling our senses and our souls? I was soldier looking at multi-verses through a poet's eyes. Everything was ancient. Everything was new. Everything was unnerving. Here were the inconceivable flowers of a universe with billions of timelines and no edges. Unhinged boundaries. Bent and stretched. Bounced. Tumbled. Hellride might cover it. Came out.

People were looking at their hands, flexing their fingers, looking at the others. Estrada stood, took a wobbly step, grinned, "Seems like I work OK." Puff crossed himself, put his christ cross to his lips and kissed it. Betty Jens went to the window. Her eyes said it; the stars were not our stars. Couple of minutes scanning, computers verified it.

"Fuckin' A," Estrada said. "*Fucking. A.*"

Captain Mack said, "It worked. Holy shit."

Our physicist Maneri and our astronomer Taborn, wooted and traded high fives. One stunned, one beaming and bouncing in his seat, both kids Christmas morning high.

I wanted to ask if they had any idea where we were, but it wasn't the Milky Way, so it was a win.

I went out back to see Davidson.

"Find a solar system and let's get rid of this damn thing. I'm ready for this to be over, Lt.," Davidson said.

I wanted to bring up using a rocket to inject the fucking thing into a sun again, but I remember what Charlie said about the influence of energy and skipped it.

Found a place. It didn't have a name, of course, and we were not going to give it one. "Secrets shouldn't have names and we are on a secret mission," Andromeda said. "Right, Lt.?" Mid-size planet, no satellites, in a small, quiet solar system of twelve planets behind a nebula in a celestial swamp Maneri named the Magus. Ninety-five percent covered with water. Trans-imaging revealed a dense world below the waves: coral reefs that were miles deep; several vast volcanic zones; deep-water current storms; billions of marine life forms, some the size of dolphins and sharks; continent-size forests of aquatic plants. Less than thousand miles apart, located at the equator, two small, uninhabited continents above sea level, no islands. Both were nothing but mountainous rock, not a single life form or plant.

Nav computer showed the distance from this planet to the next closest star was more than double Earth's sun to Proxima Centauri.

"It's certainly isolated," Taborn said.

"Secret mission be damned. I don't get to set foot on undiscovered planets every day; I've got a name for it." Maneri said. "Kylo." He looked unhappy when we didn't offer applause. "That's my mom's favorite seafood restaurant; mine, too. We used to go there all the time. Grab the corner booth, best view of the beach for fifty miles." He looked up at the ceiling. Wasn't a minute later he closed his eyes; a smile came to his face. "Fresh Dungeness crab stuffed halibut, breaded and grilled . . . topped with garlic cream and served with whipped potatoes and a hazelnut blue cheese salad. Parmesan crusted cod with red bell pepper sauce. Bottle of Black Stallion . . . their menu should have had a disclaimer: you'll need a nap after."

Estrada's face said it all; living off the space grub we were, reeling off menu items to restaurants you loved might get your ass slapped around.

Named or unnamed, everyone agreed this was as good a place as any to hide the Gate.

We put down on a stony beach. Davidson would take the Gate out to sea and drop it into the blue deeps; plan was he'd travel out for at least twelve hours (maintaining fifty knots) before dropping it in an unknown location. The part of the plan the other crew members hadn't been informed of, after he dropped it, he'd unleash the tactical nuke in our go-fast wave runner. No Davidson, no Wave Runner, and no hint of where the Gate was.

Davidson didn't know it but I was his transfer agent, and I was the only one who knew he was not coming back.

I was up at 3 a.m. GMT Earthtime. Assisted Davidson with unloading the wave runner from Bay 3 and getting it in the water. He didn't need my help, but I wanted to be there.

We did not talk much.

I stood and watched Davidson put the Gate in the 54-Q Crate and load it, using four grav-mags. Damn Gate was the size of a pack of smokes and barely weighed two pounds, but Charlie Butler had assured us the two ton container would keep the Gate where we put it. "Bury it, sink it, it should stay where you deposit it; ain't much going to budge a 54-Q," Charlie said.

Davidson put to sea at 7 a.m. Packed a porto-food locker with lunch, dinner, breakfast, snack-sticks, and bottles of stim-water. Also took one beer, "I'm going to celebrate after I cast it into the deeps." On that ocean, he only had the sky for company.

I held my requiem silently.

Dawn Fulton, our computer and systems wonk, said, "Fully weaponized. Complement like that, I feel bad for anything that crosses his path." Look on her face said her heart-rate was pinned in the swoon zone. Had anyone asked, I would have told them she was planning on Celebration Day bedding when he returned.

Standing there watching his departure, I admired his show for Dawn. I might have grinned, slightly.

We didn't exchange sentimental declarations. Didn't shake hands, or wave.

I set the alarm on my body-clock for twelve hours.

Water was dark, didn't look warm, but it was. The slow tidal waves rolling ashore were small, slow, comforting. The beach was solid stone, but flat, almost too flat. Sky was soft purple-blue. Not a beach for playing volleyball or a pig-roast, perhaps, but swimming and lounging in the sun, sure. Natural downtime pleasures are hard to come by in deep space.

After our AI Harley had completed scans of the water and approved it for swimming, Dawn and Simon were the first ones outside.

Dawn had grown up on a beach in southern California. Her father had been a semi-pro surfer and she got the *water* bug from him. "The beauty of the ocean when you're sitting there waiting for the next wave; that's soul food." She could immerse you in the zen of surf for two days without drawing a breath.

Estrada and Betty followed Dawn and Simon outside.

If Puff's *would-you-look-at-that* grin had been any wider, it might have required a theme song. "The place is really starting to look like a beach. Put a keg and some bikini babes out there you'd be halfway home. Add your basic hepcats in Hawaiian shirts doin' the hula-hula hula-hula, maybe a tiki bar set-up . . . man, that would be gnarly. Silver moonswing, right tunes, I'd be up for a slow dance with a fast mermaid."

"You don't want hot dogs, too?" I asked.

"Chow? You bet. You know me, Lt. I'm always up for chow."

Under a necklace of clouds, we heard round tones, deliberate tones, brought distance from another time.

Betty was the one who saw them first. The water filled with surfacing shapes from the sea—flying, a commonwealth of glint. They were traveling in a large pod, leaping from the water; they appeared to be playing with each other.

They came ashore like sea turtles.

Excited, thankful, Betty had her arms across her chest, her fingers knitted together. She leaned toward the creatures. "A voluptuous beginning. They might be coming home to roost."

And they did resemble turtles, a bit; some swimming and diving, the slow walk as they crawled from the sea foam, harmless creatures at play. Way they looked, round sofa-pillow shaped, set of flippers behind each of their four stubby legs, and their size, about that of a bulldog. Could have been amphibious or reptilian, but it struck me, they were tired *puppies*—maybe their eyes bent my thoughts in that direction. They had thick, short necks and small round heads, and big round eyes, hypnotic eyes—there were nebulas and stars in their eyes.

Watching them was soothing, and a bit spellbinding, the gentle pulsing and the kaleidoscopic chameleon colors changing on their skin. There was idleness to this world, the creatures, the water, the illuminations. Made you feel like you were being called. You wanted to be open and fit, wanted to be carried to the shore of healing.

They ran to us. Like little fishes drawn to our big boat.

Betty was an animal lover. Back on Earth, she owned two dogs, Giant and

Frankie, and did charity work for animal rescue and local shelters; she decided the aquatic creatures would be called sea puppies. "They're so cute and playful, makes you want to snuggle. I'm going to call them sea puppies."

She picked one up and hugged it. "Estrada, look. I'm going to call her Spell. Look at her colors changing. She's pure magic."

Estrada yelled to Betty, "I want one, too!"

Dawn was swimming and watching Estrada, another wacko dog lover, play with the sea puppies. He was petting them, and they were rolling over and slapping the surface of the water with their front flippers. You could tell Dawn wanted to play with them, too, but was wary.

Estrada screamed. He'd gone into the water up to his knees and the sea puppies had come. He petted. They played. He laughed and talked to them, "What a good boy." "Yes, you're a beauty, too." They vocalized clicks and whistles, seemingly in reply. And their pulsing became a frenzy of sharp, flashing patterns and feeding.

Dawn headed for shore, the vigor of every stroke bleeding utterly into the next. She never made it.

Simon was enjoying his, as he termed it "shore leave". Had a bunk-roll out and was laying there, earbuds filled with who knows what transgressive noise. Had I been in a gambling establishment, I'd have put down big money that he was deep into fuck fantasies with our A I Harley. I still remember falling on my ass laughing, when Betty walked into the galley for coffee one morning and found Simon trying to convince Harley, who was down on her knees, his semen wouldn't contaminate any internal elements. "Hell, Harley, its just 10cc of love lava. You can spit it out if you have to." Betty lit into him, up one side and down the other. Half the crew heard the landslide hit him, came running, and stood there grinning.

His head was bobbing, his eyes were closed. Simon never opened them—the puppies started with his face.

Andromeda Vanbeck. Brains and wit. Tall. Brunet. High cheek bones. Carried herself like royalty. Curves I've eyed and almost begged to embrace. If we were back home in a bar, or better yet, a club with a dance floor—there's a great place on Goric, on Albertina Beach—I'd walk across the room and ask, *again*. She was quite a ways out, floating. The water around her appeared to boil. I thought it odd there was no tint of red. Andromeda didn't scream. I got a dry knot in my throat, but I didn't scream either.

Gary, our engineer, was running; zigged, they zigged, zagged, they zagged. Panic, headed the wrong way. Fell. Got up. Ran. Fell again. Got grabbed. Things had him, shook him. He looked confused.

Puff Monder was jumping, marionette on strings, hopping. Seen comedy routines, clown and fool, looked like he did . . . if you take away the blood. I didn't laugh.

Betty started to run. Opposite direction of the beach. No food. No water. No weapon. No shoes. She was a good kid; sweet, reliable as clockwork, and witty. Twenty-eight years old, she had two doctorates, and was only here as window-dressing, to make the mission look believable. I saw her stumble and fall, hard; she was sitting there holding her arm. Shame she was going to die here, die the hard way.

Captain Andrew Mack had run inside and grabbed a pulse rifle. Three empty clips were at his feet . . . and the tide of puppies was still coming.

I blinked. He was down, viscera.

Our A I Harley was standing near the shore a good twenty meters apart from the other crew members. She was staring far out to sea when I shut her down remotely. I looked out at where she'd been looking. *The heart remembers,* I thought before I remembered Harley didn't have a heart. "All that intellect." *Shame really.*

I was the only one left inside. I locked the hatch, closed the viewport.

Maneri and Taborn and Pete Rechy avoided the puppies for nearly twenty minutes. They finally made their way to our craft and were banging on the hatch. Didn't check the time; they didn't bang all that long.

I sat alone, cup of black coffee. Eight hours to wait. Opened my music playlist on the ship's computer and selected an old jazz recording from the 1990's. Joe Henderson started playing the sambas of Antonio Carlos Jobim. His alto sax was sleek, sexy, airy . . . like a velvet moon it lingered. The quintet caught the wave Henderson was riding; their easy tempo moved my mind to *paraiso.* "Boto" ended "Dreamer (Vivo Sonhando)" came up; I would have like to have been on a Caribbean beach, warm waves coming ashore in the moonlight, waltzing with a tall brunet. Harmony in her arms and I'm drifting, blissful, dreaming what she dreams. Andromeda's eyes would be for me, on me, and I would not look up at the cold stars.

No fun being a cold bastard, to have people (enjoying the fruits of the truth, justice, and freedom you help provide) look at you like you're some machine built for atrocity. But I had been trained and trained, and the oath was more than just words to me. Gave up a lot of my soul, so others didn't have to. Didn't cry over it, much; you execute the mission to the best of your training, and if you make it out alive, you move on to the next. The blood and scars and loss never go away, but you keep going forward, even if some days you're not up for running at top speed.

Tried to push the knot in my throat aside with the thought that this was my last mission.

"Hide it well enough and there may be no Reawakening. If you take the artifact far enough out into the galaxy, or into another one, and lose it, bury it, maybe the fucking-thing stays lost. That's the best we can hope for. We could lock it up here—put it behind hundreds of layers of security, but war comes, and power changes hands, *or corrupts*, and people get fucking stupid ideas—might help if they let some of us shoot politicians; just a well-researched and thought-out culling. This artifact needs to be lost. If the Gate Seekers get their hands on it, the Book says, they will possess the key to unlock all the gates. We can't allow that to happen." Seven days later, Charlie Butler drowned in his pool. He was drunk, and it appeared he'd fallen, struck his head and slipped below the water; autopsy didn't mention he'd had help—from me.

Charlie spent a year putting this mission together: he hand-selected every member of the expeditionary force, he acquired our spacecraft, he kept everything off the books and away from prying eyes. He lived to preserve, protect, and defend the Union. With the Gate now somewhere below the waves, it's my turn to preserve, protect, and defend the Union. Push this button and me and the ship and all knowledge of what we did out here is gone—two hundred kilotons gone; no slip of the tongue to a lover, no not-so-veiled inference while inebriated.

"Every ship I've ever served on has had rats," Captain Mack said. "I don't like rats, so, I brought, Rattler." Fifteen-pound Maine Coon. Silver tabby. He's sitting here with me. Typical mysterious cat, he's statue still, watching me, and I haven't a clue to what he might be thinking. Chow, maybe? Davidson's POW Medal is attached to his collar; the medal wasn't there yesterday. Rattler's been here for over twenty minutes and hasn't uttered a sound; that's odd. I wonder if he knows what I'm about to do?

I stare at the detonation button. It's blood red.

"Are we sure this thing is what they think it is?" I asked Charlie the night he handed me my Transfer Agent assignment.

"Sure enough that we have to try. You've been in enough firefights; you know they're all risky, and long-term odds are against you coming out of the ass-end. That's where we are; betting on a very big long shot. But if we can pull it off, maybe it stays lost, Hank. Maybe?"

I hope Charlie was right.

(*Brian Eno* Ambient 4: On Land; *The Ventures* "Perfidia"; *The Rivieras* "California Sun"; *Vanduras* In The Dark; *The Surfaris* "Surfer Joe"; *The Hondells* "Little Honda"; *The Beach Boys* "Heroes and Villains"; *The Halibuts* "A Taste Of Honey"; *Junior Brown* "Surf Medley"; *The Shadows* "Atlantis")

§

**Joseph S. Pulver, Sr.** *is a Shirley Jackson Award-winning editor,* (The Grimscribe's Puppets *2013*). *His editorial work includes* A Season in Carcosa, Cassilda's Song, *and* The Madness of Dr. Caligari. *He has released four mixed-genre collections, a collection of* King in Yellow *tales, and novels. His fiction has appeared in many anthologies, including* Autumn Cthulhu, The Children of Old Leech, Ellen Datlow's The Year's Best Horror, *and* Best Weird Fiction of the Year. *His work has been praised by Thomas Ligotti, Laird Barron, Michael Cisco, Jeffery Thomas, Anna Tambour, and many other writers and editors.*

# When Yiggrath Comes

## TIM CURRAN

ILLUSTRATED BY
SISHIR BOMMAKANTI

THE JUMPSHIP *BARTHOLOMEW* TOUCHED DOWN ON GAMMA ERIDANI 4, ABOUT two klicks from the Terran outpost on Centipede Ridge. It was dark out there. Darker than dark—the sort of unrelieved stygian blackness you could only seem to find on alien worlds countless parsecs from Earth and the Colonies.

The sun had set some six hours previously. With GE 4's eccentric orbit, it would not rise for another five days.

Riger, the first officer, led the others out into the poisonous, methane-heavy atmosphere—Doc Kang and two techs, Sealander and Wise. The landscape was a crazy quilt of rises and hollows: sharp-crested waves of rock that looked like dunes and tall, narrow pipes of stone. The rises weren't so bad, just a little trippy in the low gravity. The hollows, on the other hand, were filled with congested, thorny vegetation that pulled and snagged at their suits. Overhead, triple-winged cartilaginous birds called trinary qualaks shrieked in the murky sky. They were also known as "piss-mongers," owing to their unpleasant habit of directing streams of corrosive urine at anything which startled them . . . which was pretty much everything.

Riger led the others over a razor-backed hillock, and there was the outpost atop the ridge in the distance. It looked like an interconnected series of multi-storied black boxes.

There had been no contact with the survey team in six weeks.

Riger got on the comm with the *Cosmo*, orbiting some four hundred kilometers above. "It's dark, real dark," he said. "Not picking up any life signs. It doesn't look good."

"All right," Captain Cawber sighed. "Go in, but go in careful."

"Aye, sir."

"Keep your eyes open, mister. God knows what kind of mess you're going into."

Riger studied the outpost, eyes fixed and worried behind the bubble of his helmet. He wore a shiny green enviro-suit known as a lizard skin. Like the others, he carried a pulse weapon. In the black sky, there were occasional phosphorescent blue-white streaks caused by bursts of ionized xenon gas in the nitrogen-rich atmosphere. They looked like a sort of tubular lightning.

He led them up the ridge to the compound. The outer fence wasn't energized. Everything was down.

Just for the hell of it, he tried to raise the survey team again. The outpost was called Starlight Station, but why anyone had called it that with the constant, heavy cloud cover and hydrocarbon smog of GE 4 was beyond him.

"Well?" Sealander said over the com. "We going in or what, sir?"

"When I say."

The terse reply shut Sealander up. They were all scared. And for that very reason, they weren't going in until he had a good feel for things. Twenty-third-century technology told him there was nothing alive in Starlight, but he trusted his instincts.

"Okay," he finally said. "Lead us in, Sealander."

"Shit," Sealander said.

Wise giggled.

Sealander got to the main hatch, scanning it with the lights of his helmet. "She's not pressurized, First," he said over the comm. "Airlock is blown."

Riger and the others came across the compound, nearly hopping in the low gravity. The shadows around them were deep, sinister pools. The beams of their lights slashed about like blades.

They went in.

"Can you get some lights going in here?" Riger asked.

Sealander shrugged inside his suit. "Sure. Probably. Generator's down. There should be four backup systems. Funny none of them kicked in."

"Maybe, somebody shut them off," Wise said.

"Now, why in the hell would they do that, son?" Doc Kang asked.

Wise had no answer, or none he was willing to share. The kid had imagination, real imagination, and sometimes that was a benefit, Riger knew. But not in a situation like this. What you needed here were level-headed, nuts-and-bolts types. An imagination could be lethal.

*If it was up to me, he would have stayed behind.*

But Captain Cawber picked who he wanted, and that was that.

Sealander studied Starlight's layout on the inside of his helmet bubble. "Looks . . . looks like the power core is below. If we follow this corridor, take a left, and a right, we should see the hatchway at the end."

"Maybe we shouldn't split up," Wise said. "I mean, not just yet."

"C'mon, kid, and zip it with that talk," Sealander said, leading him off.

"All right, Doc," Riger said. "Let's you and I find central control."

He led the way with his blue-tinged helmet lights. Kang followed. Crazy, knife-edged shadows swept around them. They checked a few rooms on their way to central, mostly labs—geo and bio—and an emergency supply closet. They saw no indication that anyone had been there in some time.

"What do you make of it, Doc?" Riger asked when they paused at the station canteen, their lights scanning row upon row of empty tables.

Kang shrugged. "Not really sure. I mean, let's face it, if anyone was still alive, they would have picked up our transmission."

Riger felt his throat tighten. "But there were fifty people here . . . they can't all be dead."

"Can't they?"

He was right, and Riger knew it. It had been six weeks since the distress call. That was a lot of time. Anything could have happened.

"At the very least," he said, "there should be bodies."

Kang shrugged again. "When I first joined the service, I was a medic on an ore-crusher, the *Dolly B.*, making the hop from Proxima D and E to the uridium refineries on C. There was an ore camp called Crater Valley. Automated but for five hardrock drillers. Nobody had heard from them in weeks, so we sent down a rescue party. You know what they found?"

"Not a thing."

"Exactly. Those boys were gone—just gone. Point being, things happen way out here, First. Bad things. Things you can't even imagine."

Riger had heard plenty of tales like that in his time. He didn't even bother commenting on it. Doc was always going on about something. He didn't believe people belonged out this far.

Riger called in to the *Cosmo*, told them there was nothing to report. Not yet.

They moved down the silent corridor and up a metal flight of steps. Their footfalls echoed out and came back at them, making it sound as if they were being followed. Had Riger been an imaginative man, he might have told Cawber that the atmosphere of the station felt corrupted, contaminated by something namelessly bleak and horribly noxious. It seemed he could feel it seeping into him like a disease. The station was deserted. He was sure of that. Yet Starlight felt unpleasantly *occupied*. But by what, he could not say.

Five minutes later when Sealander came over the comm, Riger nearly jumped. "Hate to say it, First, but Wise was right: somebody shut everything down. And I mean everything. Not just power but life support, water recyclers, atmospherics, everything. About five-and-a-half hours ago from what I'm reading."

Riger felt something chill inch across the back of his neck. *Just after sundown,* he thought.

"Can you power it up?"

"Sure, I can cold-crank the pile, but it'll take fifteen, twenty minutes to cycle it."

"Do what you gotta do."

"Aye."

Riger was standing in the cabin of the chief biologist, a woman named Freeman. As he swept his light around, he saw nothing out of the ordinary. There should have been something. Even a few drops of blood would have been reassuring.

*It's so damn quiet, so damn empty.*

"First! Over here!" Kang called over the com.

Riger rushed out into the corridor. Kang had ventured ahead into central control. He had his light on a form pressed up against a bank of instruments. Whoever it was, they wore a yellow e-suit and bubble helmet. Both were old in comparison to the lizard skins of the *Cosmo* team.

"Who is he?" Riger asked.

"I don't know. Can't get anything out of him but gibberish."

"Scans should have picked up his life signs."

"Yes," Kang said. "They should have."

Inside the helmet, the middle-aged man's eyes were huge and white, unblinking. His face was contorted in pain or terror, his mouth trembling. Every time he started to speak, it became quickly incomprehensible.

"Can you shoot him up?"

Kang nodded. He pulled a hypo from his medical kit and found the port on the man's suit. There was a low hissing as the medication transferred. Right away, the man relaxed. He blinked his eyes slowly and licked his lips.

"You . . . you got the distress?"

"Yes," Riger told him. "Who are you? What happened here?"

"Pelan," he managed, his eyes dopey and glazed. "Geophysics, Starlight Project."

"I'm Riger, and this is Doc Kang. We're from the *DS Cosmo*."

"Deep space, eh? Deep space boys." His face hitched as if he had been jolted. "It . . . it . . . there's so much. It was Henley, you know. George Henley. George and I were friends. He found the site, the ancient city by the dry ravine. That's where it started. It was Phyterian. There was no doubt. We . . . we always thought the Phyterians were wiped out by climactic upheaval. But that wasn't true. No, no, no. George proved it. The extinction event . . . it was the relic. The relic George found buried in the ruins. The relic . . . oh dear God . . ."

Riger and Kang were kneeling by him now.

"What relic?" Riger had to know. "Tell me."

Pelan was breathing hard, nearly hyperventilating. Cords as thick as the roots of an oak sapling stood out in his neck. "That city . . . it was abandoned sixty thousand years ago. That was the time of the event, you see. The extinction event. George found the relic. That's why *it* came back, the entity—Yiggura, Yiggrath . . . the Phyterians had many names for it." He was sobbing now, his eyes darting about. "The relic . . . the relic called it . . . old as the universe, pestilence old as the Big Bang, the primary cosmic generation. Don't you see? Don't you see how late it is? *It's here! It's here now! It watches us, calls to us!*"

"Dr. Pelan, you need to calm down," Kang told him.

"He's raving, Doc," Riger said, shaking his head. "He's not making any sense."

Pelan went rigid. "Goddamn you, listen to me! The Phyterians worshipped the thing! The relic was holy to them! When George found it in the ruins, Yiggrath came! Dark matter entering the visible spectrum! It is here now!"

"He's goddamn hysterical," Riger said.

Pelan scrambled to his feet. He started this way and then that. He was shivering and shuddering, *vibrating* rapidly like a pneumatic hammer. It didn't seem as if the human body could move like that. He vibrated faster and faster until his boots rattled on the deck plating.

"What the hell is happening to him?" Riger asked.

"I . . . I don't know," was the best Kang had to offer.

Pelan looked like a man being electrocuted . . . slowly. He was holding onto two modular desks as the clonic tremors rolled through him faster and faster. His voice, high-pitched and wavering, was frenzied: "D-d-d-dark matter . . . an ecosystem for s-s-such things . . . the great spiral intelligence . . . born of gravitational force . . . antimatter into a subatomic particle storm . . . writhing anti-creation, the absolute *negative* . . . it can . . . it can . . . it can be broken down theoretically, empirically, m-m-m-mathematically . . . the writhing shadows . . . the tenebrous spiraling sentience . . . do you see? Do you see? The voices . . . God help us . . . the voices . . . *seven* . . . it differentiates, it assimilates . . . it accelerates . . . it expands . . . *eight* . . . *eight point three point one-five-seven point nine-three* . . . *yes, yes, I hear it, I hear it!* The hungering star-jelly . . . no longer entombed . . . now is the time of the turning, cattle, accept me and see me and stare into the primordial riven wastes of chaos! *Five . . . five . . . five . . . six . . . seven three . . . point nine-three-one squared . . . point six point six point six point six six six SIX SIX SIX SIX SIX—*"

There was a loud, fleshy eruption, a very, *very* wet eruption of blood and tissue. Pelan launched into the air, his suit making a horrendous, grisly popping sound, expanding to three or four times its size like a helium balloon inflated to bursting in a microsecond.

He hit the floor with a wet, gelatinous sound like jelly in a plastic bag. The inside of his helmet was splattered bright red. What was inside his suit was no longer recognizably human. It slopped and rolled. Droplets of blood glistened on the suit's seams.

Kang went to him right away though he was obviously beyond hope. He pulled the pressure locks of the suit and unzipped it. He cried out as Pelan's anatomy surged out at him in a wave of red, mucid pudding that nearly engulfed him.

Riger pulled him to his feet.

"Like . . . like he underwent some massive systemic decompression," Kang said, his voice shrill.

The only thing Riger could really do was call it in. But when he tried, he got static. A heavy, droning, listening sort of static that bothered him in ways he could not put into words. It sounded as if there was something just beneath it, a low and unearthly sort of respiration. As if he was hearing the planet breathe.

"I don't get it," Kang said. "Comm was working just fine ten minutes ago."

*Yes, it was, wasn't it?* Riger wanted to say but didn't dare. He was in command, and he had to act like it. His skin was literally crawling now, and it had nothing to do with what had happened to Pelan. This was something else, something that ran much deeper. An instinctive sort of fear. He had the feeling that they were being watched, coldly appraised by an inhuman intelligence that was icy and cruel.

"Got . . . got a mountain of pure copper just over the rise, Doc. Sensors picked it up. It can play hell with communications."

Kang nodded, but it was obvious he wasn't buying it.

Riger tried the comm again, and this time, the static was so shrill it hurt his ears.

"I don't like this," Kang said.

"Me neither, Doc."

He tried to raise Sealander and Wise. At first, there was just dead air, and his heart began to hammer. "Yeah, First. Sealander here."

Thank God. "I want both of you up here right now. We're finishing the sweep and heading for the *Bart*."

Silence. A crackling. "Shit, sir, we're almost done here. Another five minutes, and we'll have this place lit up like the Fourth of July."

*Five minutes, five minutes,* Riger thought. *Do we even have five minutes?* He didn't know. He just didn't know.

He was generally a strong, secure sort of leader . . . but moment by moment, he was feeling weaker. It was this place, this awful place. It was sucking the life out of him.

"All right, five minutes. But no longer."

"You got it, First."

"At least the suit-to-suit comm is working," Kang said.

*Or being allowed to work,* Riger thought.

They found George Henley's cabin next. The walls were pasted with prints of the Phyterian city. It looked like a nightmare labyrinth of black basalt, narrow and crowded, sharp pinnacles rising high above like fangs. There were maps, too. One laid over the top of another. The city was only a few hours away.

"Look at this," Kang said.

Photos. Grainy blowups of something that looked like an immense, craggy skull made of a mottled, bluish material that appeared metallic. It looked to be fifteen or twenty feet in length with a grotesque, exaggerated, goatish appearance, like the skull of a ram that reminded Riger of medieval prints he'd seen of the Black Goat of the Witches' Sabbat. The idea made him shiver. *The devil, the devil, way out here.* Regardless, the skull was hideous, chambered with hollows and exaggerated jaws, two immense cylindrical horns rising from its apex.

"Makes . . . makes me think of ancient Egypt on old Earth," Kang said in a dreamy sort of voice. "That thing looks like the head of Anubis."

Riger only knew the image of the skull made him feel uneasy, nervous . . . *expectant.* Disturbed. The skull was dead, of course, but the feeling he got was that it was not dead *enough.*

Kang pushed the photo print closer to him. "That's the relic," he said with something like religious awe. "That's the relic that summoned Yiggrath, the unborn and undying, the endless, deathless shade from the black seams between time and space."

Riger just stared at him. "What in the hell are you talking about? Pelan never said any of that."

"I . . . I don't know." Kang looked confused. His adam's apple bobbed up and down. In the lights of his helmet, his skin was sallow and diseased, his face running with beads of sweat. "I don't know why I said it, First."

Riger turned away from him. There was a loose, repellent cast to his features. It disgusted him.

Kang found a personal tablet hidden beneath more prints of the city. As soon as he touched it, it activated a holo-journal entry. A narrow, wizened face was projected before them.

"*There can be no doubt,*" said the dour voice of the image, "*that what we now know of the Phyterian civilization and what we thought we knew are in direct contrast. For decades, we believed that the Phyterian race was destroyed by an extinction event known as the Primary Cataclysm. This climate-altering release of methane gases was from unprecedented and devastating seismic activity in the southern hemisphere in the region known as the Plain of Glass. These deposits were locked in intercrustal pockets during planetary cosmogony.*

"*At the PC—Primary Cataclysm—level of sediments, we see evidence of a mass extinction of the sort Earth experienced at the close of the Permian. Ninety-five percent of GE 4's organisms perished some sixty thousand years ago. The Phyterians, a squat bipedal, toad-like race, also went extinct. Before that, the planet was rich in biodiversity—herd animals such as the hesperhippus and bonditherms, the massive quasi-reptilian crotacoils, numerous species of land-dwelling prycops and megacytes, aquatic helix worms and fishlike icthydonts as well as plant species such as the tyrannophytes and nyctaderms, thousands of species of seed pods, club mosses, and fungi. The list is endless.*

"*Now, no one can refute that the Primary Cataclysm occurred, but we now know there was another extinction vector. What this was is difficult to explain, but the finding of the relic skull by Phyterian priests known as the Accylardu-dek-despoda, or the Sect of the Gashed Ones, was the catalyst. The skull—if I may be so bold as to apply such a descriptor—is formed of a spongy material that has so far defied analysis. I believe it is the material remains of a creature not from the space that we know and understand, of a denizen of the dark world, a creature of dark matter, a thing of dark electromagnetism from a parallel anti-universe. How it died, I cannot say, but I think that it was in a transitive interdimensional state between the exotic physics of its universe and that of our own.*

"*The Phyterian priesthood called this entity something that can be reproduced phonetically as 'Yiggura' or 'Yiggrath.' The skull opened the gates between two spheres of reality and channeled the pestilence that claimed the Phyterian world. That is a theory. That is a guess. But based upon glyphs in the dead city and my own assumptions, I believe it to be true.*"

That was the first entry. Succeeding entries became more and more nonsensical, lacking lucidity or any linear logic until they became little more than ranting.

"Doc, we don't have time for this," Riger said.

"Then we better make the time." He queued up another entry.

Henley reappeared. It was the face of a man close to madness—staring eyes, twitching mouth, trembling lips, a voice that was high and scratching, nearly hysterical.

"*The skull, the skull, the damned skull. It is in my dreams, it shadows my life. It compels, it owns, it possesses. I am not who I was. I feel I am being appropriated by a godless horror from some loathsome dimensional pit of insanity. The skull is not bone. It is dead but it lives. It is warm under my touch, pliant and fleshy. There is memory in it, memory of this world and a thousand others, exterminations and extinctions and genocide. I have touched death, and death has taught me its secrets.*"

The next entry showed an image of what looked like a very old man. His eyes were bloodshot, his mouth contorted into a grotesque grin.

"*The others do not scoff so much now, eh? They do not think that George Henley is so mad after all, do they? None will dare approach the cursed ruins of Kry-Yeb, the dead but dreaming city of the Phyterian Empire. I have returned the skull to its tomb beneath the city, though distance matters not to such a thing. It beckons to me. But I will not go there. I will not lay my hands upon it and view the carnage of dozens of worlds turned to poisoned, toxic graveyards. I will not!*

"*Only the blazing light of the sun weakens the skull. I fear the coming of night.*

"*The others? Oh yes, they feel the thing now, and they know it calls forth another of its kind. Soon will be the time of the great dying, the mass entombment, the sacred and profane interment of all that walk above the land. The time of the skinturning is at hand, may God help us all.*"

The final entry was of a broken, stick-thin old man whose back was bent and whose hair had gone a shocking white. One eye was closed, the other wide but glassy.

"*There is no escape. With great, pitiful futility, Dr. Pelan and the others have sent out a distress call. That which waits in ravening darkness only laughs. Soon will come the night, the night that lasts five Earth days. When the sun again rises, we shall all be dead. The signs of the coming of Yiggrath, the unborn and undying, the endless, deathless shade from the black seams between time and space, are many. There is a curious red haze in the sky and branching green lightning at the horizon. The winds are hot and dry, the winds of pestilence, the breath of the embalmer. No one can be sure of anything now. As another darker, malefic dimension intersects with our own, electronics and machinery fail. Time is turned back upon itself, so now is yesterday and five minutes ago is two weeks hence. The spacetime continuum is tearing open, and I alone can see what is waiting to creep out."*

After a long pause, *"It is full dark out now. Yiggrath comes. I hear the others out there, the crew of Starlight Station. They are driven to a mad frenzy, screaming and crying out, shrieking in the night like animals being butchered as they fall into the hands of the living god. And out the window . . . yes, it is Yiggrath rising high and black and diabolic above the station. His horns brush the dark, spiral holes between the stars.*

*"It comes! It comes!*

*"Inside, oh God, oh god, the hour of the skinturning . . ."*

"Shut that damn thing off!" Riger ordered.

"That's it," Kang said. "That's all there is."

They were getting out, back to the *Bartholomew* and up to the *Cosmo*. Riger wasn't going to bother searching for anyone else. They needed to come down here with a large search party. There was no way he could handle it with four men, *and why the hell didn't Sealander have those fucking lights on yet?*

As he hurried Doc Kang down the corridor and down the metal steps to the first level, he tried to call the *Cosmo*. That static, that damned static. It was as if there was no ship up there. All he was getting was the drone of the planet itself, the echo of atmospheric electrical activity.

Then he heard Captain Cawber.

"*Cosmo!*" Riger cried. "This is Riger! We're coming back up, sir. What's going on down here is more than we can handle."

He expected Cawber's usual stern rebuttal, but what he got was much worse. "All right," the captain sighed. "Go in, but go in careful."

*What in the hell?*

"Captain? Captain? Are you reading me?"

"Keep your eyes open, mister. God knows what kind of mess you're going into."

This was the transmission from earlier, after the crew landed with the *Bartholomew*. What was this? What kind of sick fucked up joke was this?

"Time is turning back upon itself just as Henley said it would," Kang mused. "Now, we'll be delivered into the hands of the living god."

Riger wanted to hit him.

*Something* was happening. Reality—the reality he had long known—was disassociating itself from Starlight Station. He felt a hot, bright sort of delirium open inside his head as time became elastic, stretching and sagging and reinventing itself. Now, the corridors were too long, stretching into black, stark infinity. He felt that if he followed them, if he ran blindly down them in some hysterical terror, he would fall off the rim of the universe and plunge into the ravening darkness. Yes, it was here, it was now, it was happening. He could feel the physical parameters of the station begin to alter, squeezing him from all sides, the walls oozing and bubbling, the angles in the corners warping, intersecting, splitting open to reveal sinister, eldritch vistas beyond time and space.

"We don't belong out here," Kang said, his face pale as spilled milk behind his helmet bubble, his eyes huge and white like goose eggs. "Out here in these awful spaces where darkness is endless and insanity takes physical form. Do you see that, Riger? Don't you see the terrible, horrendous mistake we've made by exploring deep space?

"It wasn't *our* idea at all! From the very crude beginnings of Sputnik and the Gemini missions, we were summoned into space, driven into it like herd animals, compelled to come out here!" He reached out for Riger, clawing at him. "Don't be a fool! Open your eyes and see, really *see*! It's always nightfall out here and and and *seven* . . . this planet is a trap! We followed the dark creek into the black black . . . *eight* . . . river which spills into the ocean of stars and now we see the malign shapes that hide behind them like a child behind a blanket! Here, flesh and matter and time and cold intellect intersect and and and—" He began to shake, trembling and jerking, thumping against the wall. Like Pelan, *vibrating.* "The . . . the coordinates . . . *eight point three point one-five-seven point nine-three* . . . oh God, oh God, oh God . . . here now, it blossoms! The stars are stripped away and the blackness of the cosmos opens like a great, hungry mouth and *five* . . . *five* . . . *five* . . . *six* . . . *seven three* . . . *point nine-three-one squared* . . . *point six point six point six point six six six SIX SIX SIX SIX SIX—*"

Kang's voice became a funneling scream as he vibrated madly, and there was a deafening, fleshy pop as he exploded inside his suit like a tick burned with a match. He bounced off the walls, hit the ceiling, and fell at Riger's feet, the inside of his helmet filled with a bubbling, sloshing red mire of macerated tissue and blood.

Riger ran.

He got on the comm and called, *shouted* for Sealander again and again, but there was no response. Just that static squealing in his ears, louder and louder, shrilling, screeching, making him cry out. He ran toward the entrance, and there was Wise, waiting for him.

"Wise!" Riger cried. "*Wise!*"

Then his hands were on him, and he could feel the soft give of the man's lizard skin, and Wise pitched over, his suit breaking open, and what was inside splashed over the floor.

That's when Riger knew.

That's when he *really* knew. Wise was sprawled there on the floor in a soup of his own anatomy, a husk of pulp and raw wet matter. He had been birthed from his e-suit like a slimy fetus from an infected placenta, wearing the globular jewels of his organs on the *outside*, wrapped in the moist pink tentacles of his intestines. *The turning, the skinturning.* It was how the living god received his worshippers, how Yiggrath welcomed them into his church—he turned them inside out

Riger stumbled out into the poisonous atmosphere of Gamma Eridani 4, standing and falling, rising and tripping on rubbery legs.

*This is . . . this is . . . this is the hour of the turning.*

He looked up and screamed, for Yiggrath had come. He/she/it towered above him, a glossy, obsidian-black gargoyle rising a mile or two or three into the hazy, flickering auroral, neon-slashed sky. Its jagged, spectral wings spread from horizon to horizon, its titanic body flickering and sparking with a soft blue lambency. The rising spires of its horns seem to brush the clouds. It grinned down at him, snout opening like a monstrous bi-valve that could swallow the stars.

Riger did not scream. He was struck dumb with awe at the cosmic horror of the creature, of Yiggrath, the unborn and undying, the hyper-relativistic nightmare, the multi-dimensional living god that threaded the galactic magnetic field like a needle.

Bathed in its frozen shadow, everything around him began to spin and whirl, pulled inside out and broken into a blazing cyclonic storm of energized particles like droning phosphorescent corpse-flies that seemed to move around

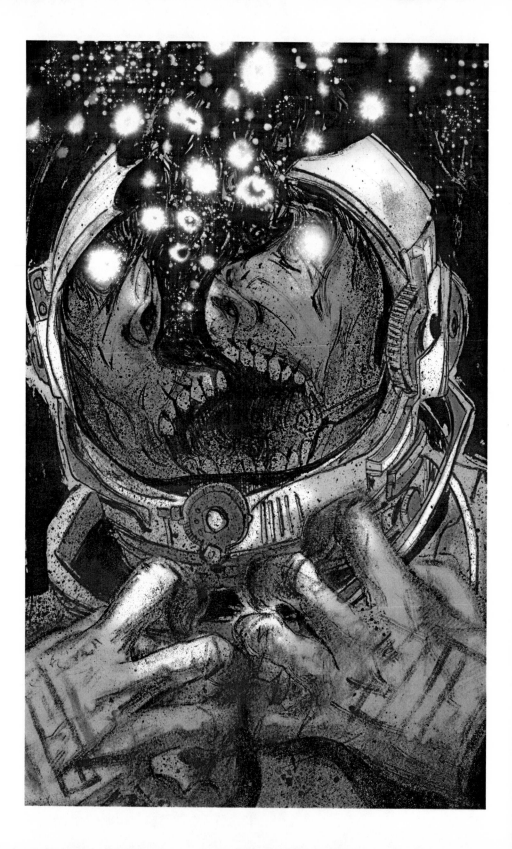

him and through him at light velocity and perhaps beyond until he was certain his head would split open like a jelly-filled gourd. And then, *then*, as his mind sucked into a black hole inside his cerebral cortex, he saw an enormous, endless plain of glittering stars forming chains and pulsating nebula and nightmare constellations that no man had ever seen and lived to tell of.

And as his eyes seemed to explode from his head, his voice rambling on and on and on—*eight . . . eight point three point one-five-seven point nine-three*—he saw the transgalactic gulf and its throbbing pulsars and glowing strata of stars split wide open, coming apart like a jigsaw puzzle in an alien spectrum of light, and he saw worlds, a million-billion dead worlds blackened into cinders in some geometrically perverse, impossible anti-space where multifaceted triangles and polygons and trapezohedrons hopped like frogs and a milky, writhing incandescence crawled, a monstrous worm a hundred light years in length. And as his voice screamed out the coordinates of his own approaching destruction with a sort of manic and rapturous mad glee—*five . . . five . . . five . . . six . . . seven three . . . point nine-three-one squared . . . point six point six point six point six six six SIX SIX SIX SIX SIX*—he knew what Yiggrath wanted him to know: that the universe, the third dimension, was all synthetic—it was a simulation, a twisted vision, a hallucination that the beast had dreamed and now had grown bored with.

This is what Yiggrath wanted Riger to understand, the lurid joke inside the punchline hidden in the hysterical cackling iridescent chaos of known space, the seed it planted in his head as his skin began to turn.

§§

**Tim Curran** *is the author of the novels* Skin Medicine, Hive, Dead Sea, Resurrection, Hag Night, Skull Moon, The Devil Next Door, Doll Face, Afterburn, House of Skin, *and* Biohazard. *His short stories have been collected in* Bone Marrow Stew *and* Zombie Pulp. *His novellas include* The Underdwelling, The Corpse King, Puppet Graveyard, Worm, *and* Blackout. *His short stories have appeared in such magazines as* City Slab, Flesh & Blood, Book of Dark Wisdom, *and* Inhuman, *as well as anthologies such as* Shadows Over Main Street, Eulogies III, *and* October Dreams II. *His fiction has been translated into German, Japanese, Spanish, and Italian. Find him on Facebook at: https://www.facebook.com/tim.curran.77*

# The Immortals

# ANGUS MCINTYRE

ILLUSTRATED BY
LUKE SPOONER

THE HALL IS VAST AND EMPTY, THE VAULTED ROOF LOST IN SHADOW ABOVE. The polished black marble of the floor reflects a line of huge columns, lit only by a glimmer of daylight that enters through the louvres of half-hidden windows.

It is a space built to impress, but the man who walks through it is not impressed. In his long lifetime, he has seen thousands of such places, places built both to dwarf and to exalt their human builders. He finds their grandiosity predictable.

He follows a red light floating in the air in front of him, taking his time, refusing to be hurried. He walks with the aid of a cane that he does not need but which is part of his present aspect. Currently, he has the appearance of a man of advanced years, with a hawk-nosed face framed by a mane of white hair, broad-shouldered, his back only slightly stooped—the very model of the distinguished patriarch. He wears a maroon beret and a black uniform whose severity is broken only by a discreet line of medal ribbons.

This appearance is an affectation or perhaps a disguise. In two millennia of life, he has been five times a man, four a woman, and more besides. He has fathered more children than he can name and given birth six times. In another decade, perhaps, he may choose to be a young woman or a fragile child whose eyes sparkle with ancient wisdom or something only superficially human.

"The others are waiting for you in the hospital annex, General Montdarau," the red light whispers. Montdarau raises thick eyebrows in mild annoyance. He has not come all this way to be chivvied by a machine.

He thinks about the word *hospital*. Nowadays, a hospital is a place of transformation. One enters a hospital as a caterpillar enters a cocoon, emerging a different being. Only on backward worlds does the word still denote a place where the sick and injured are made well or the dying warehoused until medicine can do nothing more for them. On backward worlds and, he suspects, here. The council would not have summoned him merely to witness a rebirth.

His measured steps bring him at last to the end of the hall. A door slides open and the red light flickers and winks out.

The open door reveals a smaller chamber. Around a catafalque of polished glass and metal, its surfaces alive with colored lights, four other beings are waiting for him. They turn as he enters, and he appreciates for the first time the gravity of the situation.

"General," says a tall woman with iron-gray hair cut in a severe bob.

"Madam Secretary."

At the first secretary's elbow, a round-faced hermaphrodite in colored silks bows a greeting. For Tiril of Essen to leave their homeworld, the matter must be of extraordinary importance. Behind Tiril stands Doctor-General Kamach, next to a fluted column of brass that is the avatar of the machine-philosopher Hasdrubal.

Five makes a quorum, Montdarau thinks, but what a quorum. The five gathered here can make decisions that could change the fate of whole solar systems.

"You studied the dossier?" the secretary says.

He nods. It told him little, consisting only of the technical fiche for the starship *Nerea* and the biographies of each of her crew. Significantly, it did not include flight plans or astrographic data related to the starship's destination.

Kamach gestures, and the glass and durasteel cylinder of the medical incubator tilts and swivels, a metal shield sliding down to reveal what lies within. For a second time, Montdarau hesitates.

The effects of elective surgery or genetic programming are sometimes unsettling. The wounds of war are often horrifying. Montdarau has seen both. This is worse. He knows instinctively that this is something that has been *done*, not chosen.

The face is still recognizably human, but the flesh has been burned and melted. The cheeks have flowed like wax, leaving blobs of flesh dangling from the scorched bone of the jaw. In places, the charred skin has split to reveal gray pustules that glisten and pulse. The mouth is open in a soundless scream, showing too many teeth. The lidless eyes—undamaged, the irises a bright pale blue—stare blankly at the ceiling.

The casing of the incubator hides everything below the collarbone—the flesh has been flayed from the man's shoulders, Montdarau sees, and the exposed bone is etched with tiny symbols—but what is on display is bad enough.

"Captain Merrick, I assume," he says.

"For the moment we are referring to him simply as the survivor," Kamach says. "You will see why."

"What did this to him?"

The first secretary shakes her head slowly. "It is unclear."

"No recordings?"

"The starship was lost. This body was found in a lifepod. What little we know has been pieced together from his utterances and the fragmentary records in the pod."

"Fragmentary?"

"At some point, he destroyed the pod's data core before trying to end his own life. In the latter, he was unsuccessful."

Montdarau nods. Like them, Captain Merrick had been an Immortal, his engineered body of extraordinary toughness and resiliency.

"We keep him sedated," Kamach says. "For our own safety as well as his comfort. But my doctors are convinced there is little more to be learned. His mind is gone, possibly for good."

Montdarau breathes out. "Tell me what you know," he says.

Captain Merrick is five hundred years old, but he wears the body of a young man, robust and well-proportioned. He looks as he did at thirty-five, before he won the first of his famous series of victories. His manner is easy and natural.

His quarters are modest, a horseshoe of private chambers surrounding a formal reception room. One wall of the reception room is dominated by a mural showing a man in green coveralls nestled in the womb of a great machine. With his pale skin, blond hair, and look of capable determination, the man in the painting resembles the captain so much that for a moment Lysa Tallis wonders if it is intended as a portrait.

*El Hombre, Controlador del Universo,* her mindware informs her, adding a translation and a biographical note about the artist. The painting is not the original but a copy so ancient that it must be scarcely less valuable.

The captain extends both hands. "Welcome aboard, Academician," he says.

She makes a formal reverence, but he answers with a counter-courtesy that erases the difference in rank.

"We don't stand on ceremony," he tells her. He waves his hand for the other members of the crew to come forward: Rothan, the engineer, Netts, systems artificer, and Belis, the ship's supercargo and scientist. Like the captain, Rothan is an Immortal. Despite his gray beard and lined face, he is actually centuries younger than Merrick. The others, like Lysa, are in their first lifespan, perhaps still undecided whether to undergo the complex process of genetic editing and technical augmentation that confers full Immortality.

"You'll meet our passenger later," the captain says. "He has gone planetside to secure what he described as 'essential supplies.' Once he joins us, we will be ready to depart."

"You are familiar with Doctor Erbach's work?" asks Rothan.

Lysa shakes her head. "My specialization is in planetology," she says. "Doctor Erbach, as I understand it, is a historian."

She is not being strictly honest. As the Commonwealth's designated observer, she has reviewed everything related to the mission. Erbach's published work is esoteric and hard to access, but she has studied what she could find.

She is not sure it can strictly be called history. Erbach's rambling theses span a handful of ancient disciplines, from sociology to philosophy, hermeneutics to exobiology, a rickety structure of speculation leaning heavily on disputable interpretations of paleo-archaeological data. Privately, she considers Erbach a crank. On the other hand, someone values his ideas enough to fund this mission and so give Lysa her first chance at a full observership. She keeps her judgments to herself.

The captain is smiling.

She guesses his assessment of Erbach is similar to her own.

"Did you spend much time at the University on Azzecca, Doctor?" Captain Merrick asks. He glances across the dinner table to where the observer is bent over her plate, picking at her food. Her brown hair falls around her face, like a veil, as she leans forward.

"No longer than necessary," says Erbach. "I wished to consult certain records there." He sniffs. "Records of whose importance they were, of course, wholly unaware."

He is a thin man, hollow-eyed and long-jawed. Elective surgery has made his face distinctive but not attractive, a pale oval framed by lank dark hair.

"Records supporting your . . . theories?" asks Belis.

Erbach turns to her. "I do not deal in theory," he says. "I am in possession of certain scientific facts. But what I have discovered is fragmentary and incomplete. I wished to extend my knowledge."

Captain Merrick suppresses a smile. "You must be aware that some of your . . . facts . . . are not widely accepted," he says.

"The heliocentric system, atomic theory, the existence of Coleman-Vibbert subspace matrices were all once 'not widely accepted,' as you put it, Captain. They are no less real for that." He looks directly at Merrick. "I would not presume to tell you how to run your starship, Captain," he says. "But in this matter, you must consider me the expert."

Merrick has so far treated his passenger with every courtesy, but he is not accustomed to condescension.

"Your contention, if I understand correctly, Doctor," he begins, "is that certain archaeological and cultural relics found on Old Earth are not simply products of primitive superstition but point to the existence of an actual alien species that visited the birthplace of humanity in the remote past."

The doctor bobs his head. "Not only Earth. Additional artifacts were recovered on Yttris and—"

"And this ancient race would, according to you, possess powers that can only be described as godlike. With intelligence an order of magnitude greater than human."

"An order? Many orders, Captain. Beside the least of them, we would be no more than ants."

Lysa Tallis looks up. "An exaggeration, surely," she says. "Somsakchan has shown—"

"Somsakchan has shown nothing!" Erbach snaps. "He regurgitates a hash of numbers to bolster his ignorance."

Captain Merrick, for whom metacognitive theory is something of a hobby, is unwilling to let this pass. "Humanity has encountered, Doctor, forty-six intelligent alien races. Some are more intelligent than humans, others less. But their intelligence, however you measure it, is of the same order as human intelligence. The same is true of machine minds. Evolutionary epiphenomena constrain biological intelligence; Godelian limits on self-description restrict the development of artificial intelligences. Superintelligences are the stuff of fantasy." He pauses. "I have studied Somsakchan's work. Far from being, as you call it, a 'hash of numbers,' it is elegant, formally precise, and well supported by observation."

"Nevertheless," Erbach says. "Somsakchan is a fool, and those who trust in his claims . . ." He hesitates, belatedly aware that he is on the point of insulting his host again. "They will be disappointed," he finishes weakly.

"Well," says Merrick. "That is interesting."

"Mad," says Belis. "Quite mad."

Lysa fails to hide a smile. "It does look that way."

They are in the supercargo's office, which doubles as a command center for the ship's automated laboratory. Without moving from her chair, Belis can call on analytical equipment that would be the envy of many university research departments.

"Not that it matters," Belis says. "He can amuse himself looking for his kathooloos or whatever they're called, and we can do some real science."

The two women exchange a look of understanding. In theory, Lysa's role on the mission is to observe the activity of the Chartering Party: the unlikeable Dr. Erbach. She does not look forward to trailing after him while he turns over stones and fills her ears with his messianic nonsense. Belis is offering her the chance to do actual work and put her name to a report that will not be an embarrassment.

"I'd like that," Lysa says.

The *Nerea* masses a quarter of a million tons, and her power plant puts out as much energy as a small star. Her subspace processors can rewrite the structure of reality itself to open a bridge to a tachyonic alter-universe, hurling the huge vessel across light-years in the blink of an eye.

But it is the will of her captain that commands, that sets the ship in motion and gives her purpose and direction. It is Captain Merrick who will steer the ship through the labyrinths of Coleman-Vibbert subspace and bring them safely to their destination.

Resting in his gimbaled cradle, he fuses his consciousness with the ship's systems. He slows his breathing, letting his mind empty of deliberate thought. He stretches, feeling the shape of the universe around him. Elemental hydrogen molecules crawl on his skin as he luxuriates in the warmth of the closest star.

"Stand by for transfer," he says, and Rothan brings the *Nerea's* twin reactors online. "On my mark."

He feels Netts move the crystalline capacitors into alignment. The ship has become an extension of his body, interconnected at a synaptic level. As his body melds with the machine and his mind reaches out to explore the structure of subspace, he attains a holistic awareness of everything about him. He can feel the presence of the supernumeraries aboard–Belis, Tallis, Erbach–like grains of sand in the familiar and precise machinery of the vessel. His awareness hesitates for a moment on the three long pods tucked under the ship's belly, Erbach's "essential supplies," and his eyes widen for a moment as he guesses their contents.

But he has no time to dwell on that now. The transfer window is opening. He breathes a word of command, and Rothan dumps fuel into the reactors. The space around them folds, uncoiling into higher dimensions.

A heartbeat later, the *Nerea* drops out of the mundane universe and into its shadow twin. It begins to accelerate, tumbling down an energy gradient from the dissolving gateway. If velocity has any meaning here, their speed is already many times the speed of light in the universe they left behind.

Travel is not instantaneous. Merrick, his consciousness accelerated by his pilot's augments, is aware of the passage of time. He has time to observe and to decide. His instruments paint pictures of the space around them, and he reacts reflexively, choosing the safest path through a universe dancing with whorls of unpredictable energy.

The target star system, or rather its projection in this universe, is close enough that Merrick can already sense the energies surrounding it. He feels an instant of anxiety. The system's configuration is known to be atypical. But nothing in the laconic notes of the scout who first catalogued it has fully prepared Merrick. It lies within a dense knot of force-lines, like a fist clenched in the fabric of spacetime. As the *Nerea* bears down on it, Merrick scans for angles of approach and finds none. The knot swells monstrously ahead of them, viciously involuted, rotating with lunatic fury. Whirlpools of energy blaze out from its core.

At the last instant, he sees an opening. Fighting momentum, he swings the ship around. A distortion arc, tendrils of energy tightening like tentacles, rises in their path, but Merrick has already initiated the process to open a gateway back to the physical universe. He feeds power to the subspace engines, preparing to climb back into real space.

Something kicks him hard in the ribs, and he cries out. The rusty taste of blood fills his mouth. Red lights flicker at the periphery of his vision, and he can smell burning. The *Nerea* howls like a wounded leviathan.

The gateway stabilizes. For an instant, Merrick hangs between two universes. Around him are the efflorescences and energy spikes of Coleman-Vibbert space, the barb of force that lacerated his ship already sliding astern. Ahead, he glimpses normal space, with a silver sprinkle of stars against a sable sky. Like a diver rising from deep water, he and the ship ascend, squeezing his lungs tight on the last of his air.

They are through, the gateway winking out of existence behind them. Merrick slumps in his cradle, conscious of nothing but the whooping and chattering of the alarms.

Something is wrong. Lysa sees it in the behavior of the crew. They assure her that everything has gone according to plan, but their faces say otherwise.

The ship informs her that the captain is in his quarters and cannot be disturbed. Something about the phrasing reinforces Lysa's suspicions. Like everyone else, the ship uses the language of the Commonwealth, an ancient tongue derived from the majority languages of Old Earth and capable of almost infinite degrees of nuance with layers of meaning hinted at through syntax and word choice. Reading between the lines, she gets the impression that the captain is somehow injured or embarrassed.

In the absence of the crew, Lysa has only Dr. Erbach for company. He at least appears to be in good spirits.

"A rough passage," he says, "as I knew it would be. But I knew that our captain could do it. Few other men could." His mood is euphoric, his long features animated by something like glee.

Outwardly, there is little to justify his excitement. The star is unexceptional, an F-class dwarf distinguishable from a million similar stars only by a few anomalous spectral lines. The ship's sensors have detected a handful of planets: a hot Jovian in close orbit, its outline fuzzed by ionized gas, howling all over the 21 cm line of the radio spectrum; a rocky super-Earth farther out; and a trail of frozen rock and ice balls stretching toward the system's tenuous Oort cloud. Lysa collates the data and finds it tediously similar to hundreds of other catalogued systems.

The one oddity is the presence of a moon in orbit about the super-Earth, a moon large enough to be almost a binary companion. Its presence does not fit with Lysa's model.

Erbach is unsurprised. "I expected as much. You watched my lecture on the Gebel al Mawta fragments? The double logogram in the third line, pluralizing the *duat*, clearly indicated that the throne of the god was associated with a binary configuration."

"Are you saying this system has already been described?" Lysa says.

Her disappointment must show. Dr. Erbach smiles. "Only by a half-literate scribe, six millennia ago. And his account has never been subject to peer review." He pats her shoulder, and she flinches at his touch. "Do not be afraid, my dear. You will get your publication."

On the second day, Merrick wakes to a soft but insistent chime. He rises gingerly from his bed, favoring one leg.

His physical injuries are minor: damage to the peripheral nervous system, some torn muscles, a lingering numbness in the fingers of one hand. His body is already healing.

But the passage has taken a psychic toll. In the twisted energies around the star, Merrick felt the presence of something he could not name. All conscious minds, human or otherwise, have their echo in the quantum substrate of reality. A psychically attuned pilot can easily pick out the pinpoint sparkles of consciousness from the background noise. But whatever he felt, it was not exactly a mind. It was more like—he shudders—an appetite.

He squeezes his eyes shut, trying to banish the thought. Since that fleeting contact, his dreams have been haunted. When he lies down, he is tormented by visions of places and things that should not exist. When he wakes, the nightmares vanish but the sense of dread lingers. Even the familiar surroundings of his quarters are strange, the mundane geometries seeming somehow wrong. Odd shapes crawl and flicker at the edges of his vision. Frightening voices murmur.

"Ship?" he says. His own voice sounds cracked and unreal.

"There is a priority message from Belis," the ship says.

He nods. "Connect her."

Her voice is anxious. "Captain? Forgive me for disturbing you. There is something you need to see."

The center of the room fills with a projected radar image. He sees a rugged landscape, all broken rock and jagged canyons, rendered in muted false color. As the image stabilizes, more details emerge. He begins to see signs of order: straight lines and perfect curves. He is looking down on something that might be a city.

"Where is this?" he asks.

"The moon," Belis says. "Right where Erbach said it would be."

"I see," Merrick says. He peers at the image and the details resolve, horribly familiar. He has seen these shapes in his dreams.

He dismisses the projection and sits down again. He rubs his eyes with trembling hands.

For the first time in centuries, Captain Merrick is afraid.

The city is not so much a city as a single huge, sprawling building, the only entrance a vast roofless hall lined with towering columns. From a vantage point near the entrance, Lysa watches as Merrick and Netts scout the interior.

They wear military-issue pressure suits, their armor covered by a photo-adaptive skin that generates constantly changing camouflage patterns. Lisa watches them leapfrog their way down the hall, darting from shadow to shadow, freezing into invisibility for a moment before moving on. Their equipment harnesses are hung with what Lisa suspects are powerful weapons, and it is clear that both have had military training. Despite herself, she finds something beautiful in the austere choreography of their war dance.

Dr. Erbach is unimpressed. He waits until the captain and Netts have reached the far end of the hall, then cuts in on the common channel. "The builders of this place, Captain, are long gone. There is nothing to fear here."

Merrick does not respond immediately. He and Netts continue their inspection. Finally, he turns, his chameleon suit fading to matte black. "You may approach, Doctor," he says.

Behind Merrick, the end wall is dominated by what is unmistakably a door, but one of monstrous size. Its massive hinges are twice the height of a man, and the whole surface is covered with fine inscriptions, the unfamiliar glyphs carved with millimetric precision into the metal. Erbach approaches, his gauntleted hands by his sides, staring up at it. "Magnificent," he says. "In other circumstances, I might devote my whole life to deciphering this one text." He gestures to a patch of symbols. "Here we have our Rosetta Stone: this is Old Kydelian, a description of the Acheterine Rite. By convention, the text should be repeated in other scripts across the whole surface."

Lysa cannot make sense of the writing, but she finds something unsettling about the shapes of the glyphs and the obsessiveness with which their creators covered every centimeter of the door and walls. Some of the patterns are repeated, and she guesses that the text was intended to be read or chanted aloud.

"We can bring up a deep radar set, see what's beyond the door," says Netts.

"No need," says Erbach. "I will open it."

"Do you need help with that?" Belis asks. "We have manipulator units–"

There is no mistaking the amusement in Erbach's voice. "You could pry at that door with your machines for a millennium, Scientist Belis, and it would not open for you. Even a nuclear bomb would barely scratch it."

"Say the word, Doctor," says Merrick, "and we can put that to the test."

"A kind offer, Captain, but I have a better way. I will need you to bring down the pods now."

Something about the environment blocks whisper band radio, so Merrick ends up having to walk halfway back to the lander to communicate with the orbiting starship. The landscape around him is ash grey, the rock outcrops fused and folded into bizarre shapes. On the horizon, the companion planet is a reddish half-circle filling most of the sky. It looks larger than it has any right to be; the moon orbits well inside the bigger world's Roche limit and should have been ground to dust by tidal forces millennia ago. The astrophysical impossibility is just one more factor adding to Merrick's growing sense of wrongness.

What disturbs Merrick most is the city itself. When they entered the long avenue that led to the vast entranceway, his dreams flooded back. It was as if he saw a double city. One, desolate and abandoned, its nightmare monuments shrouded in ancient dust; the other alive and inhabited by creatures of an unfamiliar species. He cannot quite make out their features; even in his dreams, he shrank from looking at them directly. They infest the periphery of his vision, writhing over the tortured landscape, scurrying and crawling like ants.

Ahead, the lander squats on the ash plain, a familiar man-made shape in this alien hell. He fights the urge to run the last kilometer, strap in, and blast off, leaving the others to fend for themselves.

With great effort, he turns his back on the lander and forces himself to face the city. He squats, digging his gauntleted hands in the dirt. He has never left anyone behind. He will not start now. If need be, he will find the courage to save even the unappealing Dr. Erbach.

He opens a connection to the starship. "Everything good?" he asks.

"Good enough," says Rothan. "You?"

"Erbach wants his pods now."

"Can do," Rothan says at last. "You want to guide them in, or shall I?"

The pods are one-shot devices, cramped cargo units balanced on a pentad of braking rockets. Merrick estimates that they have just enough fuel to land, but not to take off again.

"You guide them," he says. "Put them down as close to the city as you can."

"Copy that. What's in them anyway?"

"People," says Merrick.

The people shuffle into the hall in little groups. The yellow-white plastic of their cheap pressure suits is covered with stenciled glyphs. They move like sleepwalkers, still dazed by whatever drugs they took to let them ride out the voyage in suspended animation, crammed in their landing pods. Only a few seem alert, gazing around them at the looming walls and the vast doors with rapt expressions.

"No, no, no." Belis's voice is distressed. "Captain, we have a situation."

The suited figures stumble on, their eyes fixed on the doors and the distant figure of Dr. Erbach.

Lysa wonders what she will have to put in her report. The situation is bizarre, impossibly irregular.

"Erbach, what is this?" Belis demands. "Who the hell are these people?"

"No concern of yours," the historian says. There is an audible click as he cuts the channel. He begins to move back and forth, walking with an odd hopping motion, his long arms trailing. Puffs of dust rise where his feet scuff the stone floor.

"Lysa," says Belis. "Help me. We have to get them back to the ship before they run out of air. We can't get more than five or six at a time in the lander. It'll take us forever to move them all."

Lysa moves to intercept the closest group of sleepwalkers, but they pay no attention to her. Like automata, they continue toward the doors. When she puts her hand on one's arm, he brushes it off without looking and keeps walking.

"Captain, orders?" says Netts on the public channel. There is no response.

Another of the newcomers shuffles past Lysa. Through the plastic bubble of his helmet, she sees an eerie expression of joy.

Belis is on her knees, trying to help a yellow-suited figure who has collapsed to the floor. The man's companions walk on without looking back. Moving with blind purpose, they converge on Dr. Erbach.

Lysa starts to push her way through the stragglers, heading toward the historian. As observer, she has the authority to demand that he put an end to whatever this is. But the crowd closes in, and she is trapped, blocked by a living wall.

She is conscious of a low murmur, a vibration carried more through the stone of the floor than the tenuous atmosphere. The people around her begin to sway in time with the muted rhythm, jostling her this way and that.

Without warning, the man closest to her raises his hands to the neck of his suit. He fumbles for an instant with the collar, gloved fingers feeling for the release snaps. Then he lifts his helmet in both hands. Behind him, others do the same.

He stands for a few seconds, helmet raised above his head. A ghostly wisp of white vapor spills from his mouth, and ice crystals sparkle on his bluing lips. His eyes cloud over. He takes a step forward and falls.

It takes only moments. One instant, Lysa is surrounded by living people. The next, she stands in a sea of dead and dying. Above the bodies of his followers, Dr. Erbach raises his hands, ecstatic. He is back on the channel now, shouting words she does not understand.

She falls to her knees, trying to force a helmet back onto a woman's head. The helmet she grabs will not fit the collar ring of the woman's suit. She tries to jam it in place anyway, her vision fogged with tears.

With her attention fixed on the dying woman, she does not see the doors start to open. Only when she hears Belis scream does she look up in time to see the doors swing wide, the darkness between them filled by a huge shadow.

The screams rouse Merrick from his trance. He stands, dirt drifting from his fingers.

Above him, a dot of light blazes briefly before dimming until it is no brighter than a spent ember against the jet black of the sky. The radio brings him Rothan's last exclamation and a final burst of diagnostics, the dying shouts of man and ship cut off simultaneously.

He breaks into a run, his powered exoskeleton accelerating him toward what is left of his crew. Erbach is shouting something that makes no sense, his babble intercut with Netts' curses. Static pulses rhythmically, and through someone's open microphone, Merrick hears the distant stutter of gunfire.

He follows a trail of bodies. Not all of Erbach's cultists had the strength to make it all the way to the great doors. Many lie where they have fallen. A few still crawl toward the end of the hall on hands and knees, desperate to join with the god they have raised.

He passes Belis's body. Strange growths sprout from her opened chest. By the doors, Netts's headless suit burns with green fire. Erbach's followers lie everywhere like windblown leaves. It strikes Merrick that there is something not accidental about the way they have fallen, that their tortured shapes mimic the evil writing on the walls.

He knows what he will see. He has seen it in his dreams–the sac-like torso, the insectile limbs, and that hideous devil face with its vast black glittering eyes staring down at him with malevolent intelligence. Monstrous wings fill the frame of the doorway where it crouches, half-lost in the deeper darkness behind.

"He is risen!" Erbach's triumphant shout fills his ears. The historian is still alive, a tiny dancing figure dwarfed by the monstrosity he has woken. Almost without thinking, Merrick arms the smallest of his weapons, snaps a shot. He sees the round strike home and detonate, but Erbach's body continues to dance.

The thing emerges from between the doors, stepping almost daintily among the bodies. It straightens to its full height, shoulders level with the tops of the pillars, and looks down. It studies the pattern of the dead at its feet, its great eyes sparkling.

It stoops, stretches. With one clawed hand, it picks up Lysa Tallis from where she crouches among the fallen. Her arms and legs move convulsively for a moment before it deftly twists her head from her body and throws the pieces aside.

"You need my assent to end the life of this body and authorize restoration from backup," Montdarau says. Only a high-level quorum may vote to terminate and renew a living Immortal, and the vote must be unanimous.

The secretary shakes her head. "Yes to the first," she says, "but there will be no restoration."

Montdarau stares. If the captain is not restored, his timeline will end.

"The recorded simulacra have been corrupted," says Hasdrubal in its musical voice.

"Corrupted?"

"They exhibit the same madness as the survivor."

"That's impossible." Backup simulacra of Immortals are stored redundantly, with thousands of copies scattered across the galaxy. Even if one is lost or

damaged, there are always others available.

"Every known copy is unusable. A message arrived from Ultima Sideris just before you landed. Even the backup there is corrupt. The custodian destroyed it to avoid possible contamination."

Montdarau tries to imagine what kind of power could reach into a thousand data files scattered across tens of thousands of lightyears and alter every one. It goes beyond science.

"There is more," says the secretary.

"More?"

She nods to Kamach, who gestures again. The hull of the incubator splits apart, revealing what was hidden before.

The captain's naked body is bloated, and the pitted skin has an oily, greenish sheen. Both legs end in swollen stumps a little below the knee. The exposed muscles of the arms are jeweled with oily polyps whose tiny mouths are fringed with minuscule tentacles. The body has, Montdarau sees, both male and female genitalia.

Embedded in the doughy flesh of the torso are three shrunken shapes that might once have been human heads, their features distorted but still identifiable. Montdarau recognizes the artificer Netts, the supercargo Belis, and the observer Tallis. Their eyes are open, their faces twisted by terror and elation.

As the covers slide away, the eyes turn toward Montdarau. He sees all three mouths moving in synchrony. At first he can hear nothing, but Kamach waves his hand and a hidden speaker relays the sound, a high insidious whisper that repeats over and over.

"Iä! Iä! He is coming!" the three mouths chant in harmony. "He is coming."

---

§

**Angus McIntyre's** *short fiction has appeared in* Abyss & Apex *and* Black Candies, *in the anthologies* Humanity 2.0 *(Arc Manor/Phoenix Press),* Mission: Tomorrow *(Baen Books),* Principia Ponderosa *(Third Flatiron), and* Swords & Steam *(Flametree Publishing), and on the BoingBoing website. His novella* The Warrior Within *will be published by Tor.com in late 2017. He is a graduate of the 2013 Clarion Writer's Workshop. Born in London, he has also lived in Milan, Brussels, and Paris. He now lives in New York, where he works as a software developer. More information about his writing is available on his website at http://angus.pw/.*

## *Minor Heresies*

# ADA HOFFMANN

### ILLUSTRATED BY LUKE SPOONER

**M**IMORU STILL REMEMBERED VAUR STATION, THE SILVERY LAB CIRCLING an uninhabited water world. Spare, high-ceilinged, soft and clean, yet always crowded. Always the smell and sound of a few too many human bodies-and the Vaurians *were* human, too, no matter the alien filigree the Gods might have melded with their cells. No matter that the first generation had been grown in vats and that one Vaurian might not look the same from one day to the next. They were human, smelling like sweat and soap, coughing, squabbling, having love affairs, having nightmares. They were men, women, neither, both, and in between, and the glass and steel columns of Vaur Station enclosed them like a cathedral nave. Vaurians were an experiment. The experiment was ongoing.

Mimoru had not minded being an experiment. He had been happy to hear about the Gods, the enormous sentient computers who planned out all of human society and who had created him, too. How many people could say that they were part of a God's special project?

Unlike many, he had a mother—he was one of the first generation of Vaurian births outside the vat. The nanoscopic circuits in her cells were designed to divide as the cell did, and they bred true. It had been a major success, though he did not know that when he was small. He remembered one day, five years old, looking up at her as she fiddled with a food printer.

"Mother," he had said, "what will I be? When I'm big and old like you."

She turned and focused on him. There had always been a puzzled effort in his mother's face, a slowness. He would learn, much later, that it was the puzzlement of a woman who had never had a mother and was working out from books and guesswork how to be one.

"Anything," she said. "That's the point, isn't it?" Her cheekbones grew wider, and her hair rippled from ash-black to blonde for emphasis. "Anything at all."

"Darker than that," said Mr. Haieray behind Mimoru in the dirty mirror. "Zora are soothed by light-dark contrast. What do you think I hired a Vaurian for? Skin *dark*, like space. Palms, teeth, hair and eyes white. Like stars. And body *round*. Why can't you be female for this one? Women are rounder. We have to make this deal."

Mimoru struggled to comply, watching his—her, now—form balloon out under her loose robes. On Vaur, where everyone could do it, changing form had not been a private thing. Here, Mr. Haieray's gaze felt rude. Like peeking under Mimoru's clothes.

Everything felt dirty here, out on the edge of the galaxy. Everything was always dirty in comparison with Vaur. Everything built by humans: crooked, low-tech. But it had been Mimoru's choice to come out here.

She studied herself in the mirror. In school, Mimoru had studied humans of many nationalities—not only bodies, but mannerisms, tics of expression, styles of dress. She had seen very dark-skinned humans from Old Earth, a deeper tone than the medium brown of most other worlds. But what Mr. Haieray was asking went beyond that. It was a caricature.

She'd signed on as an accountant, not a shapeshifter-on-command. But any Vaurian was a shapeshifter-on-command when you got down to it. Refuse Mr. Haieray in one of these small things, and the short list of employers available to Mimoru would grow much shorter. She'd been foolish to think it would be different.

"More," said Mr. Haieray.

And Mimoru *was* getting paid for this. She ballooned out, further and further, until he was satisfied.

Vaurian school was taught by robots and angels: the latter were mortals who had agreed to do the Gods' bidding. Some angels were Vaurian but most weren't. Most of Mimoru's teachers had been stuck in only one body with thick titanium plates glinting at their temples where all of the circuitry connecting them to the Gods went. You always had to do what an angel said because they were the Gods' servants, and they did much more than teach: terraformed worlds, organized societies, hunted down heretics. That last one most of all.

When Mimoru was eight, the angels had started to frown at him for reasons he did not understand and to schedule more than the usual number of private talks with his mother.

Mimoru could guess what they were talking about. There was something wrong with him. The other Vaurians, by the age of eight, had established an elaborate social structure. Cliques formed and were infiltrated, betrayed, broken, and reformed; the smallest details of mannerism became shibboleths by which one group recognized another. Everyone wanted to fool everyone else, to be the best spy. That was what Vaurians were for, after all: to be a special kind of angel when they grew up. Angels who could look like anyone.

Mimoru, at eight, did not like cliques. He had been taught a great deal about emotions and social structures, so he understood what they were, but keeping up with them in practice was too much. Sometimes, even the noise of his classmates playing was too much. Mimoru liked quiet. He liked to read, count, and sort things. He liked to sit alone in the library.

"It is not unexpected," said the assessment robot to Mimoru's mother when it called her in. The assessment room's walls were crystalline on three sides. They sparkled down on Mimoru as he hunched in his chair, understanding only that he had failed. "We can't micromanage the genes of biologically born children. It was inevitable that defects would arise."

Mimoru wondered what it meant for a person to be a defect. Or what he would do, if he could not be an angel, after all.

Hex Station, where Mr. Haieray had taken Mimoru for this latest job, was nothing like Vaur. It was large, lumpy, misshapen. It had been built piecemeal over hundreds of years, a collaboration between several alien races—mostly Spiders and Aikita. The effect was a hodgepodge: carpets and hangings in the styles of dozens of worlds thrown over simple steel and ceramic bulkheads, a disorienting warren of tunnels, steps, and elevators, opening out every so often into a breathtakingly wide arboretum. Doors and corridors were wide, to accommodate alien bulk, but most rooms were no larger than they needed to be. The work space that the Stardust Interplanetary Trading Company had rented was particularly small—a meeting chamber, a shabby anteroom, a couple of offices, and a storage room that doubled as headquarters for the company medic. Hex Station had proper hospitals, of course, but most of their doctors had not studied human anatomy, so it paid to bring someone along.

They didn't need the space for long. Just long enough to make one deal. But Mr. Haieray wasn't very happy about that deal, judging from the way he paced back and forth. "The Zora should have been here by now."

"I warned you," said Bûr-Nïb, the secretary, examining her long green nails. "Zora get strange every few cycles."

Bûr-Nïb was one of Stardust Interplanetary Trading Company's non-humans. Fully ten percent of their number was alien, which was enormous by human standards—in the core of human space, one might live a full and adventurous life and never see one. Aliens gave Stardust an edge in making deals with other aliens, or so Mr. Haieray said. In practice, most aliens at Stardust worked shit jobs like Mimoru's.

Bûr-Nïb's body plan was more or less humanoid: upright bipedal and just over five feet tall with an outslung face only slightly off human proportions. She rarely spoke of Íntlànsûr, her homeworld; rumor had it that she'd been driven out. She was one of the few here Mimoru would consider a friend.

"They agreed to meet fifteen minutes ago."

"I'm aware of the time, sir."

"I proposed the time and they *agreed*."

Bûr-Nïb wrested her gaze from her nails and looked Mr. Haieray directly in the face—a sign of aggression, for Íntlànsûrans, though her accented voice remained level. "Yes, and a year ago, that agreement would mean something. Six months from now, it will mean something. But with Zor and its neighboring stars in this alignment—"

"Don't tell me how to do my job," Mr. Haieray snapped.

"They will be here," said Bûr-Nïb. "Eventually. They just won't concede that time works the way you say it does."

Mimoru shot Bûr-Nïb a sympathetic glance, which she politely—by Íntlànsûran standards—ignored. Calendars and years had always been of interest to Mimoru. The way that stars and planets moved, always changing but in a controllable, predictable way.

"What alignment would that be?" she asked as Mr. Haieray stalked away.

Bûr-Nïb waved a hand. "It has to do with Zor, Antares, Ovus-55B, and a few others. Um, but it's probably one of these things that's not polite for humans to discuss. It involves, um . . . religious rituals."

"Oh," said Mimoru.

She cared less than Bûr-Nïb seemed to think. Obviously, aliens were heathens; most of them had never even heard of a human God. Those who did, like Bûr-Nïb, seemed to prefer not to discuss it. Most humans did not like to discuss the Gods with aliens, either. If a human began to believe whatever an alien believed—to worship nature, or philosophy, or imaginary spiritual beings, instead of the Gods—they'd be a heretic. They'd need to be killed. But aliens were not subject to the Gods, so they had to make do with something else. Mimoru wasn't scandalized by that thought the way so many people were; it was just life for aliens.

"Humans," Bûr-Nïb muttered, watching Mr. Haieray pace.

Mimoru, despite his defects, was not prohibited from becoming an angel. Nor were any of his classmates forced. They didn't need to be: signing the contract and shipping out to have the neural circuitry installed, when one came of age, was simply the thing to do. A few rebels, singly or in small cliques, chose otherwise. They went down to the mortal world to spy and steal for the highest bidder. Or sometimes to act.

Mimoru did none of these things. In spite of his eighteen years on Vaur, he was a bad liar who frightened easily, hated attention, and did not think well on his feet. He was not good for much except reading and counting, and angels did not need any help with those things. So he found his way to a mortal college, worked his way through by waiting tables, and ended up with a degree in accounting.

The Gods let him go, and his mother sent him off kindly. The flaw in his plan, though, was that mortals did not like Vaurians. Nobody wanted a shifty, unpredictable shapechanger in charge of their finances—and Mimoru did not think he could hide his nature for long. Each of his food-service jobs had been short-lived, ending when a customer noticed some small unnatural shift in his skin, some inconsistency in his appearance from one part of the meal to the next, and raised a fuss. By the time he graduated, he was living off his meagre savings, eating little, growing desperate. His grades were good, but his job applications went wholly unanswered, except for the Stardust International Trading Company.

Leaving human space required some red tape. Aliens were heathens, and not just any human could be trusted to walk among them. But Mimoru, known if not exactly loved by the Gods, passed the security clearance easily.

"So, it's settled then," Mr. Haieray had said when Mimoru handed him the papers. "Now, here are the rules because I've seen what you people can do. You do as I say at all times. One fuck-up, so much as a stolen paper clip, and I drop you back down where you came from."

Mimoru had nodded automatically, like he would have for an angel back on Vaur. They were halfway to Hex Station before he realized that this might have been a mistake.

Roundness and contrast looked good on the Zora. They resembled horse-sized insects made of beads: heads, joints, and legs made of spherical segments, alternately pitch-black and chalk-white. They spoke a clicking, pure-toned language which was translated into Earth creole by an Íntlànsûran interpreter.

Mr. Haieray spent five minutes berating them for being late.

"Time moves as time wills," said the Zora.

"Time moves as we agreed, which was twenty minutes ago," said Mr. Haieray, and in spite of Bûr-Nïb's glares and the interpreter's increasingly uncomfortable fidgets, he kept on.

"We understand," said the Zora at last, "that your deal does not only involve agreements to the passage of time. There was an offer involving the transport of Zoran blacksteel to human space."

"Yes," said Mr. Haieray, reluctantly redirected. "There is great demand in certain sectors for building materials with superior shear strength. Our firm could—"

"How much demand?" said the Zora. "Specifically."

This was where Mimoru came in. Grateful for the chance to actually do something, she pulled out the pages of charts from her briefcase. "Among others, the human planet Salomta uses three hundred million tonnes of steel per year. But Salomta's seismic conditions . . ."

She was not the best at public speaking, but she liked data. Zoran steel, if a middleman brought it to human space, could improve the construction industry on many human worlds, and at a fat profit to everyone concerned.

Humans tended to glaze over when Mimoru went through data. But the Zora seemed to be paying attention. When Mr. Haieray raged, they had twitched and fluttered. But when Mimoru spoke, their gaze fixed on her unblinkingly. They asked sudden questions and sat silent and rapt for as long as the answers went on.

Unless she was misreading. She could analyze human body language by rote, but she'd never seen Zora before. For all she knew, a steady gaze meant aggression, the way it did for Bûr-Nïb. Maybe Mr. Haieray had miscalculated, and this body was an affront to them in ways that mere ranting could never be.

She went on talking anyway. She did rather like this data.

At last, one of the Zora raised one of its limbs in a curling gesture.

"We find this offer promising," they said, "and we have more questions. However, there is a pressing matter we must attend to. If you'll excuse us, please."

"No, that's not acceptable!" said Mr. Haieray. "We are in the middle of a business transaction. You can't—"

He spluttered, red-faced, as they filed out of the room anyway.

"You," he said, turning after the door shut. "You're the shapeshifter. Follow them."

Mimoru's already-too-round eyes widened.

Bûr-Nïb found words first. "Sir, that's espionage. I'm pretty sure it's also against your law. They could be doing something you're forbidden to see. You can't—"

"*Don't* tell me what to do!" Mr. Haieray roared. He pointed a finger directly at Mimoru, who shrank before him. "Isn't that what Vaurians are for? Spying?

For all we know, they could be talking to our competitors. If you want your job, follow them. Now."

The Stardust Interplanetary Trading Company staff were the only humans on Hex Station. If Mimoru wanted to be discreet, she needed a non-human form. She'd heard some Vaurians could do that, if the form was human-*ish*—two arms, two legs, two eyes, and so on, like Bûr-Nïb. But those were the most famously skilled Vaurians. Mimoru was just an accountant.

Well. If she wanted this job, she could try.

Mimoru let his cells relax back into his Vaurian base body: a slight, slender, translucent thing that sparkled inorganically when the light hit it right. He looked straight at Bûr-Nïb—mentally apologizing for his rudeness—and shifted his features, one at a time, to look like hers.

Scaly, olive-green skin. A tuft of something more like feathers than hair. Outslung jaw, long nails. Flat chest, but a swollen belly protecting what, for an actual Íntlànsûran, would have been an egg pouch. Limbs—Mimoru grunted with pain as his joints ground against each other, trying to replicate the effect he saw in Bûr-Nïb—bipedal, and with the right number of joints, but *off* just slightly, longer here and shorter there, a few degrees away from human-normal anywhere.

Everything hurt. He felt like he'd been hit by a streetcar, and he didn't even know if he'd done it right. He glanced in the mirror. He thought he looked like Bûr-Nïb, but who knew what details he was missing to an alien eye?

"Good enough," Mr. Haieray barked. "Go. We're losing time."

"Do you even want to *know* how many laws this violates?" Bûr-Nïb demanded.

They were still arguing when Mimoru slipped out the door.

He wasn't sure which way the Zora had gone. He was still dressed in a loose robe, which was not a common Íntlànsûran style, and he looked awkward and out of place. He knew only a few simple phrases of any Íntlànsûran language and nothing at all of any of Hex Station's hundreds of other tongues. He leaned on the wall, trying to slow his racing heart—anxiety, probably. Or had he screwed something up in the Íntlànsûran metabolism? Probably just anxiety. Occam's Razor.

As a child, Mimoru had introductory espionage lessons like every Vaurian. But he had failed them miserably. He was not going to manage anything suave here. He was not, for instance, going to infiltrate the kitchens and befriend someone who could steer him in the Zora's direction. He barely even had friends as himself.

He remembered the older kids talking strategy, though. The best strategy for tracking, reportedly, was smell. Mimoru had never done it, but . . .

He concentrated on his nose, on the finest level of detail, finer even than hairs and pores and freckles. What were scent receptors supposed to look like? He tried the quick and dirty route and mentally ordered every tiny structure on the inside of his nose to multiply itself tenfold.

A sharp, quick pain burned through his sinuses—followed by an assault of sensation. There were too many smells to take in: metal and ceramic, dust, a dozen fabrics, the reek of cleaning chemicals, the musk of thousands of bodies. He gagged. How had he never noticed what a burden it was to smell things?

He leaned on the door and waited for the nausea to subside. There were so many stinks in this corridor, most of which he could not identify; he could not remember what, if anything, Zora smelled like. He put a hand to his head. The Zora would be an organic smell. They were carbon-and-water-based, and since they had just been here, their smell would be the strongest organic one. Right?

There it was. A watery, reptilian, faintly familiar smell, starting at the door.

Mimoru followed the trail. Aliens passed him here and there on their way to meetings or meals or whatever else. He did not greet them and kept his eyes downcast, like a proper Íntlànsûran. Smells twisted, turned, and mingled, making him retch.

What was he doing? Bûr-Nïb had said this was illegal. If he brought trouble to Stardust, he'd be fired. If he saw forbidden things, religious things, like Bûr-Nïb had mentioned, he might be investigated. But the Gods knew Mimoru was no heretic. And if he refused, he was even more sure to be fired.

What was she afraid he'd see? Zora praying, chanting, preaching sermons at each other?

Here he was, three turns later, at a closed door in a narrow, vacant side-hall. It was button operated, like most doors on this station, steel, and windowless. It was undoubtedly locked. Mimoru smiled in relief. Definitely, when he pushed the button, it would be locked. He could tell Mr. Haieray, *I'm sorry, I followed them to their room but the door was locked. I did the best I could.* That would solve all of his problems.

He pushed the button.

The first thing that registered, when the door slid open, was the smell. Like blood and rotten flowers, like seafood going bad, like an immense inorganic sea that hated him, specifically.

The Zora were in the room, all six of them, crouched down in what might have been a supplicatory position. But the room—

The room was not a room. Somehow, even though they were comfortably ensconced in miles of halls and corridors, the room opened out and out on the whole galaxy. Mimoru could see all of it, staggering in its size, and behind it, infinite blackness.

Something was alive in that dark. Something bigger than a galaxy, watching with dark eyes bigger than stars. Looking back at the Zora, through the angles afforded by the way the stars aligned. Wondering—Mimoru was certain of this, the way one is certain in nightmares—wondering if it was worth the effort not to destroy them, this time.

Two Zora turned to look at him.

As their heads turned, something in space twisted, like elastic pushed to its limits, and lurched the other way. The room spun and slammed shut, and it was just a room again, a dinky corporate room, like Stardust's, with a set of woven blankets spread over the floor. Just a room. But he'd seen what it was before.

The Zora made a noise, but Mimoru didn't understand. They moved toward him.

Mimoru ran.

By the time the gnawing panic left Mimoru's head, he had already run back to the meeting room on autopilot. Shed his Íntlànsûran disguise almost by reflex, yowling in pain when his joints and scent receptors reverted sharply to their usual forms. Babbled out a half-coherent story to Mr. Haieray. Been sent to the company medic, a squat, usually bored-looking woman named Ushiwo, who had looked him up and down with sudden alarm, dosed him a puff of panic-suppressant gas, took out her diagnostic book, and began a thorough battery of psych tests.

Mimoru's heart rate slowed enough to register that the doctor was on the questions about hallucinations. This was the third time.

Had he hallucinated? Did that explain all this? It would be a relief if he'd hallucinated. It would mean that massive being wasn't still out there.

*I've ruined it,* he wanted to say. Maybe he said it out loud; he wasn't thinking clearly. *I distracted them, and now, they can't placate that thing, and maybe, we're all doomed.* Out here in alien space where the Gods could not save them.

"In the last six months," said Ushiwo for the third time, "have you experienced anything else you couldn't explain? Flashes of light, spots or shapes in front of your eyes, insects on your skin, voices other people couldn't hear?"

"No," said Mimoru. "Not at all before this."

Ushiwo's initial alarm had subsided into an intense concern. Every few seconds, she frowned, flipped several dozen pages in her diagnostic book, and scowled more deeply.

"Have you taken any recreational substances, legal or illegal, or any medicines other than the ones in your file?"

"No," said Mimoru, his mind still churning. "Listen, are you trying to diagnose if I'm crazy? It's okay if I'm crazy. I'll believe that."

Ushiwo sighed and, for the first time in at least ten minutes, put down her diagnostic book.

"No. I don't think you're crazy. You have no symptoms of anything, aside from the mild Asperger neurotype in your file and this . . . um . . . experience. You're not even mood disordered, for fuck's sake."

"But there could be something wrong with my brain," Mimoru babbled. "I was—shapeshifting unwisely. I tried to look like an Íntlànsûran. My joints were out of alignment. I was modifying my scent receptors totally untrained. Who knows what I might have done to my brain? Cranial pressure could have . . . anything could have . . ."

"Did you, at any point, modify the size and shape of your skull?" asked Ushiwo.

"No, but—"

"Did you make any attempt, however minor, to physically modify any part of your brain?"

"No, that would be crazy."

"How about the inner workings of the cardiorespiratory, endocrine, or any other systems that can chemically affect the brain's workings?"

"I modified my scent receptors."

Ushiwo looked at him impatiently. "In your brain or in your nose?"

"In my nose."

"Anything else?"

"N-no."

"Then that doesn't count." She picked up the book again. "Shapeshifting has nothing to do with this."

"You don't know that," he said, feeling desperate. "You've never worked with Vaurians. You don't have the specs for Vaurians."

"No, I don't," said Ushiwo. Her mouth had flattened. "What I do have is training in the Gods' official health standards for humans traveling outside human space. I've now run you, more than once, through the full testing that any such human with a report of strange and disturbing sensory experience requires. The results are clear. Your experience today wasn't a hallucination, Mimoru. It was heresy."

Mimoru stared at her and spluttered, his mouth suddenly so dry that he had to work through the muscle movements several times before he could speak.

"Alien heresy," he said. "Alien. The Zora were heretics, not me. I didn't do anything. I didn't know they were doing—whatever it was—when Mr. Haieray sent me to find them. I just—walked in on it and ran away. I didn't do any of what they were doing. I don't believe what they believe."

Ushiwo smiled a bitter little smile with no humor in it. "You believe," she said, "on some level, that there is a great horrible being beyond the galaxy who can be placated through the Zora's ceremony. A being more powerful than the Gods. No matter how you deny it, how you attempt to repress the memory, that belief will remain. And it is a belief that cannot be allowed to defile human space, Mimoru. No matter the cost."

"But—"

But that isn't fair, he couldn't say. When had he ever called the Gods unfair?

*But what will happen to me?* he wanted to say.

Ushiwo sighed and tucked the book away, heading for the door. "The Zora weren't on our list of dangerously heretical species. Their specific beliefs were unknown. Obviously, they'll have to be listed now, and this business transaction will be cancelled. The rest of us will go home cranky. You, well, you'll have to wait here. The angels will come for you soon."

"But—" said Mimoru.

The door swished open, and Ushiwo stood at the threshold a moment, regarding him.

"I didn't make the rules," she said, a pained twist at the corner of her mouth. "I'm sorry."

She turned away. The door swished shut, and the lock clicked.

Heretics were terrible people. That was one of the first things they'd learned in school. In between the ABCs and addition, they'd watched history vids about heretics. Watched heretics cut the terrified throats of children, to feed the blood to false gods. Watched heretics blow up buildings, scattering bodies across the ground, just because they didn't like the real Gods. When little Vaurians slept, they feared heretics, not bogeymen, under the bed.

Vaurians had been created to stop them. That was why the Gods had given them so many good things. Being an angel was hard, and the Gods didn't force anyone. But a Vaurian angel could infiltrate heretic groups in ways no other angel could. Tens of times more heretics would be caught, the teachers promised, if Vaurians did their duty. Hundreds. The world would be so much safer.

Only much later had Mimoru learned about minor heresies, degrees of heresy. You didn't have to blow up buildings to be a heretic; you just had to believe the wrong things.

He hadn't known that, yet, when his fifth-grade class was summoned to the amphitheatre, a wide, bright room in the centre of Vaur. They'd huddled together on the plush steps while a group of angels dragged a struggling heretic out in front of them.

He remembered the man: a slender middle-aged man with disheveled black hair. He was the first non-Vaurian, other than angels, that the class had ever seen face to face. Mimoru had memorized that man, in the automatic way that a Vaurian memorized any face. The lines on his face, wrinkles, pockmarks, scabs. He had clearly been tortured. He was trembling. His legs shook so hard, it was a wonder he could stand. The class, callous like most children, giggled. For weeks afterward, in the corridors of Vaur, Mimoru and his classmates had mimicked that man's struggling walk. Jeering to cover an unease they scarcely had words for.

The angels had read the man's crimes to the class and shot him very precisely in the head. There was an immense amount of blood. The class sat silently a moment, shaken, staring. Then a ragged cheer broke out.

What child wouldn't cheer when their bogeyman died?

Mimoru considered all this as he sat, shaking, in the excuse for an infirmary.

He did not think Ushiwo had ever seen an execution. Not close up, at least. Not in anything other than a vid.

He felt ashamed of his fear. The Gods were good, weren't they? You could kill a few people, if that was the law, and still be good. Maybe what he'd seen really did make him dangerous.

But he was afraid, and he wanted to run. Even if it meant running back to the Zora.

*You don't know what the angels will do to me,* he thought in Ushiwo's direction.

When the door swished open, it wasn't angels or Mr. Haieray. It was Bûr-Nïb. She looked furtively from side to side and gestured for him to follow.

"It's no use," said Mimoru listlessly. "The angels will find us. When they get here, they'll search the station top to bottom."

"Which is why I'm getting tickets on the next transport out. To Glupe, Blackball, Eta Carinae, wherever. You'll stick out, but human Gods can't do as much with extradition orders as you'd think. We'll figure something out."

"They'll find us first."

"Not if we hurry."

He shook his head. "I like you, Bûr-Nïb. I don't want to make you an accessory to . . . to . . ."

To whatever this was. Not heresy, he thought, in spite of the Gods' rules. More like—seeing what was inconvenient to see.

"Do you think I'm not?" said Bûr-Nïb. "Do you think I haven't played that scene in the meeting room over a million times? I could have stopped it. Argued harder. Said more."

"More about what?" Mimoru tilted his head, a new horror dawning. "Did . . . did you know what would happen?"

Bûr-Nïb turned, picked up Ushiwo's diagnosis book, and abruptly tore it in half, throwing both halves to the ground.

"*Humans!*" she shouted, so loudly that Mimoru expected someone to come running. "Humans! Of course I knew! Everyone knows that you're a homicidal theocratic cult! Everyone knows you're crazy. I even told you the Zora were leaving for religious practices. I just didn't—I couldn't get enough words out in time, not ones Mr. Haieray would listen to. And I thought even Zora in full-on cult mode would have the presence of mind to lock their door."

Mimoru's skin rippled as he tried to digest this. "Ushiwo said nobody knew."

"About Zora? I hope not. There are a million things nobody tells humans because we know that as soon as you find out, you'll cut off contact with a whole species and execute any humans who met them. Humans!" She bit her lip, fighting for control, and took another heaving breath. Mimoru had never seen her this angry, not in the face of Mr. Haieray's worst excesses. "And I wouldn't even be telling you this much. I wouldn't stick my neck out for a human, not even a friend. Except you're not really one of them, are you? You're not a human."

"Vaurians are human," Mimoru said. It was automatic, a phrase he'd repeated constantly since leaving Vaur.

"So?"

He wasn't a very good human. And he wasn't a very good Vaurian, either.

He didn't want to die. He might be damned anyway, even if he escaped. The Gods would find his heretic soul, in the end, and visit upon it all the punishments he'd avoided in life. But until then . . .

What would he be leaving behind? Mr. Haieray. A vast array of worlds that didn't want him. Vaur, which he had left behind anyway, for better or worse. A family that had already moved on.

He took a deep breath.

"Okay," he said and followed her out the door.

Mimoru watched Hex Station spiral away through his tiny porthole as the Aikita transport launched. The station had not been destroyed yet. Maybe the Zora had carried on after his interruption and fixed it. He hoped he would never find out.

He remembered flying away like this from Vaur Station, his first year of college. Not knowing what awaited him.

Vaurians were an experiment. The experiment was ongoing. Mimoru's part of it had failed—but, then, he'd known that long ago. Maybe it was time to stop judging by the standards of a species that didn't want him and start judging by his own.

Bûr-Nïb shifted beside him, her gaze fixed on her nails. The violet glow of the warp drive flared out around the porthole, and the station disappeared from view.

§

**Ada Hoffmann** *is a Canadian graduate student who is trying to teach computers to write poetry. She has published over 60 speculative short stories and poems, which were totally not written by computers. Her work has appeared in professional magazines such as* Strange Horizons, Asimov's, *and* Uncanny, *and in two year's-best anthologies. She is a winner of the Friends of the Merrill Collection Short Story Contest and a two-time Rhysling Award nominee.*

*Ada was diagnosed with Asperger syndrome at the age of 13 and is passionate about autistic self-advocacy. Her Autistic Book Party review series is devoted to in-depth discussions of autism representation in speculative fiction. She is a former semi-professional soprano, a tabletop gaming enthusiast, and an active LARPer. She lives in southern Ontario with a very polite black cat.*

*You can find Ada online at http://ada-hoffmann.com/ or on Twitter at @xasymptote.*

# A Superordinate Set of Principles

## BOGI TAKÁCS

### ILLUSTRATED BY LUKE SPOONER

*BUILD YOU INTO AN INCONQUERABLE FORTRESS, A CAVERNOUS WOMB, shells upon shells protecting the small and wounded. I, Armor Maintenance Specialist Ishtirh-Dunan, shall serve you until my last, fading breath.*

I hold onto the feeling as I bare my palm, place it upon the interior shipsurface—to maintain, to re-sanctify. Ever smaller tentacles curl upon themselves between the layers, the flowering fractal pattern straining against interior and exterior surfaces. Active defense: if the armor bursts, all the carefully prepared material will come gushing out at the attacker. Is it biomimesis if our engineering is biological at heart? My thoughts run along the coiled tendrils and stewing sacs of abrasive chemical soup—everything appears in order, everything checks out.

I bow my head in respect to the living ship, infinitely more complex than my fleeting sentience, and proceed to the next task, surveying the exterior. I am still sitting in the airlock, patiently growing vacuum-resistant skin over my limbs, when Head Surveyor Ebinhandar steps in and scratches at the newly grown chitinous patches over her cheeks.

"May you fill your niche," she greets me, friendly but vaguely distracted.

"For the benefit of all," I respond.

"I've been looking for you—figured if you weren't responding, you must be working with the ship," she says.

I nod wordlessly, still entangled in Presence. She goes on.

"The ship is sensing further sentients down planetside. Core-Steering wants you to grow the armor to level-three preparedness."

I look up at her, really seeing her for the first time. The gray of her skin is pale and mottled with agitation. "Is something wrong?" I ask. "This sector should only have some traveling humans."

She looks away. "They just have different allegiances is all."

She leaves me to my work after a few pleasantries and declines to exit the airlock with me. I don't understand why grow new skin, but I don't want to bother her with the question. I focus on my task, going through the motions of cycling through the airlock with the outward appearance of measured calm, but inside me, an ever-rising sense of dread jangles my nerves.

What could conceivably be wrong with humans? Humans are quite similar to us in basic body shape if little else beyond that. They have limbs like us, heads like us. We have a human on the ship. She fills her niche very nicely, and I like her. As I plant growth-promoting nodules into the outer shipsurface, my thoughts wander. I should talk to her. I need to pause every now and then, waiting for a new nodule to solidify in my glands—I did not expect a need for level-three armor.

Calm is increasingly difficult as I sense the consternation emanating from Core-Steering and moving its way along the ship in great, towering waves. I do not shield myself, but when I cough up the next nodule and it slips away from my trembling fingers, I begin to wonder if I should. But I do not want to isolate myself from the collective, even if it means sharing in the negative emotions as well as the positive. Instead, I pull myself closer to the outer surface and kiss it, the nodule hurtling up my throat as the next cough wracks me, striking the surface and embedding itself. I work it in with my tongue, make sure it's attached properly.

My taste receptors don't work in space, and I miss the familiar, coppery sensation.

I make my way across small, snaking tunnels, cavern-bubbles, storage sacs. On foot, slowly, with the justification that I am checking the interior systems—but they all check out well, and there's no reason to investigate them further.

Navigation Specialist Anihemer is lying in her berth, and I crouch by the small zero-entry pool.

"Does the Navigation Specialist have a minute to spare for me?" I bow my head and ask.

She sends a yes and slowly turns upward, detaching from the ship connections, closing her gills. She sits up and grins at me. "Always glad to see you," she says, and for a moment, I wonder why the informality. Then again, she's a human with human customs, even if she went through the transformation to be more like us. She doesn't spend much time going out and about in the ship. I have heard other humans are outgoing, so maybe, it's just her—or maybe, it's us. Is she uncomfortable?

"How do you feel?" I ask, trying to match her level of formality. I hope the casualness doesn't come across as forced. "Are you all right on the ship?"

She tilts her head sideways and laughs.

"Where did this come from, Navigation Specialist?"

I offer her my thought processes; that's the easiest. She turns serious. "I'm quite all right, thank you. I enjoy being here. I very much like navigation, and I have three friends."

I'm ostensibly not one of her friends? Sometimes, it's hard to understand what she's implying, but she doesn't offer me her thought processes. Still, she seems earnest. I bow my head. "I am glad you enjoy having joined. But you seem gloomy."

"I'm worried about these people planetside, like you." She pauses. "Ishtirh-Dunan, *you* are one of my friends! What troubles you troubles me, too." She offers me her thought processes, and I accept.

We sit for a while, mulling over the situation. The Flowering has been in communication with the Interstellar Alliance, the largest organization of humans—but the humans claimed this system was uninhabited and devoid of organic life. Our ships do not want to take other people's land, but it is budding season, and it would be preferable to be inside a planet's gravity well. Yet this one seems taken by humans entirely unknown. The Alliance professes ignorance, and they claim to have no resources to investigate.

We are on our own.

We are strong. We are powerful. But we don't want to cause harm. We only want to grow in peace.

Anihemer sighs, switches back to speech. "The ship asked me to go planetside with the investigation team. Do you think you can also reinforce my armor? I'm concerned."

"I certainly can if you allow me," I say with a measure of relief.

She gets out of the water. "The Assistant Navigator is also on duty and will be for most of the rest of the day. You have time to work on me."

There is a medical pod close by for occurrences such as this one. We walk, and I support her on her feet—she's still unsteady after the disconnection. She detaches her suit from her skin and allows it to be reabsorbed by a bulkhead. She lies down on a tray, and it molds around her body.

I cup my palms and disgorge the nodules that had generated in my body while I was making my way along half the length of the ship. This amount should be enough.

She lets me access her physiosystems, and I adjust the thalamic switchover. "You will not feel pain, just pressure," I say. I gently rub the nodules into her skin with my long fingers, push them deeper to nestle among bundles of muscle. I work on people less often than I do on the ship, but the smaller scale can also be comforting.

She's entirely relaxed but not asleep. I can feel her thinking, but I don't know the content of her thoughts.

"Do you think you can also do something about my light-channels?" she asks.

My fingers halt in the folds of flesh. Blood wells up, is absorbed by my skin, and recirculated to her body. I don't quite understand the question. "What would you have in mind?"

She is uneasy. "I'm afraid I might need to, um, rapidly externalize power . . . ?" Her voice trails off.

"I'm sure they will send people to do that should the need arise," I say.

She insists. "What if I get separated?"

I know that fear. I have held it close in my own heart. I focus on my breathing to calm myself. Separation is hard for our people.

"I can set up a layer for that, but in order for it not to interfere with prediction for navigation, it needs to be rather . . . restrained," I say.

"If I can just have enough power to hold people off for a bit, that should do," she agrees. She is a good pathfinder, and I know she wouldn't want her ability to be compromised.

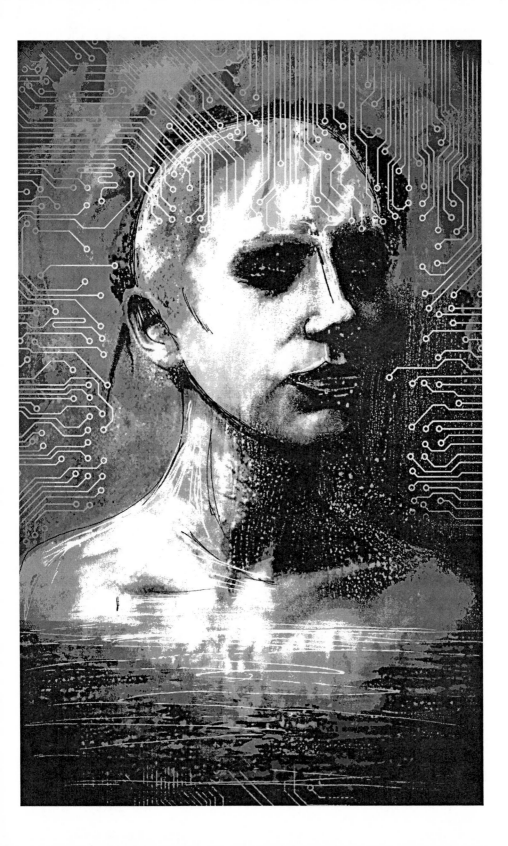

Yet I cannot relax. She might need a good defense. A good, active defense. I know all too well that the best defense is sometimes offense.

I reach out to the ship with my mind, petition to be allowed planetside. There is acknowledgement but no immediate adjudication. I'll have to wait.

I finish installing the nodules and close up her back, smoothing out the skin but not hardening it, yet. I direct her to the med-pool, and she sinks in, kneels on the bottom to look at me. Our faces are level—this pool is elevated. The fluid laps at her shoulders, and she looks interested, not frightened. She kept many of her human features, but she doesn't look alien to me. Will those people—

I peel off thick strips from the bulkheads, hold them in two bundles. "This, this will hurt," I say. "Not the installation as much as the synchronization. No matter how I adjust cortical inputs, it's not possible to hide from the everglowing light."

"That's all right," she says and—seeing that I need encouragement?—adds, "I went through a quite drastic transformation when I joined, remember?"

I cough nervously, swallow back a nodule that arose unbidden. "This is definitely not that radical."

We begin. I share my thought processes with her just to explain the procedure, but I tell her not to reciprocate—it might be too distracting for me. I step up to the pool and hold her as she floats facedown, gills open. The strips form tubes, thinning out toward the front, that worm under her skin with their tips. Two to run parallel with the spine and some smaller auxiliaries. This goes easily. She turns, stands—shaking slightly, not from any pain but from the body reacting to the change. The pain will come later. I support her with an arm around her, leaning into the pool. The other strips are easier swallowed. I access her physiosystems, adjust her gag reflex. So much material is still hard to swallow. I hold her as she struggles with it, but the strips have enough autonomy to burrow forward. I can see the movement inside her abdomen, her chest cavity. She is shuddering strongly, but I hold her firm.

"This is good. This is good," I repeat, "easy, easy now."

"I'm all right," she says, voice hoarse.

"Synchronization is easier in your usual berth," I say, and she lets me carry her back to Navigation in my arms, ease her into that pool.

"Thank you," she looks up to me and whispers, and I wish she wouldn't thank me yet.

It is painful to readjust. I allow her to cope any way she can. The ship doesn't want to cause her pain—not unless she wants that, and she doesn't. But it is difficult to have these larger modifications.

She screams, she cries, she hugs herself into a ball entirely underwater. I wish I could say she doesn't need this modification, and maybe she doesn't, but there is a sizable chance she might.

She left her people, and they might not like that.

We're going downside, planetside in a small landing pod, just three of us—Anihemer, me, and Defense Operative Mezvamar. The defense operative is rather unhappy with Anihemer's latest transformation.

"I can protect us all," Mezvamar says. "The Navigation Specialist might have better capability for self-defense, now, but without practice, there is no skill. Allow me to demonstrate."

A globe of brilliant multifaceted light turns around inside the landing pod, inside our minds, inside the universe—it is filled to bursting with power, and I would strain away from it if it weren't everywhere. After completing one rotation, it vanishes as fast as it appeared.

Mezvamar exhales. "This kind of control. This kind of skill."

I look uneasily at Anihemer. Nothing we did was forbidden, but maybe it wasn't necessary either. We didn't want to inconvenience the defense operative, and especially not anger her, but she looks angry now.

"Our apologies to you," Anihemer says. "I asked the Armor Specialist to do it."

I want to protest, but the defense operative interrupts me. "If the need arises for you to employ your self-defense, we are better off aborting the mission. I can jump all three of us back shipside."

She is right—though I suspect part of her wants to show off, to let us know she can jump while carrying two people besides herself.

"Let's hope it won't come to that," Anihemer says.

But even before our pod touches down, burst fire hits its outer light-barrier.

We step outside with trepidation. The shots haven't even managed to touch the armor, let alone weaken it; they were absorbed by the light-barrier strengthened by the defense operative. But the intent has been made clear.

Anihemer cringes when she sees the men—all men, in antiquated envirosuits painted with a crude pattern. I understand this because she opened her thought processes to me. The resemblance truly goes no further than the bare configuration of limbs. Beyond the men rises a set of . . . objects, and my mind struggles to interpret the sight until it is joined by Anihemer's memories. These alien structures with their threateningly sharp edges are buildings.

"Greetings," she says in Alliance Common.

About five different heavy weapons are aimed at us, and while I don't expect any of those to do much damage, I don't envy the defense operative who will try to deflect their projectiles before they can reach our armor.

The one closest to us—their leader?—says something gruffly in response, and I only understand his words due to Anihemer's understanding. He's asking her if she speaks his language. This is only implied, but I get it loud and clear: he is not going to stoop so low as to speak Alliance Common.

Mezvamar nudges me with her mind, and we also connect—I quickly appraise her that we stepped into some kind of aggravating intra-human conflict. We arrange our minds into a three-node cluster as Anihemer speaks.

"Why are you shooting at us?"

He steps back in startlement.

"The monsters speak _____?"

I can't parse any specific words, let alone proper nouns, just the intent.

"We are not monsters," Anihemer says. "I am from _____, just like you. I grew up eating pieces-of-cereal-in-a-whitish-fluid for breakfast."

He steps forward again. Blood suffuses the vessels in his face, and his skin changes color. "I didn't grow up eating pieces-of-cereal-in-a-whitish-fluid for breakfast with no monster."

"Life is change," Anihemer says. This is not going well.

Incongruously, Mezvamar thinks she'd like to try that dish.

"Are you Isolationists?" Anihemer asks. This concept is common enough in the universe that I understand the name with ease.

"Why should I tell a monster? We are no Isolationists. We came all this way with the power of science and progress," he boasts.

Shooting at us must qualify as progress in their minds.

We still try to assimilate this when some of the other men leer from the back. I still do not understand the words, but I try to grasp the concepts better—they are the names of . . . tentacle monsters? Us? They see us as—? My brain struggles to assimilate the wildly different perspective conveyed to us through Anihemer speaking their language. Everything that is beautiful in us, everything that is elaborate and complex and organic and soft and kind—it is to be eradicated, disinfected, scrubbed clean.

Anihemer asks them, "What does progress mean if—"

She never gets to finish the sentence, for this is when the ground splits open and the giant shape arises, soil clumps streaming down its sides.

The men cheer. "Progress! All hail the Manifestation! The Manifestation of Progress!"

It is unbearable. Terrifying. The shape is entirely inorganic; it is devoid of everything that is good in the universe. It makes no sense to the mind, and the mind must turn away in fear of the unassimilable, the cruel and lifeless. It is a shape demarcated in its entirety with straight lines.

The humans do not turn their gaze away. They beam at the bright yellow ▲, their faces aglow.

"The summoning succeeded!" they murmur. "Our intent, reaching out to the most fundamental of the Ancient Ones! Taking form, taking shape!"

Then the turquoise ■ ascends.

"Technology! The Manifestation of Technology!" The men weep in utter joy and hug each other, pat each other in the back.

Our feet are rooted to the shuddering soil birthing unimaginable monstrosities.

Anihemer is the only one who can withstand the mind-shattering sight. In her thoughts, I can feel an unfamiliar geometry reassert itself—a geometry not built on recursion and self-similarity or on curves and time-courses, but one built on straight lines. Disjunct points. Forming ▲ and ■ and . . . my mind struggles with alien concepts. How have these people ever built a spaceship?

The ■ descends again, followed by the ▲, thumping at the ground as we struggle to maintain our balance. An infernal, grotesque jumping spectacle. I try to avert my eyes, but I am forced to watch as they begin to shoot spikes of light, a malevolent twisting of the Everglowing. One of the nearby buildings—I now understand, made up of ■s for some obscene reason?—shatters from the impact. Bodies in charred envirosuits soar through the air. I watch this because even this is easier than facing the ▲. Progress and Technology begin to decimate their surroundings.

The men chant louder.

The two gigantic shapes cease their jumping and turn toward each other while they keep on shooting—seemingly at random in every possible direction. The gap between them begins to glow. I can feel space itself attenuate. The thinning-out mercilessly draws my attention even as I do not know what it is that I see. Emerald-colored glimmers appear in the gap and fade away. I sense a bottomless, all-permeating hunger emanating from the shapes.

I know that I see rigidity and destruction, the antitheses of life and natural growth, but to my utter horror, I also begin to understand that these shapes have a certain appeal—in their vast simplicity, in their uniformity, in their mind-numbing lack of variation.

They appeal to Anihemer, who grew up with pieces-of-cereal-in-a-whitish-fluid and learned about ▲ and ■ but turned away from them.

They appeal to me—a friend. A sharer of thought processes.

They appeal to—

Mezvamar is the first to unfreeze, by necessity: she dodges an incoming bolt, moving with raw muscular grace, and shouts at the ■ towering above her. "WHAT HAVE I EVER *DONE* TO YOU?!"

The humans shudder, awakening from their trance, and train their weapons on us in unison. They take aim, ready to fire—

Anihemer pulls at the newly built structures within herself, flings light out toward the humans. Rapid exteriorization of power.

It does little: the forceful push rapidly devolves into a faint breeze. But it clears her mind. It confuses the humans. It gives us a moment of opportunity.

Mezvamar roars and jumps forward. A wave of burning hot power pushes the humans away, and they scatter in the air like pollen whirling inside a ship-cavern.

They do not get up. But the ▲ begins to move toward us. It has no color gradations or anything that would give it a semblance of reality beyond its yellowness. It's homogenous and entirely unfathomable. It is the manifestation of progress built on annihilation. Progress defined by pushing ▲-shaped spacefaring vessels into the great beyond, ▲s that have no Presence or mind and that move by burning away more inorganic matter instead of merging with the everglowing light.

The ▲ makes a monstrous grinding noise as it approaches, sliding on the ground. This is even harder to bear than the jumping. It grates at every single one of my senses.

"DOES IT HAVE A WEAK POINT," Mezvamar screams.

Anihemer thinks frantically, and we think with her.

Where do the two geometries intersect?

Can we subsume these shapes in ours?

Can we incorporate—

Recursion. Self-similarity.

Active defense. Defense I have set up—and set up well.

"If this backfires and we end up with a gazillion angry ▲, we are *so* screwed," Anihemer yells. "Let alone ■!"

We perform what our mind-cluster has decided.

Mezvamar gives power to Anihemer, enough power to reach the ship, reach out to the assistant navigator.

Mezvamar gives power to me, and I check the armor one more time—all ready to go.

The ship lurches sharply planetside, rushes, singing with the joy of motion strengthening the Presence.

The ship rams the ▲, outer armor layer bursting, coils of tentacles springing out.

Our cluster strains as we try to constrain the coils into an entirely unfamiliar shape.

A ▲ and another ▲ and another ▲ and another ▲. They latch together in a fractal pattern, subsuming each ▲ into a growth of many ▲s. Turning toward the ■. Moving. Subsuming. Self-similar and self-replicating. An integrated function system, building itself into curls and whorls, plantlike—or like smoke rising on the wind.

We were worried the ship's armor layers would not prove to have sufficient material. But the material of these alien shapes molds readily to the new pattern. The new kind of progress. A superordinate set of principles.

Nature itself.

"Heck yeah, _____," Anihemer mutters. "I studied math for this moment." She turns to us, grinning with tears. She suspends mind-contact for a moment and enunciates slowly and clearly, so we can pay attention to the phonology. A name. "Heck yeah, Sierpiński."

And I see that _____, planet of these humans, has always held seeds of a different progress.

We reestablish contact and hold hands as above us curlicues glow against the emptiness of space.

Anihemer cries, and we can sense that she is finally free.

We wait companionably as the black-clad humans of the Alliance jump in, mostly in groups of three. Mezvamar grins, eager to comment. "See, that's how it's done," she says. "Good and proper."

A human walks up to us, armor almost covering their entire body—sturdy and modern but not of their own self. Through their visor, we can see their face: it's round, brown-skinned, firm, but friendly.

"Well met," they say in Alliance Common. "I'm _____ ___ _____ of the Free State of _____, delegated to Alliance Treaty Enforcement."

Anihemer understands from the choice of grammar that this person is a woman. But I'm frustrated I missed her name. I ask Anihemer to repeat it for me, sound by sound: Anayāun ta-n Oronesun.

Anihemer turns away from me and steps forward. "This is not Alliance space."

The officer readily agrees. "No, and we make no claim to it. But you have alerted us to a threat endangering Alliance space."

"Indeed?" All three of us are skeptical, but only Anihemer can speak to the Alliance representative with ease.

"We detected jump point generation from here to Alliance Central, the Emerald Spires." I have heard of that place before, so this is easy to understand. The Emerald Spires are the locus of Alliance decision making. It makes an eerie sense to me: if one desperately wants to eat, why not start with the richest, most nourishing portion? So many people, so much wealth.

I hiss as I understand the immensity of what we have accomplished. What we stopped.

My gaze lingers on the symbols on the Alliance officer's helmet, patterns I had taken to be imitating thorns—and my blood runs space-cold as I realize they are made up from interlocking ■. Something inside me has irrevocably changed.

The officer grins—for a moment, so similar to Anihemer—and she gestures at the whorls above. "What do you propose to do with all that material?"

"We can incorporate it into our growth," Anihemer says. "What do you propose to do with all these people?"

"They are _____-humans and _____ wants to withdraw from the Alliance. It's a politically delicate situation." The officer grimaces. "We will take them, but we'll see what happens."

Anihemer is not even surprised. She says, "_____ wants to withdraw after spending so much effort on joining? I've been away far too long."

She glances up, follows the twists and turns overhead with her gaze. "Or rather, I haven't been away enough."

Mezvamar and I step next to her, flanking her. Supporting her with our presence. Her mind leans into the closeness of our minds, and her muscles relax ever so slightly with the relief of it all.

"Well then," she says. "Let us grow."

§

**Bogi Takács** *is a Hungarian Jewish agender trans person currently living in the US as a resident alien. E writes and edits short fiction, poetry, and nonfiction. Eir work has been published in venues like* Clarkesworld, Lightspeed, Strange Horizons, *and* Uncanny, *among others. You can find em at http://www.prezzey.net or as @bogiperson on Twitter and Instagram. E also writes about books at http://www. bogireadstheworld.com and has a webserial in the same continuity as this story at http://www.iwunen.net.*

# The Sixth Vital Sign

## WENDI DUNLAP

### ILLUSTRATED BY MICHAEL BUKOWSKI

T O PROCREATE IS THE ZEITGEIST OF EVERY PRIMITIVE CULTURE, THRALL TO every base whim and instinct. It is a narcissistic impulse on par with psychiatric disorder. With social evolution comes the realization that the point is not reproduction but prolongation of life with as much vitality as possible.

Weh understands this. The desire to prolong life has governed his species for millennia, a race distinguished by their morality and strict principle to do no harm. They've sought to maintain this harmony throughout the universe. But times have changed.

In some circumstances, even the evolved find themselves in the accidental predicament of creating life. Of course, with these situations comes a wave of ego, titillating that primordial vanity to replicate oneself, to create a mirror image that is different in one, single aspect: its perfection. But there is also deep regret when one must become a god. Reproduction, after all, tends to fall short of expectation, and nurturing is not necessarily innate. The creator is often disappointed by the offspring's inadequacies and its own failings as progenitor. And as always, pain follows disappointment.

*Or does it cause it?*

These are the musings that plague Weh, a scientist on a space laboratory orbiting Vhrool in the twenty-third nebula. Each rotation marks the end of a year, and the deadline for another progress report to a council whose impatience is surpassed by their physical and mental deterioration. The new year is mere hours away and Weh is no closer to a solution than he was a year ago. Instead, he fears that what he does have is something else entirely.

*If creation leads to disappointment and disappointment leads to pain, can we then conclude that creation is pain? And is destruction than pleasure? Death a release?*

Weh rubs his temples with brown tentacles, suctions gently massaging in a futile attempt to stay the oncoming migraine. These are not rational thoughts. The Shesmu sickness has begun to spread. In some, it starts with the mind, others the body, eventually coursing through both. His team wasn't tasked with a cure, only to create a sustainable system of organ and nerve regeneration to halt its progression. But time has finally run out.

He sinks into the murky waters of the rehabilitation chamber, opening his wide maw to inhale the nutrient-infused liquid. After several minutes, he rises with a dramatic exhale that shakes the metal, foliage-covered walls of the ship. He lifts his massive bulk across the sleek, moss-covered artificial stone and onto the cool soil covering the floor. He can still feel the cold, unnatural metal underneath. The humidity is so high that a thin mist hovers in the air, but it is not enough. Already, his pores are drying out, his eyes red orbits, his tentacles shriveling and sore. His wings shrink into the base of his back to escape the aridity. He visits the rejuvenation chamber more and more these days. Another sign that despite the distance, the disease has found him here in space. Even the brains of Zaoth could not thwart its advancement.

*I don't want to die here.*

He misses the deep oceans and shallow lagoons of home, moisture everywhere, plant-life green and lush and lifting to the moons, the dirt warm and fertile. His pulse would synchronize to the squawks and splashes of the other sea creatures, his breathing steadied to the motion of the water.

There is no nature in space, only artifice with chemically enhanced waters, replicates of totems and statues, a depressing mimicry of home. Here, the black void is pierced occasionally by blinding white suns, and the only creatures are the abominations caged within the bowels of the laboratory.

"We cannot afford failure," the council admonished.

So for the last year, he's hidden the truth.

*The macabre shrouded in cold emptiness, the cries of the suffering swallowed by the blackness of space.*

He shakes his head to clear the negative thoughts. But the guilt is inescapable. Anything with a conscience would feel the same, but Weh is certain Shai no longer has one.

"Bountiful risings!" she greets him as he walks stiffly into the laboratory, her tentacles wave merrily around her face. She is the picture of physical strength: skin moist and glistening, tentacles taut, eyes bright and focused. But her physical strength is merely a façade. Shesmu has found her, too, and she is almost completely insane.

As the specimens mature, Shai's arousal is undeniable; she invents fresh tortures to inflict on these creatures in the name of science. Yesterday, she beat the male until his flesh broke and fluid ran from its eyes. She insisted she needed to test how quickly it could heal. "Sedation is out of the question," she argued. "It may impact the speed of regeneration." And of course, she insisted on inflicting the beating herself, questioning the efficacy of the neuralgia machines.

He hates her.

"Council update at 1200," she reminds him unnecessarily. "Have you thought about what you're going to say?"

"The truth," he answers.

Shai snorts in derision.

And he hates himself for lying with her last night. But her insanity fuels an enthusiasm that brings his weakening body to new heights of pleasure. They twisted and intertwined for hours before he was lulled into deep subconscious by the unrelenting pulsing of her body against his own. Her soft quivers of pleasure set tone to visions of colorful explosions erupting from the tips of tentacles and the soft sweetness of her core. But when he awoke, she was gone. Done with him, he suspected she had gone to copulate with the specimens again. He caught her at it once, already.

"I'm testing the sensitivity of their nerve responses," she dismissed his horror and continued with psychotic brazenness.

Or perhaps she had them fight again. "To test durability," she'd explained. She'd prod them with electrical shocks until they clawed and kicked at one another to avoid the pain they knew would come if they stopped. Titillated by the display, she'd watch while discreetly reaching tentacles deep into her folds to stimulate herself.

Worse still, the creatures are now sentient.

This was not the plan. The specimens were intended merely for organ and nerve growth to remedy the symptoms of the disease. But in attempting to manufacture neurological regeneration, awareness emerged. Perhaps, he shouldn't care. Wiser creatures, creatures deserving of consciousness, would have sought comfort in one another. At the very least, they should have a rudimentary sense of self-preservation to conspire against a common foe. But Shai has conditioned them to be at war. Now, no longer in need of external provocation, the specimens attack one another at random and compete for the most basic of resources: food, water, even Shai's affections.

*Monsters beget monsters.*

It is only a matter of time before he is just as sick, his desires decidedly less amorous than his colleague's. Millions of years of a strict vegetarian diet, and now, the disease has awakened a primordial desire for flesh. He salivates at the sight of them. Their warm, tender flesh growing riper with each passing moon. Fortunately, there is only Shai to judge, but he knows she would like to watch. Consuming flesh—never mind a product of one's own body—is abomination, and these days, there is nothing Shai likes more. He wants to be better than her, but he knows he is not. He will consume these creatures before long.

"Well," Weh sighs, "let's prepare the report while we still can."

"Transmission start," Shai commands and Weh begins.

"This is Vhrool Space Laboratory 696, progression status 7 prepared for the R'lyeh Scientific Council. The subjects of this report are specimens α-12 and ε-13, harvested from Ω-strain materials 360 moons ago to redress the deterioration caused by the Shesmu virus. Live matter extracted from both scientists was used to create scaffolding with greater stability than previous specimens.

"Specimens grew rapidly with essential systems to sustain life, including respiratory, circulatory, and digestive. Scaffolding became an endoskeletal structure, the base for a functional bipedal form. Attempts at tentacle replication failed. Twenty digits have formed from arm and leg extremities, growing sufficiently to support movement but lacking the size and dexterity to adequately replace our failing limbs as specimens are relatively diminutive in size. This is no doubt due to the calcification of scaffolding, which at this point cannot be removed without killing the specimens."

"This was attempted with specimens ξ-5 and ς-6," Shai interjects. "Each specimen sedated and a complete laminectomy performed."

*A task she took great pleasure in performing,* Weh wants to add but instead says, "Actually, the specimens were completely deboned."

"Only to collapse when revived and expire several minutes later," Shai continues unabashed.

"And it appears the specimens felt great pain during this process, despite sedation," Weh adds.

Shai dismisses the notion, "There is no conclusive evidence that any of our specimens have awareness beyond simple nerve reaction to stimuli," she responds coolly.

But Weh can remember the screams.

"The scaffolding is essential for the viability of the organisms," Shai continues with scientific detachment. "Muscle development is insufficient as sole support for the specimens. Organs and nerve tissue were harvested and refrigerated. Organs ceased to function just six hours later, supporting the previously established critical window for successful transplant."

Weh sighs. He never wanted to create life. Becoming a god was not an ambition. He studied philosophy before surrendering his mind to the science program. He seeks comfort in the false truth that he may be saving his species, but each day, he is confronted with his futility.

Still, they continue the charade.

"Back to specimens α-12 and ε-13, reproductive systems have formed as binary genders," Weh explains, "specimen α-12 becoming biologically male and specimen ε-13 female. Once the reproductive cells began to regenerate on a chromosomal level, they seem to have an intention all their own."

"Of course, this means that if sexual organs are needed for transplant, we must replicate twice as many specimens for harvesting," Shai adds. "Time and cost implications are well known. We have started to grow a third, dual-gender specimen to course correct. Until then, we are observing the distinctions in the genders as this may impact organ function. Muscle development on the male surpasses that of the female, resulting in increased physical strength. But interestingly, the female has greater tolerance to both stress and pain. We recommend further neurological study to determine exactly why, but this should be noted when harvesting and replicating from male specimen α-12."

Shai gestures for Weh to proceed.

"Less progress has been made with nerve repair to thwart the psychosis of the virus," Weh begins.

"Transmission, pause," Shai commands, turning to her partner. "Are you sure you want to do this?"

Weh hesitates, but Shesmu has yet to completely devour his mind. After a moment, he nods. Shai exhales and commands, "Transmission, resume."

"Neurotrophins like nerve growth factor, or NGF, are produced naturally by the specimens at lower than sufficient levels," Weh begins. "In addition, we have created an organic-based neuroprosthetic prototype and implanted into ε-13, the female. Full cognitive impact is unknown at this time. It is possible that NGF levels in the specimens have been compromised due to the stress of the testing environment and chronic pain." He glances at Shai, who simply looks away. "But we are no longer in a position to alleviate either of these conditions," Weh finally admits. "NGF has been extracted from specimens and injected into both myself and my colleague with little effect. Despite treatment, our mental deterioration progresses steadily, manifesting in sado-sexual impulses . . ."

"And a growing appetite for flesh," Shai interjects with a smirk.

*So, she knows.*

Weh flinches but continues, "We regret to report that there will be no further progress within this laboratory by either myself or my colleague. We are in the process of full mental deterioration and reversion to primitive states. We request the removal of specimens immediately for the continued viability of the work. Transmission end."

The report is sent instantaneously along with samples of the specimens' DNA. Weh and Shai wait in uncomfortable silence for a response.

Shai is the first to break the tension, "You did not tell them the whole truth."

"I said enough," Weh responds.

"Still, it's over for us."

"This report is the one moral thing we've done since boarding this laboratory."

"You've condemned us," Shai accuses.

"I've saved us," Weh answers. "Surely, you have enough sanity left to see that. You've become a monster, Shai!"

Enraged, Shai puffs up into an aggressive stance, her tentacles waving, wings unfurling to beat against the laboratory walls, "Do you think I'm proud of my behavior," she shouts. "Do you think I'm unaware of what I've become? Perverse, barbaric. I cannot help myself, you self-righteous dhole! And you are no better. I see you licking the tissue samples, nibbling at the specimens when you think my back is turned. Slicing pieces from where you don't think I'll look. I see your sickness too, partner!"

Weh simple nods. "Then we agree. This should end."

Seconds later, the communication monitor flickers.

"Don't interfere," he warns Shai as a figure appears on the screen. It is a bulbous, misshapen mass of tentacles, obviously implants from various specimens grown in laboratories across the galaxy. It is a monstrosity. A set of eyes barely visible amidst the swirling extremities indicates a semblance of a face.

"Hastur, is that you?" Weh gasps.

"Yes, Brother, it is I," the voice is strong despite the chaos of its container, the tenor unmistakably his half-brother and junior member of the R'lyeh Council of Elders—too junior to respond to an official annual report on unsanctioned biological regenerations conducted on a covert space laboratory. "Your report has been received."

"What?" Weh asks. "Where is the council?"

"I'm afraid few have the physical or mental capacity to continue to serve. I am sorry to hear of your own decline. Great progress has been made, though, in impeding the physical decline of this disease on your ship and others. As you can see, my own body, though unsightly, has been restored in no small measure due to the work done by scientific pairings such as yourselves."

"I am glad that we have at least contributed that," Weh responds.

"As for the psychosis, I'm afraid the other teams have been just as unsuccessful. I fear we may be doomed to immortal insanity. We have ordered all mentally afflicted to Xoth, where minds wiser than ours continue to work on a cure."

"Xoth is a secure medical facility," Shai protests, her worst fears realized. "We will be prisoners!"

"For your safety and ours," Hastur replies, "isolation is the best course of action. But my sincere hope is that it will be a temporary stay."

"And what of the specimens?" Weh asks.

"Sedate and transport back to Vhrool where they will be replicated and harvested for their parts."

"But . . ." Weh begins.

"Is there anything else that should be considered before we conclude here?" Hastur asks.

Weh and Shai exchange an uncertain glance.

"Let me be very clear," Hastur continues. "Your work and the work on the other laboratories is critical to the survival of our species. I know that during the performance of your duties you may have felt compromised. Your work may have had unfortunate consequences. And you may feel a certain attachment to what you've created. Guilt even. You were, after all, attempting to replicate yourselves. But the fact remains, we need these specimens. We need their organs, we need their cells, we need their nerves, even their fluid and their bile. We need every bit of them. They are of us, and they are ours to use as we see fit for the survival of our species. Now, again I ask, is there anything else that should be documented in this *official* council report before we conclude?"

Weh answers hesitantly, "No. You have it all."

"Then, your work here is done. Now, let us care for you. Are you able to transport to Xoth, or shall I send an escort?"

"We can make it there on our own," Shai responds.

"Gratitude. I will check back in a day to ensure you both have arrived." With that, Hastur disappears.

Resolved, Weh and Shai approach their creations. The specimens huddle naked, shivering in adjacent cages with barely room to stand. The creatures stare back with terror and—worse still—understanding. They heard everything. The male knocks over his water bowl in frustration. The female reaches through the bars of her cage toward her creators, seeking compassion as if a tangible thing.

It is natural to want to protect one's offspring, even for a species unfamiliar with the notion. This evolutionary imperative is hard-coded even when science has negated the need. A deep genetic mantra whispering, "survive, survive," setting tempo to all critical life decisions. Even in civilizations where survival is more invention than reproduction, that biological instinct persists.

Weh and Shai prepare their specimens for transport in solemn silence, each processing privately the extent of this final abomination. Uncertain, they strap the creatures into travel units before inducing stasis.

Clarity comes with a sneeze.

*Cthulhu,* is the sound Weh makes following an oozing of thick green mucus from his pores, a physical symptom of the disease. Three violent sneezes follow: *cthulhu, cthulhu, cthulhu.*

"Idh-yaa," Shai curses as she is inadvertently covered in Weh's fetid fluid. "You are a mess!"

The female creature speaks first, her tongue thick and uncertain but with determination. She points to Weh and repeats, "Cthulhu," and then to Shai, "Idh-yaa."

The words hang in the air as Weh and Shai pause over the bound bodies of these beings. They stare with wide eyes, tentacles frozen, as they take in this final proof of sentience.

"She thinks those are our names!" Shai exclaims in horror.

"Yours is fitting." Weh laughs nervously.

Shai ignores him. "I'm not doing this," she finally decides. "I'm calling the council. Someone besides Hastur."

While she frantically attempts to call the council—her back turned to her partner, shouting commands and pressing buttons—Weh stares bewildered at the creatures.

"Cthulhu," the male attempts to repeat, more of a grunt than the careful pronunciation of the female.

"Cthulhu, Cthulhu, Cthulhu," they chant together in desperate reverence.

"Shesmu help?" the female asks. "Shesmu cure. No," She declares, "No more. No more!"

Weh backs away.

"What have we done?" Weh shouts, but Shai only waves her hand to silence him.

"I'm getting the council," she repeats.

The female continues to ramble, attempting to communicate to save her life. But she is doing the exact opposite.

Shesmu is rising and Weh is suddenly ravenous.

Her brown skin is radiant under the soft glow of the laboratory lights. The light dances off round thighs, her body shaped in angles and curves, so unlike his own bulbous form yet created from it nevertheless. Her eyes communicate intelligence, but Weh is distracted by her neck. Long and angular, veins pulsing. She twists a head covered with sponge-like fur. He touches it.

*It's so soft.*

She is bound but snatches her head away.

He grips it, holds it steady, leans forward to let her fur tickle his tentacles. She becomes very still, quiet. He sniffs. She smells like sun, the hot beaches of home. He extends his broad pink tongue and licks her entire face in one aggressive flick, tasting. Fluid pours from her eyes, like sweet saltwater. He cannot stop. He leans in and bites down gently into the plump flesh of her cheek. A single

trickle of blood tickles his tongue.

"No," she cries.

Weh pulls away, "I'm sorry."

Arms bound, she rubs her bloody cheek against her shoulder and whimpers softly from the pain. She looks up at Weh and nods as if to say, *Apology accepted.* She forces a reconciliatory smile.

"Cthulhu," she whispers.

"I'm sorry," Weh repeats before turning to the male and pouncing.

There is screaming and there is blood, but Weh is no longer aware. There is only the hot flow of fluid and flesh down his throat as he tears through layer and layer of the creature's chest, down to the scaffolding. Unable to stop himself, he rips out a rib, raising his head to howl with the bone still lodged between his teeth.

Shai is there, pulling him away, slamming his body repeatedly into the wall until he sinks to the floor.

"What are you doing!" she screams.

She races to the male, pressing hands against the gaping wound where blood sprays out like a geyser.

Weh shakes his head to clear it, realizing the gravity of his actions.

"Did I kill it?" he asks.

"Not yet," Shai shouts. "Grab a clamp!"

They work in silence to repair the wound. The female is quiet, the male unconscious. When Shai and Weh finish, both creatures are alive, the male strapped to a gurney and the female locked inside of her cage. Blood covers their bodies and the once-pristine walls of the laboratory. Meat still hangs from Weh's tentacles and teeth. Despite himself, he sucks it off.

Wiping the blood from her suckers, Shai turns to Weh in disgust, "What were you thinking?"

"You've done worse!" Weh cries.

"That's a matter of debate."

"The female was talking," Weh tries to explain, "So I went for the male . . ." he shakes his head before looking up hopelessly at Shai. "I couldn't help it."

Shai sighs. "I know a little something about that. Well, what now? We can't just turn them over for harvest. Or replication.

"Did you get the council?"

Shai shakes her head, "No, I had to stop my colleague from devouring a sentient being. The council doesn't know yet. Not that it would change their minds. They're desperate. You heard Hastur."

Weh just shakes his head.

"Okay," Shai decides, "so we send them away."

"You forget that they hate each other. They'll tear one another apart."

This, too, Shai thinks through. After several moments, she nods, "Then, we inject them with enough oxytocin to inhibit adrenocorticotropic hormone in the hypothalamic-pituitary-adrenal axis. This should simulate the feeling of love. It will not last—but perhaps long enough for the female to care for the male's injuries. She's capable. I'm certain of that; I designed her neuroprosthetic myself. And hopefully in the process, they will learn to cooperate. It will give them a fighting chance."

"Is this what it feels like to be a parent?" Weh asks.

Shai laughs wickedly, recalling her frequent illicit couplings with the creatures, "I certainly hope not, or this is a really twisted universe. But we created them. We're responsible now for what they become."

Weh's discomfort increases.

"Let's just find them a home," he says, "before we're both completely mad."

Finding the wormhole is easy enough. It leads to a known galaxy; though charted and visited many times, it is far enough. Together they carefully examine each planet for the ability to sustain life, starting with the nearest to the sun. They ignore the frequent and frantic calls from Hastur. They know that they have precious little time before their own extraction is ordered and they are remanded to Xoth, their children stolen and murdered to feed their dying species. Fortunately, the third planet from the single sun offers the most promise—already brimming with life but with no detectable sentience above ground. They prepare their children for transport.

The credibility of creators and their intentions has always been questionable. Yahweh and Shaitan, known as Cthulhu and Idh-yaa by their creations, did the only conscionable thing they could with the last remaining threads of their sanity. They set their creations free, saving them from future torments, giving them an opportunity to live on as they themselves decline.

But hopelessness clouds their mercy. They fear that there is no saving these corrupted creatures who were born out of selfishness, forged from the basest of appetites, their consciousness brought forth in pain. The madness that is eating away at their own morality may one day consume their progeny.

Moreover, the universe is not as big as it once was, and time is relative. Parent and child may very well meet again, unaware of their connection except for a vague, genetic familiarity. In some distant future, will the created meet creators who have completely succumbed to rage, lust and hunger? On that day, will the work of the council be fulfilled, the creations slaughtered in service to their creators? Yahweh and Shaitan do not know. They can only hope that if that day does arrive, their children will be strong enough to withstand.

# The Temptation of St. Ivo

# CODY GOODFELLOW

ILLUSTRATED BY
DAVE FELTON

**S**TRANGE QUICKSILVER RAIN FELL FROM HIGH ABOVE THE CLOUDS UPON the face of the sulfurous mudflats and glaciers of frozen ammonia on the morning of the first day. From the deceleration corona of *For His Own Glory*, a briefcase-sized nanoprocessor ship circling the unsurveyed world in its abusive binary orbit around a bloated, moribund red giant and a blue daystar in an Oswalt density near the center of the Milky Way. The microscopic compiler-impregnated rain immediately began to order and accrete native molecules, but they sprang to life and industry only when the narrow strictures of biology and polity had been satisfied, only when the presence of primitive yet promising lifeforms were examined and their genotypes and vestigial souls holographically vivisected for signs of readiness to receive the word of the Evolved Christ.

Out of the mud rose a bowed spine and spoke-like spires of new-minted marble and windows of brilliantly hued stained glass, a humble tabernacle with the general outline of a chambered nautilus, and out from its yawning doors was disgorged the steam-wreathed likeness of a man.

Father Ivo Tsieh-Mondragon of the Mendelian Brotherhood knelt upon the trackless mud and suffered the primary lifeforms to come unto him. He took in his silicon gauntlets a Bible, opened its cover of ivory and horn, and began to read holistic code from the Amended Genesis, the Lamarckian Psalms, and the Song of Selection with such elevated passion that three of his teeth cracked, owing to a shortage of hydroxyapatite in local soils. Drawn into its coruscating radiant light, squirming meta-amoebas like beached jellyfish arched and contorted their opalescent membranes in an ecstasy of mindless enlightenment, vestigial organelles pulsating with electrochemical sparks of quantum uplift, the deathless words inscribed in letters of holographic fire in the dead-end helices of genetic script.

And as the sun set upon the First Day, Father Ivo looked up from the Bible and said, "Amen," and he saw that many among the numberless swarm of amoeboid pagan babies regarded him with crude free-floating eyespots with the same irises of cold cornflower as his own eyes, and he saw that it was good.

Even when the prophets of the empirical method and the scholars of the mystical finally united and linked arms to discover and celebrate the Grand Design as humanity's highest purpose, the path of the Church of the Evolved Christ was ever beset by thorns.

As humanity faced the wreck of its only begotten homeworld and stagnation and speciation in scattered solar system niches, the Mother Church's last flagellants accepted the age of the universe and the intelligent design of all life as His greatest miracle. Science cracked the method, or at least *a* method, by which the Creator enacted His work in the encoding of anti-entropic light. First a tool for education and indoctrination for its encoding of any amount of information into full-spectrum visible radiation, it soon proved useful for quantum gene therapy. Such combination accelerated the diaspora of genotypes until organisms couldn't exchange bacteria, let alone procreate, but it also allowed the syncretic church's early inquisitors to spread the human "meme" far beyond humanity's reach.

The first interstellar seedships to leave the Black Eye of Pluto and successfully make landfall on inhabited worlds found not only the seeming universality of the double helix and the humanoid form but also strange artifacts of psychobiological corruption even among aliens with no morphological kinship to humanity—gangster planets, gladiator planets, brachiating octopi Nazi Stormtroopers, and ambulatory fungi flower children with ancient hippie folksongs in their mangled DNA.

The galaxy's reprisals for these early errors of cosmic cupidity were swift and horrendous in their world-burning fury. Humanity was hunted and wiped out in hundreds of systems, forced to reinvent itself as the Word that lived in the Light and became flesh only at the will of spontaneously authored nanocompilers. Suffered only to minister to the lowest lifeforms on uncolonized worlds with dying primaries in the margins of the Milky Way, the church's ministers yet had spread the Word to tens of thousands of worlds in the first eleven millennia of their mission, and everywhere, they found fertile soil for their message of uplift, of the kinship of all lifeforms in their shaping by the Hand of the Almighty, and of the grace awaiting them when their forms reflected His divine face.

On the morning of the Second Day, Father Ivo was taken aback to find his charges engulfed in a schism.

After a gruesome but swift and wholly necessary purging of the unmutated, the surviving membranous sacs, inspired to develop eyes and ears, had been set upon by a faction that had shrewdly turned vacuole orifices into jawless mouths lined with silica teeth. Formerly content with ingesting plankton analogues and eubacteria colonies to supplement chemosynthesis of their mineral-rich habitat, the uplifted blobs now thrived upon cannibalism, further complicated by the move from mitotic reproduction to sexual conjugation of offspring. The females quickly became much larger and far more rapacious than their unlucky mates.

Clearly, the victors in the internecine warfare at his feet would be those favored few with both adaptations as well as the first outgrowths of teeth and rude skeletal features, but the resulting bottleneck would leave a depleted population, slower to respond to the chatoyant Light of his evangelization. The Bible must have sensed his nagging guilt over this, for it refused to heal his broken teeth and subjected him to a rigorous catechism.

In his unnumbered incarnations over ten thousand years of ministry, Father Ivo Tsieh-Mondragon had converted 793 species to accept the spirit and image of the Evolved Christ and had been martyred 3,889 times. But it was a function of his undying faith, as well as his hastily compiled bodies, that he was more agonized by the scrutiny of the only book he had ever read with every examination.

"Why, O my son," spoke the thunderous voice of the Lord, "did I create all that lives?"

"To revel in the glory of creation and its creator."

"And why did I make all that lives in such a multiplicity of forms?"

"Each life is a note in the Grand Design, pointing to the glory of His image, which is writ in the form of mankind."

"But why, O my son, must all that lives know pain, fear, hunger, and death?"

Ivo hesitated before answering, the biting cold strumming the exposed nerves of his broken, ill-made teeth. "The devil Entropy assails the web of Life to unmake it but, by testing it, allows the Living to come to know uplift to a higher order of complexity, allows the promise of sharing the form of the Creator and dwelling with Him forever when heat death claims the universe."

"And what is the duty of those blessed few who know the shape of their Creator?"

"To witness after the model of the Evolved Christ, to demonstrate his fitness and deliver even unto the least of these the Light of His Word . . ."

Sometimes, unworthy thoughts assailed the serenity of his faith when he could afford it least. Sometimes, the only thing more absurd than traveling across the galaxy as an immortal hologram, reincarnating on every godforsaken terrestrial body out of thin air to witness the self-evident divine lineage of a Bronze Age hedge magician who performed catering miracles at weddings, was the absurdity of dying five thousand times on as many worlds to spread the gospel of a messiah who only died for one world's sins once (and may have faked it, if some were to be believed). That and constantly having his motives attacked by a weak AI with a split personality derived from the two antithetical depictions of God in the Old and New Testaments.

On the morning of the Third Day, the snares of the devil Entropy were out for Father Ivo as he was attacked by his food supply.

Where, yesterday, the crop of native foliose lichen had presented a piebald field of chemosynthetic bladders and scabs on a substrate of spiny crystalline boulders, it now was a hydra-headed snarl of carnivorous barnacle geese with razor-beaks of black glass and gummy tendrils that salivated muriatic acid as they snapped up the stupid worms drawn wriggling into the crop with their rudimentary notocords glistering with lightning strikes of arousal.

Father Ivo nearly lost his hand along with the sleeve of his raiment when he tried to pick a sheaf of the rubbery rock-meat for his matins meal. The practical and political value of eating wherever possible of the same food as his flock was not lost on him, but even before the attack, the dismal flavor had him pining for the memory of his own recycled bodily wastes.

He did not wait for the Bible to interrogate him about how this ugly miracle had come to pass. The lichen had somehow absorbed the Light or at least had ingested the tissues in flux when it began devouring the slowest of his flock, but it hardly mattered. For all he knew, he would be raked over the coals for failing to recognize in the lichen a fitter candidate for conversion and quantum uplift.

Best not to leave the Lord any choice.

On the Bible's narrowest dilation, Father Ivo seared the unruly lichen with the Light of Revelation until he'd razed it to its semi-ambulatory roots and fused the mud to a convex lens of steaming obsidian. Entropy is the devil, he told himself, and its snares must be spotted and slipped for His own glory. Every neck that stretches does not reach the Tree, but every stretch brings the Head closer to the Face of God.

The ground seemed to belch in approval of his words, thrusting up alarmingly until a bubble of mud twice his height flung him backward. The bubble burst, and a fountain of white fire and a pyroclastic cloud engulfed Father Ivo who, stunned with excruciating pain and swimming in molten glass, could not appreciate the Extreme Unction his Bible recited for him even as the sinkhole produced by the explosion engulfed him.

On the morning of the Fourth Day, Father Ivo Tsieh-Mondragon emerged from his tabernacle to find his flock had vanished. Still shaky from his hasty incarnation upon receipt of the death notice from his previous body's Bible, Father Ivo was further disturbed by his first waking memory: that of an incomplete body compiling in the tabernacle's glandular pantry. The living chapel apparently did not place much faith in his survival, for he noticed there were more resources allocated to compiling successors than into replacing the torched food supply.

Icy wind sliced through his robes but did little to quash the stench of ammonia, sulfur, and bacterial blooms. The mystery of the missing mendicants, at least, was easily solved. From the spawning bogs where they painfully ascended through half a billion years of evolution in three days, the stamps of lobe-finned migration herring-boned up the slimy slopes to the slag-capped sinkhole and pointed down a narrow lava tube of dripping crystal that Father Ivo managed to penetrate only with some difficulty and shedding of armored garments.

That their trail coincided with the location of his lost Bible was a source of both comfort and alarm. Their simple nervous systems might quiver with religious ardor for the book that lifted them out of oblivion, but they might also be attracted to its leaking quantum radiation and so grow into the shape of the Unmaker.

With all the detachment he could muster, he examined the last sensations of his old body until they were like a stranger's personal effects. In his panic, Father Ivo had ignited a pocket of methane clathrate suspended beneath the lichen and been sucked under when the explosion had collapsed itself. He came rather unexpectedly upon the Bible, fused to the wall of the tube by a thin crust of glass, smeared with the slime of the passage of his wayward parishioners and embossed with a poignant handprint of caramelized flesh.

They had crawled over the source of their salvation in their morbid haste to reach the bottom of the tube, which terminated in the apex of a dome-shaped cavern that resisted every attempt to gauge its size with visible light and sonar. But what his light did bring into shocking relief, suspended on a rack of spear-like stalagmites of smoky crystal, was his own mortal remains.

Father Ivo had beheld his own dead form more times than he cared to count, but this tableau in particular quickened him with an almost mortal awe at the sublime beauty at the heart of his often maddening, seldom satisfying faith. Though this death had come about in no small part due to his own cupidity, this particular body almost embodied, to his new one, the ideal of Humanity.

Suspended in a supine position with limbs splayed out to demonstrate the elegance of its bilateral symmetry wedded to a linear asymmetry, of complexity yoked to the simplest possible form that could claim the stars. Digits fanned out in supplication, facial features rigid in ecstatic excruciation, transformed by the fatal breath of the divine. In death, he attained a universality, ascended to iconography. He was St. Theresa, San Sebastian, Vitruvian Man, Adam waiting to receive the spark of life from the hand of the Lord, and hanging above him, Father Ivo could not but look upon him as the Lord must have looked upon the First Man on the day that blessed mutation finally shattered the chains of Entropy, stood upright, and looked at the heavens to utter the First Word in praise of his Creator. Hundreds of species more "advanced" than humanity existed, but with few exceptions, they were decadent, detestable races declined into a twilight of over-specialization, kept alive in a selective vacuum by the toil of lesser, often humanoid, slave races.

Father Ivo found himself short of breath, eyes tearing up for want of blinking. The second skin of rippling, mottled glass like a stylized halo of holy light, the seven needles of crystal piercing his torso, only gave the tableau the brittle, unreal brilliance of the doctrinal visions drilled into his head just before he awakened, and the fact that the body was identical to his own in every way made it impossible to look away, even as he could not quite accept its reality.

The cult of saints had become thicker than a planetary census within a century of the first wave of missionaries, and the criteria for martyrdom had risen to ignore all but those who suffered true death with the failure or corruption of reincarnation from a tabernacle hatchery, yet Father Ivo was moved to record the image and request that the Bible submit his predecessor for beatification before he could move himself to deploy nanomites to decompose it.

It was perhaps a noble impulse to do justice to so total a sacrifice or perhaps a stirring of insecure conscience that led him to explore the cavern further. Father Ivo assiduously avoided examining his own motives as he extruded a braided rope of his own hair to the floor of the grotto of metamorphic lava rock encrusted with a corona of towering stalagmites radiating from a spherical feature nearly a hundred meters in diameter that yet bore the unmistakable contours of an architectural feature, rather than a topographical one. His flock was gone, and he was not inclined to lose his coming day of rest for having to start over.

The floor of the grotto was blistered with moguls of tortured rock. The trail of the wandering worms was a prismatic carpet he followed to the underbelly of the sphere where an orifice of sorts admitted entrance to an interior space lit by viridian phosphorescence, once he shattered a phalanx of crystal spars. The sphere seemed to sweat the crystals with an urgency that must be reaction to his presence, for he could hear them growing like mineral lightning, throbbing with subtle stresses under the weight of his Bible's light or under the subtler pressure of his gaze. The concave walls of the sphere were corrugated with sinuous markings he was forced to credit as deliberate. Though it bore little resemblance to any known script the Bible had ever encountered, it was yet unmistakably the result of some agency.

But even this could not hold his attention when he beheld the thing at the center of the temple.

A trembling elliptical mass, nearly touching the stalactites, floated suspended above a circular pit in the floor at the spherical chamber's center. It would have served as a fitting idol, an eidolon of whatever was once worshiped here, were it not composed of the wriggling bodies of his missing flock.

Countless thousands of worms in a rat-king swarm, a cluster so dense it tensed and relaxed like a vast heart with the naked ardor of a spawning orgy, yet as he watched, they seemed to eat each other—no, they simply merged, one into another with a sickening fluidity, skins dissolving together and organs entwining in a perverse reversal of mitosis, engulfing each other before his eyes until only a finite number of vast blobs of glittering protoplasm swirled and strained in a shapeless form that drove Father Ivo to his knees with unbelieving awe when it finally deigned to speak to him.

Not in words but in the language with which humankind first spoke to the universe: in immersive holographic memetics that rescripted the reader into the spirit and image of the author.

Found himself in an impossible body as inexplicable in its byzantine, fractal intricacy as was the labyrinthine sophistication of its brain. His species wore and shed bodies like clothes, leading a parallel existence inside the mirror universe of an aggregated AI. Power inseparable from godhood, yet when all mystery had been gnawed down to mere knowledge, when all pleasures had left the nerves insensate, the soul empty, they asked their foremost prophet to find God for them.

She looked out into the void and into the depths of species memory, into the boutiques of black market body-shops that would modify her in ways the collective mind would never allow, the better to secure her vision.

When she returned to show them God, the entire planet vibrated with anticipation as it had not since long before her race renounced the empty game of interstellar conquest a score of eons past. Few were told that she had had all her exterior sensory organs surgically disabled and had gone, by any standard of her senescent and libertine species, quite incurably insane.

She uttered a brutally primal ululation of mindless exultation and, before she could be stopped, committed suicide in a most barbaric fashion involving removal and devouring of her own head. Within moments, the world computer had integrated her self and become infected with her vision. Instantly, everybody on its network was stricken blind, deaf, mute, and dumb to olfactory and equilibrium stimuli. The world computer accepted a pandemic of suicides and deaths by misadventure in the ensuing panic but refused to decant new bodies. Those trapped within the world computer were made to share the prophet's vision and the joyous shedding of decadent complexity, to join her in tearing down all science, art, philosophy, memory, until nothing remained but the essential spark that had driven them to seek, in their greedy ennui, the hand of God.

Cut off from the superficial shimmering of their world and the distracting bleatings of each other, they found the universe quivered with the stirring of gods beyond number. They felt it showering down on their blind, awakened faces from the dark spaces between the stars as a diffuse rain of cosmic obscenity too profoundly convoluted for lesser minds to unravel and perish at its implications: abominable neutrino screams of eternally embryonic gods writhing in the cores of stars and the bowels of black holes, and at the galactic core, the echoing roar of the source of all that lived, of all that was, of the blind idiot Creator early humans knew as Azathoth, which had convulsed in an ecstasy of parthenogenesis and extruded a billion galaxies . . . but which was yet a fleck of jetsam in the eye of Yog Sothoth, a mindless paroxysm that secreted bubble-universes like so many dead skin cells . . .

But loudest of all, they felt the vibration of godhead within their own flesh and knew they alone were cut off from the music of the ever-unfolding Creator . . . unless they sacrificed all that they were, all that they had achieved, all that they knew, and even knowing itself . . .

From the metaplasm of Azathoth had come all physical matter and antimatter, and in its shapeless chaos lay the divine energy that species across the universe had worshiped with varying degrees of accuracy. In the detritus of the stars, its infinite progeny gestated in cycles that measured the deaths of stars as trimesters. In unkindled gas giants and in the molten cores of terrestrial worlds, they slept and, in their dreaming, sometimes begat miracles, sometimes monsters. So many worlds where life had emerged and evolved and arrogantly clawed its way to the stars were little more than cracked eggs, where the sleeping potential to hatch a godling was squandered in mortal species that deluded themselves into thinking they were the pinnacles of creation. But if evolution had no end, it could easily turn a circle.

Besieged by a billion gods with no use for their prayers, his species eagerly extinguished themselves and emerged from the world computer's crèches as shapeless meta-amoebas, slipped out of their last ruined cities as the climate controls failed and the mud buried all their eagerly forgotten works, and returned to the primordial soup with no regrets, resonating in blind idiot joy with the eternal echo of Azathoth birthing the universe . . .

It is arguably a harder thing to learn that one's whole existence is built upon lies and the promulgation of lies than it is to learn how unimaginably alien is the true nature of the face of one's creator.

Father Ivo recovered from his vision to find that the pillar of worms had merged into a single convulsing mass with no discernible axes or symmetry, no stable organs, but primitive buds of ur-organs erupting forever out of its fitfully simmering membrane, seething with the eagerness to become anything. All his work undone . . . and worse—

The long forgotten inhabitants of this godforsaken planet had regressed as far as their madness allowed, but only with Father Ivo's genetic meddling were they awakened to their true purpose. Now, the unified thing, yet eons from its pupation into something like a god, it began to force itself into the pit in the floor.

His mind all but unhinged by what he'd seen and relived, Father Ivo could only throw open the Bible and read from it as its light skewered the shapeless monstrosity, this first begotten Nephilim of the unacceptable one true God.

The light stabbed deep into the unholy thing, and Father Ivo nearly buckled as the anti-entropic radiation was sucked out of the Bible faster than it could be produced. The abomination seemed to shrivel into itself or to succumb to the divine program and assume lateral symmetry, but a tentacle of boiling membrane thrust out at him to smash him down or snatch the Bible from his hands . . .

For a moment, he believed he'd won.

The tentacle split open and twitched as its liquid mobility surrendered to the commandments of muscle and bone. The tentacle flattened and fanned out an array of bony digits with a shorter one in opposition in awesome imitation of a human hand.

It was exactly as he imagined it . . . indeed, it might have been plucked out of his imagination, from his earlier memory of God touching Adam. Indeed, he trembled beneath the gigantic hand and closed his eyes in reflexive expectation of the bestowal of some indescribable blessing . . .

The hand fell upon him, its weight nothing like he expected, but its touch was electric upon his skin. It burned . . .

Burned . . .

He burned with invisible fire. His garments disintegrated. Face, hands, limbs, body, burned as something took him apart at a molecular level. It must be his own nanomites, the ones deployed to build the tabernacle, but they were programmed to autophage after he was completed. But they were only another living thing, in the end, and far more liable to hear the call than one who heard only the unending blather of its own voice . . .

The hand retreated back into the mother mass of the shapeless child of God as it shrank into the hole in the floor, and Father Ivo yearned to go after it, but the pit, when he reached it, proved to be little more than a crack in the floor. His body yielded to the narrowing of space with some degree of pain, but he found himself able to fit quite handily once the last remains of his skeleton were ejected out of his anus.

On the morning of the Sixth Day, Father Ivo Tsieh-Mondragon emerged from the tabernacle and looked with disfavor upon the work of his previous bodies. His memory of what had befallen him cut off shortly after he descended into the sinkhole and recovered his Bible, and the new one he had been issued forbade him in its most saturnine voice to investigate it further.

Little else remained to be done to try to salvage the mission. It was becoming harder to chastise himself for the sins of his previous bodies, but it would be his fate to be disintegrated with the tabernacle when *For His Own Glory* was recalled to rejoin the mothership *Skycake* before it migrated closer to the galactic core where it was hoped more fertile unclaimed worlds would be on offer.

Of the teeming population of meta-amoebas cataloged in the initial planetary survey, Father Ivo observed only one specimen, and none of the progress his predecessors logged was on display, though it made such a nuisance of itself, flailing nets of sticky cilia at Father Ivo and piping from its gasping vacuoles a susurrant noise he imagined sounded like a lipless whisper.

"You not I. I am I," the abortive amoeba rasped at him until Father Ivo was moved to squash it with his boot.

§

**Cody Goodfellow** *has written five solo novels and two more with NY Times bestselling author John Skipp. Two of his collections,* Silent Weapons For Quiet Wars *and* All-Monster Action, *both received the Wonderland Book Award. He wrote, co-produced, and scored the short Lovecraftian hygiene film* Stay At Home Dad, *which can be viewed on YouTube. As a bishop of the Esoteric Order of Dagon (San Pedro Chapter), he presides over several Cthulhu Prayer Breakfasts each year. He is also a cofounder of Perilous Press, a micropublisher of modern cosmic horror. He currently lives in Portland, Oregon.*

# A Dream, and a Monster at the End of It

# NADIA BULKIN

### ILLUSTRATED BY LUKE SPOONER

THE *REMINA* LANDED ON ELIJAH WITH A BUMP AND A SCRAPE AND THE certain satisfaction of its arrival having been foretold. The solar ring's best scientists had all agreed: on Elijah's last sail through the neighborhood, it had come closest to Sarai. It was only fair that Sarai should be the first to land upon it, the first to drill it, the first and only to mine its riches. The prodigal planet; the stranger from afar.

Sarai had eagerly awaited its return for a thousand years, committed to it songs and films and cigarette brands and about a hundred of their eldest sons' names in this year of its perihelion, and across the solar ring, so had everyone else. Three dozen refugee communities were waiting with desperate colonization requests that the ICG would never read. Tero was waiting to capture Elijah with an arsenal of illegal push-missiles, even though Elijah wasn't theirs to claim by any standard of interstellar law. Everyone else was waiting with telescopes because Elijah was just that beautiful, coming into habitable space like a chariot not of fire but ice.

The only one not waiting a second longer was Sarai, because fortune favored the brave in the interplanetary age.

Captain Kadan brought out the bottle of wine that he'd smuggled onboard and promised that they would open it after they made first break. "We're going to drink it all," he told his crew, "and then we're going to stuff the bottle with a note that says 'Go Fuck Yourself,' and we're going to throw it out the airlock and hope it hits Tero. With any luck, they'll think it's a message from their great-great granddaddies."

His crew laughed.

It was easy to laugh at that overgrown planet that thought everything was theirs. Easy to laugh at all the Callers perched on the cliff, yelling nonsense at the abyss—so convinced they were that somewhere out there was humanity's true home, some great empire that had lost track of one of their outposts. But *out there* had become *in here*, and through all the cracked mud and subterranean lakes and water vapor, there was no one yelling back. They were alone. They were alone, they were alone, they were alone; praise God, they were alone.

"Xenia is a Caller too, you know," said Ariq, slyly.

Xenia always tried to play it down. She'd say, *I grew up in a religious community on the Eastern Plains, called the Good Garden. They were believers,* she'd say, *but they weren't Callers. Oh, no. They were actually the opposite of Callers: they were cautious.*

"But tell him *why* you're cautious," Ariq goaded.

Xenia shrugged. "Because we don't know what's out there," she replied, trying to be matter-of-fact because it was matter-of-fact, wasn't it? They couldn't possibly know.

Captain Kadan stared at her for a second and broke out in uproarious, hearty laughter—the laughter of a man who knows he's fulfilling a destiny that's been foretold. "You *are* a damn Caller," he told her. "You're just a really pessimistic one."

Captain Kadan and Ariq left to do the honors. The captain had been waiting his whole life to drive that rig into Elijah's face in Sarai's name; Ariq was the one who knew how to work the machine.

"Happy hunting," Xenia said. From the safety of the *Remina*, she watched their rover roll along on the SAR, the size of a small insect and about twice as vulnerable. A sense of abiding cold had seeped in from Elijah's pale ice hills and methane lakes when she wasn't looking, and she had the wild thought that maybe Elijah caught a cold somewhere out there at the other end of its stretched-out-rubber-band orbit? For the first time since they left Sarai—to the cheers and claps of their comrades chanting "First Break! First Break!"—she wished she hadn't agreed to this detail. Should have listened to her parents. They alone didn't herald Elijah with trumpets. They called Elijah "Hellstar," mostly because it had spent the past thousand years crossing through a whole lot of *nothing*: not *nothing* because they knew for sure that it was empty but *nothing* because it was silent, like a held breath. Elijah had spent the past millennium in—*(hell)*.

"Hey, Zee. What exactly do you think is out there? Is there a bug hunt I can join?"

She pressed the microphone closer to her chin. "We'd be the bugs, Captain." Over the comms, she heard the two men laughing and tried to will herself to laugh with them.

But before they reached the pre-assigned site for first break, Xenia spotted something a mile left on the SAR: a tiny, perfect circle inside a tiny, perfect heptagon. She asked the rover to hold.

"Are you sure it's not a mountain?" Captain Kadan asked, eager to continue this most noble quest before the Great Tero Starfleet was able to close in with their ship-sized drills and claim first break, claim that Elijah belonged to *them*.

She was sorry to have to give him the worst news he had perhaps ever heard. "It's geometric," Xenia said. "It looks manmade."

Of course, Xenia had dreamt about Elijah. They all had. She had friends who dreamt of seeing peppermint-colored Elijah in their lover's eyes or of dogs running up to them on the causeway with Elijah tucked between their teeth, a lovely saliva-covered marble. But in most of the dreams *she'd* had since childhood, Elijah was enormous instead of shrunken, swollen far larger than the minor planet ever could have been in Sarai's sky a thousand years ago and growing larger by the minute. Her father would be pouring out oil onto a fire nearby, glumly saying, "No good, no good," and Xenia would try to point to the rapidly approaching planet, but her father could never see.

Even as Elijah filled the half-light of the sky; even as a large rift opened along Elijah's equator and revealed a gigantic, all-seeing eye, visibly rippling with veins and blood vessels; even as that eye fixed its ne'er blinking gaze upon Xenia and her father; even then, he didn't see it.

No one spoke while the rover drove over to the structure. No one wanted to say what they were all thinking: that they had lost the race, even though they had had a figurative eternity to plan and deployed every resource possible—including a formidable army of spies—to ensure that they came in first on Elijah. The *Remina* had hid behind a long-period comet on its way out of habitable space and rode the momentum until the drop down to Elijah's soft, slushy surface. And yet, for all this, they had lost. Someone had outsmarted them. Someone else wanted Elijah more. The fact didn't seem possible, considering their desperation for its sweet silicates, its delicious platinum and palladium.

Once Captain Kadan and Ariq reached the heptagonal structure, Xenia didn't have to switch to their video feeds to know that whatever it was, it meant first break. The slew of curses coming over the comms was evidence enough. Slugged by a wave of nauseating unfairness, she briefly rested her head on her arms. First break was an awful rule, but Sarai had signed onto it because it beat the alternative: to the captor go the spoils, which would have worked solely in favor of the large and heavy, like Tero. When she raised her head again, her eyes briefly lingered on the view from *Remina's* perimeter camera: the distant foothills of ice and glimmering misshapen methane swamps, all dark, all the time. All dark, yet Elijah had seen it all.

"What is it? Whose is it?" she said, turning on Ariq's video. She saw the tips of white boots she assumed to be Captain Kadan's. The corroded hexagon lined a round tunnel burrowing into the ice, all glowing a sharp, military green. Whoever built it hadn't gotten very far; there was nothing but black at the bottom of the well.

"They must have done it the last time Elijah was in habitable space."

"Last time?" Captain Kadan scoffed. "You mean a thousand years ago?"

"Probably more like nine hundred and ninety years, but yeah."

Xenia cut in. "I don't see any Tero markings on it. But there's something else . . ."

The two men stopped, and Ariq stooped, zooming in on the etchings carved into the hexagon. It just looked like knife marks to her eyes, but when the computer took a look, the cuts became words: "Property of the Free Paaten Nation. Hail Elijah, Our New Home."

There was a lot of angry mumbling that she couldn't quite hear because her mind had been swept away by thoughts of the long-suffering Paateni, hiding on the peripheries of Tero's storms like beaten animals. She had read a sad statistic about them in school: no other nation-group had filed so many colonization requests and been denied every time. Nobody wanted to make Tero angry, so Tero got away with everything. And because the "Free Paaten Nation" would have still, technically, belonged to Tero, Tero was going to make off with Elijah too.

"We have to destroy it," Captain Kadan said.

Silence. That went utterly against first break's principles, though neither Xenia nor Ariq wanted to say that out loud. Ariq's video tilted up toward Captain Kadan's greenlit face, and their fearless leader looked downright skeletal: eyes bugged out, cheeks hollowed-out with terror.

"No one knows about this," he went on with escalating desperation. "Tero clearly doesn't know. The ICG doesn't know. We're the first ones here . . ."

"They were the first ones here," said Ariq. He was an engineer. He believed in laws.

"And where are they now?" Captain Kadan hissed. He slid a little on the sludge, only pretending to be looking for a thousand-some-year-old astronaut, because what if something in a vaguely man-sized suit actually shambled forth? "They were stupid enough to land on Elijah while it was swinging out to aphelion. You know they're all dead. The ICG sees that tunnel, all they're going to think is 'better hand it over to Tero, one of *their* crews made first break.'"

And then Xenia actually saw something behind Captain Kadan—a shadow, a shape, a mountain-sized presence at once there and not there, sitting up under the ice like a—*(body)*. She clapped her hand over her mouth to stop herself from crying out because surely it was just a trick of the unfamiliar terrain? There were crags on Vanyez that looked like saber tooth fangs.

"Captain, there's something over there," Ariq said. She almost yelled, *Don't!* but Ariq was pointing at something else: a much smaller, coffin-sized lump a few yards away. At first, it looked like tholin heaps that were starting to come uncovered, but when they chipped away the ice, the shape beneath it was too familiar. An astronaut. A Paateni from Tero. Preserved.

That time, Xenia let slip a little whisper to God.

The last time Elijah passed though habitable space, just a bit closer to Sarai than to Tero, Sarai and Tero were looking elsewhere. The Hammarskjöld asteroid was

passing between them, and Tero was illegally flanking it with fighters as they sent an army of miners to the surface. They mined so aggressively that, even though they didn't have push-missiles back then, the asteroid lost so much mass that it eventually fell into Tero's orbit. Hammarskjöld was now just a mute little moon that the Tero had renamed Lojala, the Loyal.

It had been a blatantly illegal seizure of a new habitat. Sarai lodged vocal complaints to a sympathetic ICG, but all they could do was voice disapproval. No one wanted to anger everyone's best trading partner. And while all this unfolded, Elijah sailed through habitable space, noticed primarily by poets and cults and only the most reckless of separatist groups.

The Paateni astronaut was mummified, her suit melted into her body as if polymers and flesh had been liquefied and re-frozen. Her helmet had collapsed inward, and her eyes, nose, and mouth were pressed outward against a crystal-coated visor that must have half-melted, making a sort of sculptor's mold. They could feel the curve of her nose and lips and her closed, bulging eyelids but not the flesh or bone or cartilage. She was kissing the veil. She looked like a grotesque, bulbous marble statue that had been painted a sparkly, silvery gray.

Captain Kadan had gone back out to the site of the Paateni break. He had kept his distance from the body after they hauled her in, throwing water sachets and gobbling protein bars in the mess instead. Xenia and Ariq only knew he had left the *Remina* because they watched him drive the rover out of the hold while they soaked the body in medical fluorescent light.

"He lived for this," said Ariq, who had served with the captain before on the botched comet capture mission Magical Lasso. "He kept saying, if we don't stop them from taking Elijah from us, they're going to take everything. We're not going to survive. He kept saying they might even take *us*." He shook his head. "I told him that was crazy."

If Xenia had learned anything from the Good Gardeners, it was that there was no such thing as crazy, not where the cosmos was concerned. But she didn't want to think about everything that the failure of the mission might mean, so she focused on their new charge. "What do you think happened to her?"

"Time," Ariq suggested, and he was right—time was the enemy of matter.

"But why does she look like she's been covered in chromium? There isn't any on Elijah." She delicately traced the curve of the astronaut's nose. "What is this stuff?"

And then the mouth parted. Her jaw fell open, like long-clenched masseter muscles had finally relaxed, revealing a cavernous throat clogged with the spacesuit's cables and coated in silver. It would have been bad enough without the distinct, melancholic sigh that accompanied the event and sent Xenia and Ariq jumping back, Ariq grabbing a scalpel. For what felt like ten minutes but in truth was only one, nothing else happened. "Air escaping the body," Xenia whispered, but then, there was the sound of *inhalation*, ragged and weak, but breath all the same.

"My Sarai," said Ariq, letting the hand that held the scalpel go slightly slack, so the little knife swung back and forth between his fingers like a pendulum. "She's alive."

But Xenia could see this was not life. Not the way life had ever been understood anywhere in the solar ring, anyway. Maybe, it wasn't death either. Nor was it some prehistoric attempt at cryogenic sleep. But maybe things happened differently *out there*. Her mind's eye went racing past the planets and moons and asteroids and satellites of the solar ring, past all the libertine space-villages and corporate spacelabs, out of habitable space, into the cold uncharted deep. Racing, racing, racing toward something hidden with a gravitational field more powerful than the sun . . .

Xenia quickly pressed her palms against her eyes. *One thousand, two thousand, three thousand.* This was how her parents had taught her to spend exploratory science class in primary school, kicking away her nerves, insisting to the teachers, *no, no, I don't want to know.* By the time she opened her eyes again, the Paateni astronaut was moving her mouth. Stretching her chrome lips. And Ariq was leaning over her as if to listen, hissing at Xenia to bring the microphone over.

Because she was speaking.

The Paateni's eyes never opened, thank God. Perhaps, eyes did not survive the transformation into this state of being.

It was hard for the microphone to pick up her words, and it was just gibberish at first—a lot of *cold* and *end* and *light*—so Ariq tried to orient her. He told her the year and the place—"you're still on Elijah"—and asked her the last thing she remembered, mostly to see if she still had memories.

*"We were long-sleeping."*

"Sleep?" Xenia whispered. "They made first break and then went to cryo-sleep?"

Ariq snorted in a derision that wasn't unearned. Even now, no one had successfully awoken from cryo-sleep past one hundred three years. The hippie space village Mauna Pica had just jettisoned the preserved body of their one-hundred-ten-years-asleep founder to save room and money, saying with a shrug, *if it's meant to be, someone will pick him up, by-and-by.* "What kind of cryo-sleep would a separatist colony have had back then? More like permanent suspension hooked up to an ultra-low-power battery." He shook his head. "This was a suicide mission."

But Xenia thought it was rather beautiful, if very sad, the amount of trust they had placed in their brethren to not only find a way to claim them but to wake them, one thousand years later. *"We're on a suicide mission,"* she noted. When Ariq silently tightened his fist around the scalpel, she wondered, *and maybe, so is every human, aimlessly shuttling around the solar ring knowing that they had fought their way out of the primordial soup only to be greeted not by trumpets but silence.*

*"I woke. Alone. But not alone."*

"What woke you?" Ariq asked into the microphone, which robotically repeated him in archaic Paatenese.

The lips pressed together and opened like a blooming flower. *"God."*

Ariq bristled. "Fucking Callers, can't even think proper—"

But then the words started spilling fast and frantic from the microphone, from the astronaut's wildly contorting mouth: *"God is wrath is God is death is God is hunger is God is chasing me is God is eating everyone . . ."*

Tend your own garden. Keep your head down. Xenia glanced at Ariq, and she could tell by the flicker in his eyes, like a frightened prey animal, he was trying not to process this, trying not to come to the same inevitable conclusion that she was spinning toward.

Whatever terrified rapture-dream had overtaken the Paateni faded, and she tried to orient herself again: *"You are not Paateni."*

"No . . . we are from Sarai. The Paaten rebellion . . ." Xenia paused, searching for words that would cause the least hurt, "was ended two hundred years ago."

And then the mouth stopped moving. Not even a cry.

Ariq muttered that they should have lied because they both knew there was one more question—the most important question.

Xenia quickly leaned down and asked, "Where is God, now?"

It took five heartbeats for the Paateni astronaut to answer, and when she did, it was nothing more than the softest of clicks. "*Hiding.*"

She was about to turn around, tell Ariq that she understood he didn't believe in extraterrestrials, let alone *space monsters*, but to please trust her, just this once, trust that something inhuman had found its way onto Elijah and now they had to *go go go*—but she heard him loudly say into the comms, "Captain? We think you should head on home. We think Elijah may have run into some weird shit out on the aphelion . . ."

The cottonball haze of relief at having been believed was immediately pounded out by Captain Kadan's unintelligible voice, thin as a nylon thread beneath the din of an enormous un-living roar. Unintelligible, except that he was screaming.

They rushed to switch his video feed onto the head-up display, bringing it up just in time to see a rush of incomprehensible movement as a distant ice-mountain slid into motion, less like an ice-sheet slipping and more like a blanket being pulled off a bed. Crystal sparks—*silver? chrome?*—filled the feed, glittering against the endless night as their captain's garbled yelling turn to static.

Behind them, Xenia thought she could hear the Paateni astronaut laughing, but she was wrong: it was a manic, cable-clattering seizure, as if the gunmetal chrome that now grounded her every cell was trying to dislodge, to spit out what remained of her bones and her plastic suit and run free toward whatever it was that was dancing *out there* in the dark.

Calling is a sin, and Callers are tempters. Tend your own garden. Keep your head down. If you're lucky, the vulture passes you by. Goodness doesn't need to be invited, but evil does. Good listens, evil answers. Good abides, evil seeks.

The children in the compound instinctively understood the advantages of being small and quiet, of crouching under floorboards and holding their breath—*one thousand, two thousand, three . . .*

The adults in the compound usually only arrived after the world had shattered them somehow—perhaps a death had left them convinced that any god was a bastard or that the government was hiding an apocalyptic truth. More rarely, they'd encountered something that had shaken everything they thought they understood. An impossible voice on a radio, a cave painting, a hieroglyph, a dimming star. A string inside had been plucked as if to sing, *you are not alone,* and they had reacted not in jubilation but in fear.

They forgave Xenia for leaving them but not for joining the Sarai Aeronautic Force, even though the government was grounded and their missions looked for minerals, not microbes.

*You will be undone,* her father said. *Go and you will be undone.*

Her mother died in the Garden. Xenia didn't find out for two years.

At first, Xenia and Ariq just sat on the floor of the *Remina*, waiting for whatever had reached out from under Elijah's ice blanket to find them and kill them. The sound of its roar, like a bullet train rushing through a mountain tunnel, had stilled any possibility of rushing to the flight deck and escaping. The thought, *better to die,* bounced between them, though they could neither speak nor meet each other's eyes. *Better to die than live in a world where this is true.* Xenia saw her parents every time she pushed her palms against her eyes, digging in the dirt with their heads down like moles. *Hellstar Elijah. Hellstar Elijah is coming back infected. You just wait and see . . .*

What finally shook them back to life was the radar's automated warning of an incoming aircraft. Even before they had visual confirmation, they knew it could only be an envoy of the Great Tero Starfleet, come to collect what they thought was their due.

No questions were asked before the *Remina* was jammed and crippled and rendered into a heap of trash metal. Their life support systems were put on a thirty-minute clock, to give them time to get into their suits.

"They can fucking have this fucking planet," Ariq muttered, putting on his helmet.

Xenia briefly considered dragging along the Paateni astronaut—who had twisted in on herself like an action figure thrown by a child and who might, now, actually *(hopefully)* be dead—but then reasoned that such a fate wouldn't be fair to the Paateni, to sleep for a thousand years only to be lit on fire by the very people she'd been trying to escape.

The Tero fleet had turned on Elijah's lights, staking enormous LEDs on poles into the ice sludge. Xenia and Ariq could only see the dimmest outline of the Tero cargo plane, humming contentedly like a well-filtered air conditioner. From the nose alone, they could tell it was enormous. And in front of it, eight astronauts waited in red and white suits, holding sleek black guns with sleek black gloves. One of them barked a command that their microphones near-instantly translated in an androgynous voice as "Stop!"

They stopped, sliding a bit on the ice.

"You don't have permission to be here. What is your business on Elijah?"

Nothing felt worth explaining, anymore. Ariq mumbled, "Obviously, trying to make first break," and had to repeat it at gunpoint when they couldn't quite make it out.

"What do you mean, first break? This planet belongs to Tero. We have listed it within our catalog of territories for almost a thousand years . . ."

Xenia's eyes drifted toward the darkness where she knew the mountains would be. The mountains and God, hiding in the chrome. She thought of the other children in the compound hiding under the floorboards, mischievously twiddling their fingers against their knees, eyes hidden in shadow but curiously sharp teeth glowing and—*(hungry)*. She thought she was picking up a sound. A tectonic moan. Bones grinding. And a strange, steady hum.

She suddenly realized that Ariq was yelling. "You don't understand! We have to go, all of us! There's something here, and it killed our captain . . ."

"I repeat. Please, be quiet."

"We are all going to die unless—"

Xenia barely even saw him raise his hand. The gesture was so fast, there wasn't near enough time to understand its intent, though she assumed he was trying to point to the mountains and the hiding god. But it was enough. Two lights zipped from two guns, just two of the briefest flashes in the dark, and converged at the very center of Ariq's heart. He buckled and fell, the burn in the wound slowly smoking. Something that had been held very taut inside Xenia, some tiny emotional muscle she hadn't even known was there, snapped and broke.

"Hostile gesture," said one of the other members of the starfleet. "Judgment call."

The starfleet officer who'd spoken the most took a long pause to stare at the trigger-happy subordinate, and then nodded toward Xenia and started turning around. No translation was needed. Power is the universal language. Even before the two officers in red-and-white reached her, she felt her arms going slack, her knees unlocking, the decision between *resist* and *obey* tipping toward acquiescence.

And then a larger power intervened, as she had known that it would. She had the jump amid the screaming and the chaos, running with big, bounding, half-flying leaps across the ice toward the site of the Paateni break—but this time, Xenia could also look back over her shoulder and see.

When Captain Kadan was killed, it had all happened too quickly and over too much digital interface to register much more than movement: massive displacement of matter that seemed far too large and violent for Elijah—the little prince. But now, only a cloudy visor and the length of a standard space station separated them; now, she could see the spinning, singing, sinning faces in the chrome; now, she could see the arms like enormous silver lava tongues wrap around this most beloved prodigal planet. Now that she had seen the glory of its victory over *(everything)*—she could see how the Paateni astronaut could have mistaken this ravenous presence for a god.

She used to have another dream about Elijah, though this one she never told anyone. There was a hollowness to the vision that used to make her sick to her stomach, sicker even than the dream about Elijah's eye. Elijah was passing over, nothing more than a small white cable car, and her mother was still alive and speaking to her so quietly that she could not understand the words except that her mother seemed to be speaking about the transience of the flowers at their feet. A kite string floated down from the heavens—from Elijah—and her mother smiled and grabbed hold of it and flew away, one of hundreds, no, thousands of sailing refugees.

Xenia sometimes ran after them but never, ever managed to catch a kite string. The older she got, the harder she tried, not because she wanted to go but because to be abandoned seemed unspeakably worse. Yet she would inevitably be left curled on the now-dead grass, thinking, *I wish there was nothing. I wish there was nothing out there.*

All but one of the Teroan officers died during the assault, some bodies sent flying and breaking on impact, some bodies taken up and eaten. The only survivor was the officer who had done most of the talking, who had followed Xenia into the well that the Paateni had dug a millennium ago. Her name turned out to be Bree Bonan, and she had been a captain before all of that became irrelevant. Now that the LED lights had been swatted down and both the Tero craft and the *Remina* pried apart by eager, searching arms, the two women stood on built-up sludge with their backs against the wall, injured past the point of feeling pain. Xenia saw Bonan whispering to herself—what she assumed to be a prayer to the keepers of that lost empire that Tero was always trying to foolishly call out of the dark—and was struck by a sudden savage thought.

"Did you know?" she spat at Bonan. "Did you know that"—*God, God, God*—"thing was out there? Did it reply to one of your little SOS calls, say, *ready or not, here I come?*"

Bonan looked genuinely, momentarily horrified. Of course, they had had a very specific vision of what their great ancestral birthright was going to look like when it finally stepped out of the anonymous expanse—God and mother and father, all at once—and it was nothing like this. "No. We never got any . . . no, we didn't know."

"Well then, I guess it's a true miracle," Xenia snorted. "How very proud you must be."

Bonan let out a little feral growl. "Don't you see that it doesn't matter now?" she hissed. "We've already started bringing Elijah in. Everything is . . ." she squeezed her eyes shut.

Xenia realized that those were tears Bonan was trying to stop. And she knew, too, that their homeworlds lay so near each other that the Hidden God would be able to jump to not only Tero's gleaming razorblade cities but to Sarai's too, if it wanted. And by the way it tore through matter here, ripping apart Elijah's skins of ice and nitrogen, Xenia knew, like a stone in her gut, that it wanted everything.

Something wet fell from the darkness above and landed on Xenia's shoulder, filling the muscle there first with a frozen numbness, and then with the deepest, most perfect pain. She strained to turn the little outside light on the helmet onto it, only to watch a small puddle of viscous chrome seep through the suit as if to burrow, to *hide*. She could hear Bonan sobbing—the woman was holding her shaky, black-gloved hand up to her helmet. Straining to understand what had just seeped in even while more liquid oozed down the walls of the Paateni well. Only for a moment did Xenia contemplate scrambling up the smooth walls, like a rat in a toilet bowl, before the pain in her shoulder pulsed that, of course, there was no running from God. *I told you,* the pain was saying, sounding eerily like her father, *I told you you'd be undone.*

"Your radar will see it," Xenia said, when she could no longer feel her limbs. But there were graves, and gardens, that needed protecting. "Your radars will pick it up. Even if it's hiding. And then your missiles will blast Elijah to pieces."

"No. They won't." Bonan still had her eyes closed. Now that God was hiding inside her, she probably would never open them again. How very much like the Paateni woman she looked, Xenia thought. And she, too, would be indistinguishable from them, in the end. "We would never destroy something we love so much. Do you know how long we've waited . . .?"

"A thousand years," said Xenia. "Yes, I know."

The chrome was falling faster now; more like a rain. But from her scalp to her toes, she understood that everything was all right because she had been chosen for something more. There would be no death, no abandon, only oneness, eternal. Purity filled her heart as elements organic and non-organic were remade for posterity—first, split open.

Then. Reconnected.

§

**Nadia Bulkin** *writes scary stories about the scary world we live in, three of which have been nominated for a Shirley Jackson Award. Her stories have been included in volumes of* The Year's Best Horror *(Datlow),* The Year's Best Dark Fantasy and Horror *(Guran), and* The Year's Best Weird Fiction; *in venues such as* Nightmare, Fantasy, The Dark, *and* ChiZine; *and in anthologies such as* She Walks in Shadows *and* Aickman's Heirs. *Her debut collection,* She Said Destroy, *was published by Word Horde in August 2017. She has a B.A. in political science, an M.A. in international affairs, and lives in Washington, D.C.*

# BROKEN EYE BOOKS

### NOVELLAS
*Izanami's Choice*, by Adam Heine
*Never Now Always*, by Desirina Boskovich

### NOVELS
*The Hole Behind Midnight*, by Clinton J. Boomer
*Crooked*, by Richard Pett
*Scourge of the Realm*, by Erik Scott de Bie

### COLLECTIONS
*Royden Poole's Field Guide to the 25th Hour*, by Clinton J. Boomer

### ANTHOLOGIES
(edited by Scott Gable & C. Dombrowski)
*By Faerie Light: Tales of the Fair Folk*
*Ghost in the Cogs: Steam-Powered Ghost Stories*
*Tomorrow's Cthulhu: Stories at the Dawn of Posthumanity*
*Ride the Star Wind: Cthulhu, Space Opera, and the Cosmic Weird*

*Stay weird.*
*Read books.*
*Repeat.*

*www.brokeneyebooks.com*

*twitter.com/brokeneyebooks*
*facebook.com/brokeneyebooks*